FOLLOWED BY THE DARK

THE DARK SERIES *Book Five*

Followed by the Dark

Copy Editing: Jenn Lockwood | Jenn Lockwood Editing

Proofreader: Rosa | My Brother's Editor, Mary | On Pointe Digital Services

Cover Design: Danah Logan

Interior Formatting: Danah Logan

ISBN: 979-8-9851796-3-7 (e-book)

ISBN: 979-8-9867063-0-6 (paperback)

ISBN: 979-8-9867063-1-3 (paperback – discreet cover)

ISBN: 979-8-9867063-2-0 (hardback – discreet cover)

A NOTE FROM THE AUTHOR

Trust Denielle and Marcus.

This was, by far, the hardest book to write in the series. You will experience sides of Denielle I never anticipated when she first "came to life" in *The Dark Series* trilogy.

Each book in *The Dark Series* is unique to its main characters. They write the story; I'm just along for the ride. As they get older, their characters grow throughout the series, make mistakes that can have you either relate to, like, or dislike (possibly even hate) them. They are raw and flawed, but we love them anyway.

Followed by the Dark (FBTD) is the **FIFTH** book in *The Dark Series*. While the romance in FBTD is a standalone, the plot is a continuation of events that began in *The Dark Series* trilogy. **It is strongly recommended to read the previous books prior to reading FBTD.**

Denielle's story within _The Dark Series_ is set three years after the last chapter (not epilogue) in _Because of the Dark_ (Book Four).

This series is intended for **MATURE (18+)** readers. _Followed by the Dark_ is a dark, enemies-to-lovers, age gap, romantic-suspense novel and features strong language, violence, explicit sexual scenes, and situations that may be considered **TRIGGERS** for some. **Reader discretion is advised.**

(For a more detailed list of potential triggers and tropes in this book, scan the below QR code.)

*For Kezia, my bestie and "therapist." Thank you for never second-guessing why I'm texting you at all hours about topics that would be considered—what's the word?—concerning to most.
I promise it's book-related research.*

"Glass House" - Machine Gun Kelly
"Familiar Taste of Poison" - Halestorm
"Never Got to Say Goodbye" - Payton Parish
"Idol" - Hollywood Undead feat. Tech N9ne
"No Light, No Light" - Florence + The Machine
"Venom" - Eminem
"Mirror" - Lil Wayne, Bruno Mars
"Cut" - Plumb
"Sandstorm" - Darude
"Proximus" - Lauro Picotto
"The Nights" - Avicii
"Steal my Romance" - Ghosts On The Radio

PROLOGUE

MARCUS

I cross my ankle over my knee in a failed attempt to stop my leg from bouncing. All I achieve is for the itch to switch to my other limb. My knee starts to bob up and down, and I swallow the growl that's been steadily building in my throat since boarding the jet. I glance at the Garmin on my wrist and calculate our remaining flight time—one more hour.

I shouldn't be here.

I'm not afraid of flying. At thirty-seven years old, there is not much that scares me. I was thrown into hell well before I was legally an adult. I fought and clawed my way out of the black pit that kept my soul hostage since I last held her. I'm alive, but I'm not. I'm in purgatory. To the clueless observer, I am having a case of aerophobia as my nails dig into the buttery soft leather of the armrest. I'm not. My heart rate has been somewhere around one-twenty, and the oxygen supply to my lungs is as delayed as the restocking of toilet paper during the pandemic a few years ago. None of this should be the case when your ass is planted on a private jet approaching a multimillion-dollar vineyard in Northern California.

I'm a mess.

I'm not supposed to be working. I've never worked this week —not in the fourteen years I've *served* under George Weiler. He knew the date when he hired me for his security team. It was my one and only condition.

When Lilly and her husband, Rhys, informed me that they decided to move their daughter's first birthday party to the family's private estate, it was a win-win situation. The place is a fortress. Ever since becoming Lilly McGuire's bodyguard before she came out to the public and took over her family's empire six years ago, I've felt guilty about leaving her side for a whole week. She and Rhys are not just my employers; they are my friends. The closest I will ever get to having a family again. Knowing she would be shielded during my absence was a huge relief.

Then, I got the call.

George was not able to accompany Lilly on the jet as planned. He is the head of security for Lilly's family, including the business side. He runs the show. Being his second-in-command for almost a decade—and Lilly's *Shadow*, as I was named—it would fall on me to make sure the family arrived safely. Everyone under George is qualified. He trained us all. But neither he nor I are *able* to give up control when it comes to Lilly's safety. It's personal for us.

I've replayed the phone conversation in my head numerous times, searching for a clue as to why George would force me to be here. I came up blank. It could only mean one thing: something came up with Lilly's brother. If George doesn't want to talk about it, you'd have more success digging through a three-foot-deep concrete wall with a plastic spork than getting answers out of him.

Don't get me wrong, this job saved my life, which is why I will never refuse an assignment. I care about the McGuires and, of course, want to make sure their guests are secure. But being in *her* vicinity for longer than I already have had to be since her arrival in LA—

Her. Denielle Keller. Lilly's best friend since the two were prepubescent teens.

I lift my head, and my eyes immediately zero in on the perfectly curled, dark-brown hair spilling over the backrest two rows up. I purposefully chose the single seat in the front in order to limit having to face the woman to boarding and deplaning.

I attempt to be courteous with her, but ninety-nine percent of the time, that goes out the window. Her presence triggers a deep-rooted hatred I didn't know existed for more than one person. Most still believe it is because she clocked me in the nuts six years ago, and I had to physically restrain her for hours—I let them believe that. The last thing I want is to lose my position because of my dislike for Denielle *"The Bulldog"* Keller. This week, though...I have no fucking clue how I'm going to do it. I can't escape the same way I can in LA.

She laughs at something Rhys says to Lilly, and my jaw clenches of its own volition. A wave of heat spreads through my body—the unpleasant kind. Besides the physical assault, which I can somewhat excuse, given the circumstances, her presence sets me back years—not something I ever thought I'd have to go through at this age.

A ripping sound redirects my attention to the present, and I close my eyes in resignation when I take in the tear in the leather where I've dislodged it from the seat.

Well, fuck. This is going to be a long trip.

CHAPTER ONE

DENIELLE

Two weeks earlier

I NARROW MY EYES, attempting to decipher the flutter in my chest as I stare at the mover's back. Nervousness? Relief? Excitement? All of the above?

He rolls the last stack of boxes out the door and...that's it. I didn't expect it to be such a blur. Five years coming to a close in a matter of two days.

But what did I expect? I called my best friend in the middle of the night, declaring I'd be moving in with her on the other side of the country. Lilly McGuire doesn't do anything half-heartedly.

We've been best friends forever, but life took turns neither of us would've seen coming when she had walked into Butler Gymnastics Academy that day in middle school.

My vision blurs as the door swings shut, and I stand alone in my empty apartment. The walls suddenly seem too white, the cherry hardwood floors too dark. I pivot toward the floor-to-ceiling windows and scan the buildings surrounding mine. New York was supposed to be my home, my future...

Lilly didn't ask a single question about why or what happened. She just took care of it—or her assistant did. I doubt she called the moving company herself, as busy as she is.

My BFF is the heiress to a multigazillion-dollar family hotel empire. But that is only half the reason she is *famous*. When she was six years old, she was kidnapped by *The Babysitter*. While she escaped then, he tracked her down ten years later.

Lilly is as well known to the public as it gets. She's on a first-name basis with the heads of all the major media outlets. She took over parts of the business, expanded it before graduating college, and now runs the whole empire like she was meant to. If she needs something done, it gets done. Someone will bend over backward to get in her good graces. Not that she's a bitch or anything. That would be me in this (*platonic*) relationship. I'm *The Bulldog*, a title I equally loathe and embrace. If you mean harm to the people I care about, I will bite down and not let go until you submit. But when it comes to me...well, that has become a different story over the last few years.

Lilly simply keeps her inner circle to a minimum. She has trust issues, but who can blame her? The past has shaped how we approach our future. We should all probably be more fucked up than we appear, but not everything lives on the surface. I'm the best example of that.

My phone vibrates in my hand, and I lift it into my line of sight. I stare at my other best friend's face on the screen, and my heart slows. Guilt creeps through my veins. *Shit.* He found out that something happened. Otherwise, he wouldn't call. We spoke mere hours before—

My fingers tighten around the device as if I'm holding on to Wes like I have so many times. He has been my rock for years. But this time, he can't help me. He has his family, and I have to do this *alone*—as much as that's possible when moving in with your bestie, her husband, their baby girl, and...*Marcus Baxter*.

. . .

OF COURSE, Lilly sent the jet. I could've easily taken a commercial flight to LA, but her usual mode of transportation was already en route when she informed me of the time the movers would arrive to pack up my life.

A few years back, she upgraded to a large-cabin jet, fully equipped with a small bedroom in the back. I made fun of her for a whole week. Who the hell needs a plane this size? But after our first trip with all our friends, I suppressed any further smart remarks. It beats having to deal with multiple layovers.

So, I'm now buckled into one of the twelve plush seats that could easily hold two individuals. Joel comes over the intercom, letting me know that we're waiting to get cleared for takeoff. He has worked for Lilly's family forever, and he's as familiar to me as my father's driver.

My father.

Victor Keller is going to throw a fit when he realizes I abandoned my condo overnight. Technically, it was forty-eight hours, but I doubt the semantics will make a difference. That place had been my home since I started college. I loved the apartment and neighborhood.

Quitting my job without notice will also have its consequences. But with yet another deceit by the male species, I've finally chosen to follow my friends out west. Not that I cared too much about the male. The humiliation from his actions was the reason to pack up and start over. It's only a matter of time before the entire office finds out. I'm not sticking around for that.

As if he's read my mind, my phone lights up. Settling in earlier, I had placed it on the small table separating the seats. His name is like a spotlight aimed at my retina, and I flutter my eyes closed with a drawn-out inhale. *Calm down.* I pretend I don't see the texts. However, the repeating vibration against the wooden surface forces me to acknowledge their existence.

Has he finally figured out that I am gone? Took him long enough after he came home to his empty apartment—or he had to digest what I left out in the open for him to find.

Inhaling to the count of four, I hold my breath for four before exhaling at the same rate. Curling my lips under, I blink and reach for my phone.

I swipe across his name and begin to read.

Collin: Where are you?

Collin: I just got to your place. All your stuff is gone.

Collin: Max said he saw movers.

Max. My nosy doorman—former doorman.

Collin: Hello?

Collin: Sweetheart, where are you?

Sweetheart, my ass.

Collin: Answer me!

Collin: NOW, Denielle! We have the Pomodor Benefit tonight.

That's more like him.

Contempt ignites my insides with every new line inscribing itself into my brain. He can shove his precious benefit where the sun doesn't shine. All the way up to his— How dare he give me orders. He is the last person with the right to demand anything. I tighten my hold around the phone until the skin over my knuckles begins to burn, imagining it is his throat. The scene replays in front of my mind's eye, and heat slithers up my neck. My thrashing pulse is drowning out the jet's engine that just came to life.

I contemplate sending him a selfie of me flipping the camera off but decide against it. He's not worth the potential fallout if the picture got out. And it would get out. We were together for nearly two years. I know him. He'd do anything to save face. Collin's family is from the Upper East Side and is a controlling force in my industry, especially his mother—my (as of today) former employer.

In her eyes, her son can do no wrong, no matter how

degrading and despicable his actions are. I would get the blame somehow, and a picture like that would be the final nail in my career coffin.

Instead, I power my phone down. As soon as I'm in LA, I'll change my number. It's time to leave the past in the past.

As much as that's possible with my new house enemy.

With my purse in one hand and my sunglasses in the other, I duck through the jet's door. I'm momentarily blinded by the California sun, and despite the rays warming my skin, a chill runs down my neck and back. I slip my oversized LVs on and focus on my friends waiting for me near the hangar in their Escalade. Lilly exits the passenger side, smiling in my direction. Before I can overthink it, I rush down the short flight of stairs. It's been too long since I've seen her.

After a hug that is entirely too short, I slide into the back of the SUV.

Leaning over my goddaughter's infant seat, I coo, "Hi, pretty girl. How is my favorite shopping partner?"

"Oh, Jesus," Rhys groans from behind the wheel.

Lilly barks out a laugh but then turns to meet my eyes. "She's excited to have her Auntie D around twenty-four seven."

"Yeah. So great," Rhys mutters under his breath.

"Fuck off, McGuire." I reach around the headrest and smack him against the back of the head.

"Language, babe," Lilly admonishes, and I can't hide my snort.

How times have changed.

We merge into traffic, and with every passing mile, I chip away more of my white nail polish. I despise the habit I've picked up whenever I'm about to be in close quarters with Marcus Baxter. I probably should just neglect my manicures for the duration of our cohabitation. Anything else would be a waste of money.

"What happened, D?" Rhys breaks the weighing silence.

I anticipated an interrogation the moment I exited the jet. They either didn't want to ambush me, or...does Lilly already know? It wouldn't surprise me if she found out with her talent for information gathering. No, there is no way she would've looked in that direction.

I meet Rhys's brown eyes in the rearview mirror, his concern hitting me harder than I thought it would. He has been a close friend for years, but not as close as I am with Lilly or Wes.

He continues, "Don't get me wrong, D. We are happy to finally have you on this side of the country, but..."

Rhys doesn't have to finish the sentence. This cloak-and-dagger operation is beyond uncharacteristic for me. I've had my future planned out since entering Westbridge High freshman year—with color-coded Post-it notes and a meticulous time line written out in my phone's calendar. My career was set to be in New York.

I avert my gaze out the window, the landscape fading away to memories.

SIX YEARS AGO, I had expected finishing high school without my friends to be torture. I missed them, but in the end, it was a relief neither of them was a witness to my new reality. They were focused on getting their own derailed lives back on track, unsuspecting of what had come to light in mine. And I kept it that way.

Lilly and Rhys stayed in LA, dealing with the fallout of her family's secret, the kidnapping(s), and her stepping into her role within her *new family*. The press ate it all up. In addition to dodging the paps, her and Rhys struggled to move past what had happened to her. She almost got killed, and to say it messed Rhys up would be an understatement. He became the embodiment of a paranoid, overprotective, clingy boyfriend.

Some of his guilt for not being able to protect the love of his life drove him to take actions that, in the end, ruined his friendship with Wes. With a brief separation, while the McGuires were stationed in North Carolina, the two had been joined at the hip since grade school. Rhys lived with Wes for years while he avoided Lilly to maintain his family's secret. When the truth finally came to light, Wes was there. He stood by Rhys, Lilly, and me, never once wavering in his loyalty. While he used to be Rhys's best friend, Wes and I had formed a bond that was uniquely ours.

Just when we had thought the nightmare was over—Lilly was safe—our group of four fell apart, and I was trapped between my two best friends. Lilly was my sister in every sense of the word except the blood relation, and Wes...he had been my constant. He was there when Lilly withdrew after she recovered her first memory—another fun side effect of her hidden past—not to mention when I found my long-term boyfriend, Charlie, cheating on me at a frat orgy. Wes helped me through it.

Neither of them made me choose. They never would've done that. However, the constant pull to defend Lilly and Rhys and to sympathize with Wes's resentment and anger were gradually corroding my insides.

We all entered the public limelight when Lilly announced who she was. We were there when it all started—and ended. But Wes was hit the hardest. He was dropped by his dream school to avoid unwanted public attention. He lost the future he worked his entire life for and had to move to Stonebriar, Montana to get a degree. He broke off contact with everyone but me for years.

I returned to Westbridge, Virginia and finished high school. While the paparazzi followed me too, they mostly observed. The occasional photo of me flipping them off made its way to the internet, but I was left alone in the end. There was nothing to report—at least, nothing the vultures knew about.

. . .

FINGERS SNAP next to my ear, and I zero back in on the interior of the vehicle. Lilly is partially turned in her seat, scanning my face. Once she has my attention, she begins to stroke the light-blonde fuzz on her daughter's head.

"Babe?" Her one-word question is laced with worry and curiosity.

I sigh, and my shoulders slump. The distance between New York and LA has allowed me to keep up my charade, but this is done now. How much I will have to disclose is still in question. The potential that our friendship could change doesn't sit well with me—but neither does keeping secrets from her. Talk about a rock and a hard place.

"I was seeing my boss's son," I state—a fact she knew, but that was about it.

"Yes, but I didn't think it was serious." Her eyes narrow.

It wasn't serious in the sense she's insinuating, at the same time, it was. Nothing I'm particularly proud of, sitting here.

After I found Charlie pounding into that sorority bimbo, I limited my relationships to surface-level, scratch-the-itch urges. None of them were able to reach any deeper than their fingers or dicks—nowhere near my heart. Until Collin. Not that he was the love of my life, but we complemented each other—ambitions, meticulously planned future, *and between the sheets*. Or so I thought.

"A lot has changed the last few years." I lean my head against the back of the seat and watch as her brows knit.

Lilly lets go of Audrey and places her hand on my knee, squeezing. "Do you want to wait until we're at the house?"

She still reads me as she did when we were in high school. It's as unnerving as it is a relief, because somewhere over the last six years, parts of that Denielle got buried under the rubble of my crumbling reality, also known as *my* family's secret.

I peek at my goddaughter. Not that she would understand, but it still feels weird to discuss that part of my life in front of her.

"Yes, let's chat later over a glass of the fancy wine stash you inherited," I joke and force a smile on my face that is as sincere as when grocery store greeters want to know how I'm doing.

By a miracle, my archnemesis is nowhere to be seen. Unfortunately, that does nothing to ease the knot in my stomach. I've been waiting for him to appear in the doorframe, throwing his distaste my way. Distaste is putting it mildly. Marcus Baxter has made it clear over the years that he downright loathes me. I don't blame him.

I settle into the mini-suite Lilly assigned me.

This used to be her father's house—*mansion, cough cough*—and after her past came out of the dark, it became her home in LA. The second floor used to have two guest bedrooms in addition to the library, her father's office (Lilly's office now), an art studio, and a playroom. Over time, Lilly and Rhys remodeled parts of the estate, updated furniture, etc., and creating this space was part of it. Lilly has never said it, but she holds out hope to one day bring her family together under one roof. She knows her only living blood relative wouldn't want his original bedroom. For now, though, the vineyard is his place of residence, and this space will be my temporary home. When we arrived earlier, Lilly informed me that Marcus had moved out of his bedroom and into the guesthouse. I didn't ask if I was the reason for it. I was.

I'm placing the last pair of my sleep shorts in the bottom drawer of the dresser when a soft knock makes my heart jolt. My hand flies to my chest. I need to get a grip. Marcus is not going to smother me in my sleep—I hope.

Inhaling, I swivel toward the door. "Come in."

The knob turns, and I catch myself holding my breath. *It's not going to be him.*

Lilly's head appears in the gap, and I exhale with a whoosh. *Good grief, Denielle.*

"Can I come in?" Her genuine smile eases my nerves. This is

where I belong. Lilly and Rhys are my family in every sense of the word.

"Of course, babe."

Lilly pads across the room and drops onto the sofa set against the wall. The large room contains a small sitting area, desk, and king-size bed with nightstands on either side and a bench at its foot. I stand there like an idiot, unsure if I should plant my ass next to her or on the matching armchair, the bench, the desk chair—*Jesus*. This girl has been my best friend for over a decade. I mentally slap myself against the forehead and make my way over to Lilly.

Her eyes crinkle, and she turns toward me, tucking her legs under. "I think it's time we talk." The seriousness in her statement catches me slightly off guard, but there is no anger in her tone. She is just Lilly, my best friend.

"Where is Audrey?" I peer over at the alarm clock. It's not nap time.

"Rhys took her out to the pool. She has her weekly swim lesson."

I can feel the wrinkle form between my brows. "But she's not even a year old."

"True." Lilly shrugs. "But we have a pool, and we want her to be comfortable and safe from an early age."

"So, when does the fight-and-weapons training start?" I joke. *Not really.* This family has the skill and artillery to survive a medium-size gang war. Scratch that, the zombie apocalypse.

"Fighting, probably as soon as she can walk straight without falling over." She laughs. "You know Rhys."

Not surprising.

Her hand lands on mine. "Talk to me."

My front teeth dig into my bottom lip as I peer at the barely existing polish on my nails. Here goes nothing. "Collin and I were more serious than I let on. But not because—" *Fuck*. I sit up a little straighter. I made the decision. Now I have to stand up for it. "Not because we were in love. Don't get me wrong, I care for him—cared," I correct myself, "but mostly, we complemented each other. He had the same goals, the same interests. And he was good in bed." A smirk pulls on the corner of my mouth.

"Okay," Lilly says slowly, slanting her head so her ear rests on the back of the couch. She cozies in and pulls the throw from the armrest to cover her legs. "That doesn't sound that terrible. I mean, I'm all for love, but if you were happy, that's all that counts..."

"I found Zithromax in his bathroom." My tone is dripping disgust.

Lilly's eyes narrow, and I hold her gaze, elaborating, "He was not *sick*."

She ponders my words, and I can see when it clicks. Her brows pop. "NO!" The shock is imminent.

I avert my gaze and fight against the rage and humiliation slowly burning its way through my insides and spreading through every cell. I recall the evening, two days ago, while focusing on a spot on the opposite wall.

"I went to his condo. He was working late, and we planned to order food when he finished. I was getting a glass out in the kitchen when it slipped and shattered on the floor. I cleaned everything up, but a tiny shard embedded itself into my finger, so I went to get tweezers. Collin was very much into manscaping." I roll my eyes at the fact. "In the bathroom drawer, where he keeps all that stuff, was a bottle of Zithromax, prescribed not a week ago." I pause, inhaling slowly to calm my thudding pulse. "I thought that was weird because he'd been fine. I'd seen him at work and at night most days."

I'm not necessarily proud of what I did next.

"I logged into his laptop that he always keeps at home." Pause. *Just spit it out.* "And into his patient portal." I avert my gaze until I can no longer look away.

Lilly presses her mouth in a thin line, and I can't help myself. "Don't judge me! You hacked into Katherine's social media for revenge. And not to mention spying on King for, like, ev— Just because you run this massive empire priding itself in its security—"

My BFF's demeanor shifts, and my next words remain lodged in my throat. Her devilish expression is not the response I expected to me word vomiting the morally gray actions she took at times.

She clucks her tongue. "Please. I would've done the same thing. I would've gotten that information for you any day if you had asked. I may run a business now, but when it comes to my family..." Lilly lets the statement hang.

"You're not disappointed?"

"Why would I be? The douche kept a secret from you—his *girlfriend*."

"Fiancée."

"What?"

"From his fiancée," I clarify quietly.

"You are engaged?" Lilly squeaks, and I wince.

"Was engaged." The ring was the only item I left in New York. It should've been delivered to Collin by now.

She rubs her temple. "I'm...confused."

"Collin's mother wanted him to settle down. His partying was not good for publicity. He needed to represent the image she created for the brand, and with me working for her, it was the perfect setup in her mind. I didn't care. As I said, we complemented each other."

Lilly nods, and the glistening sorrow turns her hazels dull.

"You know that, after Charlie, I refused to let anyone in all the way again. I was going to tell you at the vineyard in two weeks. I didn't want to do it over the phone."

If one person believes in a soul mate, it's Lilly. There is no relationship without love for her, but that's because she grew up with her other half—even if she had no clue until her life came apart like a frayed thread you pull on, unraveling until you have so many pieces you can't put it back together. The guy I naively thought was my other half cheated on me, and after that, I chose to protect myself from the hurt. Not that it helped. Even the guy I didn't *love* love managed to hurt me—by humiliation.

"I found the test results for an STD test his physician ran. He has chlamydia."

"Fuck." She shakes her head. "I— I don't know what to say. Did you get tested?" Lilly scans my face.

I put on the mask my friends have seen for as long as they've been around me—*The Bulldog*, as they call(ed) me. "I had my annual exam last month. Everything was fine, but I will go get checked out again. We always used condoms, but better safe than sorry." I shrug as if it's no big deal, yet my insides feel like a balled-up piece of paper. "Who knows where he got that shit from. I'm mostly embarrassed and—"

It's at that moment that my phone begins to ring on the other side of the room. We both glance in the direction of the intrusive sound. "I need to change my number." I don't have to tell her that it is probably Collin. Again. He's called and texted in thirty-minute intervals since I turned my phone back on to call my brother, Oli. One person in my family should be aware of where I am until I find the courage to face my father.

She grabs my hand and pulls me up. "Then let's do that."

I squeeze her fingers, bringing her to a stop. "What about Rhys and Audrey?"

Lilly lets go of me and hooks her arm around my shoulders. "Daddy can take care of his princess for a few hours. I need some quality time with my best friend."

CHAPTER TWO

MARCUS

"Bax." King drops herself in my lap, forcing me to abandon my forward position with my elbows propped on my knees.

"Monroe," I reply without averting my eyes from the disaster in the making.

Wes, King's husband and one of Lilly and Rhys's best friends, is in the pool. He has Rhys on his shoulders while their friend Hudson climbs on top of Kiwi's—the four of them about to battle it out like a bunch of high schoolers, not four adults in their mid to late twenties.

King hooks her arm around my neck. "You know Monroe hasn't been my name in years." She takes a swig of her beer.

"You know my name has three more letters," I counter, mimicking her by lifting my bottle to my lips. We arrived at the vineyard two days ago, and so far, I've holed up in my bedroom in the east wing. I always stay near the family, while the guests are in the west wing. When we arrived, I swiped supplies from the in-house bar and limited my meal hours from one to four a.m. I told myself that intermittent fasting would be good with my current *liquid* calorie intake. I did my job by bringing everyone here. Now, I'm off the clock until we head back to LA or Lilly leaves the grounds—which is not likely to happen, but it's the reason I can't return home for the remainder of the week.

King barks a laugh and tightens her hold on me. "Touché, *Shadow*."

We go through the same spiel whenever we see each other. And if I'm honest, I need it today. Besides Lilly and Rhys, Kingsley "Monroe" Sheats is my closest and sole friend.

When she showed up on the playing field four years earlier, I didn't trust her. I would even go so far as saying I would've shot her on sight if she so much as lifted a finger toward Lilly the day we met. She was the enemy. Fast forward to now, and I'd eliminate anyone who tries to harm her or her family. I misjudged her —a fact I can admit.

Lilly had me follow King before I escorted her back to Montana, and I quickly learned that she was dealt every shitty card life had to offer—similar to my upbringing. She was a fighter, though. No matter how often she was pushed to the ground—face first—she would get up, flip fate off, and keep going. Something I didn't learn until it was too late. I had let the darkness consume me until I was no more than a bruised shell unable to feel. Something I will regret for the rest of my life.

Nothing brought King down, which was one of the reasons I was drawn to her. I saw part of myself in her, other parts I *wanted for* myself. We helped each other in ways not many could relate to, which was probably also why she asked me—over Kiwi, her childhood best friend—to be her daughter's godfather. It was the second time in my life I had tears in my eyes that were not caused by physical—

"Where is Nugget?" I inquire in order to divert my thoughts before diving further into the black hole this week has ripped open. She used to call her daughter Nugget before she was born and had a name: Haddie. I continued the habit.

I wrap my arm around King's waist and look up at her. Warmth expands behind my rib cage as she smiles and leans her temple against the side of my head. A sense of peace settles in me, my muscles uncoiling for the first time since boarding the jet. I should've sought her out sooner, but I've been avoiding everyone. Today is Audrey's first birthday party, though, and I have to make an appearance.

Wes scans the area, and when he finds his wife, he focuses back on their little wannabe war play. He didn't condone King's friendship with me in the beginning. I never figured out if his possessiveness was out of fear of losing her (again) or because he saw me as an actual threat. The woman is sex on legs, no point in denying that, but she's never done it for me. Plus, a blind person could see that she's only ever had eyes for his ass. So, he quickly changed his tune. These days, we hang out when I am in Stonebriar, and King has class or is working at The Grizz.

I probably should consider Wes a friend. A distant one. My hesitation simply lies in not letting people—

"She's passed out in the west wing living room," King interrupts my internal self-psychoanalysis.

My spine stiffens, and I sit forward, ready to push out of my chair—dropping her in the process if necessary. "Who is watching her?"

She puts her beer on the table next to us and guides my face to hers with two fingers. When she has my full attention, she says, "Heather is inside. Audrey is taking her nap in the Pack 'n Play next to Haddie."

There is no humor in her statement. Besides George, King is the one other person I've let in on my past—why, this week, each year, I go off the deep end. And why I am *a bit* overprotective of my three-year-old goddaughter.

The spike of adrenaline fizzles out. I cover my mouth with the fingers not required to hold on to my bottle, and I sink back. "Fuck, Monroe. I hate you sometimes."

Haddie is safe with Rhys's mother. Everything is fine.

She pulls my hand down and covers it with hers. "How are you holding up?"

Her head is turned, not making eye contact. We're both following the still ongoing water fight.

If anyone else were to ask that question, I'd say, *"Fine."*

"I don't want to be here, *King*." I only ever use her first name when we're serious. And even then, it has to be a near life-and-death situation.

In my peripheral vision, I notice her curl her lips under. She remains mute for so long that I assume she won't respond.

"What do you need from me?" If she wasn't married and if I were to feel anything beyond sisterly/best-friend affection for her, I would have had my cock in her a long time ago. But that's all she is: my best friend.

Before I can stop myself, I growl, "Keep Keller away from me." Just speaking her name makes my internal temperature rise.

King sighs. She knows why I am the way I am, but my hate for Denielle Keller... That's the one secret I have not divulged to her. Once more, she proves to me why we are this close. Most women would push and nag until they got what they wanted. Solve the big mystery. Not Monroe.

"Okay." After a pause, she adds, "Why don't you and Wes take Haddie on a hike tomorrow? She loves when you boys have your little outdoor excursions."

I smirk. "Outdoor *excursion*? Big words, Monroe."

"Fuck you," she huffs and snuggles closer as we witness how Kiwi dunks Rhys with a battle cry resembling a hoarse hyena. We both crack up as the four boys disappear under the surface.

My amusement, however, gets stuck in my throat as the person who shall not be named exits through the patio door, and my arm involuntarily puts King's waist in a vise.

"Owww," she hisses.

. . .

A LITTLE OVER two weeks ago, I was waiting for Rhys to show up for our five a.m. training session in the gym when Lilly marched in instead. Her initial determination dissipated before she opened her mouth and stabbed a verbal icepick into my eardrum. "Den's going to stay with us." She hollowed out her cheeks and scanned my face.

Everything halted—my heartbeat, my motion to grab one of the training pads off the shelf. I couldn't move. I didn't know how long I stood there before time snapped back into place, and my pulse began to thrash through my veins.

"Why?" was my profound response.

Her shoulders slumped. "I don't know. She called last night. She needs to leave New York."

My eyes narrowed. *Leave New York?* Denielle was obsessed with her career. It was her only positive trait—because it kept her far away from me.

"I had Makaila organize a moving company that will pack her things. Joel will pick her up tomorrow once the movers are done."

Makaila was Lilly's assistant. She started working for her a few years back, and after some intensive vetting of her background, she was deemed trustworthy enough to move freely around the McGuires. We'd learned our lesson from the past. George didn't let anyone near Lilly or her family without us knowing their preferred brand of toothpaste.

"O-kay." I forced the two syllables out and focused back on the shelf with the equipment.

"Marcus?" A hand landed on my forearm, and I glanced down at Lilly.

I held her gaze, and she chewed on her upper lip before speaking. "She is my best friend. I need to be there for her. Something isn't right."

My chest constricted as I took in the conflicting emotions flittering across her features. "I understand." I pulled the corner of my mouth up, hoping to give her some assurance.

I must've failed because she amended, "You can stay in the guesthouse. I'm not kicking you out, but I thought that might make it easier."

It would.

"Yes. I appreciate it." I drew her into a hug. "Thanks."

She returned the embrace.

It had been clear to everyone for years that I couldn't stand breathing the same air as her best friend. Despite Lilly and me never having openly discussed the reason, she knew. She took it upon herself to unearth the corpses responsible for the animosity between Denielle and me, and since she was my employer, I understood the necessity. She didn't treat me differently for it, which I appreciated.

When she pulled back, her eyes ping-ponged between mine. "We'll work on your schedule for the foreseeable future. Maybe Ethan can also help out when he's here."

"I'll be fine, Lilly. I've been around her for years. I can separate my job from—"

"That's not the point, Marcus." She switched to her mom voice, and I chuckled. "You are my friend as well, and I care about your feelings. We'll find a solution that works for everyone. She's only here until she finds a job and can move into her own place."

"Yo, Shadow. Sorry, I was—" Rhys halted in his tracks and cocked his head. "What's going on?"

Lilly faced her husband. "D is moving in with us."

I SPENT the rest of that day carrying my belongings from my room to the guesthouse. It had two bedrooms, a small open-concept kitchen and living room, and one bathroom. More than I'd need, but the kitchen would make life bearable. I made sure to stock the fridge and pantry so I wouldn't have to track to the main house to scavenge for food much.

Before his shift, Ethan showed up at my door. As usual,

he made himself at home before I could greet him. With a protein bar—still in its wrapper—between his teeth and a bottle of water in hand, his ass got comfortable on the couch. He spat his snack out on his lap before eyeing me up and down. "Heard I'm taking over when Keller is around."

Ethan was technically my subordinate, but that had never kept him from speaking his mind.

"Shouldn't be too often. I'll still cover my shifts," I said, sitting down opposite him. I just wouldn't hang out at the main house like I used to.

"Well, I don't mind watching her ass." Crumbs fell out of his mouth while he chewed.

"You were hired to guard the McGuires, not chase pussy. If that's too much, I can replace you," I barked. My fingers curled to fists on top of my thighs, and his eyes widened.

I wouldn't consider us close, but we had spent enough time together to joke around and even *share* some female fun. If his desired object to play *"dip the dick"* wasn't the one person I blamed for everything, I may have joined in. Did she deserve my wrath for the full extent of what transpired? No. But the original cause had been eliminated. She was merely second best—the one I could get to.

Ethan lifted his hands, palms toward me. "Whoa, B. I know you hate the woman, but I'm not losing my gig over some ass. You just tell me where you want me."

That was better.

I nodded. Pride kept me from admitting that my outburst was unwarranted. Ethan was a good *soldier*, one of my best. George hired him a couple of years after me. You could say our boss took in the misfits and made sure they found their place— like he did when his tragedy struck.

We put on a game and kicked back until it was Ethan's time to report for duty. All of us rotated through the day and night shifts, three blocks of eight hours. George made it clear that we needed to be able to focus whenever necessary, and that required us to adapt to random sleep schedules.

Once the door closed behind him, I called it a night. I had the first shift tomorrow, which meant I'd be off when *she* arrived.

I HAD no clue how long I had been out when I jolted upright in bed. My heart was hammering against my ribs. I couldn't draw in the air I needed to feed oxygen to my lungs. My chest burned, and my hand automatically reached to the side, finding its target. As soon as my skin connected with the cool metal of my H&K, the pounding of my heart slowed. I curled my fingers around the grip and inhaled slow, deep breaths.

It was just a dream.

I repeated the exercise, a.k.a. breathing, as I studied the ceiling above me. This was not my room. Every other person would panic from waking up in an unfamiliar place. Not me. I was trained to remain in control. Without moving, my gaze scanned its surroundings, and I recognized my location. I was in the guesthouse—my temporary home.

Every inch of my body was covered in a sheen of cold sweat, my white shirt clinging to my skin. Strands of my hair stuck to the side of my face, and I regretted not tying it back last night. I was gonna have to shower before my shift started in—I peered at the red digits on the alarm clock—two hours.

It was three in the fucking morning.

With my pulse returned to a normal rhythm, I clasped the corner of the comforter with my opposite, not-armed hand and threw it back. Sliding my legs out of bed, I sat hunched forward, forearms resting on my thighs, my gun ready.

Despite my steady beating heart, my mind was anything but. With my eyes flicking over the objects in the room, I recalled my dream. Nightmare. *Memory.* Bits and pieces fell into place, and with every new picture forming in my mind, the sweat started coating my skin anew. It hurt to inhale.

I could smell the coppery scent of her blood. Saw her contorted body. Her eyes were closed. I fell on the hot asphalt next to her. No, no, no. The pain receptors in my body screamed at me to get up. I could sense the gravel biting into my bare knees, the heat from the day still lingering on the surface. My hands were trembling. I was scared to touch her, but at the same time, I needed confirmation that she was alive. Her chest. Was she breathing? Please breathe. More screaming in the background. It was all a blur of sound. Tilting too far forward, I caught myself, my palm landing in something sticky. I tuned it all out. She needed to breathe. I couldn't lose her. I couldn't lose her. I couldn't—

DROPPING THE H&K next to me on the mattress, I shoved my fingers into my hair. I fought the urge to yank on the strands, making the pain overshadow the memory. I hadn't had that dream in years. I spent hours upon hours working through the suffocating torture of reliving the last time I saw her chest move.

This was *her* fault. Denielle showing up here indefinitely had caused a crack in my carefully constructed armor. I would not let her ruin my life a second time.

I pushed upright and grabbed my sweatpants from the bottom of the bed. There was no going back to sleep. I might as well get my workout in early today.

CHAPTER THREE

DENIELLE

I HAVE NO IDEA HOW I'VE AVOIDED HIM FOR THE BETTER PART
of two weeks.

Every corner I round, I expect Marcus to intercept me and
finally follow through with his hate. We've evaded each other for
years, but now I'm *invading* his life—and job.

The first time I ran into him, the second day after I arrived
in LA, my stomach plummeted, as if I were bungee jumping—
without the cord. On cue, he glowered at me, his lips parted, and
I expected one of his verbal barbs. Instead, his focus shifted, and
I no longer existed. I caught myself, on several occasions,
seeking out his eyes simply because confusion knotted my
insides. I had no idea how to handle the change. I was torn
between wobbly legs, a dry throat, and insomnia—relief, paranoia, *and* suspicion about what game he was playing.

Ethan was around more than during any of my previous stays
at the mansion. I didn't complain, yet I wondered if the adjust-
ment in Lilly's security was caused by my residency in her house.
That followed a whole rabbit hole of questions: Who initiated
the change? Marcus rarely left her side since he took over for

George. Did Marcus request to be spared my presence? Was my secret no longer hidden in the dark? Did my best friend dig into my past? Or did he fill in the gaps to his animosity? Was I imagining it all? If Lilly knew, why wouldn't she tell me?

I needed to find a job and a place of my own ASAP.

The few times we ventured out, Marcus went back to being glued to Lilly's heels, but again, he ignored me. He did tense up whenever I would say something, and, one time, I caught him curling his fingers into fists until the whites of his knuckles showed, but that was it. He didn't throw his usual disdain at me. At times, he seemed almost distracted. Lilly said this was a hard time for him.

I knew.

Since I changed my number, Collin switched to email. His desperately ridiculous attempts to explain himself started to grate on my nerves. How do you justify cheating? Continuous cheating with some chick that *works* the club scene, as I found out from a mutual friend. When Phyllis Liberman's name popped up in my inbox, I had reached my limit. I deleted all five unread messages and blocked everyone associated with Collin or Liberman Fashion.

I didn't want to get a new account—yet. I had had that email since high school, and all my professional connections reached me through it. This was my fresh start. Unfortunately, from scratch since I wouldn't receive a reference from my previous employer, but...fuck it. I could do it. Marcus Baxter may be able to intimidate me, but not this sex-crazed excuse of a man who couldn't even use protection when he cheated on his future wife.

Wife. God. What was I thinking?

When Wes found out, he all but ripped me a new one. King had to take the phone away from him when he got so loud he was about to wake Haddie up. He was right, though. Being away from my friends, immersed into my world in New York, part of me believed this was the right decision. It was not. Being around them for the past fourteen days had opened my eyes.

· · ·

WE'VE FINISHED Audrey's birthday lunch and are waiting for the little ones to wake up from their nap before we have cake. After helping clean up the kitchen, I make my way to the heart of the estate. I love coming to the vineyard. Despite what happened here, it always gives me a sense of peace—seclusion from the world.

My gaze is out the floor-to-ceiling windows in the first-floor great room. Lilly called it the big sitting room when she first described this place—big being about as accurate as referring to February in Montana as *mildly chilly*. (I've vowed never to visit Wes during that time again.)

The windows face the back of the property. From my spot, I observe the guys being their obnoxious, childlike selves. A laugh bubbles up, and I shake my head as Rhys climbs on Wes's shoulders. This is not going to end well. Movement to the side pulls my attention away from the boys. I follow King as she drops into Marcus's lap. A hollowness settles in my chest. They have a bond only two people who've experienced similar trauma can understand. Before King took her place at Wes's side, Wes and I were those two people. We were there for each other when everything else had fallen apart around us. *But* despite him being my rock, I never confided in him about what revelation turned my already broken world to rubble six years ago. At times, I wanted to tell him—anyone—but then I remembered that this would ultimately not just change my life. It would unravel a string of carefully woven lies.

"What are you doing in here?" I jerk around as Lilly steps to my side. The magnitude of the room caused her question to echo.

I plaster the smile on my face that has become a permanent fixture there. My mind struggles between the pull of happiness for being here with my friends and dodging the knife threatening to cut the string tethering me to my future—dangling in front of me how I ruined someone else's.

"Heading out now. I was helping with the cleanup."

"Oh my gosh, you're the best." She hooks her arm around mine. "He refuses to let me do anything." She rolls her eyes, and I genuinely laugh. Witnessing Lilly's eyes light up from being around her *whole* family causes a flutter in my chest that makes the dread of my reality disappear—for a little while.

She tugs on my arm. "Let's go outside while we wait."

My heels automatically dig in. Marcus is by the pool—with King.

Not that King would take his side; that's not who she is. After spending time with her, King has become one of my favorite non-*best* friends. I always look forward to hanging out with her. She is loyal to a fault, kind, a kick-ass mom, and she makes my best friend happier than I've ever seen him.

THREE YEARS AGO, Wes and I arrived in Stonebriar after he had fled to New York. His life had been turned upside down once again, and he was drowning himself in the high percentages. He loved King, but was that enough? I was worried, after what he'd already been through. After spending several days talking, discussing all his options, and me giving him a piece of my mind, we flew back together. I would always have his back, no matter what his decision would've been in the end. But it only took one glance at King with Marcus, their friendship newly formed, and Wes went alpha male on the *Shadow*. Besides my precisely aimed kick to his manhood, that was probably the only other time someone had surprised Marcus Baxter and got a hit in on him. Instinctively, I stepped between the two. Marcus could've eviscerated Wes in a matter of minutes. Wes could hold his own, but not against a trained soldier who had been working under George "*The Ghost*" Weiler for years. In my hasty decision, I made the mistake of touching Marcus. The brief connection jolted me to the core. I could see the hatred oozing out of his pores. He didn't hold back either when he put me in my place in front of the entire bar. King was the first to step in. The girl who crushed my friend's heart comforted me. Tears of hurt, humiliation, and guilt ran down my face. She probably assumed I hated her for what happened between her and Wes. *For who she was.* Yet, she still wrapped her arms around me like we'd been friends forever.

"YOU CAN'T AVOID him for the rest of your life, D." Lilly's words are like a slap to the face.

What does she mean by that?

When I don't speak, she swivels me to face her head-on. "Listen, I..." She blows out a breath. "I know, okay?"

My heart stops. She knows? The thumping in my chest slowly picks back up. My mouth opens and closes several times. Heat spreads through every limb, and I sense the flush in my cheeks. "He told you?" My question is anything but steady. I can't help but peer toward the tall windows for a fraction of a second.

This time, she closes her eyes and imperceptibly shakes her head. He didn't tell her. That means... "You dug into my past?" my voice rises with my now thrashing heart.

"D, I'm sorry." Lilly is pleading with me. "I had no idea until... I was checking Marcus's background, and..."

She found out years ago.

"FUCK, babe!" I shriek. I dig the heels of my hands into the sockets of my eyes before being able to face her.

Lilly shrinks away, and I attempt to get my battling emotions under control. My arms drop. I'm rooted in place.

"Lilly? What's going on?" Her brother's calm voice coming from the archway to the kitchen interrupts the crackling silence.

Lilly whips around, and I take that as my chance to rush toward the patio doors.

Fuck. Shit. Fuck!

Does she know everything? Or just my part in the chain of events? What about before *the accident?*

My bare feet hit the heated marble patio, and I ignore the stinging pain. Instead, I welcome the hurt. It overshadows this new development.

I take two steps, and my eyes automatically find his. His gaze narrows, and a squeak of pain from King drifts over to me. Marcus jerks his head to the girl in his lap, and I follow the silent exchange between them. King's eyes briefly flicker to me, and she gives me a forced smile. I mimic her sentiment and set one foot in front of the other until I reach the lounge chairs where Elle and her sister are sunbathing.

They haven't noticed me, their lids most likely closed behind their dark shades, and I embrace the solitude. I lower my own glasses and settle into the chaise. Behind the security of my over-sized Louis Vuitton's, I let myself find him again.

The day my life changed to what it is today begins to play out in front of me like a movie.

"WE'LL GET YOUR LUGGAGE," Ethan announced as I unfolded myself with a groan from the seat Marcus had held me hostage in. Despite the age difference, I had considered him hot. Now, all I wanted was to kick him in the junk again. My best friend had been kidnapped, and her father and head of security forced Wes and me to fly back home. We were in the way of the rescue mission. Who wouldn't be freaking out at that?

If I so much as moved a muscle, he would tense, ready to pounce and restrain me again.

What did he think I would do? Skydive out of the jet and walk back to LA? Maybe his damn ponytail was too tight and had killed some of the blood flow to his brain.

I nodded at Ethan and ignored the asshole still glowering at me as I slowly trailed Wes to the exit.

Wes glanced over his shoulder and smirked. "That was kind of entertaining."

I smacked him against the back of his head. "Keep walking, Sheats."

He hooted, and for the first time in hours, the crushing weight constricting my airflow eased. To cope with our situation, Wes had put his headphones in and damaged his eardrums with Linkin Park to the point that I was sure Joel could hear it in the cockpit. The fact that he was listening to one of Lilly's favorite bands was not lost on me either. Wes blocked everyone out and left me alone with my thoughts, drowning in the unknown of whether or not I would see my best friend again.

With the tightness in my chest returning, I slipped my hand into my oversized LV, searching for my phone. I needed to know if there was news. With one foot on the top step, something red drew my attention. I halted in my tracks. There, next to the hangar, was my father's RS7.

He's in town?

I hadn't spoken to him or my mother since my drive from LAX to Lilly's home. He didn't know I was coming back, and I assumed I would be riding with Wes and his dad.

Dizziness turned my vision hazy, and I latched on to the frame of the door.

Wes was already down the steps and halfway to his father's SUV before I could make my legs cooperate. In my head, I was going over my father's travel schedule. He should've been in Chicago.

I slowly placed one foot in front of the other. By the time I reached the passenger side of the sedan, Dad had made his way around and was opening the door for me.

"Honey." That was as affectionate as my father would get.

He gestured for me to get in, but I paused. "Dad. What are you doing here?"

"Tristen called about the situation in Los Angeles, and we figured it was better to be here when you arrived."

Do they have news? Is Lilly safe?

I knew better than to ask, though. Not here. Instead, I read between the lines. He had to check personally if I needed to see my therapist.

I was about to bow under his arm resting on the hood and drop into the passenger seat when Marcus approached with my luggage. My heart fluttered, and I had no idea why, but my spine stiffened. Of course, my father noticed my shift and dismissively peered behind him.

When his eyes landed on Marcus, his brows hitched, and he turned farther. With his change in position, I had a direct line of sight to my best friend's bodyguard. What I saw next shocked me to the core.

Marcus's face paled, and he froze midstep. His eyes locked on my father. With one lightning-fast move, he dropped my luggage and drew his gun, aiming it at—Dad?

A wave of adrenaline crashed through me, and I couldn't stop the screech that built in my throat. "What the fuck?"

I frantically searched the airfield for Wes or Ethan—anyone who could stop the madness. I noticed the taillights of Wes's dad's SUV leave through the gate. He didn't say goodbye.

What is going on? Where is Ethan?

With the gun aimed at my father's forehead, Marcus approached in a way I've only ever seen on TV. His locked jaw and tight mouth accompanied the hatred in his eyes, and a cold shiver ran down my spine.

My father took a step away from me and squared off to Marcus. They were mere feet apart, and if Marcus pulled the trigger, it would've been a point-blank shot.

I leaned sideways to get a better look at my father's face, and his demeanor had gone cold—colder than usual, I meant.

"Marcus Baxter. What a surprise." My father didn't sound surprised.

What the fuck is going on?

"Keller. I told you if I ever saw you again that I would kill you."

What?

Marcus's tone was so low that even if anyone were in the vicinity, his words would've been only audible to the three of us.

"You are not going to shoot me." My father chuckled. "Not here. Not ever."

I tried to make sense of what was happening but came up blank.

With his head cocked, the corner of Marcus's mouth pulled up in a sneer. "And how do you know that?"

My father turned to me. "Get in the car."

The pounding against the inside of my rib cage made it hard to breathe. My lips parted, but no sound came out.

"Now, Denielle!" The command was clear, and as it had been

programmed into my DNA for years, I followed. I slid into the seat, but before my father slammed the door shut, I heard him answering Marcus's question.

"If you were half the man you pretend to be now, you would've saved her back then."

Her?

The door closed, and I was waiting for the sound of the gunshot. Instead, Marcus lowered his weapon and resembled a statue. He tracked my father as he rounded to the driver's side.

Dad halted with one foot on the floorboard and his forearms resting on the roof and door. I couldn't see his face. All I heard were the words that would throw my life into another tailspin.

"You never had the balls, Marcus. Don't pretend to be someone you are not."

Every muscle in my body tensed, and I couldn't look away from the man I had come to dislike over the last several hours for how he treated me. But for a fraction of a second, those feelings vanished. My father's words had hit their target. It was written across Marcus's every feature, and my throat ached. Then, his brown eyes found mine, and the ache turned into a choking lump. His gaze narrowed, and I shrank into the soft leather of my father's current toy. I was unable to break the stare down as the knowledge burned itself into my soul that whatever the reason Marcus knew and hated my father for...it was now extended to me.

Dad peeled away and sped toward the gates of the airfield.

"Dad! My luggage!" I swiveled in my seat and watched the distance between Marcus and the car increase. He hadn't moved, and I couldn't make out his face.

"You have enough clothes," was all he replied before we left the airfield.

That night, my life changed forever. Again.

CHAPTER FOUR

MARCUS

EVERYONE'S BEEN ASLEEP FOR HOURS. WHO KNEW THAT A
party for a one-year-old could be this exhausting? And I didn't
even have to participate much.

I stop at the NCC before heading back to the sanctuary of
my room. The NCC, short for *NASA Command Center*, is the
heart of the estate's custom security system located on the
second floor. Lilly named it that during her first stay on the
property because of the numerous monitors on the walls and the
desk that sits in the center of the room. The windows that
would've faced the vineyard side of the property had been
removed during the initial remodel. You could only enter if you
passed all three safety measures: fingerprint, retina scan, and
voice recognition. I'm sure my eyebrows were attached to my
hairline when George first introduced me to the room. I was
used to high-end security, but this... It made sense, though, given
who developed it: Lilly's brother, Nate. So, it didn't surprise me
that he also found a way to turn the NCC into a massive Faraday
cage. Nothing could penetrate the inside, yet the technology it
housed was unaffected.

I rattle off my passphrase, and the dead bolts in the steel door disengage. Stepping over the threshold, I halt. A tall blond figure is sitting at the desk, with George leaning against the side of it. Both heads turn my way, and I narrow my eyes.

It's three thirty in the morning.

"Boss. G." I nod at both. To this day, I have a hard time not addressing George with *sir,* but he insists that his military times are over.

"You're still maintaining your schedule?" George cocks his head. He is fully aware that I avoid everyone with a pulse. He even went so far as to apologize for forcing me to be here—a gesture I would've never expected from him yet appreciated beyond measure.

"Yes, I will make sure to adjust back to rotation once we are in LA." I don't have to say it, but at the same time, I do—for my own sake.

George nods his head in acknowledgment before turning to the man who employs us—next to Lilly, that is. He gave Lilly the majority of his shares before *leaving* for six years, ensuring she'd always have the final say in any decision above the boards. Now that he's back, we will see how much he gets involved again. For the time being, he is acclimating to life here at the vineyard.

"I'll talk to you in the morning. Let me know if she needs anything." George shifts his focus to me after he gets a lazy thumbs-up. "While you're up, check the feed, then find me tomorrow to discuss your departure next week."

My departure?

"You're staying?" I didn't think George would be required here anymore.

He oversees the physical security of the business, including *The Garage,* as we call it. *The Garage* is located under the original Altman Hotel, housing the maintenance and local motor pool the hotels supply their guests with when requested. Lilly has turned the family empire into one of a kind, putting the skill she and her brother share to use. People all over the world choose the Altman Hotels for their safety, security, and discretion.

"For the time being." His stoic face doesn't give shit away, and before I can reply, he pushes past me and is out the door.

I let the new information sink in before taking the spot against the desk George vacated. Nate briefly glances up at me before his eyes find one of the monitors once more. He's only two years older than me, and given the trauma we both went through in life—albeit different, but trauma nonetheless—there is mutual understanding and respect.

Working for George for years before I became Lilly's *Shadow*, I'd automatically been around our employer. We never spoke more than the occasional greeting and superficial pleasantries. Not because he considered us (his detail) employees, but he was merely private by nature. Later, I found out the extent of *why*. For a hot second, I considered quitting, but then, who was I to judge? None of us were saints. I continued to accompany Lilly on her visits with him, and the meaningless small talk quickly turned to deeper conversations and shared interests. We both cared for Lilly's safety, and I liked the man.

I follow his line of sight, and it clicks. "Does Lilly know she's here?"

Without averting his eyes from the sleeping form in the bed, he replies, "Yes."

I'm not surprised. He doesn't keep anything from his sister. Never has. "No one else has seen her," I state. I'm only privy to the information because I ran into her during my first nightly food hunt. She didn't anticipate anyone else would be awake and almost gave me a heart attack.

"Wes saw her when you arrived but hasn't put together that she was not one of his friends. He was too preoccupied with King once Haddie was in bed."

I chuckle and can't swallow the comment. "Don't tell me you've used your little creation for anything but security purposes?"

He closes his eyes and draws in a calming breath. "Dude, I wanted to bleach my eyes after witnessing..." He shudders. "They're like family. It was like catching your kid sister—"

I blink, scanning his features. My mouth falls open, his mortified expression a dead giveaway. It's like a switch flipped, and I double over. My shoulders shake as I attempt to suppress the laughter. Straightening, I slap his shoulder. "Man, don't tell me you did..."

He whips around. "Not on purpose, fucker," he growls and pushes me with so much force I stumble to the side.

This is too good.

"I've always been alone. The system sent an alert about *unusual* activity. I fixed the sound alerts quickly after that," he mumbles the last part.

I bend at the waist again and howl. My side cramps as I try to draw in the necessary air. I needed a distraction but didn't expect it to be this humorous. It feels good not having to force the positive emotion—great, even.

"Fuck you. I'm going to bed," he announces with a huff before pushing himself out of his chair.

I straighten and mock salute. "Sounds good, boss." Another chuckle bursts out. He doesn't spare me a backward glance.

ALONE, I plant my ass behind the desk. Pulling my phone out of the pocket of my sweats, I unlock the device and click on Spotify. Being the mastermind he is, my boss created his own network inside the walls of the estate. You cannot bring technology inside unless he allows it, but everything works perfectly normally once you're permitted access—even inside the steel cage I'm currently sitting in. Tapping on the radio based on my most recent playlist, I place it next to the keyboard and lean back in the chair. I let my gaze flit across the screens. Everything is quiet. I watch him enter his bedroom, and my fingers hover over the keys before I type in the commands, transferring the feed to the six monitors on the wall. Each screen now displays another six windows. The estate has hundreds of cameras, each individually accessible. I let the system my boss developed from scratch when he was in his midtwenties do its thing.

The man is a true genius.

The pictures switch every couple of seconds, and my eyes swipe over the frames. The feed changes again, and I sit up straighter. There is movement by the pool. The property has an underground gym, a running track, and an indoor lap pool. I enlarge the frame and narrow my eyes.

What the—

In the back of my mind, the song coming out of my phone's speakers registers. "Glass House" by Machine Gun Kelly fills the air.

How ironic.

Denielle sits at the edge of the pool. She is still in that ridiculously oversized, long-ass dress she wore earlier today, the material pulled up to her thighs as her feet dip in and out of the water. I zoom in further and pause. The water of the pool is reflected on her glistening cheeks. My brow creases, and I tilt my head to the side. I don't think I've ever seen the woman cry. No, not true. There was one time. The day she thought I was about to kill her BFF for clocking me in the jaw. The idiot threw a jealous tantrum because of his own indecisions about his now wife. Keller stepped between us. I didn't stick around to see the full extent of her little breakdown after I made it clear once again where we stood. However, I'm aware that Denielle Keller doesn't show weakness. She got her nickname for a reason.

Studying her features, I follow the movement of her fingers swiping under her eyes, and my curiosity peaks. Why is she hiding down there? And in the middle of the night.

I grind my teeth as a bitter taste coats my tongue. *Why the hell do I care?* I don't. If she's upset, she probably deserves it.

I'm about to minimize the window when Denielle leans forward and slips into the water. Fully dressed. I blink. The fuck?

Her head goes under, her dark hair the last to disappear. Holding my breath, the beat of my heart accelerates while I wait for her to come back up. What is she doing? I glance at my watch and back at the monitor. When the ripples in the water smooth out, I press my palms onto the armrests of the chair, ready to push out of the seat. No matter how much I loathe this woman, blame her for her part in what happened to McKenna—my eye twitches as I force myself to think her name—I'm not letting Denielle harm herself on my watch, let alone under Lilly's roof. What the fuck is wrong with this wom— Her head breaks the surface, and I exhale sharply. She treads water for a few minutes before she swims to the edge and pushes herself up. She faces the camera, and it's apparent that her tent of a dress is weighing her down. A diabolical grin pulls at the corners of my mouth, enjoying her struggle. I cross my arms and lean back, waiting for her to— The amusement dies in my throat, and I choke on my spit at her problem-solving: Denielle sinks back into the water and strips out of her clothes. A flutter *unsettles* my core. She is not wearing a bra, and where my gaze dips... *NO!*

I avert my eyes from the screen. This is not happening. *But it is.* A tingling that has no business being there floods my body. The music filling the background switches to "Familiar Taste of Poison" by Halestorm, and my cock stands at full attention from the short glimpse. My fingers curl around the armrests, and I squeeze, battling the urge to look back. I lose.

My stomach rolls in complete contradiction to the rest of my body. This woman is the physical reminder that McKenna...*Ken* is no longer with me. This is not some peepshow on Pornhub. But my groin region doesn't get the memo. Blood continues rushing to my cock, which, with my growing hate for Keller, causes a physical conflict I have no idea how to handle. Hate is black and white, dark and light. Either you do or don't. This is neither. I despise Denielle with every fiber of my being, yet said fibers have a will of their own. I shift and lean forward, grasping the edge of the desk as irrational thoughts fill my mind: intercepting her on her way to her room, pressing her into the wall, her legs wrapping around me and— My dick throbs in my sweats. I lock my jaw, and deep-rooted anger (at my body) slowly replaces the heat fueling the need to feel her perky tits on full display. She pulls herself out, her dress hanging limp from her fingers. She's standing there next to the in-ground pool, chest rising and falling, staring at nothing. The only fabric covering her is a black lace thong, and I can no longer stop myself from scanning her body. Denielle Keller is painfully beautiful—even with all my contempt and resentment, I have to admit that. Her subtle curves are the right amount of athletic and feminine. Her flat stomach shows a hint of muscle but not to the point of a six-pack. Her tits are the perfect handful, not too big or too small. My fingers itch at the thought of squeezing them, rolling her nipples between my thumbs and forefingers. She emanates everything I've always been attracted to in a female. Jesus, why couldn't it have been King? Or even Elle or her sister? Elle is my type of brunette, but she's taken. And her sister is as blonde as it gets. *Fuck!*

Denielle drops her dress and reaches back to wring out her wet hair. My eyes greedily follow her movement, and I move one hand from the desk to fist my cock through my sweats. This is so many shades of wrong, yet the rapid thudding against my chest won't subside. Instead, it ramps up, and after a brief hesitation, I untie the string of my sweats. My fingers tremble as I pull the band of my pants down, letting my dick spring free. Every muscle in my body is coiled. I fist my shaft, moving up and down once, and my eyes roll back inside my head. When there is no visual connection anymore, rationality slams back into my brain. I'm not doing this. Not with her. I tighten my grip until I'm forced to hold my breath, nerve endings screaming at me to stop. Just when I'm about to grunt from the self-inflicted punishment, I let go of my cock and pull the waistband back up.

Not waiting for Denielle's next move, I turn off the feed and grab my phone. I'm out. The need to numb myself takes over, and I exit the NCC, not bothering with the lights. Taking two steps at a time, I make my way down the double staircase to the first floor, aiming straight for the bar in the grand room. Peering at my choices, I grab the bottle with the most amber liquid inside. I don't care what it is. It'll do.

I turn to head back up to my room when something catches my eye. Someone. Denielle, wrapped in a white towel, hair still dripping wet, and her dress clutched to her chest. She pads toward the foyer and staircase, not paying any attention—probably not expecting anyone to be here at almost four in the morning.

Before I can stop myself, I step away from the wall and in front of one of the floor-to-ceiling windows. My shadow appears on the floor as she is about to step into that spot. Denielle shrieks and drops her dress, holding on to the towel at the last moment. She whirls in my direction, and our gazes collide. A buzzing current fills my veins. She sucks in a breath, and I revel in the emotions flitting across her face. Surprise, confusion, fear, and... She scans me up and down, her tongue wetting her bottom lip. My eyes narrow. I hadn't seen that since our first meeting—before I knew who she was. I slant my head as I slowly advance. My adrenaline spikes, and I revel in the feeling of the hunt, stalking my prey. I expect her to cower, as she has done for years, being fully aware of her guilt. She does the opposite. Denielle pulls her shoulders back, not dropping her eyes from mine. I *need* her to retreat. She is tall, but I tower over her nonetheless. When I'm less than a foot away, she cranes her neck.

"What the fuck do you think you're doing?" I growl, putting extra disdain in the question. I know very well what she did. I watched her like a fucking Tom. But there is no way I will ever let her see what her little show did to me. I'm in denial myself. She is the reason... With that thought, my fingers curl inward, and I breach the gap between us until my nose almost touches hers. I can barely make out my own words over the rushing in my ears. "Get the fuck to your room, Keller. You have no business being here."

Awake or here, as in the sense of the property, she can draw her own conclusion to the meaning. I need her to submit. This is how it works.

Her lips press into a thin line, and she scowls. This is not how this is supposed to go. I wait for her to throw some type of retort my way. She raises her chin, indicating that, for once, I'm not intimidating her. The flutter in my lower half tells me I want her to push back. No. She is not allowed to be strong when it comes to *us*. But then she dips her head, crouches to pick up her fallen dress, and walks away without a backward glance. Her spine is straight, and my disgust has reached a new high. I am in charge. She is not! Her feet connect with the first step, and I whirl around, hurling the bottle against the massive fireplace.

She does not get to cause any emotion but pure hatred in me.

CHAPTER FIVE

DENIELLE

What just happened?

The hammering in my chest makes it hard to draw in air. I lean my back against the door. My legs tremble, and I sink to the ground. Placing my forehead on my knees, I exhale a shaky breath. Water from my still-wet dress seeps over the floor, making contact with my feet and exposed ass. The towel barely covers my boobs and thong at the same time, hence my bare behind being planted on the hardwood floor.

Not being able to shake Lilly's confession, I wandered through the mansion until I ended up on the lower level. Water has been my *calm* for as long as I remember. Submerging myself under the surface, peering up at the muted world above... It severs me from reality.

So, when my best friend informed me that she knew the truth—the secret I had carefully maintained for years—I was catapulted back to being five years old. I don't have many memories from that year, except hiding underwater until my lungs burned and black spots appeared in my vision. That remains clear as day. How it started. The whole messed-up chain of events that led to the encounter a few minutes ago.

I replay the scene in my head. I had no idea anyone else was still—or already—up. At the same time, I'm not surprised that *he* was the one I ran into. Marcus was absent during the day, so he had to leave his room at some point. It made sense it was at night.

Goose bumps run in waves down my arms and legs, and I shiver. The water on my skin has dried, yet my hair is anything but. Wearing drenched underwear doesn't help either—drenched in so many ways.

Jesus.

I could still sense the heat radiating off Marcus's tall frame. His very broad, muscular frame. Something new overshadowed his usual hatred, something I couldn't decipher. His proximity caused a tingling sensation in my core that made me clench my thighs. He had a full bottle of booze in his hand, but when he breached the distance, and his breath mingled with mine... I could taste his earlier beers on my tongue. I hate beer. On him, though...

A feverish flush spreads through me anew, and the chill turns into a whole new trembling. I shake my head at myself. I'm being ridiculous. This is Marcus Baxter.

His slanted head, how he regarded me with a crease between his brows, appears in front of my mind's eye. He seemed almost...confused? Irritated by something. Someone. Me? What was he thinking? Was it because I didn't tuck tail?

My fingers fidget with the hem of the towel.

Why didn't I run? That's a mystery to me.

I take emotional stock. My lungs hurt from... I almost didn't come up in time. The burn felt too good. It pushed all the other feelings aside, exhausted me physically.

Craving my pillows, I didn't pay attention to my surroundings, which was how he managed to surprise me. Ever since moving in with Lilly, I have been on constant alert. But pushing the limits—my limits—my mental battery was drained. Then, he acted very atypically to his usual loathing. Throw it all together, and I stood up to the man for the first time in six years. And I liked it. I reveled in the satisfaction that he was not happy about it. That I caused him...whatever that was—even if it was increased dislike. I felt in charge. It was all an illusion. I understood that. But the brief shift in power was exhilarating.

My thoughts drift to Lilly. She dug up my skeleton—the one my father has buried so deep in our walk-in closet behind a thick concrete wall that no one outside our family knows about it. Except for her now. I curl my toes, the urge to go back to the pool and dive in speeding up my pulse. Not tonight, though. I need sleep and to form a plan for how to approach my best friend—alone.

THE SUN IS high in the sky when I finally emerge.

Going to bed after four in the morning has resulted in sleeping long past lunchtime. When I attempt to peel back my eyelids, they feel like I have an entire beach under them. Eyedrops? Coffee! *Eyedrops...* I can't decide what I need first. A caffeine IV drip while using my eyedrops. Yes! That would be ideal.

But since that isn't going to happen, lubricating my eyes comes first. On my hunt for my liquid energy, silently praying I don't run into Marcus or my best friend (I'm not ready to confront her), I take two steps at a time down the back stairs. It's a shortcut that leads from the hallway where the guest rooms are located directly into the kitchen. I'm about to hit the bottom one when King appears in the opening.

"You're awake!" She beams at me, carrying a travel mug.

A high-pitched squeal escapes me as I scramble backward, almost falling on my ass. My palm flies to my chest, attempting to reassure the hammering inside that everything is okay.

Good Lord.

Righting myself and dusting off invisible lint, I smirk. "I'm up. I'm still working on the awake part." I cough the last word, and the sting in my lungs makes me wince. I overdid it last night. I wasn't smart. Giving in to the urge to cut ties with the outside world was something I hadn't done in years. There hadn't been a need to. My episodes slowed when I hit puberty. Lilly and I met, and I stopped using my parents' pool as escapism. Toward the end, I was able to hold my breath for almost two minutes. But that was when I submerged myself every other day. This time, I counted to ninety-eight before my body revolted, forcing me up.

King cocks her head. "You okay, D?"

I blink. "Where is everyone?"

She taps her forefinger to her lips, peering to the ceiling. "Umm... Elle and Hazel are outside by the pool. Lilly, Rhys, Wes, and Marcus took the kids on a hike. I haven't seen Heather or Tristen. And the rest of the boys are downstairs, doing some workout drills."

"Marcus is awake?" The question is out before I can stop myself. *Well, crap.*

King's eyes narrow. "What do you mean?"

I don't acknowledge his existence. Ever. "I, um... I ran into him last night on my way to bed." Why do I feel the need to explain myself? "I was at the pool. He was stocking up on his booze when I went upstairs." I attempt to put up a front, making myself as disgusted by him as he treats me.

The fire creeping up my neck tells a different story as the memory of his proximity floods my brain.

King studies me longer than I'd like, then nods. "Let's get you all caffeinated up. Then, we'll join the girls outside. The others won't be back for at least two more hours."

God, I love this woman. My shoulders sag in relief, the tension I was holding melting away. If Wes hadn't married her, I totally would. Dropping the topic, she hooks her arm around mine and leads me deeper into the industrial-sized kitchen.

• • •

I AVOIDED LILLY ALL DAY. Avoid in the sense of making sure we were not alone. On the one hand, I itched to hear what she had found out about me—Marcus and me. No! Me. There was no Marcus *and me*. But on the same hand (not even the other hand), the idea of her revealing her knowledge to me made my stomach roll, a clench that forced me to swallow hard. I don't get queasy easily, but this...situation took my appetite. Dinner was one of my best performances to date. I ate, complimented the chef, swallowed the tasteless but delicious looking meal, smiled, forced the bile down whenever my best friend made eye contact, and didn't look around to potentially find Marcus lurking in the corner, ready to hate me some more. He was never at dinner or any other mealtime. Why was I waiting for him? It was Oscar-worthy. But once everyone finished up, I excused myself under the pretense of catching up on sleep.

I wasn't ready to talk. Yet.

IT'S WELL PAST MIDNIGHT, and I'm lying in my bed, scrolling through my various social media accounts.

I haven't been online much since leaving New York, mainly because I am avoiding nosy questions. I sent my new number to the friends I trust not to hand it over to Collin. The rest, mostly business acquaintances, either got emails or (the more casual ones) messages via social media.

Getting up late has inevitably resulted in not being tired when it is time to hit the pillow. Propping my phone on my stomach, I stare at the blank screen forever. I want to check what everyone is up to—also, what they have heard about my sudden departure. Eventually, I cave to curiosity and log into my apps.

I've just started commenting on a friend's post, which shared a picture at my favorite restaurant, when a knock interrupts my typing.

I don't ask who's there. "Come in, Lilly."

A colony of ants is marching up my stomach walls. I watch the gap between the frame and the door widen, and Lilly's face appears. "Can I come in?"

And with those four words, the suffocating anxiety turns to a faint prickle in the back of my head. This is Lilly: my best friend, victim of *The Babysitter*, girl who became a billionaire heiress overnight, and seasoned hacker. I've never considered her anything but the girl I met at Butler's. None of the attributes change who she is as a person. Why would she treat me differently? She hasn't. That's not who we are.

Last night's episode instantly seems unnecessary.

Was it, though? It felt...*right*. Experiencing the familiar sting, separating myself.

I curl my upper lip between my teeth, shoving all the questions and doubts to the back of my mind. Smiling, I pat the mattress next to me.

Lilly approaches slowly. Is she waiting for me to change my mind? Send her away? She lowers herself next to me and, after a moment of hesitation, leans against the headboard. Her gaze locks on something on the far wall. "I'm sorry about yesterday. How I sprung it on you."

I mimic her position, shoulder to shoulder, chewing the inside of my cheek. In my peripheral vision, I notice her thumb flicks against the other four fingers of her hand. She is a nervous mess. The tightness in my shoulders lessens.

"How long?" My tone is slightly above a whisper. I don't have to ask in a full sentence; she understands the meaning.

She inhales and holds her breath before she confesses, "Since Marcus disappeared for the first time."

Almost exactly six years.

"Why did you never say anything?"

Her fingers twist together, halting her tic. "It wasn't my place."

And this is why this girl is my best friend.

"So, Marcus hasn't told you?" I need to make sure.

She smirks, peering over at me. "Do you really think he would ever share something regarding his personal life? He works for George."

Warmth spreads through me, and I crack a smile. "You have a point there."

I'm scared to ask how much she uncovered, but I can't avoid it forever. "What exactly did he *not* tell you?"

Lilly snuggles closer, leaning her temple against my shoulder. I shift and reach for her hand, interlacing our fingers. Sweat begins to pool between our palms. The wait for her to start talking is pure agony, but this isn't a topic that can be rushed for either of us.

"You have no idea how many times I've wanted to bring it up, ask you why you never talk back to Marcus. You are one of the strongest women I've ever met, but with him..."

"I deserve his hate," I murmur with a sigh.

Her head whips around. "No, you don't! It was not your fault."

She doesn't know the whole truth.

I don't reply. I can't. The words are stuck in my throat.

After a moment, she squeezes my fingers. "The first time Marcus took off, I was confused. He never so much as left five minutes early. I went to George, but he shut me down, saying this was the one week each year Marcus was not available. My inner paranoia took over. After everything we'd been through with... I couldn't accept his explanation."

She's referring to her brother's employee who betrayed her family—slipped past George's security.

Lilly continues, "I looked into Marcus's past. He was in the military for four years before he started under George. I didn't find much about him. He was always private. I could've dug deeper, but at the same time, I didn't want to. Then, I discovered the reason he enlisted."

"McKenna," I whisper her name.

"Yes." We sit in silence. Lilly flexes her fingers. She is trying to suppress her tic. "I think it was his way of punishing himself. He blamed himself for the accident."

Accident? I was never privy to the full story, only what my father relayed to me—allowed me to know. He didn't divulge how or why McKenna ended up in his OR. Just that she did. And that she never woke up like she was supposed to.

"She got hit by a car. Landed on the hood and then got thrown onto the street. Her head hit the curb."

Oh god.

That explains the surgery. Why a neurosurgeon—my father —was operating on her.

"From what I was able to dig up, she would've made it. They rushed her to the hospital in time, but something went wrong. When I read your father's name on the report, I...I stopped. Now I was also invading your life, and...I couldn't do it. There had been too many secrets in the past. I accepted that Marcus was gone every year on the anniversary of the accident. And after that, the argument he and Ethan had after they got back from dropping you and Wes off in Westbridge made sense. Marcus saw your dad. He put two and two together. He channeled all his hate toward you."

"My father was called out," I explain quietly. My tongue feels too heavy. The ache in my throat makes it hard to form the words. "There had been an...incident that night." My breathing accelerates, and my chest feels too tight. "They called my dad out of the surgery to check on me."

Lilly's head whips around. "You?" She sits up straight, facing me head-on. "What happened?"

Suddenly, the fear of her seeing me in a different light scares me to death. My eyes search the room for a sign, anything to help me figure out what to divulge to her.

"I fell into the pool." Coiling every muscle in my body to hide the tremor racking through me, I relay the story my father had told many times over. "Oli found me, but I wasn't breathing. Obviously"—I gesture at myself with my free hand—"it turned out fine, but my mother panicked. The EMTs and, later, the ER doctor assured her I was in no danger. I passed all their tests. But she insisted on my father checking on me. They pulled him out of surgery to verify what others had already confirmed." The words have been scripted, rehearsed, and carved into my brain since I was five years old. This is the story. This is the truth—the puppet show—they made everyone believe. I hold myself so rigid my back feels like it's about to snap in half.

Lilly scans my face. I see in her eyes that she is trying to decipher the missing piece, the detail I'm withholding.

"They were pretty much done. My father put his fellow in charge to finish up. He was about to be board certified the following week. Something went wrong."

Lilly's eyes widen and gloss over. "Oh no!" Her hand grips mine. "This is not your fault, though. It was an accident."

I slash my mouth. I want her to believe it, so I nod. I don't want to lie any more tonight. Lilly has heard enough. Not everything, but enough.

Maybe one day I will come clean with everything. But for now, I'm glad there is one less secret between us. It changes things. Two and a half weeks ago was my fresh start. A strength I haven't felt in a very long time spreads through me.

CHAPTER SIX

MARCUS

Today is the day everyone, but Nate and George leaves the vineyard.

I hadn't seen Denielle since our *meeting*. When I first laid eyes on her this morning, it was clear that something had changed—not just between us. She carried herself differently. Where she used to cower, avert her eyes, she held my gaze. Challenged me.

After arriving at the airfield, I stand next to Joel, listening to him give me another rundown of the flight plan. I bite my tongue to stop myself from reminding him that I came up with the order of the stops. Lilly, Rhys, Audrey, *Keller*, and I would be dropped off first. The jet will then take the others to Montana. Elle and her entourage will stay there for a few days with Wes and King before heading home to Colorado. The rest of the McGuire family had left a day early because Heather had been called back into the office for an urgent case.

My gaze drifts over everyone unloading the two SUVs. King is arguing with Wes while holding Haddie's hand. I wink at my goddaughter, and she grins. The corner of my mouth tilts up.

Wes found his match with King. She doesn't take shit from him, and I love it—sometimes even egg her on just to get some entertainment. I'm an asshole.

I check the next group. Lilly is handing Audrey to Rhys before leaning back in to undo the car seat, and Denielle is digging for gold in her oversized purse you could hide a body in.

Her head whips up as if sensing me watching her. As soon as our eyes lock, I expect her to turn away and refocus on whatever she is fishing for. She doesn't. Instead, she quirks a brow, her mouth remaining in a flat line, unreadable. My chest constricts, but I refuse to acknowledge it for anything but distaste. The flutter spreads to my lower belly, and I widen my stance, crossing my arms. Not butterflies. Killer hornets. Cockroaches. Yes, cockroaches sound about right. Something you want to grind under the sole of your shoe until it's nothing but a splatter of exoskeleton and intestines. A voice in the back of my mind laughs at my denial. The buzzing current in my veins doesn't help. I refuse to look away first, which seems to amuse her. The stoic expression changes to a sparkle in her eyes. The twitch at the corner of her lips is visible across the distance. I zero in on the movement and tighten my hold on my cuffed biceps.

Not. Happening.

I have no idea how long our standoff lasts. Someone, Joel, calls my name from right beside me, and my head slowly turns in that direction. I don't break eye contact until she is out of my line of sight.

"Are you good with the plan?" Joel's tone rings with exasperation.

"I came up with the plan. What do you think?" I snap, and he stumbles back.

My reaction was uncalled for. I had ignored him, not the other way around. I sigh. "Yes, sorry. Plan sounds great."

Joel bobs his head, not convinced of my sincerity, and I take that as my cue to check in with Ethan to make sure everything is set for our arrival. Whatever is going on with Denielle...I don't like it.

The flight was mostly uneventful.

Mostly because Keller continued to not act like herself. Since the day I connected her to the man who had abandoned my sister on the operating table, she never sought me out. She would do anything not to make eye contact, the guilt carved in elegant cursive across her forehead. That has suddenly shifted to something...unpredictable. Not only did she openly challenge me before our departure, but as we settled into our seats, I caught her peering at me through the curtain of her brown locks. Her eyes were unfocused, yet I was acutely aware of her watching *me*. A flush trailed up her neck, and she finally aimed her attention at the task at hand. I followed her every movement as she stowed her belongings away, ignoring the knot this shift had put in my stomach.

When we were finally ready for takeoff, I inserted my wireless headphones into my ears. Lost in my head, I drowned everyone out with "Never Got to Say Goodbye" by Payton Parish as soon as the wheels left the ground.

The anniversary had passed, but the void that usually accompanied me for the next fifty-one weeks had not set in yet. I hadn't been able to visit Ken, have our ritual of me telling her what happened this past year and her not answering—no smart remark or funny quip, how it used to be. I would have to find a way to see her on one of my days off. Lilly would give me personal time without hesitation if I asked, but...I wouldn't. It was time to get back to my routine. Maybe Ethan and I could hit up *The Club* one of these nights. I could use some *playtime*.

I stare at the ceiling of the guesthouse. My growl of frustration breaks the silence.

This has never happened.

Once again, a side effect of having *her* living on the property. We've been back in LA for two days, and I can't adjust back to rotation.

I want my room back. I like it in the main house. Even after Audrey was born, it never felt crowded. Granted, the mansion can fit the house I grew up in ten times over, but still. The McGuires are family. The thudding of my heart increases with every breath, and my irritation steadily grows. I'm on second shift this week—one in the afternoon until nine at night—but no matter what I do, I can't sleep. The only time I get shut-eye is long after the sun's up and then also no more than a couple of hours. Soon, it'll impact my ability to perform my duties.

For that alone, I want to march to the main house, kick in her door, and throttle the woman. Anything is better than admitting that whatever happened at the vineyard's pool has been fucking with my head. Her tight, naked body, with her wet hair cascading down her back, walking along the edge of the water, repeatedly flickers in front of my mind's eye. Every time I run into her during my shifts, an image of her perky tits forms. I swallow the images, which are accompanied by a sour taste down my burning throat. Yesterday, I found her bent over, looking for something in the freezer drawer, and have gone so far as mentally removing her thong in my visions. My fingers have been itching to wrap around her throat for an entirely new reason.

Denielle doesn't help eliminate the issue either. I caught her numerous times sneaking (and holding) glances. While she doesn't give any indication of what the meaning behind her newfound interest is, it is present whenever we are in the same room. A crackling sensation that I refuse to acknowledge as anything but disgust. With whom, I am still analyzing—definitely her, but my mind and body's treacherous betrayal comes in at a close second.

Fuck!

I throw the covers back and slip out of bed. I went to bed in basketball shorts and a tee, expecting this to happen. Shoving my feet into my gym shoes, I swipe my H&K and phone from the nightstand. Another early morning workout it is.

Crossing the short distance to the main house, I hug my torso. It's chilly, and I want to blame that on Keller, too. My irrational side is slowly taking over, and I grind my teeth. I'm a grown-ass man, for fuck's sake.

I let myself in through the kitchen patio doors, finding Ethan sitting on one of the barstools, scrolling through the security feed on his tablet. He's on third shift and peers up at me when I pass him on my way to the basement entrance.

"Can't sleep again?" he quips.

"Fuck off," is all I reply as I pass him, and his laughter drifts after me down the hall.

I open the door to the basement stairwell and take two steps at a time. The farther I descend, the slower my feet move. The thuds of someone running on the treadmill echo through the gym. Who the hell is down here at three in the morning?

When the soles of my shoes connect with the hardwood covering the entire bottom level, I swivel in the direction of the two treadmills situated at the far end with the other cardio equipment.

You've got to be fucking kidding me.

There is no way Ethan wasn't aware of Denielle being down here, running for her life. That's how it looks based on the sweat pouring down her face and onto the treadmill. It's also not safe. It looks like someone emptied a bucket of water on the band.

My concern is quickly replaced with a new round of discontent. Now she's ruining my workouts as well. I cannot escape this woman. Her increasing presence doesn't help the steadily growing tug-of-war inside my head. Blame and hatred battle against *I want to bend her over and fuck her raw.*

The fingers of my hand not wrapped around my gun flex and curl at the image forming in my head. An unwanted flush crawls up my neck. Denielle bent over, propping herself up on the weight bench while— Ken's face replaces the picture, and the fire in my veins turns to ice. I didn't protect her. It's Keller's fault that she's not here. She never gets to have the babies she always dreamed of.

I need to do something. The violence demanding revenge slowly overpowers the drive to make her tiny body mine. Neither is an option, though. An idea forms, and as much as the new visual excites me, I am fully aware of the fact that it's nothing more than an immature prank. Anything is better than...

Denielle hasn't spotted me. Her gaze is on her reflection in the mirrors mounted along the entire wall of the basement. Her eyes are unfocused. Tilting my head, I briefly wonder what's been going on with her—nope, I don't care.

I place my gun on the shelf next to me and fish my phone out of the pocket of my shorts. Swiping it open, I start scrolling. Nope. Nope. More scrolling. *Perfect!*

I make sure my phone is connected to the gym's surround sound system. Rhys and Lilly, equally, try to blow out their eardrums when they work out. When they spar against each other, the entire estate shakes, despite the soundproofing. It's a miracle they have functioning hearing.

I lean with one shoulder against the wall and cross my legs at the ankle. Devious anticipation hums through me. I peer up at Denielle to ensure that she hasn't noticed me. She has not. Her wireless headphones won't matter in a second. Turning the volume all the way up, I press play on "Idol" by Hollywood Undead feat. Tech N9ne. It's not as much about the lyrics— though they fit, to an extent—as it is about the sound. If you don't expect it—

Denielle trips as the bass shatters through the speakers and catches herself at the last moment before diving off the tread- mill. The adult in me is aware that my actions are anything but safe. She could've gotten seriously hurt, but— Her head jerks around, and her wide eyes narrow. Whether her chest is heaving from her run or my surprise is the question—both probably.

The hum has turned to a buzzing, my muscles tense in anticipation.

I straighten from the wall and fold my arms over my chest. *What are you going to do?* One side of my mouth stretches up and forms something between a sneer and a grin.

Keller rips her earbuds out. "WHAT THE FUCK?"

She jumps off the exercise equipment and marches toward me. *Come fight me.* Her face resembles a wet tomato and is anything but intimidating. I bite the insides of my cheeks to not start laughing. She stops right before our feet touch. I can sense the gravitation. Scanning her up and down, her skintight, dark-purple shorts and matching sports bra burn themselves into my retinas. I don't allow my mind to go where my dick is already heading. My chest constricts, and the only option I have is to surrender and walk away, or she will see that one part of me does not loathe her.

I move around her as if she hasn't spoken at all. Striding casually to the weight bench, I shove my phone into my pocket and utilize the motion to adjust my hard-on.

"MARCUS!" She's seething.

Not turning, I study the weights lined up in front of me. I stroke my chin with my thumb and forefinger. I'm acutely aware of her following my every move in the mirror.

This game is beginning to be fun. Game? What the fuck? I don't play games with a target. And that's all she is—the target of my hatred.

The sound suddenly cuts off. I slowly lift my eyes to hers. I slant my head. "Did you say something?"

Her fingers ball up. Livid Denielle Keller is a sight to be seen. Something I've never been privy to since she has always submitted to me—until now. I understand where her nickname came from. But I know her little secret. She doesn't intimidate me. I consciously recall the last time I held Ken in my arms—her closed lids, her face battered, and her hair caked with blood until the paramedics wheeled her into the operating room. After that, I was never able to wrap my arms around her again. I couldn't.

"You could've killed me, asshole. What if I had tripped?" She props her tiny fists on her hips and tilts her chin up.

I slowly swivel on my heels and approach her. I study her features before scanning her body up and down. Her breathing has slowed, but the closer I get, the quicker the rise and fall of her tits. I don't stop until the heat radiating off both of our bodies mingles. For the first time, I don't fight the pull and lean in. My nose trails her cheekbone to her ear. Her breath hitches, but she doesn't move away. When my lips align with the shell of her ear, my tongue darts out, swiping over the skin. The salty taste from her sweat registers, and desire shoots to my groin. A whimper escapes her mouth, and I close my eyes.

"Who says I didn't want to kill you?" My tone is ice, and her spine stiffens.

I take a step back and casually fold my arms over my chest.

Give me your best, Keller.

I watch her carefully as her gaze locks on something past me. I don't turn to see what it is. She doesn't make eye contact when her lips part. At first, nothing comes out, but then she surprises me. "How did you find out?"

My short nails dig into my biceps, leaving crescent-moon imprints on my skin. I expected pretty much anything, but not this.

Denielle's eyes slowly focus again and shift to my face. She stops on my lips before her gaze flitters back and forth between my eyes. She waits for my response when all I want to tell her is to *fuck off*. How dare she bring that up?

My muscles strain against my skin until my body vibrates. I draw in slow, deep breaths in an attempt to stop the images flashing in front of my eyes.

I WAS BACK in the hospital.

After they informed me Ken would never wake up again, I lost it. I trashed the waiting room until security escorted me outside. I sat on the curb for hours. My head in my hands, I cried. No one attempted to help the kid from the wrong side of town. My clothes showed it. The blood still staining my hands showed it. After the adrenaline rush had left and the emotional exhaustion set in, I stared at the slightly rounded edge of the cement next to me. It wasn't even sharp, yet it took her away. No! The curb wasn't at fault. Ken fled from him. I yelled at her to run. I wanted to save her. But she dashed into the street, her eyes behind her, on me taking the beating for her. The car couldn't stop. Ken got thrown off the hood and—

I enlisted in the military that same week. I needed to do something with my rage and grief, direct it toward something of worth. I refused to disappoint Ken. She always dreamed of us having a future far away from this. It was during boot camp that I got introduced to a guy who knew a guy who knew someone else.

I got a credit card, maxed it out, and wrote a check. Then, I waited. Less than two months later, I had answers. Some. To this day, I have no idea how he dug it all up. It couldn't have been through legal channels, but I knew.

Ken's neurosurgeon, Victor Keller, had recently lost his wife. It was ruled an accident, but he remarried mere months later. He had two children with his late wife, Oliver and Denielle.

I should've put it together immediately when I met Denielle, but it didn't click until I saw her with her father at the airfield in Virginia.

The night of the surgery, Denielle had run away. Apparently, she was having problems—as my PI phrased it—since her father remarried. She was seeing a therapist regularly. But that time, it had been worse. She had fought with her stepmother and disappeared. Somehow, she ended up in the pool. She had had swim lessons since she was a baby, and she showed no other injuries when she arrived at the hospital. Denielle simply decided *not to come back up.*

Her brother, who had been looking for her, found her submerged in the water. She couldn't have been under that long because she was revived without problems. But the stepmother threw a hissy fit for her husband to check on her himself. Immediately. I didn't think a surgeon would just abandon a patient. The procedure was pretty much over when Victor Keller put his fellow in charge to finish up. It should've been routine, but Ken went into tachycardia and a blood vessel in her brain burst. The fellow couldn't find it in time, and... I lost the person I loved most in the world because Denielle took a swim.

Later, my PI was the one who introduced me to George. They had served together, and he thought I would fit in with the crew my boss was building.

"MARCUS." Denielle's calm tone severs the connection to the past, and the visual reminders dissolve like paint being washed off a canvas.

I focus on the woman in front of me. "You mean, how did I find out that you are the reason my sister didn't make it out of your father's operating room?"

Her lips press into a thin line, but she bobs her head.

"I know everything about you, Keller."

She inhales through her teeth.

"Your spoiled little ass didn't like that Daddy remarried, and you didn't get all his attention anymore. So, you threw a tantrum that almost killed you. But instead, you took my baby sister from me."

My throat feels like I swallowed a thousand razor blades with every new word. The tension in my muscles turns to lead, and I'm aware that if I don't move away from the woman, I will do something I'll regret. What, I don't know yet. The woman has the ability to force me to my knees with her beauty and my loathing for her existence equally.

I shift and stalk toward the staircase, grabbing my H&K on the way. Before I make it to the second step, her voice rings through the gym.

"Then you don't know everything."

CHAPTER SEVEN

DENIELLE

"WHAT THE HELL DO YOU MEAN YOU MOVED TO CALIFORNIA?!" My father's crimson face covers the screen of my phone. Spit flies out of his mouth with every word.

Fucking Oli, I made him swear not to tell them.

I bite the insides of my cheeks, aware of my father not nearly being done chewing me out. I'm a little surprised that it took him this long to figure it out. My parents knew that I was going to California for Audrey's birthday and probably assumed I had left early.

I was dead asleep from my late (or early) workout session when the buzzing on my nightstand began. He had to call three times before my foggy mind comprehended what the obnoxious sound was, which didn't help temper his mood. One doesn't ignore Victor Keller. If he doesn't have his eyes on you personally, he uses cameras to do so. Hence the security system in my childhood home, and him purchasing a condo with a doorman (whom he paid off to report my comings and goings) and video surveillance on every entry. Not unusual for a New York high-rise, but strategically planned by my father. Why my former doorman didn't report me leaving, I don't know. Nor do I really care. Probably because his extra cash flow would cease.

I'm done with the spying.

My friends always assumed that it was because of our financial status. None of them would've guessed the real reason. My father didn't like to be in the dark about anything, but his travels would force him to leave, and my mother would accompany him. Celine Keller may not be my mother by blood, but she raised me for most of my life. She has always wanted what's best for me but only ever had eyes for him.

After McKenna Baxter, my father took on more of an adviser role in his field. He still performed surgeries in very special circumstances, but his primary area of expertise became theoretical—another reason my father never treated me the same again. I ruined not only Marcus's life and future that day, but his, too.

I went to bed early after spending hours sending emails to every single business acquaintance on this side of the country. It's time to get back to work. I need to find a place of my own, get away from Marcus. I will never be able to fully shake him, but living on the same property...it's too much for both of us. Whenever I replay the departure back to LA, how his eyes had darkened when he scanned my body, a shiver runs down my spine and settles in parts that have no business being affected by him.

My father's rant continues. "I bought you that condo because you *had to be* in New York to fulfill your dream. A dream, I might mention—"

"I got it, Dad!" There goes my intention to let him finish. My tone is harsher than I'd usually dare address Victor Keller with, but as soon as I was ripped out of the black void of sleep, the constricting weight settled back in my chest. There is no denying it. Something had been between Marcus and me down in the gym—something other than hatred. A crackling electricity had engulfed my whole body in flames. Things have changed since I stood up to him after the night at the vineyard, but the guilt still festers deep in my core. At the same time, I can't with-stand the force drawing me to him. He also showed some of his cards last night—or more like which cards he is still missing. The same card I refuse to reveal to Lilly.

I inhale deeply. "I was going to tell you this week. I was at the vineyard for Audrey's birthday, and we just got back last night." That's a lie, but who cares. "Oli shouldn't have—"

"Your brother didn't rat you out, Denielle," Dad sneers, and I pause. "You know as well as I do that Oliver always covers for you."

"Then who?" The crease between my brows will require Botox.

"Collin called. You ended your engagement!" he gets louder, and there is movement in the background.

"Hi, Mom." I sigh. Of course she would be listening.

"Hi, honey," her soothing voice filters through the speaker. This woman never raises her tone, contrary to her husband. She is calm personified—one of the qualities I love about her.

Yet, she never could calm you the same way water could.

"Your engagement, Denielle." Dad redirects my attention to what's important to him.

"Is over. Collin cheated on me," I inform him, lacking any emotion. "Did he tell you that?"

Showing my father that something gets under my skin will result in him questioning my mental state—I've done that myself enough lately.

That makes my father pause. "He did not, but—"

Of course there is a *but*. "I found out because I found his STD medication."

My father's face sours. Whether he is upset because of Collin's actions or because I will no longer be marrying into one of the richest families on the East Coast remains to be seen.

The phone suddenly switches hands, and Celine's face appears. "I'm sorry, honey. That's unforgivable. You should've told us, though. You know your father doesn't like when we are not aware of where you are."

Your father, not we. She always does what he says. "I'm an adult."

"We're just worried that..." She looks past the camera.

"I'm not relapsing. I've been fine for years." I wait for them to call me out on the second *fib* I've told in the last five minutes. The craving to dive has been a constant since that day a week ago. It's like I got a fix of something I had stayed *sober* from for the last decade. My saving grace (or reason I don't give in to the need) is that Lilly and Rhys only have an outdoor pool, and I would have to face whoever is on night shift to explain my actions, which also would, no question, get back to my friend(s).

"If you do feel like you need to...you will call us?" Celine's hopeful expression makes it hard to continue with my charade.

"Of course," I lie with a smile that's anything but genuine. But she takes it.

"OK, good." Her shoulders sag, and she glances to the side, no doubt at my father. "We are really sorry about Collin. That's unforgivable."

I can't stop my brows from shooting up at her words. Unforgivable? Seriously? Thankfully, I swallow the snort in time before I drop my pretense completely. I love Celine, but she is the last person who should call cheating unforgivable. She was forgiven after all.

"I gotta go. I'm helping with Audrey this morning." Why not continue the untruths?

"We love you, honey." She blows me a kiss and turns the camera to my father.

"Bye, Dad." I force the corners of my mouth up.

"I expect you to call us twice a week." The thunderclouds over his head linger.

"I will. Talk to you soon." No point in arguing. For the first time in my life, I am out of his reach, no cameras or spies to report back to him, and he doesn't like it. If I don't give in to an extent, I wouldn't be surprised if he takes matters into his own hands to secure his control. I tap the *end call* button.

Staring at the phone that just held my parents' faces, restlessness begins to spread through my veins. My legs are too tired for another run. I exhausted myself last night like never before. It helped because I fell into a dreamless sleep as soon as my back hit the mattress. Normally, the itch would keep me up, which was why I attempted a new way of turning it off.

My thoughts drift to Marcus and how he made himself known last night. I wanted to punch him for his fucking *prank*. What are we? Twelve? Suddenly, my cheeks feel funny, and I lift my free hand to my face, tracing the smile that has formed on it. Marcus showed some of his cards. He also revealed something else he didn't mean to. He thought I didn't notice how he adjusted his dick when he walked away, but I did. The full-length, wall-to-wall mirrors don't hide anything in the gym.

Except when you're zoned out on a treadmill so you don't submerge yourself in your friends' pool.

I affect him, and he doesn't like it. Probably loathes it as much as he hates me breathing the same air as him. My smile turns into a joker-like grimace, and my pulse quickens. A sense of power surges through my limbs, the exhilaration lifting the weight in my chest that my parents' call put there. I can work with that. If he wants to play games, who am I to put a stop to it? Let's play.

TODAY IS the first day since leaving New York—fuck, no—the first day in years that I've felt like myself. After the conversation with my father and Celine, I checked my emails, and by a miracle, one of my contacts had replied. I had worked with Denis Perrin on several occasions during my time at Liberman. He owns a boutique called *La Déesse* here in LA and is known for his designs. His prices are outrageous, but his clientele doesn't care. His store manager recently quit to become a personal shopper for some heiress, and he needs a replacement ASAP. The position involves running the shop, ordering materials for his *creations*, overseeing the production, and managing the staff. It's more responsibility than I had at Liberman, where I barely saw a sketch, let alone was involved in any of the actual processes. Denis had seen my creativity even before I attached my drawings to my *casual* email inquiry. He assured me I had potential, which is high praise coming from him.

To celebrate, Lilly and I spent the day together. We went for brunch, taking turns holding Audrey in our laps while we ate and letting her nibble on our food.

I'm taking my life back, building my future. And Marcus's perma-scowl whenever I hold his gaze, wink at him, or push him further even made me laugh out loud on one occasion.

We decide to feed the press a bread crumb when Lilly and I take a selfie in front of the restaurant. The news coverage about her is back to the obsessive level of six years ago. Now that her brother has returned, everyone is speculating about what will happen next. I post the picture with the caption, *"Reunited! To new beginnings and a lifelong friendship."*

"I bet Lancaster will show up within twenty-four hours," she jokes as we walk to the SUV Marcus pulled around.

"Oh, Lord. Is he still around?" I roll my eyes. How can a grown man be that pathetic?

"On and off. We haven't seen much of him in the last two years, but the occasional blog post still surfaces. We expect him to show up sooner or later." She shrugs nonchalantly.

Lancaster was—*is*—a reporter obsessed with Lilly's past. But his fixation didn't end when everything was put out in the open. He redirected it to all of us—anyone who was connected to Lilly. He followed each of us regularly. However, after Lilly and Rhys, Wes saw him the most. First, when Wes lost his future, then when King surfaced four years ago. You would've thought Lancaster had won the lottery. He stalked Wes and King for months but eventually got bored when nothing new or exciting happened. The two were brand-new parents and domesticated, nothing Lancaster could blog about forever. I haven't seen him in years either, which is why I had forgotten about him.

"Do you think he'll use you to get to Nate, now that he's back?" I ask curiously. "You think he'd be dumb enough to try and sneak onto the vineyard?"

We're settled in the back seat with Audrey between us. I hear a snort from the front seat and meet Marcus's gaze in the rearview mirror. When I hold his stare, his eyes narrow. Reluctantly, he redirects his attention back to the road. He despises giving up first, but he has no choice when maneuvering us through traffic.

I peer at my friend. Lilly missed the exchange, her focus on straightening her daughter's bow. Absently, she retorts, "If he tries, he'll have a rude awakening."

Lilly is referring to the security measures built into the vineyard's outer defense. The wall surrounding it has some type of technology built in that will fry every device that is not permitted on the property. The only way to keep your electronics intact is to come through the (open and disarmed) main gate. And even then, they won't work until you are allowed to connect to the internal Wi-Fi of the estate. It's like a massive bubble shields the property.

"Maybe he should. It would at least give us some entertainment," I muse, and we both laugh. Audrey giggles at her mom, and I look at my goddaughter. "You guys are so screwed when she grows up."

Lilly sighs and leans back against the seat. "Don't I know it? Can you imagine what boys will have to endure between Rhys and George?"

"Don't forget her uncle and extended family." I mock flex my biceps, and we both lose it.

TWO DAYS LATER, I have my official interview at *La Déesse*.

Ethan drops me off in front of the boutique, informing me he'll wait until I'm done. At my reply that I can Uber it home, he cocks a brow, and I understand. He's following my BFF's orders.

Denis shows me around the store, which consists of the showroom on the main level, and his design studio, a few offices with the alteration room, and a small kitchen on the second floor. The actual collection is made off-site. His paranoia about anyone finding out his fashion secrets is off the charts, and I suck in my cheeks to not laugh at it.

He pushes open a door and gestures for me to head inside. "Here we are. This will be your office."

"Mine? I assumed you, uh... had more questions for me," I stammer. I didn't expect this to be it.

He waves at me dismissively. "I've seen your work. And anyone who can stand up to Phyllis is more than capable of running *La Déesse.*"

Wow!

"Collin will be out here next week to go over the contract with you so we can start production," Denis continues.

Wait, what?

"Wh-what do you mean?" My heart rate thickens. What did I miss?

Denis slants his head. "The fall fashion contract? Liberman Fashion will include three of my new designs in their upcoming collection."

Fucking great.

My internal temperature rises, and I speak before I can put a stop to it. "Is that why you're giving me this job? My connection to Liberman? Collin and I broke up."

Denis purses his lips and crosses his arms. "I'm aware. Phyllis informed me of the unfortunate circumstance."

What the fuck does that mean?

I have no idea how to respond. What unfortunate circumstance? That Collin cheated on me? Or that I didn't sit back like a demure, soon-to-be filthy rich fiancée and let it slide? My thumbnail digs into the pad of my middle finger—the only gesture I manage to not fully form fists.

When I don't speak, Denis continues, "I've known Collin since he was ten years old. He's always been a spoiled little shit. It was a miracle he remained faithful to you for as long as he did." He ends the last sentence with a sneer.

My brows shoot up. *Oh.*

"However, the contract stands. I want to hire you. I do believe we can create extraordinary things together. You are very talented, Denielle. So, my question to you is: can you suck it up and work with your scum ex-fiancé for the sake of fashion?"

A snicker bubbles up, and I let it escape before I think twice about it. Denis is...*something*. I don't have to consider his question. I want this job, and it's not like Collin broke my heart. I stretch out my hand. "For the sake of fashion."

Denis squeezes my fingers tightly, and his face lights up. "Excellent!"

CHAPTER EIGHT

DENIELLE

ETHAN INSISTED WE STOP AT THE CAFÉ LILLY AND I WENT TO
the other day and pick up a celebratory treat. Ethan is fun to be
around and a nice distraction from enduring Marcus the majority
of the time.

With my macchiato in one hand and a bag of fancy cookies
in the other, I duck under Ethan's arm, entering the house. The
garage is situated opposite the basement door. My attention is
behind me, laughing at Ethan, who is challenging me that I
could never eat all the treats myself, when I slam into a wall. No,
not a wall...a body. A very hard body.

I stop short, and before I can turn, I know who it is. I recognize the person without visual confirmation. Between a scent
that is uniquely his—a combination of fresh laundry detergent,
leather, spice, and currently sweat—and every cell in my body
instantly experiencing a draw toward said body, I slowly pivot to
meet Marcus's glower.

No, he doesn't glower at me. He's pinned Ethan down with a
stare usually geared in my direction. Was he supposed to be back
sooner, and I kept him from his job?

"Yo, what's up, B!" Ethan slaps Marcus's shoulder and moves past us down the hall toward the kitchen. Is he ignoring his boss's animosity, or did he not notice it?

Marcus doesn't grace Ethan with a reply. Instead, his head dips to focus on me. Fire courses up my neck, and I straighten my spine. I expect some type of vicious remark, but he remains mute.

"What?" I lace my one-word question with irritation.

A groove forms between his brows, and he cocks his head, scanning me up and down. I follow his perusal but can't find anything out of place. I wore a burgundy pencil skirt, a white cap-sleeve blouse, and my black patent Louboutins to the interview. The outfit is more conservative than I would typically show up in for work, but not knowing how stringent Denis is with his employees' dress code, I was going for safe over sorry.

"What's your problem?" The initial heat in my neck has transformed into an unpleasant burn on my cheeks, and I despise Marcus having this effect on me.

The corner of his mouth quirks up, and I follow the small movement. He leans closer, and his scent envelops me, urging me to lean into it. Before I can give in to the need, though, the Marcus I've known for six years is back.

"You're my problem, *Keller*." His proximity is painfully close, and any warmth in my body is snuffed out, reminding me why Marcus and I can never be friendly or civil with each other.

Without another word, he steps back. He strides in the opposite direction of Ethan, toward the door leading to the side of the house and yard—to the guesthouse because I made him leave his home.

The guilt that snakes through me and settles in my chest is halted by my phone vibrating in my hand that's also holding the bag. A sigh escapes me with a whoosh, grateful for the distraction.

I head into the kitchen and set everything down on the island. For a brief moment, images of my first time in this room appear like flashes in front of my eyes, and I shiver. The destruction, the blood... I shake my head. No. That's in the past, and it will never happen again—not with the security measures that have been put in place since.

I let my gaze drop to the countertop where my phone lies, still lit up. A frown forms on my face.

Huh?

A messenger notification sits at the top of my missed emails and texts while I was at *La Déesse*. I hadn't checked it after Ethan and I left, too distracted with the excitement about my new employment.

Charlie York

My heart stutters and then picks up speed. I haven't seen this name on my screen in years. Part of me wants to delete the message unread, but curiosity about what he could possibly want has me clicking on it. The device unlocks, and I get my answer.

Hey, D. I saw you moved to LA. I was wondering if we could meet for coffee or drinks sometime?

I didn't expect that.

Before I can think about a potential response, Rhys walks in, downing a bottle of water. He is in swim trunks and has a towel draped over his shoulders.

"How did it go?"

"I got the job!" I jump in place, clapping my hands.

Rhys's expression lights up. "That's awesome! I knew you would!" He crosses to where I stand, enveloping me in a bear hug before I can protest.

"Ew, McGuire. You're wet. Gross." I attempt to wiggle away, laughing.

He drops his arms. "Sorry." His sheepish smirk makes him appear boyish, and he reminds me of the kid I grew up with. "Have you told Calla yet?"

Rhys's nickname for Lilly makes me smile. He uses other endearments, but the majority of the time, he addresses her with

Calla. It's been like that since the moment she declared her love for calla lilies years ago.

"Not yet. I just got back." I glance around the room and out the tall windows toward the backyard. "Where are your girls?"

"Audrey's napping, so Calla wanted to get some work done. She's upstairs in her office." Rhys heads toward the fridge and pulls out another bottle of water.

I nod. "OK. I'm going to change out of these clothes and then go see her."

"Sounds good," he replies absently with his head now in the pantry.

UPSTAIRS, I strip out of my skirt and blouse, leaving me standing in front of the tall mirror in my white lace thong, bra, and heels. I bite my lip. "What would Marcus think of this outfit?" I whisper to myself.

I shake my head. *God, what's wrong with me?*

I unclasp my bra and reach for the maxi dress I discarded at the foot of my bed yesterday. Stepping into it, a sigh of comfortable relief escapes my lips. This is much better. I make a mental note to check with Denis on what he expects me to wear.

Picking up my phone again, I remember Charlie's message. He wants to meet me. After six years. I haven't heard so much as a peep from him since the night he went to his frat party and left me at his apartment—not even when he discovered what I had done to his possessions after I found him doggy-styling some skank the following day when I went looking for him.

I no longer hold a grudge. I don't feel anything for Charlie. The hurt and hatred slowly morphed into indifference, and eventually, I rarely thought of him at all. His actions led me to guard my heart against another hurt, but even when being careful not to fall in love, I got slapped in the face with another man's infidelity.

My fingers hover over the digital keyboard for a moment.

Me: Charlie. This is a surprise.

Keeping it pleasantly neutral.

It takes less than a minute before the banner slides down again and interrupts me catching up on emails. I tap on it.

Charlie: I know. I saw you are in town and wanted to reach out.

My curiosity is piqued. Charlie never had any intention of moving to the West Coast. He always talked about staying close to his family after college.

Me: You're in LA?

Charlie: For about two years. Mom passed, and I needed a change of scenery.

Oh, no. A lump forms in my throat. I adored Kelly York when Charlie and I were dating. After the...breakup, I lost touch with her. It was too awkward. No doubt she figured out what had happened.

Me: OMG, I'm so sorry. What happened?

The speech bubble appears and disappears several times.

Charlie: Any chance you would meet me for coffee?

A flutter quivers in my stomach. Would I? My eyes sting, and I blink. Kelly is gone.

Me: Yes, sure. When?

Charlie: How about two hours? The café you like so much?

How does he—? Oh, my last few social media posts. I haven't been active in so long, and then the only times I've posted were when I went to The Baking Room.

My initial panic evaporates.

Me: See you there.

Sitting on the bench at the foot of my bed, I digest the news. Lilly is no longer in her office when I reemerge. I find her downstairs in one of the sitting rooms with Audrey playing on a blanket. Rhys and Marcus are standing near the open patio doors, freshly showered and engrossed in a passionate debate. Getting closer, the words *exhaust* and *suspension* drift over, and I tune them out immediately. Car talk is as fascinating to me as if I were to try to explain the difference between an accordion and a knife pleat to anyone outside of the industry.

Despite my disinterest in their conversation, I catalog Marcus's outfit in meticulous detail. His signature ripped jeans are paired with one of his many solid cotton tees—today's color of choice is navy blue. He's wearing brown Red Wing Heritage Classic Mocs in the same shade as his shoulder holster. His hair is still wet and hangs in loose strands around his face. My fingers itch to comb it away from his forehead.

I force myself to shift my focus before anyone catches me gawking. Marcus ignores me as usual.

Approaching my friend, I suppress a grin at the sight of Audrey balling her tiny fists at her mom when she is attempting to make her stand and walk to her for the toy she wants. "She has your pigheadedness."

Lilly rolls her eyes and focuses back on her mini-me. "If you want Lola, you have to come get her." She waves the little stuffed turtle in the air in front of Audrey. I swear, if she knew how, she'd flip her mother off.

"Hey, babe?"

Lilly side-eyes me while keeping her attention on her daughter. "Hmm?"

I inhale. I don't know if I'm nervous about what I'm about to ask or why I'm asking. "Can I borrow one of your cars this afternoon?"

In my peripheral vision, I see Rhys's and Marcus's heads whip in my direction. Before Lilly can respond, Rhys inquires, "Why do you need a car?"

I bite my lip. Lilly doesn't help the situation either by saying, "Ethan can drive you wherever you need to go."

I guess I don't get around to revealing the why.

"I'm meeting someone."

"Someone?" The sharp bark makes me scrunch my shoulders up. Marcus has never publicly addressed me.

I choose to give him the cold shoulder as he does with me all the time and answer Lilly instead. "I'm having coffee with Charlie, and I don't know how long it'll be."

"Charlie York?"

"Your Charlie?"

Rhys and Lilly simultaneously exclaim with confused expressions.

"Yes." I don't want to elaborate about Kelly until I know more.

"Well, um...sure. Take the G-Wagon. The keys are on the board." The frown on my friend's face is still in place.

I lean forward and give her a side hug, followed by placing a kiss on the crown of Audrey's head. "Thanks, babe. I'll text you if I'm late."

Lilly and Rhys exchange a look. "Okay. Be safe."

Standing up, I wave to Rhys before heading toward the other side of the house, ignoring Lilly's *Shadow*.

IT IS one in the morning, and I'm running at seven miles per hour on the treadmill. I need to be faster, crave to run faster, but my body won't comply. I'm at my limit. It's only been twenty-three minutes, but running at this pace is no easy feat for me. I'm no runner.

Before I even left The Baking Room, I needed to go under. My lungs were constricting, and the sense of uncontrollable suffocation overpowered me. There was no way to face my friends in my condition. I texted Lilly that I was grabbing dinner with Charlie and would be home late.

Lilly: R u ok?

My actions were anything but typical.

Me: Absolutely. We're just catching up. See you later, babe. *heart emoji*

Obstructing the truth was starting to become natural.

Instead of eating dinner with my ex-boyfriend, though, I sat on a side street, exercising every breathing technique I had ever learned from the various therapists my father sent me to. All of them helped for no longer than a few minutes, the conversation replaying in my head on a loop.

Charlie had already been there when I arrived. Seeing him after such a long time and after the news he gave me over the phone, tears instantly spilled over. He had hurt me more than I ever admitted to anyone, but this was not about us. He stood as I entered the café. As if it had been yesterday, he read me, and I stepped into his open arms.

"I'm so sorry," my voice broke.

"Thanks, D." He held on until I was ready to let go.

We settled in the small booth he somehow snagged up—the three booths had an hour-long wait time every time I'd been there.

I ordered my drink, and we remained silent until the barista placed the tall glass with my iced latte in front of me.

"D, I—"

"What ha—" We started at the same time, and Charlie grinned crookedly.

The flutter in my chest reminded me of how it used to be between us. I returned the expression. "You first." I motion for him to continue before picking up my caffeine fix and taking a sip.

His chest rose as he drew in a long breath. Holding my gaze, he said the last thing I expected to hear. "I owe you an apology."

I didn't let my surprise show, keeping my face blank. "Thank you."

While it was too late to repair the damage, I no longer held on to my hate.

"I should've contacted you years ago." He lowered his gaze to his coffee in front of him and wrapped his fingers around it. "But

I was too... It doesn't matter. I ruined something great, and I'm truly sorry for that."

I had no doubt that his remorse was genuine. "I appreciate you saying it." The corners of my mouth tilted upward on their own. I didn't have to force the sympathy on my face.

"I came back to Westbridge after college. I ran into Oli one day, and he told me you had moved to New York. I may or may not have followed you online for years," he admitted coyly.

"My brother never told me." I slanted my head, searching my memory for Oli mentioning seeing Charlie.

"He clocked me good that day," Charlie massaged the side of his chin.

"He what?" I sat up straighter, clenching my teeth. That explained why he didn't confess. Oli knew I wouldn't have wanted him to defend my honor. I did that all on my own when I *donated* Charlie's belongings.

"I deserved it." My ex shrugged. "I was high as a kite and in a drunken stupor most of my freshman and sophomore year. I took the whole college experience too far. I wasn't coping well."

Confusion spread through me. "Coping with what?"

"My parents were separating. They kept it from me until I was out of the house. Then, they didn't have to keep up the charade any longer, and things fell apart quickly."

"Why did you never say anything?"

His hold on his mug tightened until the tendons on his knuckles showed. "Why does anyone decide to keep secrets? Insecurity? Embarrassment? Avoidance?"

A hollow sensation settled in my chest. If he only knew how spot-on he was with that.

"I understand."

This time, I shocked him. "You do?"

"We all keep secrets from the people we love at one point or another." I pressed my lips into a thin line before I elaborated any further. "What happened to Kelly?" I needed to redirect the topic—not that this would be a less emotional conversation.

Charlie let go of his drink and rubbed his palms over his face. Leaning back in the bench seat, he folded his arms across his chest. "It was an accident."

Holding my breath, I waited.

"Mom was visiting my aunt at her beach house. We went there once..." He trailed off as he looked to the upper left, probably recalling the trip we took his senior year at Westbridge High.

"I remember," I whispered. His aunt's vacation home was on a small island connected by an endless bridge to the mainland.

"Mom was heading into town. Aunt Carol said Mom wasn't feeling well—she had been having headaches for a while—and wanted to go to the pharmacy for some migraine stuff. She had run out, and my aunt didn't have anything strong enough. Aunt Carol had a broken foot, which was why Mom was visiting in the first place. So, she couldn't go get it for Mom."

Icy suspicion slowly began to slither through my veins. I didn't like where this was going.

"The medical examiner said she blacked out while she was on the bridge. Her car went through the rail, and..." Tears were running down Charlie's face.

Please, God, no!

I couldn't breathe. My fingers curled into fists, and I dug my nails into the palms of my hands.

"She drowned." Charlie choked as his eyes found mine. The anguish in his depths was too much.

Bile rose in my throat while dark blotches appeared in front of my vision. Kelly drowned. Alone in her car. Was she in pain? Did she know what was happening? Or was she unconscious? It didn't matter...she was all alone. No one helped her. I pressed my fists to my chest. Even if someone else had been on the bridge and stopped, the water was too far below. They couldn't have gone after her. She never had a chance.

Charlie reached out. "D..."

"No!" I shrank back in my seat. "Don't." *Don't touch me.*

My skin was too tight. I peered around the café. None of the other guests were paying us any attention. I needed to get out of there.

Kelly drowned.

I reached for my purse and almost landed on my ass as I hastily slid out of the booth. "Charlie, I—" I couldn't finish the sentence. I needed to be out of there before I lost it completely. I needed water. Go under. Calm. I couldn't. Oh god...

"No Light, No Light" by Florence + The Machine is thundering through my earbuds. The sound hurts, but not enough. I want it all to stop, and for that, I need the pain before the numbness sets in. I trip and catch myself at the last moment, jumping both feet to either side of the band.

Without pausing, I prop myself on the sidebars and start running again, not fully touching the band until my feet keep up with the speed. I slowly lower myself, my legs nearly buckling. Each muscle in my legs is rubbery. I refuse to slow the pace.

Not one minute later, I stumble again. One of my wireless earbuds falls out and is catapulted somewhere behind me. But this time, I don't have to break my stride. One ear with music will have to do. I can't stop. Suddenly, the emergency stop is pulled, and I hit the screen of the treadmill.

"Owww!" My ribs collide with the edge. The stabbing sensation causes stars to pop up behind my squeezed eyelids. I wrap my arms around myself, bending over.

"What the fuck are you doing?" The thrashing pulse in my ears drowns out the seething demand.

Breathing in and out through my nose, concentrating on the slowly subsiding agony, I ignore him. Strong fingers curl around my biceps and pull me upright. "KELLER!"

The abrupt motion intensifies the burn, and I whirl around. My throat aches, and tears sting my eyes, but I pull my shoulders back and rip my arm out of his grasp. "My name is Denielle, *Marcus*! Stop fucking addressing me by my last name. I'm not my father."

A new emotion settles in the pit of my stomach. I needed a distraction. The pool wasn't an option. Running didn't do it for me either. Standing up to Marcus Baxter, however...the insensate urge to drown myself shrinks to a bearable level. I submerge myself in the craved numbness his presence evokes.

His hand still lifted between us, Marcus regards me with a mix of curiosity and disdain. "What the fuck are you doing, *Keller?*"

As he leans in, he lowers his palms on the sidebar of the treadmill to support his weight. Our noses almost touch as he growls my last name once more. It's his way of establishing his dominance. We both silently agreed to the rules of our little game. Tonight, though, I don't care. I bridge the gap and copy his motion from the other night—my cheek against his until my lips align with his ear. His slight stubble causes friction against my skin that instantly makes heat shoot to my core. I fight the need to shift my stance. Next, I do something I would've never in a million years expected from myself. The tip of my tongue darts out, and I lick the soft skin under his ear. Marcus goes rigid but doesn't pull back. Out of the corner of my eye, I witness his hands curl around the bar of the treadmill in a knuckle grip. One would think he is livid if it weren't for the barely audible groan he can't suppress.

I lower my voice. "Go. Fuck. Yourself. *Marcus.*" I press my lips to his flesh once before pulling away, meeting his shocked gaze. His nostrils flare with his mouth in a thin slash. I take a step back, pivot on my heels, and put one foot in front of the other. I can sense his stare on the back of my neck, but even if I wanted to execute one more power play by winking at him, I have to put all my concentration into walking out of here. My legs can barely support my weight, and for the first time in hours, I feel like the old me.

Thanks to Marcus Baxter, the man who hates my guts.

CHAPTER NINE

MARCUS

*W*HAT THE FUCK? *W*HAT THE ACTUAL FUCK?

I trail Denielle's swaying ass out of the gym. Still latched onto the treadmill, I want to crush the plastic underneath my fingers. My heart hammers at an unnatural pace, and I struggle to draw in a breath with sufficient oxygen to supply my lungs. The heat in my core fuels the contradiction shredding my insides. Part of me wants to chase her down, bend her over the nearest exercise equipment, and spank the sass out of her while watching my cock driving in and out of her tight little pussy. The other half of me itches to wrap my hands around her throat and squeeze until she can no longer talk back. Her audacity to *pretend* she is in charge, she needs to be taught a lesson.

I have no desire to work out now. My dick is throbbing, yet I refuse to give in and allow my body what it craves. For a brief moment, I debate following through with the hunt, but then shake my head. That would just prove to her that she's won this round. And that's a big, fat *hell no!*

Instead, I put my body through a workout that makes me question my ability to report for my shift in a few hours.

. . .

Despite struggling to lift my arms to slip my holster on (or walk), I show up on time.

Lilly and Rhys are in the kitchen. Audrey sits in her high chair and hand-feeds herself something resembling macaroni and cheese—at least, I hope it's that.

"Denielle is starting her new job on Thursday," Lilly interrupts my scrutiny of her daughter's nourishment. At first, I think she is addressing me, but then I realize she is talking to Rhys.

I slip into the bench seat and pull my phone out of my back pocket. Holding it in both hands, my thumbs hover over the display as I eavesdrop on the conversation.

"That soon?" Rhys swivels toward Lilly and hands her a dirty plate, which she loads into the dishwasher.

"The previous girl quit overnight, and apparently, there is a big contract happening with Liberman."

"*Denielle's* Liberman?" He sounds shocked, and my curiosity is at a new high. I'm aware that Keller was employed by Liberman Fashion until her sudden relocation to LA, but what's the big deal if—

"Collin is the main contact between Denis and his mother. Den said he'll be here next week to oversee the fabric choices." Lilly bites her bottom lip as she eyes her husband, waiting for his reaction. Rhys halts in the middle of handing her more dirty dishes.

"Are you shitting me? And she took the job?" His tone has lowered to a dangerous growl I don't often witness—unless his family is somehow threatened.

"I can handle my ex-fiancé," Denielle's voice comes from behind me. Both McGuires shift their attention to the doorway, and the sound of bare feet padding across the tiled floor tells me that she is coming closer.

The hair at the nape of my neck stands, and I tense. Her nearness causes my stomach to roll and my heart rate to pick up at the same time. Contempt and *I want to fuck her raw* are battling for control. As she appears in my peripheral vision, my fingers tighten around my phone. Another part of my body also throws his opinion into the mix. She is wearing cutoff shorts that barely cover her— uh...scratch that, they don't cover it at all. Her perfectly round ass peeks out from under the frayed hem, and my cock wins the fight. A flutter in my core accompanies my now hard-as-a-rock dick.

My grip slackens, and my phone clatters to the tabletop. All eyes in the room shift to me, and I grind my teeth.

Fucking great.

Denielle studies me with an arched brow before she refocuses on the other people in the room. She drapes her arm over the back of Audrey's high chair and strokes the little girl's cheek with the opposite hand. Audrey gapes up at her godmother with stars in her eyes.

"This job is not something I can refuse. It allows me to build a new life here and away from Collin," Denielle elaborates as she makes her way over to the fridge.

And move out of this house.

"After the manwhore is back on his side of the country," Rhys deadpans.

Manwhore?

I definitely missed something. With one hand on the handle of the fridge, Keller glances over her shoulder. Her gaze lands first on Rhys, then flicks to Lilly, glazing over me like air.

Lilly shuffles her feet. "I told him. I'm sorry."

Told him wha—

Denielle's eyes snap to mine, assessing how much attention I'm paying to the conversation. The corner of my mouth pulls up. I'm fully invested. Anything I can use to put her in her place is of interest to me.

"It's fine, babe. I didn't ask you to keep it a secret." She doesn't break our stare down, closing the fridge absently.

"I know, but I still feel like I should've asked first." Lilly takes a step toward her friend, and Denielle diverts her focus.

My shoulders drop, and I realize how stiff my spine was until now. I slowly inhale through my nose until my lungs can't take in any more oxygen. Holding my breath, I let the aggravation of her hold on me seep through every limb. When it reaches the tips of my fingers, they curl inward, and my trimmed nails dig into the palm of my hand.

Denielle moves around the island and stands next to her friend with her back to me—*cheeks* once again on full display. My cock twitches. Thank fuck the table conceals my physical state.

No one is paying me any mind. I lean back in my seat, folding my arms over my chest, following the show.

"Babe, half of New York knows. There is nothing that stays under the rug at Liberman, especially when it pertains to Collin. He made his bed when he bragged about his extracurriculars to the office gossip guy. Now he has to lie in it." She casually lifts her shoulder.

Huh, the idiot cheated on his fiancée. And she doesn't care?

I slant my head, waiting for what comes next. I overheard Ethan tell one of the other guys that *the hot ass staying on the property* recently broke off her engagement to some rich tool. I didn't stick around to find out what had put a stop to Keller joining the ranks of the East Coast high society.

"But he didn't just cheat once, D." Rhys throws his hands up, exasperated. "It went on for weeks, and he could've given you his fucking STD."

Whoa.

Heaviness in my chest suddenly overshadows the glee of her being the victim of her poor life choices. This tug-of-war is grating on my nerves. There is nothing positive about Denielle Keller—besides her fine body. Maybe.

Denielle interlaces her hands on top of her head, glancing toward the ceiling. "He didn't, though. There was no way I would've let him near me without a condom. I wasn't risking getting pregnant. Everyone knows the pill is not a fail-safe, and kids are not in my future."

Keller doesn't want kids? Not that I'd judge anyone who chooses not to have children. I never saw myself as a father, but Denielle Keller has a knack for her friends' offspring. Haddie and Audrey equally love the woman.

She drops her arms and lets them hang by her sides. Her tone changes, and I sit forward again.

"I left New York because of the humiliation he caused for me, not because I cared. I told you that I wasn't in love with him. I wouldn't make that mistake again after Charlie."

Rhys snorts. "D, this is fucking bullshit. That was in high school. Are you telling me you will never care for another man again? Plus, you just hung out with Charlie for, like, twelve hours the other day."

What a freaking soap opera.

Paying close attention, the subtle shift in Denielle's posture registers in my brain. I've been studying this woman for weeks to unearth any weakness she may have. I can probably read her better than her lifelong friends. Her palm is tapping her thigh, the movement increasing in speed. She's getting agitated.

"I had coffee with Charlie," she snaps at Rhys, and he stumbles back. "One fucking iced latte. His mother died. You know how close I used to be with Kelly." Her voice rises with every word. Lilly's wide eyes reveal that she is as shocked as the rest of us by her friend's display. Denielle stands with her profile to me, and I narrow my eyes at the tremble in her chin.

"I thought you guys had dinner as well," Lilly whispers. "Where were you, if not with Charlie?"

Denielle's head snaps to her best friend, and it's clear she got caught. I'd like to know as well where she was. She didn't show back up on the property until the middle of the night. My daily check of the security logs revealed that tidbit to me.

"I was out." She slams her bottled water on the counter,

pivots on her heels, and marches out of the room like her tight ass is on fire.

What the fuck?

I DON'T SEE Keller for the rest of the day. Lilly had to run to the office for a few hours, which, therefore, included me as her *Shadow*. Rhys stayed with Audrey, and by the time we got back, Lilly headed straight upstairs to tuck her little girl into bed. I beelined to the guesthouse to hit the pillow for a few hours of not sleeping.

When I get to the gym for my—now regular—early morning workout, Denielle has already left. The puddle around the treadmill tells me that much. A check of the feed confirms my observation. She went down to the gym shortly after midnight and left around two thirty. We don't have cameras in every room, like at the vineyard, but enough to track the movement of the property's occupants—or intruders, if anyone was ever dumb enough. Again. The need to find out why she is putting herself through this self-torture in the middle of the night is beginning to distract me more frequently than I'd like—which would be *never*.

The following day, Lilly and Keller act as if nothing had happened when I report for my shift at one. Denielle ignores me, and I gladly reciprocate the sentiment. I've officially entered the stage of permanent exhaustion, resulting in the grudging decision to pause our game. If it wasn't for my family history, I'd consider pharmaceutical help in getting me back on a semi-normal sleep schedule. I've been acting like a juvenile high school bully who has to show his opponent who's in charge—not that there was ever a question about that.

Is that right? a voice laughs sardonically in my mind.

I ignore the internal taunt.

Days blur together, and I'm starting to get back to a routine. I'm back to being the *Shadow*. We fall into the same rhythm as before *her* arrival.

Denielle has spent the last few days at her new place of employment. Being open seven days a week, she either got the short straw, or she's trying to prove something. Or she's avoiding being at the house.

IT'S MONDAY, and Lilly is at home. Rhys left for the office early for a conference call between the different heads of security. With the Altman Hotels being global, each country (or group of countries) has its own head to hire the local staff, set up schedules, etc. Essentially, all of them report to George, but Rhys, with his business degree, is the operational lead. George prefers to handle the in-person aspects, not the administrative paperwork.

I'm on first shift. I technically clocked out two hours ago, but I'm doing rounds through the house, per usual when Rhys is off the property. It's not necessary—the rest of the guys have it covered—but my friendship with Lilly and Rhys has caused me to take extra precautions with the female McGuires when they're sans Rhys at home.

My phone vibrates in my pocket, and I pull it out. An alert from the main gate tells me someone is coming up. I step up to the nearest window on the second floor and track the sleek, black Maybach as it rolls to a stop in front of the main entrance. We aren't expecting anyone, and I don't recognize the car, which makes me pause.

The passenger side door flies open, and Denielle scrambles out of the pretentious vehicle, seat belt halfway wrapped around her body. My eyes narrow, and I move closer to the glass.

What the—?

On the driver's side, a tall blond guy emerges. Collin Liberman. I did some research after the recent kitchen conversation. He is the embodiment of a spoiled rich brat. My sources confirmed that he couldn't keep his dick in his pants. Not to mention the coke habit no one has mentioned. I wonder if that's common knowledge. His white dress shirt is tucked into charcoal slacks, loafers completing the picture. I snort at the joke of a man. Peering down, I scan my attire of green tee, washed-out blue jeans, and black boots. My Parabellum shoulder holster is the finishing touch of the ensemble. I smirk at realizing that I matched my holster color to my shoes. I could've grabbed the tan one. *I guess I have one subconscious fashion weakness.*

Just as I peer back up, the dude grabs Denielle by the wrist, jerking her around to face him.

My adrenaline picks up, and I grip the window frame to remain in place. I'm not getting involved in— Denielle attempts to pull out of his hold, her eyes flying around wildly. She's acting like a cornered animal.

Soon-to-be-*dead* Collin latches onto her other arm and roots her to the spot. He's saying something to her. His face is flushed. He's barely holding on to his control. From my vantage point, the tears in Denielle's eyes are clearly visible. She keeps tugging, but her wrists are shackled by his fingers.

With my senses on alert, confusion accompanies the spiking heat. Why isn't she forcing her way out of this situation? She had no qualms about kicking me in the balls for much less. I watch for another moment, but when her chest begins to rise and fall rapidly, I have had enough. The thrashing pulse in my ears drowns out the sound my boots make with every step I take down the staircase. I rip the front door open with enough force for it to slam into the wall.

That'll make a dent.

Her quivering voice drifts toward me. "Collin, plea—"

I stop at the top step, letting my arms hang at my sides. "Get in the house, Denielle."

Both heads whip toward me, and Denielle's eyes widen. She is pale as a ghost, her makeup smeared like a bad horror movie. Her lips part, and I widen my stance so I don't march down and knock the fucker's lights out right there.

"Who the hell are you?" the dimwit asks, still not releasing her.

I ignore him and hold Denielle's gaze. She looks small. Scared. Nothing like the woman that has held her own against me the last few weeks. An unknown weight settles in my chest. Even when I was the one in charge of our game, she never reacted like this. She was resigned to her guilt. Never terrified of me. She is terrified now. I shouldn't care what happens to her. I don't want to feel anything except blame and dislike. The weight gets heavier and—

"Den." Her name is out of my mouth before I can think about it. Not once, in all these years, have I addressed her with the nickname her friends have for her. She's always been Denielle or *Keller*.

Asswipe's fingers go slack, peering confusedly between both of us. She uses this as her chance and frees herself from his hold.

"Let's go," I gentle my command. I grip the back of my neck with one hand. I can't recall using this tone with anyone but Ken. The all-too-familiar cockroaches are back.

Slowly, Denielle takes one step backward, then another, never letting Collin out of her sight. When she is far enough away, she pivots and speeds toward the house. She doesn't stop until she stands parallel to me—me facing the man she just escaped and her with her back to him. I glance at her. Her lips are trembling, and the need to wrap her in my arms overcomes me. Breathing suddenly feels like a strenuous chore.

Instead, I shift closer, the back of my hand grazing her knuckles. An electric current shoots up my arm, setting my insides aflame. She stiffens but doesn't move.

I don't break the connection, and, for the first time, I direct my focus directly at the guy. "Leave."

"Excuse me?" His whiney pitch makes me want to draw my gun to bring my point across.

"You heard me." It takes every ounce of self-control not to remove him myself.

"You have no right—"

There go the good intentions.

My H&K is in my hands before he can finish his sentence. "Now." I clench my teeth, breathing steadily through my nose.

Stay calm.

"This is ridiculous. Denielle," he huffs like a little pussy.

Aaand the safety comes off.

With both of my hands on the gun, the physical connection between Denielle is severed until she places her hands on my forearm. She doesn't put pressure into the touch. The tips of her fingers are like feathers. A shudder rolls down my spine.

I peer down at her, and she shakes her head imperceptibly. The way her brown eyes beg me puts my insides in knots. I dip my chin and lower the weapon, putting the safety back in place. Without acknowledging the dude, I pivot so my front faces her side.

I don't have to say anything. She starts walking through the still-open entrance, and I follow, leaving the almost corpse in the driveway. I shut the front door, pulling my phone out of my back pocket at the same time.

It rings twice before Ethan answers. "What's up, B?"

"Make sure Collin Liberman leaves the property and put him on the *do-not-enter* list with the gate. If I see him here again, I will put a bullet through his brain." I end the call before he can reply. I'll have to explain myself later, but for now, I have another concern—a concern I don't want to have.

CHAPTER TEN

MARCUS

My muscles uncoil, and I can inhale freely again. The whole scene couldn't have lasted more than five minutes.

While relaying my orders to Ethan, I followed Liberman's every move through the narrow window beside the entrance. He got back into his car but didn't drive away. Shifting my attention to the inside, I see Denielle round the corner on the second floor.

Oh, no you don't!

Again, two steps at a time, I give chase.

"Denielle." My tone is harsher than it should be.

She stops in her tracks but won't turn around. "Don't, Marcus." Even quieter, she adds, "Please."

Her plea hits me straight in the junk. Denielle Keller has also never pleaded with me. She has either taken my hate or, as of recently, pushed back.

"Why did you let the douche manhandle you?"

She doesn't turn. Her head dips forward, and I take a step closer. Her response is barely audible. "I can't do this with you."

With me?

"What the fuck is that supposed to mean?" My fingers tighten around the grip of my gun while my other hand curls into a fist. A muscle in the side of my neck begins to twitch.

Suddenly, a door on the first floor opens and closes, and Lilly's voice echoes through the foyer up to us. "Have you heard from D? I thought she would be home by now."

Silence.

"The guy cheated on her. She would never take him back!" Conviction rings in her statement. "She is not moving back." She's on the phone.

Denielle's back goes rigid.

Footsteps come closer, and before I can think about my actions, I shove the gun in its holster and lunge for the woman in front of me. My sudden attack startles a screech out of her, and I wrap one arm around her waist while I clamp my palm over her mouth.

At that moment, Audrey begins to fuss, and it clicks. It's bath time. Lilly is heading upstairs.

I adjust my hold and lift Denielle as if she weighs nothing. With the hand that had just prevented her from exposing us, I open the nearest door and maneuver us inside the...the fucking laundry room. Of course I end up with her in the most cliché small space. I want to slap my forehead. Why did I care if Lilly saw her? Or us. For some unknown reason, I knew that Denielle would not want her friends to witness her current state.

The only illumination in the room is the LED night-lights built into the outlets. Still in my embrace, she shifts and reaches for the light switch.

"No." I wrap my other arm around her as well, restricting her movement. My lips graze her ear when I speak, and Denielle sucks in a breath.

Neurons in my brain fire one contradicting thought after another at me. Why did I intervene in her lovers' spat?

It's not a lovers' spat if she is not with the guy.

Is she still with him? Again? She was scared of him. I

shouldn't be in here with her. I don't like the woman. She's hot as sin, but that's where it ends.

Does it?

Denielle's chest rises and falls rapidly against my arm. My other hand is splayed across her lower abdomen. With the tips of my fingers, I apply the slightest pressure, wanting to guide her closer. She complies without hesitation and melts against me. Her back molds to my front, and only one thought forms in my mind: her body was made for me. She leans her head back into the crook of my neck. Another perfect fit. Why is that? She is not meant to be mine.

She is not mine. She is the reason—

I refuse to finish the thought. Not now. Will I regret this later? Probably. Definitely! Though, it feels...right. However, right or not, that doesn't mean we can't *play*. Adrenaline begins to spread through my veins. Denielle Keller has always awakened the most primal urges in me, and this is no different.

My arm around her chest loosens, and I trail my index finger over the fabric of her top. I let it glide from her shoulder to where her sleeveless blouse dips in a deep *V*. When my hand reaches the spot where silk gives way to skin, I stifle a groan. *So soft.* The moment my fingertips make contact, I'm hyperaware of her—her breathing the only sound in the room.

Denielle trembles against my hold on her lower half. The urge to slip my hand into her blouse and cup her perfect handful is overpowering. Instead, I bite the inside of my cheek. I want to play.

A voice of reason yells at me to stop, especially after what I just witnessed outside. Something was very wrong with her. She wasn't herself. She didn't want to be touched, let alone manhandled by her ex. She was...scared. And what I want to do to her is anything but gentle. At the same time, in the deepest part of my brain—the part I keep closed off to anyone—a certainty settles in that she will not fear *me*.

We've been challenging each other for weeks, pushing our fight for dominance to its limits.

I slide my hand from her chest up until my palm loosely wraps around her throat. I let it settle there, waiting for her reaction. Is my instinct correct, or— A low moan escapes her throat, and I have my answer.

Light-headedness forces me to close my eyes. I lower my lips to the shell of her ear. "This changes nothing." It is a mere way of regaining the upper hand over her.

Denielle presses back into my groin, the firmness of her ass amplifying the sharp exhilaration of my swelling cock straining against the zipper of my jeans. The friction is equally intoxicating as it is revolting. This is Denielle. She attempts to look at me, but I force her to remain in place. "You do as I say, understood?" I growl.

"This changes nothing," she confirms, breathy, which is all I need.

I guide us forward until she is close to the built-in shelves storing linens and spare towels. My hand glides from her lower abdomen to settle on her hip while I continue to let the other rest against her throat. She swallows, and I apply the slightest of pressure. She still doesn't run. I'm impressed.

I adjust my hold, not breaking the connection to her skin as my thumb and trailing forefinger chase around her collarbone to the back of her neck. Gliding down her spine, her muscles vibrate under my touch as a low purr echoes through the room.

Squeezing both her hips, I say, "Hold on to the shelf."

The sound cuts off, and her head turns ever so slightly. I expect her to tell me to go fuck off, but she surprises me when she lifts her arms in compliance.

"So, you do know who's in charge," I attempt to mock her, but the lust in my tone betrays me. I don't want to want her, but I can't deny that I do. She remains mute, and it somehow tells me that she is aware of the bull I just spewed. She could call me out, but she doesn't.

On autopilot, my palm first glides across the small of her back and north until it settles between her shoulder blades. Her body submits to my intention as she arches into the shelving, positioning her ass perfectly for me to admire her curves.

The agonizing restraint of my jeans becomes unbearable, and I let go of her other hip. Unfastening the button, I thrust my hand inside, reaching around my raging cock to cup my balls screaming for release. The coolness of my palm, combined with freeing my dick, causes the endorphins in my brain to spike. My mouth goes dry at the sudden release of pressure.

What am I doing here?

Uncertainty throws a shadow on my need to take her like this. "Den." Her rasped name feels right on my tongue. I don't want it to.

She doesn't move.

"Look at me," I command. I need to see her eyes. Her eyes always have betrayed her. They're the reason I knew something was wrong downstairs. That I had to intervene.

Her head slowly tilts in my direction. She only turns enough to peer up at me through her lashes. She holds my stare before biting her lower lip. Neither of us speaks, yet we both think the same. She faces away again and widens her stance.

Jesus fuck.

My chest squeezes, and I trail her from head to toe. I didn't pay attention to her heels until now. She's porn come to life, her blouse slightly untucked. Her already short skirt has ridden up, the rounds of her ass cheeks peeking out beneath.

My palm digs into her flesh as it glides back south to the slope of her butt, tracing the outline of her thong with my finger through the material of her skirt. My other hand fists my shaft, stroking up and down. The grasp of my hand confirms there is no doubt at this moment. Reaching the top again, I run my thumb over the swollen head, swiping the first milky drop of precum off my tip. It's like the final warning of what's to come.

Clasping the hem, I push her skirt up until it bunches around her waist. She's wearing a bright-red lace thong, and my length jerks at the sight. Saliva pools in my mouth, and I can't decide if I want to taste her or pound my cock in her. I rarely eat pussy. There is something too personal to it that I generally don't allow myself. And this is Keller. I'm sure her cunt tastes phenomenal, but she is the last woman on earth I'd give that pleasure to—or myself.

I hook my finger around the fabric nestled between her cheeks and pull it to the side. I don't give her a chance to react before plunging two fingers between her warm folds. So wet.

"Oh, god," she moans as I pump in and out.

Not stopping my assault, I murmur in a tone that doesn't leave any room for negotiation. "Do not make a sound. Understood?"

Her head bobs up and down as she pushes against my hand pleasuring her. She takes what she needs. I want her to have it as much as I crave for her to submit to me being in charge.

Her legs begin to shake. I withdraw from her heat, settling my palm on her ass lightly before slapping it once. Denielle whimpers, and I wonder how far I can take this.

I fist my dick harder, moving up and down. "I want you to beg for my cock." I wrap my hand that just left an imprint on her ass around her long, dark hair. Angling her head until she has to look at me, I say, "Beg."

Denielle holds my gaze steadily. Then, it dips to where I am touching myself. Her tongue darts out, and she peers back up at me. I struggle not to roll my eyes back inside my head. She's dirtier than I ever imagined. A smirk pulls on the corners of my mouth. "I'm waiting."

Is this the moment she puts a stop to it?

She removes one hand from the shelf and reaches back until her small fingers are wrapped around mine. She squeezes once before guiding me to her entrance. Her heat radiates against my tip. I shiver as the flutter in my core increases.

"Give me your worst, Baxter." With those five words, she

almost puts me on my knees. She turns forward and repositions herself.

Fuck.

I'm lined up with her, and before I rethink the colossal mistake I'm about to make, I push my cock inside her tight cunt. And tight it is.

"Fuuuuck." This time, my eyes do roll back, and I pause, not to let her adjust to my size but to not immediately explode from the rush of sensation. Her heat grips around me, and I clench my jaw. I inhale slowly through my nose, calming my senses. When I regain control over my sixteen-year-old self that has suddenly resurfaced, acting like this is the first pussy we've stuck our dick in, I start moving. I don't hold back, either. I can't go slow. Slow is for sex. Slow is for someone you want to please. This is fucking. Nothing more, nothing less.

I thrust into Denielle, and she arches her back to give me an even better angle. With my hand still around her hair, I pull. A suppressed moan reverberates between us. She follows my order of not making a sound—or at least tries to.

I grip the soft flesh above her hip with my free hand, digging my fingers in. I increase my speed, my cock swelling. I struggle to follow my own command to keep quiet. I can't count how many partners I have had in the past twenty years, but this…this is different. I grind my teeth as I drive in and out, nearing the point of no return. I almost stop just to prove to myself that this is nothing—means nothing. But Denielle's cunt has other plans. She tenses around me as I tug on her hair once more, and this time, she doesn't stifle the moan. The sounds coming out of her as she milks my cock are too much. I squeeze her hip, and her moan turns to a whimper. I'm leaving marks for her to remember later how she submitted to me.

Two more thrusts, and I can't hold back. I drive forward, lifting Denielle onto her tiptoes with the sudden explosive movement. Her ass and hips roll as I thrust, my cock pressing into the limits of her body deep inside.

Stars explode behind my closed eyelids, and I still, letting the overstimulation of all senses overpower me. I groan as the last wave racks through me, and my knees threaten to buckle. I don't want to admit to myself that this is one of the best orgasms I've ever had. I can't. Not with her.

My throat burns as a bitter taste settles on my tongue. Regret is setting in, and I'm still balls deep inside of her.

I withdraw and pull my jeans back up. I tuck my still-hard, pulsing length into my briefs as my body continues to betray the thoughts that have already entered my mind.

I don't bother fastening the button before I pivot and exit the room, leaving Denielle there, holding on to the shelves, gasping, with my cum dripping out of her.

CHAPTER ELEVEN

DENIELLE

THE HEAT OF THE WATER SCORCHES MY SKIN. I'VE BEEN UNDER the spray for so long that my fingers and toes are pruned to the point that I doubt they'll ever recover.

What did I do?

This day turned from bad to unsalvageable.

I'D BEEN WORKING my ass off since I started my new job last Thursday: getting acquainted with how Denis runs things, meeting the girls working at the showroom, finding my place at La Déesse, and avoiding my BFF, to an extent.

I lost it last week when Rhys mentioned my coffee date with Charlie. As soon as he spoke his name, Kelly's face flashed in front of me, visions of her being submerged underwater, fighting to flee the confinement of her car. Charlie informed me the medical examiner concluded she was unconscious when her car filled with water. Nonetheless, my mind came up with its own version, soon replacing Kelly with— I couldn't breathe. The need to run pulsated through my body, and the more I attempted to stay and explain myself to my friends, the harder it became to supply my lungs with oxygen. Saliva began to pool in my mouth, and my stomach clenched. I couldn't form the words. The pictures flashed faster and faster in front of my mind's eye. Charlie and me in high school—happy. Tracking him down at the frat orgy—cheating. The sorrow on Kelly's face the last time I saw her when she dropped off the things I had left at their house. Her driving. Kelly going through the side rail, her car plummeting toward the water. Kelly's face morphed to my mother's—submerged underwater, her dark hair fanning around her. A visual I've suppressed for years. A wave of nausea racked through me. I raced out of the kitchen and locked myself in my room.

Needing to turn it off, I did the only thing I could think of. I filled the claw-foot tub in my room to the rim. Eyeing the shimmering surface, I propped myself on the side and stepped one foot into it, then the other. The water reached right underneath my knees. Fully clothed, I sat down. My drenched shorts and shirt weighed me down in a way that allowed me to pretend I had sunk to the bottom of a pool.

The tub was a decent size for being freestanding but not large enough to comfortably support my five feet, seven inches, which is why I hadn't used it for my *therapy* until now. I draped my legs over the edge, letting the water drip from my feet onto the white-tiled floor, my upper body automatically submerged. It didn't give me the floating sensation I would get in a pool, but all I wanted was the burn. Pushing my limits. Making it stop. I blinked my eyes open, staring up at the blurred ceiling above me.

I stayed like this until my lungs were spasming and forced me to surrender. I repeated my ritual until my mind was numb from exhaustion, and, only wrapped in a towel, I fell into a dreamless sleep on top of my mattress.

As soon as I woke, I dressed in workout clothes and headed to the gym to exercise—my new way of turning it off. Thankfully, I didn't run into Marcus that night. I couldn't have held my own against him.

The next day, Lilly tried once to ask me about my meeting with Charlie, but I just murmured that I needed time to process while chugging my entire mug of coffee, not to have to respond further. Whether she accepted my reply or just indulged me remains to be seen. She could figure out where I was, given that all her cars were supplied with trackers.

Fast forward to today's disaster.

I'd been taking Lilly's G-Wagon to work. It allowed me the freedom to come and go when I wanted. Not knowing how long I had to stay at the boutique, Lilly didn't try having one of her guys chauffeur me. I would get my own mode of transportation as soon as I saved up enough—not that Lilly cared. But I wanted to start fresh on my own and with no one's (financial) help. Be one-hundred-percent independent for the first time in my life.

With Collin arriving in LA early Monday morning, Denis and I met Sunday and went over the designs he planned to *loan* Liberman for their fall collection. The sketches were breathtaking, and when Denis asked me for my input on the fabrics, I couldn't stop the grin that stretched across my face. Phyllis had never asked for my opinion.

Needing the time to prepare myself, I arrived two hours early. I'd refused to take Collin's calls for weeks, ignored his emails, and blocked him on social media.

Maybe taking this job was a bad idea.

La Déesse didn't open until eleven on Mondays, which allowed me to hide in my office while one of the salesgirls made sure the showroom was in order.

I was reading an email inquiring about an appointment for a custom fitting when a knock on my door diverted my attention. My lips parted in surprise, and my gaze flicked to the gold-framed clock on my wall.

"You're early." I steadied my voice, despising the knot in my stomach.

"I flew in last night," Collin replied as he strode into the room. "The girl downstairs let me in." He sank into the plush pink chair opposite my desk and crossed his legs, interlacing his fingers around his knee. "How are you, sweetheart?"

He did not...

I wanted to dive across the tabletop and throttle him for his audacity to use the endearment he always addressed me with during our relationship. Instead, I leaned back in my identical chair and folded my arms over my chest. "I'm well. How is your chlamydia?"

The corner of his eye twitched. I had struck a nerve. While I never submitted to him (like I did with Marcus for years), I also never let him see *The Bulldog*.

"It was an error in judgment. I—" he began, and my snort interrupted his pathetic attempt at an explanation.

"Don't bother, Collin." I angled myself forward, placing my hands on either side of my keyboard. "I am prepared to work with you to fulfill the contract Denis and Phyllis agreed upon. Other than that, I have no desire to exchange more than the necessary words with you."

The tic in his jaw told me he was not used to me standing up to him like this, let alone putting him in his place. The knot in my belly loosened, and lightness settled in my chest. The *game* Marcus and I had been engaged in since the night at the vineyard had changed things for me. Collin had nothing on Marcus's intimidation. I also didn't carry any guilt toward my ex-fiancé. I didn't owe him shit. I pushed out of my chair and waved toward the door. "Shall we?"

Collin nodded curtly, but the thin line of his mouth told me he was not pleased with the change in our dynamic.

The morning passed relatively civilly. Denis showed up soon after, and he and Collin engaged in lengthy discussions on what was Liberman appropriate. I internally rolled my eyes so many times I made myself dizzy. Collin may have been the heir to one of the biggest fashion empires, and he was able to dress color coordinated, but his actual sense of fashion—what was up and coming—was as developed as a chimpanzee's.

Denis took us to lunch at a small but fancy (and overpriced) Italian restaurant not far from the boutique. The tables were too small to allow for sufficient personal space, and Collin and I ended up pressed against each other. I didn't think it was appropriate to all but sit in my boss's lap, but when Collin's hand landed on my thigh, I regretted my choice.

Denis (and the potential accusation of sexual harassment on the job—toward my boss) started to become the lesser of the two evils. I wrapped my hand around Collin's fingers and squeezed until his knuckles cracked. He winced but didn't make a sound. Loosening my hold, I placed his hand on his thigh, patting it once while smiling sweetly at him.

Don't you dare touch me.

We walked back to La Déesse. Collin and Denis discussed options where Collin could have dinner later, and I scanned the crowd around us until my gaze settled on a familiar face. A flutter of surprise made me stop abruptly, and Collin halted as well, touching my elbow. I couldn't avert my eyes from the person sitting on the bench outside of the boutique.

"Excuse me." I shrugged out of Collin's grasp absently before walking over to Charlie. His head snapped up at my approach, and his set mouth turned at the corners. So different from the man I spent the last two years with, yet nothing stirred inside of me. Our time was over.

"Hey." I lowered myself down.

Out of the corner of my eye, I watched Denis entering La Déesse. Collin openly studied us before following at a much slower pace.

"Hey," Charlie replied after we watched Collin disappear. "I hope I'm not getting you in trouble."

"How did you know where I work?" The pinch between my brows forced me to smooth out my features.

He wiggled his phone, and I smirked as comprehension set in. I posted a selfie in front of the window display last week after my first day.

"The girl inside said you'd be back from lunch soon. I wanted to give you something." Charlie reached behind him and revealed a small gift bag.

I attempted to mask my confusion with a smile, scanning the offering. "What's this?"

"Open it." He looked almost shy.

Pulling the handles apart, I peered into the bag and sucked in a breath. Tears instantly pricked my eyes, and I swallowed hard. "Charlie," I exhaled.

I wrapped my fingers around the large scarf. It was part of a whole outfit his mom had given me for Christmas during my junior year—the last Christmas we were together. In my hurt and anger, I had given it back with Charlie's stuff when she brought me mine. I had forgotten about it.

"I thought you might want it." The hopefulness in his tone made the slight pain in the back of my mouth morph into someone shoving razor blades down my throat.

My grip around the fabric turned to a vise, and I pulled it free from the small paper bag, clutching the material to my chest. My inhales and exhales sped up, and a tear escaped the corner of my eye.

"Awww, D." Charlie reached out, but I jerked away on autopilot.

With my back against the armrest, I found myself facing the man I once loved from the other end of the bench. The metal pressed into my lower back, yet my skin and muscles were numb to the sharp sensation. I saw him, and at the same time, my mind was catapulted back and assaulted by visuals of my childhood. Charlie's palms were toward me in a disarming gesture as I fought against the constricting agony in my chest. It hurt. I pressed my mouth together and tried to draw in air through my nose in slow, deep breaths—how I was taught to do in these *situations*. It wasn't working. Sweat formed under my silk blouse, and it stuck to my clammy skin. Pedestrians were starting to slow. Somewhere far away, Charlie's muffled plea for me to look at him registered. Something wrapped around my wrists, and a cry burst from my lips. I was in public. I needed to get it together. I couldn't. If Denis saw me like this, I was going to lose my job.

"What is going on here?" Collin's voice entered the mix. *Had he always sounded so nasal?*

I tried to answer, but all I managed was a croak. Someone tugged on the scarf, and I pulled back. No!

Don't take it from me.

"Denielle. Answer me," Collin shouted. "What have you done to my fiancée?" my ex exclaimed, and I finally managed to look at the men in front of me.

Fiancée? Has he lost his—

Charlie blanched, while Collin was bright red.

Concentrating on my surroundings slowed my thrashing pulse.

Suddenly, Collin reached out and cuffed my upper arm with his hand. No, no, no. His touch felt like needles, causing my heart rate to spike anew. I whimpered, writhing in his grip but unable to dislodge him. Where did my strength go? A wave of nausea rolled through me, and I clamped my free hand over my mouth. Black spots appeared, and my legs began to tremble.

"Walk away now, or I'm going to have you arrested," Collin threatened Charlie, whose mouth just opened and closed like a fish. I wanted to apologize—not that I could give him an explanation of what just happened.

Collin steered me toward La Déesse where Denis observed *the show* from within the doorframe, a frown on his face. I stumbled over the threshold, my blurry vision obscuring where I was being dragged. All I could do was follow as I tried not to vomit on the hardwood floor in front of me. My hair clung to the nape of my neck, and waves of icy shivers racked through me.

"I'm taking her home. She must've eaten something wrong," Collin explained to Denis, who nodded with disbelief marring his features. I was going to lose my job and couldn't do anything about it. I couldn't form the words necessary to communicate the lie I was brainwashed to repeat.

We don't talk about Denielle's condition, my father always insisted.

Collin didn't stop as he led me through the showroom toward the back of the building. We exited through the back entrance, reserved for our private clientele, and he dragged me over to what must have been his rental. My ankle rolled as I tripped over something on the ground, but Collin's grip simply tightened.

"Oww," a cry burst out.

He didn't stop until we were next to the passenger side. I wanted to tell him that I could drive myself home, I had a car, but I only managed a wheezing sound. My thudding pulse made it hard to breathe.

Collin halted, scanning my face before he shook his head and hissed, "Get a grip, Denielle."

What?

He looked at something behind me, but I couldn't muster the strength to check. Opening the door, he deposited me in the seat and buckled me like a child. The door slammed shut, and I jumped.

Collin slid in on his side and, without looking at me, started the car, peeling out of the parking lot.

Why is he so angry?

My fingers tightened around the soft material still in my hand, and I lifted the scarf to my face. Closing my eyes, I pressed the fabric against my skin, letting the visions batter down on me. I was helpless to the onslaught. As helpless as I was every single time in the past. The pictures were accompanied by the sound of water splashing. Someone screaming. Me. The burn intensified, and I realized I was holding my breath.

Kelly's present was yanked out of my grasp. No! Where did it go? My eyes darted around the small space, and I tracked the scarf flying into the back seat. My heart skipped a beat as I scrambled after it. Fingers clamped down on my shoulder, and the car swerved.

"What the fuck are you doing? SIT DOWN!" Collin barked. "Jesus, your father never said you would act like such a lunatic."

My father? Wha— Collin knew? My father told him about my...condition? How is that even possible?

Collin's hand wrapped around my wrist, and all mental clarity evaporated. He knew. I pressed my body against the door in a failed attempt to get away from him. Had this all been a game? His manicured nails cut into the inside of my wrist.

"STOP IT!" His command hits its target as if he'd back-handed me. My vision began to cloud further. "I'm taking you home. We will talk about this later."

My eyes fluttered closed, and my body went slack. Not because I gave up, but I needed him to release me, even if it was just for a second. The longer he held on, the harder it was not to scream. And I knew that once I started, I wouldn't stop. And then I'd most likely end up in the hospital. Or worse. Medicated.

My father had told him.

I managed to keep it together until we reached the gates leading up to Lilly's estate. A new wave of panic crashed down on me. I would have to face my friend. She was home. She wouldn't accept a halfhearted excuse this time. Collin stopped at the gate, and the guard peered through the window, recognizing me. I must've nodded, because we were granted access. Did the driveway get longer? I needed to get out of the confinement of the car.

We slowed in front of the main entrance, and I reached for the door handle. Collin's hand landed on my leg, and this time, the screech burst out. I managed to throw the door open but forgot about the seat belt. It delayed my escape, and he caught up to me.

"Collin, plea—"

"Get in the house, Denielle," the last person I ever wanted to see me like this boomed from Lilly's front door.

CHAPTER TWELVE

DENIELLE

I'M STANDING IN FRONT OF THE FULL-LENGTH MIRROR IN MY bedroom, clasping the edges of the cream towel together over my chest. My skin is flaming red where I let the hot spray pelt down on me. My dark hair hangs in nearly black tangles down my back.

What did I do?

I flutter my lids closed and breathe in deeply. Slowly blinking, I loosen my death grip and uncurl my fingers. The towel pools around me on the floor as I hang my arms to my sides. My gaze trails over my body, starting at my lips. He didn't kiss me. Lower to my throat where he held me. I should've been afraid. He had threatened to choke me on more than one occasion. The mere thought of letting Charlie wipe away my tears had caused my chest to tighten. Collin's hands around my wrists had felt like barbed wire, not to mention— My pulse picks up, and I divert where my mind is heading again.

I'm drained, my limbs heavy with exhaustion. I can't handle another panic attack today. I trail farther downward, over my breasts... The moment the tips of Marcus's fingers moved from my blouse to flesh, every nerve ending in my body was set ablaze. The heat that spread through me like an inferno was almost too much to bear. At the same time, it was all I wanted to feel. Heat had pooled in my core, dampening my underwear. The need for him to touch me eclipsed everything—the panic, the helplessness—I had felt before he interfered in front of the house. I'd never been this embarrassed and relieved at the same time. No one could stand up to Marcus Baxter, least of all Collin. Marcus pulled his gun on Collin. For me.

Why?

I settle on the four small bruises on my hip, where he dug his fingers in as he thrust in and out of me. Warmth floods me, remembering the sting accompanied by the fullness of his cock.

This changes nothing.

While that may be true, it changes everything. Maybe not for him, but for me. For years, the only thing capable of helping me escape was water, submerging myself... Or drugs—the legal kind. The kind my parents convinced me I needed. I hadn't touched any of the prescription bottles in years, tossing them as soon as Celine sent the ordered refill from my father.

Marcus's nearness was like a drug, his touch what water never accomplished—no matter how long I remained under. He made me forget and feel everything at the same time. He wasn't gentle or even kind. He had left me, legs spread, standing in my best friend's laundry room. Yet, I couldn't be upset. He touched me at my worst, his connection like a life-line bringing me back to myself. Not to forget the orgasm none will ever measure up to. I have to clench my thighs, just thinking about it.

Thank God I've been on the pill for years—the first thing Celine did when Charlie and I had become more serious. Yet, neither Marcus nor I made any attempt to protect ourselves. I had never been that careless, which saved me from the STD my fiancé got himself. Maybe subconsciously, I never trusted Collin, no matter how long we were together. But Marcus...he isn't that type of man.

Is he?

No. From what Lilly mentioned on the rare occasion we spoke about her *Shadow*, he barely left the property. Never had a relationship. He lived for his job. It was his twisted way of redeeming himself after not protecting McKenna.

I glide my index finger over each of the small imprints, pressing down ever so slightly. The sting causes me to bite my bottom lip.

This changes nothing.

THE NEXT MORNING, I descend the stairs. With every step, the nervous tingle in my chest expands. How do I explain to Lilly where her car is? Entering the kitchen, I find Lilly and Audrey engaged in a one-sided argument, my best friend begging her daughter to try some scrambled eggs. Marcus leans against the island, hiding his amusement behind a mug as he watches.

His eyes snap to mine, and the smirk vanishes. He doesn't look away but also gives me no indication that what happened in the laundry room was of consequence for him. Holding his stare, my bruises begin to tingle with the memory of how he ran his fingers in excruciating slowness down my spine to—

"Hey, D.!" Lilly's greeting forces me to break the visual connection. A feverish flush burns itself from my neck to my cheeks. I need a distraction.

Flipping my attention to Audrey, I scan the tray in front of her. "What's going on, little miss? Why are you giving your mom such a hard time?" I pick up a piece of cold egg and plop it in my mouth, pretending the cold orange-yellow blob is the most delicious meal ever. It isn't, but it does what I had hoped. Suppressing a gag as I swallow the gooey mass has snuffed out the desire after coming face-to-face with Marcus.

Audrey eyes me skeptically before slowly fisting a big chunk of egg. She peers between her mom and me, and I nod encouragingly.

"Hmmm, if you don't eat it, I will," I purr. Let's hope I can at least lie to a one-year-old.

She hesitates one more moment before shoving the entire thing in her mouth. Everyone in the room holds their breath as we watch the tiny human determine if she likes her food. Audrey swallows and immediately reaches for a second helping. Lilly throws up her hands in defeat, and I burst out laughing.

"Why couldn't you have come down thirty minutes ago?"

I cross the distance and hug her to my side. "Can't make parenting too easy for you now, can I, babe?"

She returns my embrace with a huff.

Pulling back, I scan her features. "Hey, um, could one of you give me a ride to work this morning?"

Lilly frowns. "Why?"

Before I can answer, Marcus speaks behind us. "Ethan picked up the car." His tone drips with disdain, and I jerk around.

My brows pull together, waiting for him to elaborate—anything that would explain (a) why someone picked up the SUV for me, and (b) how this warranted such hatred.

I haven't deluded myself into thinking that we're suddenly on civil terms just because he fucked me raw and gave me the most mind-blowing orgasm. But this? He must've initiated for Ethan to get the G-Wagon. No one else knew I didn't drive it home.

"Oh," is all I manage.

Lilly's gaze flickers between us, and I don't want to know the questions piling up in her head. Avoiding the interrogation, I blurt out, "Collin drove me home after work. I had a few drinks at lunch. Denis's treat." I swivel on my heels and speed to the espresso maker, my pace matching my drumming heartbeat.

With my back to the room, I get busy. I sense my best friend's stare boring into the back of my head. The hairs at the nape of my neck stand at attention.

"We have to get going if you want to make your meeting," Marcus tells Lilly.

There is a moment of silence, and I wait for Lilly to shut him down, curiosity and suspicion probably gnawing at her.

"Give me fifteen." She pauses, and I don't have to turn to know that she is throwing another glance in my direction. "Can you let Rhys know that we're leaving? Laurin will be here in thirty."

Laurin is Audrey's nanny whenever Lilly and Rhys both have to be in the office. It isn't often, but they pay the girl well enough for her to drop everything when she's needed. She is one of the board member's kids, which helped vet her background down to her panty size.

Audrey protests. She must still be going to town on the eggs when Lilly picks her up. "I'll see you tonight, D.," Lilly calls out as her retreating steps inform me that she is heading upstairs.

"See you later, babe," I reply, wanting to sag against the counter.

I'm finally getting to work on my caffeine fix, but before I can pour the grounds into the filter, someone steps up behind me. Heat radiates off his body, and my stomach flips. I turn my head sideways so he gets my profile.

"Can I help you, Marcus?" I lace my question with acid. We're back to our game—level two.

He steps closer, his entire front fitting to my back, and I fight the need to push my ass against his groin. My breath instantly speeds up as my body remembers how it felt when he dominated me yesterday.

His warm breath fans over my cheek. "How about a thank-you, *Keller*?"

I tilt my head far enough to meet his eyes. "Sure, I will catch Ethan later and thank him for picking up the car." I smile at Marcus as he hollows his cheeks in frustration.

I take a step back, forcing him to retreat. Pivoting on my heels, I face him, placing my palm over his chest. The thudding underneath tells me he's anything but unaffected, but he also doesn't dislodge my hand.

I raise myself to my tiptoes until our noses almost touch. His eyes narrow. I slant my head, letting my gaze move back and forth between his eyes before pressing my lips to the corner of his mouth. Marcus goes rigid, and his hand shoots out, gripping the same hip he bruised the day before. I don't flinch at the sudden attack. Instead, I pull back, and he peers down at me.

"Thank you," I breathe before sidestepping him and walking away—without my espresso.

I KISSED MARCUS BAXTER. Well, not kissed *kissed*, but close enough. My lips were on his mouth. The corner of it. What the actual fuck was I thinking? I couldn't stop myself. Being in his vicinity makes me feel...different. No! Not different. He brings the Denielle I used to be to the surface. The girl I was in high school. The one who didn't take shit from anyone. Even with his dislike for me and what I represent to him, I can't help the surge in power his presence gives me.

I'm halfway to La Déesse when the car announces an incoming call through its speakers. Oli's name flashes over the display in the console, and the corners of my mouth automatically pull up. I haven't talked to my brother in a few weeks, and it's time to catch up. I press the button on the steering wheel, accepting the call.

"Brother dearest!"

His deep laugh echoes through the surround sound of the G-Wagon. "You're in a good mood, Nelle!" My brother is the only one who calls me that. He couldn't pronounce Denielle as a toddler, and my parents didn't approve of shortening my name. It used to be D'nelle, and eventually, Nelle stuck. We are Denielle and Oliver to our parents, not Den, not D., not Oli. The tic in my father's jaw is ever present when we address each other with our nicknames.

"I am." *I surprised Marcus Baxter.* "I'm on my way to work. What's up?" The lightness in my chest expands hearing his voice.

"How's that going? Do you like it there?" He always wants to know what's happening in my life. We might not have been as close as Lilly was growing up with her "*brother*," but he's always been one of my best friends. Maybe because he's also the only one who knows the full truth. He was there for me when my father tried to hide me from the outside world.

"It's good. Denis is great. Nothing like Phyllis." Collin's mother's name leaves a sour taste on my tongue. Did she know as well?

"That's awesome. You deserve it. I never saw you fitting in with Liberman. You're too..."

I can picture him grasping for the right word and cackle, "I'm what?"

"Free spirited," he supplies.

I roll my eyes. "How long did it take you to come up with that *endearment*?"

"It was Elena. I was gonna say bitchy." The grin is audible, and I shake my head.

"You're a dick," I chuckle. "Where's Elena? Let me talk to her."

My brother and his girlfriend have been together since college, when I was still in high school, and everyone is waiting for them to take the next step. They are in no rush, though.

"She's out. But that's why I'm calling."

"Oh?"

"We're in San Diego for her friend's wedding and thought about driving up to see you."

A surge of excitement flutters in my belly. "YES! When?"

"Ha, who do you want to see more? Elena or me?" he jokes but continues before I can reply, *Elena, duh*. "Friday. It's short notice, but we didn't know if we could make it until now. Chloe moved the rehearsal dinner to Thursday, and the wedding is Saturday."

I mentally go over my schedule, which, besides work, is wide open. "I'll check with Denis to see if he needs me. He and Collin should be done with contract *negotiations* by then."

Oli must've been drinking something because a choking sound followed by violent coughing comes through the speakers.

"Are you okay?" My eyes fly between the call on the screen and the road.

It takes him a few more coughs to regain his composure. Oli clears his throat. "What do you mean, Collin and Denis? What's going on, Nelle?"

I sigh—no point in playing it down. "Collin is in LA. Denis and Phyllis had an agreement that Liberman includes some of La Déesse's designs in their fall collection."

"Ugh," my brother harrumphs, "and Denis didn't reveal that tidbit before he offered you the position?" He's pissed.

"He probably assumed I knew." I try to play it down. "Oliver?" There is something I can't play down, though.

"Yes?" His hesitation tells me he won't like what I have to say next. I rarely call him by his full name.

"Collin knows. I, uh..." Fuck, I don't want to say it. Not that Oli would ever snitch to our parents, but I don't want him to worry. I hold my breath and then blurt, "I had an episode." I limit it to yesterday's incident and omit what happened at the vineyard.

"What happened?" he whispers. My brother has seen me at my worst. He used to fish me out of the pool more times than I could count when I was younger. Or stay and watch to make sure I would come back up when it became apparent that I needed the *water therapy*.

I replay the morning to him and end with Collin driving me home. He is as shocked as I was when I repeat Collin's words about our father.

"That makes no sense. Why would Dad tell him?"

"I have no clue, but I don't like it. It gives him something to hold over me. And I wouldn't put it past him to use it to his advantage." I sound small.

I'm parked behind the boutique now but don't disconnect the call. I need to confide in someone, and Oli is the only one I can.

"Nelle, promise me something." His seriousness makes me sit up straighter.

My feet are both propped against the floorboard, and I press my palm on my knee to stop it from bouncing. "What?"

"If he tries to pull something on you, you need to go to Lilly."

The thumping in my ears mutes my response. "I can't."

"Denielle Keller!" My brother rarely gets angry with me. He is now. "Lilly is your best friend. Why would you not tell her? You did nothing wrong. This is not your fault."

I know his words are the truth. I didn't choose this. "I don't want her to see me differently," I admit. She already knows about what happened with Dad and Marcus. In my retelling, I also confessed that Lilly is aware of our father's hand in what happened with McKenna Baxter.

He softens his voice. "Why would she ever see you differently? You didn't change your opinion of her when she revealed her secret to you, did you?"

"No?" My meek response sounds more like a question.

"You didn't," he states firmly. "And neither would she. Nelle, you were a child when you witnessed— You couldn't do anything about it, and your mind chose a...coping mechanism. Everyone deals with trauma differently. And you had the predisposition for it to be triggered. What happened to McKenna...that would've happened with Dad there or not. No one could've foreseen that. Brain surgeries are unpredictable, or have you forgotten Dad's trademark statement during every lecture he holds?"

"You're right," I concede.

"Are you appeasing me, or do you really believe it?" Skepticism drips from his words.

I don't lie to Oli. Ever. "Both."

"Please think about talking to Lilly."

"I will." I shut off the car. "Call me when you have the time for Friday, 'kay?"

There is a brief pause before Oli agrees. We say our good-byes, and I enter La Déesse, hoping I still have a job.

CHAPTER THIRTEEN

MARCUS

My feet are rooted to the tiled kitchen floor. I dig the heels of my hands into my eyes. Did she really just do that? Denielle Keller took my control over her, over our *game,* and shoved it up my ass.

Dropping my hands, I reach one to my groin, adjusting my cock straining against my jeans.

And I liked it. When her soft lips touched my mouth, the organ behind my ribs stuttered before breaking into a sprint like a fucking racehorse. My fingers itched to wrap themselves around her slender waist, digging into her flesh while turning her sassy peck into something entirely different. If she hadn't broken the connection, my self-control would've snapped, and we would've had a repeat from yesterday—in the pantry this time.

Fuck!

After leaving her in the laundry room last night—*fleeing,* a more accurate term—I went straight to the guesthouse. Walking in, I barked at Alexa to play music and turn it up. The surround-sound system shook with "Venom" by Eminem, and standing still in the middle of the room, I let the bass vibrate through me. Letting the playlist do its thing, I moved to take the coldest shower in the history of warm-water shortages. I needed to over-power all my senses.

By the time I allowed myself to shut the spray off, my body was trembling uncontrollably. My muscles spasmed from the torture and their attempt to stay warm. I wrapped my towel around my hips, not drying the icy droplets off my skin. I needed to prolong the physical pain for as long as possible.

I had fucked Denielle Keller. Bare.

I'd never done it without protection. *Ever*. She's on the pill—that much I gathered from her exchange with Lilly and Rhys the other day. I'm clean. I get that shit tested regularly, despite my usual OCD to suit up. Emphasis on usual. What the fuck was I thinking? I wasn't, that's what. Fuck. The woman was the reason I lost my sister. If she hadn't gone for her little swim, her father would've been in the OR, able to stop the aneurysm. Or that's what I've convinced myself of for the past two decades. He had been the best on the East Coast. When a nurse informed me he was operating on Ken—who he was—I had hope. Hope that was splattered like obliterating a bird with a large-caliber rifle. His spoiled little brat of a daughter didn't like the dinner her new mommy cooked—or whatever her tantrum was about—and fell into the pool. Victor Keller had left the OR, and my sister died.

My hands curled around the edges of the vanity as I stared at myself in the mirror. From the living room, the sounds of "Mir-ror" by Lil Wayne and Bruno Mars drifted in, and I huffed noncomically. *What a joke*. The memories began to resurface—memories I only allowed myself to relive once a year, on the anniversary. Being at the vineyard, I didn't get to mourn the way I was used to.

. . .

*"W*OULD *you like to see her? Say your goodbyes?" the elderly woman in scrubs had asked with pity in her eyes after the doctor had left.*

See her? My stomach rolled as I forced the bile back down my throat. I couldn't.

I didn't want to remember her like that. Bloody and bruised. Her long blonde hair plastered to her sun-kissed skin. I wanted to see her bright smile when I thought of my baby sister. The way she had beamed up at me when I came home that evening, presenting her with a large burger and fries from the diner she loved. We didn't spend money on fancy food, but that night, I had finished a project at the garage I worked at part time, and my boss had paid me an extra fifty. That could technically feed Ken and me for two weeks on PB&Js, but I wanted to treat her to something special.

"MARCUS!" she had squealed and tackled me so hard that I dropped the paper bag with the present on the floor. Untangling herself from me, she chastised, "You shouldn't have wasted your money on this." Ken peered down to my feet. The longing in her gaze was all I needed.

I hugged her to me. "You know I will always take care of you."

Always being two more hours.

We had sat on the couch, watching something on our ancient TV that was so fuzzy I had no clue how Ken could even follow the plot, when our father came home.

Ken instantly stiffened, and I leaned closer to her until our arms touched. She relaxed into me, but the strain around her eyes told me she was anything but—an emotion I could relate to. I reminded myself that if we didn't acknowledge or bother him, he would leave us alone—or so it normally went.

The refrigerator door opened and closed, followed by the pop of uncapping his beer. The paper-thin walls in the house hid nothing. When there was no sound coming next, I realized my error. We had thrown the burger wrappers in the bin next to the sink—instead of taking the trash straight outside to the dumpster where he couldn't see it.

"WHAT THE FUCK IS THIS?" his bark traveled across the hall to the living room, and Ken shrank into the cushions next to me.

Ken's hand landed on my thigh, her fingers curling into my muscles.

"Go to your room and lock the door," I whispered.

My sister's eyes flew between me, the doorway, and our only other escape: the window.

"GO!" I hissed, and she jolted up.

She wasn't fast enough. Dad appeared in the frame, one hand around the neck of his bottle, the other clenching the orange-and-white wax paper.

He waved it in front of Ken, who stood frozen in the middle of the room. "Did you spend my hard-earned money again, you little shits?" His narrowed eyes traveled between us before he settled on me. He was swaying, a.k.a. he had stopped at the bar after work.

The beating of my heart thundered in my ears as I slowly raised myself from the sofa, not letting him out of sight. He was unpredictable when he was drunk before coming home. Most of the time, he didn't start until his ass was planted in his recliner, but on especially tough days, he started early.

The threat looming over us made sweat form on the back of my neck, and my knees barely supported my weight. I needed to put myself between him and Ken. Not that our father was overly tall or muscular. We were the same height, with Ken reaching my shoulder, but he got fed at the factory—the one benefit his job held. Compared to him, Ken and I were scrawny, living off the little money I made—whatever didn't go toward paying the bills. My feet glided over the ratty carpet, my soles never leaving the stained surface. I ensured to maintain a balanced stance at all times. We never knew when he would snap and his fist would come flying. I could handle it, but my sister...

"I ashked ou a quesh'n!" he bellowed, and Ken stumbled back. The words were slurred.

This was not good. He was already too far gone to see reason.

"Mike ordered food for the garage, and I brought mine home for Ken," I lied.

"BULLSHIT!" He took a step toward my sister, and that was it. I jumped in front of him at the exact moment the back of his hand impacted with the side of my head—the blow meant for Ken.

"RUN! Go to Mrs. Benson." We hid at our neighbor's at least once a

week. It wasn't unusual for one or both of us to show up at her doorstep in the middle of the night.

Ken whirled around, scrambling for the window instead of the front door—another tactic we had developed over the years. I would hold him off long enough for her to escape.

Dad attempted to sidestep me, but I blocked him, my palms pressed against his chest. I turned my head to confirm Ken had made it. She was straddling the windowsill with one leg outside when a hard object impacted on top of my head. A flash of agony shot through my scalp and down my spine. My legs gave out. I crumpled to the floor, clutching my uncut hair as warmth trickled down my temple. My vision faded in and out, and I zeroed in on the discarded bottle next to me as our father took chase.

"LEAVE HER ALONE!" Panic eclipsed the searing pain, and I scrambled to my feet. "I bought the food! Ken has nothing to do with it!" She couldn't hold her own against his violent streaks. Neither could I, but better me than her.

He ignored me as he latched onto her ankle before she fully made it outside.

"Ahhh!" Her ear-piercing scream was what I needed for my brain to focus. I threw myself forward and tackled him to the ground, forcing him to release my sister.

He bucked, though, throwing me off, and I landed on my back. The wind got knocked out of me, immobilizing me momentarily. He used that as an opportunity to straddle my legs. His fist was raised high, and I covered my face. I was prepared for the impact when tires screeched outside. The silence that followed was quickly replaced by shouts and cries of devastation.

My father froze, and ice punctured my heart as the sounds traveled through the open window. Using his temporary distraction to shove him off, I flipped to all fours and started crawling. I was unsure if my legs would support my weight. When I reached the front door, I pulled myself up and twisted the knob at the same time. Dizziness forced me to hold on to the frame before stepping through.

My breathing was labored from the struggle. My eyes adjusted to the *scene in front of me, and my thoughts raced to catch up with the message it received. No! I locked on Mrs. Benson standing in her faded robe on the sidewalk, her mouth covered with her wrinkled hands. Someone else kneeled on the street—the driver of the car. I followed the man, who had a cell phone pressed to his ear, to where his other hand hovered over a body. No, no, no. My lungs refused to take in oxygen as I staggered down the cracked walkway. I knew what I would find but refused to accept it. With every step, more of my sister's form came into view.*

"Marcus, don't—" Mrs. Benson's voice called out, sounding like I was underwater.

The pounding in my ears made it hard to concentrate. All I saw was Ken's bloodied face.

I PULLED my arm back and let my fist soar forward, shattering my reflection. I pounded the mirror over and over until there was nothing left to destroy. Shards covered every part of the sink and vanity. The sharp sting traveled from my knuckles until the burn reached my shoulder. My chest heaved as I propped myself on the edge. My body was coated with sweat, yet at the same time, I was still shivering. With hunched shoulders, I scanned the damage. Crimson dripped from cuts across my knuckles onto the white porcelain, and more memories flooded my mind.

Sitting on the asphalt with my baby sister was the last vivid memory I had of her. After that, everything was a blur. The cops and paramedics arrived, I rode with Ken to the hospital, they wheeled her away, and...she never came back.

Our father didn't bother to exit the house that evening. He never checked on what happened outside, why his children didn't come back into the house. When I finally made it home in the early morning hours, I found him passed out in his worn-down chair. His mouth hung open, saliva dripping from the corner.

I stared at him, letting the hollow cold spread through me like a glacier slowly melting in the warm sun. I remembered trembling all over, the tips of my fingers numb to the point of them hurting. I could've stood there a minute or an hour. I had no idea. Nothing mattered. I had lost the only person I cared about. I didn't protect her. I failed Ken. That would never happen again.

I haphazardly wiped my fingers on the towel wrapped around my lower half.

They took my sister from me. He. She. My father. Victor Keller. Denielle. She was a piece of the puzzle that destroyed my life. And I had given in to this beautiful shell—fucked her.

I WALKED out of my father's house with him passed out. All I had were the clothes on my back, a small duffel in one hand, and Ken's favorite stuffed tiger in the other. I was eighteen. It had been a miracle he hadn't kicked me out months ago. But then, he needed my meager salary.

I enlisted that day and didn't return for my revenge until months later.

Ironically, I found my father in the same position as I'd left him. However, he was the one still the same—I was not. I advanced to where his feet hung off the leg rest of his recliner, studying the man who gave me life and took it. I was breathing, my heart was pumping blood through my veins, yet I was not alive. I always thought it sounded ridiculous when people said they turned off their emotions, their ability to feel. It wasn't difficult at all. All you needed was to lose what you cared most about and let revenge drive your sense of purpose.

I sidestepped the chair and reached for the ratty cushion on the couch. My adrenaline should've been through the roof, my blood thrashing through my veins. My conscience should've screamed at me to stop. Don't do this. None of it was present. There was nothing. Darkness had settled in my chest the second I saw the doctor entering the waiting room. Not Victor Keller. Another medical professional did his dirty work.

My fingers curled around the edges of the pillow, clutching it until the ancient fabric tore under my nails. I scanned his blotchy, red skin. Years of alcohol abuse had permanently changed his appearance. I waited one more moment, waiting for hesitation to set in. When it didn't come, I lowered the object over his face and pressed my fists into either side of the headrest, putting as much pressure behind my reason to come home as my newly trained strength allowed. I cut off his oxygen supply. First, he didn't move. My father had too much booze in his system to wake up when he was about to die. Then, his limbs started jerking. I didn't startle at the sudden movement, simply tightened my hold. One hand grasped for me, but it never made contact. His arm flailed in the air without finding its target. His legs twitched. I didn't let go. The whole scene was over faster than I'd expected. Even after his palms landed in his lap and he stilled, I didn't let up. I had to make sure he would no longer be a threat.

MY FATHER HAD TRIGGERED McKenna's fate. Denielle Keller had been a nail in her coffin. I repeated the sentence in my head over and over as I bandaged my knuckles. I had let my dick take over my thinking. No matter what was going on with Denielle and why she was terrified of her ex, it was of no consequence to me. I let my grief for not protecting my sister cloud my judgment.

Dressed, I had placed a call to Ethan. I should have let Keller run face-first into her wall of lies. Lilly was supposed to be her best friend. She opened her home, yet Denielle kept a shit ton of secrets from her.

I had done it for Lilly, my friend.

"B?" Ethan had answered, confused.

"Have one of the guys pick up the G-Wagon at La Déesse." I didn't give him any further explanation, using the *I'm your boss,* to justify myself. He knew better than to question my orders, regardless of what a smart-ass he was at other times.

"Uh, okay?"

I hung up, peering at the clock on the stove. It was only seven, not time for bed, but I also didn't want to go back to the main house. Opening the fridge, I propped myself against the door. A flutter of relief and excitement swirled in my stomach.

Ethan had forgotten the remnants of the six-pack he had brought last time he came over, leaving four for me.

Not how I had planned on spending my evening, but everything was better than reliving the moment my cock entered Denielle's pussy. Heat instantly flooded me, and I grabbed the first bottle from the shelf, forgetting about my error in judgment —until she placed her lips on the corner of my mouth the next morning.

CHAPTER FOURTEEN

DENIELLE

I find Denis in his office slash studio. Thankfully, Collin is nowhere in sight. I knock on the frame and wait for him to acknowledge me. He's hunched over his desk, sketching. His pursed lips clue me in that he is in his own world—I've seen that on a few occasions in the short time I've worked for him. It takes two more taps before he notices me.

"Denielle! How are you feeling?"

"Better, thank you." My mouth runs dry as I take a step forward. Wringing my hands together, I hesitate. "I, uh... I wanted to apologize for yesterday." *Please don't ask what happened.* I don't want to lie to him.

"No need. We all go through things, and unless it impacts your ability to do your job, I won't pry." Denis glances between me and his sketchpad. Is he trying to get rid of me, or does he mean it? I slant my head, scanning his features. He appears genuine, but suspicion gnaws on my insides, especially after what Collin revealed.

"What's on today's agenda?" I decide not to press the issue, topic, whatever you want to call it. If he doesn't, I certainly won't.

Denis twists to the side, hitting a few keys on his laptop. "You have a consultation in an hour. The request came in last night. She has one of my previous designs—a few years old—and wants some alterations. You can handle it."

Um, wow. I've been here less than a week, and he saw me lose it in the middle of the street, yet, nonetheless, he hands me a new customer. "Are you sure? I mean, after... and, you know..." My gaze flitters across the room, everywhere but at my boss. Disbelief urges me to get additional confirmation.

He waves me off, peering down at whatever he's working on. "Absolutely. I must make a few changes before your *darling ex* returns at three." The way he sneers his words indicates he enjoys Collin's company as much as I do.

Immature satisfaction pulls at the corner of my mouth. "Okay. Let me know if you need anything. I'll be downstairs." When he doesn't respond and ferociously begins to put pencil to paper, I take it as my dismissal.

I drop off my purse in my office. Stopping in the small kitchen, I finally get the caffeine fix I forwent earlier, thanks to my grand idea to put my mouth on Marcus Baxter.

Standing in the small space, I eye the lined mugs in the open cabinet. Images of fresh linens flash in front of me. My fingers wrapped around the edge of the shelf while Marcus... A tingling sensation begins to stir in my core and spreads while a flush creeps up my neck. I raise my palm to my face. *Jesus, I need to get it together.* My cheek is feverish, and my eyes flutter closed. That was, by far, one of the dumbest decisions I've ever made.

At this rate, I won't be able to focus on the client, who is supposed to be here in—I open my eyes and glance at my watch —twenty minutes. I inhale slowly through my nose and hold my breath until the burn begins to spread before releasing it with a whoosh. This is in the past, all of it. None of it ever happened— at least that's what I'll pretend.

With my coffee in hand, I head back to my office. Grabbing my laptop from my desk, I pause. At the corner of my desk sits a pink orchid.

Was this here earlier?

I scan the room as if someone will pop out of thin air, revealing themselves with widespread arms and a loud *ta-da*. I was just across the hall, but I had my back to the corridor. Wouldn't I have heard if anyone had passed me? Paranoia slithers up my spine, and I jump at a noise outside the room. Whirling around, I stare at the empty doorway, then realize the sound came from Denis next door. Curses and words like *too midwestern, not enough glamour*, and *country bumpkin* travel through the walls. I'm guessing something went wrong with his work in progress.

Focusing back on my office, I slowly make my way around the desk. I admire the beautiful flower. A small, folded card is attached to the stem, and I clasp the corner between my thumb and forefinger. Bending it open without removing it, my brows furrow.

You deserve everything you get.

MY HEART SKIPS, and I pull my hand back as if the paper has cut me. No signature. What the fuck?

Is this a compliment or a threat?

And who sent it? Orchids are my favorite, always have been. The same way calla lilies are Lilly's. My friends and family know that, and...Collin. No. Why would he send this? The message doesn't make sense.

My desk phone rings, and the number from the showroom scrolls over the display.

"Hello?"

"Hey, Den. It's Cassy. Your consult just walked in."

She's early.

"I'll be right down." I hang up before Cassy can reply. Looking down at myself, I straighten my blouse. Satisfied with my outfit—not that I could've done anything about it now—I pick up my mug and head downstairs, grateful for the distraction from the surprise delivery.

Cassy is chatting with a dark-haired woman in her early thirties. Her hair is a similar shade to mine, curled in glossy waves, and her clothes scream wealth. They turn at my approach, and I plaster a smile on my face. I extend my hand. "Good morning, I'm Denielle. Denis asked me to assist you today."

Her large brown eyes shine with delight, and her smile could put men to their knees. She has perfectly straight, white teeth, full lips, and skin you only see in dermatology ads. She holds herself with confidence but doesn't come across as arrogant. She has a Birkin bag draped over her arm, and I have to swallow not to start drooling. I've grown up with money, but not that kind, and for someone who adores purses, this one is a dream.

I fight the urge to recheck my outfit, suddenly feeling like an ugly duckling. *Don't be an idiot.* I'm anything but plain. Despite my...condition, I've always had healthy assertiveness when it came to my appearance.

She places her palm in mine. "It's so nice to meet you. Please call me Em. I try not to be too formal when I'm not around my family." She smirks mischievously. "Denis spoke highly of you. I can't wait to see what you come up with."

Good grief, even her voice is beautiful.

I gesture to the sitting area at the other end of the room. "Let's sit. I was told you're looking to have some alterations done?"

"Yes, I have one of his older designs. I love the dress. It holds special meaning to me, but I would like to add some of the detail he's been using in his latest collection." She laughs when she takes in my frown. "Here, I'll show you. It sounds worse than it is."

We settle in the cream velvet tufted chairs, and Em pulls several pieces of paper out of her purse. One is a photograph of herself in the gown, and the others are magazine clippings from articles about Denis's recent designs. After a brief explanation, I'm relieved to see that she didn't play down the work. It will take some time to complete the alterations and at least two to three fittings, but nothing impossible that would be easier accomplished by purchasing a new one.

"This will be stunning," I assure her. My pulse quickens with giddiness. This is a huge opportunity to prove myself to Denis. I'm excited to get started. "If you'd like, we can schedule an appointment for you to bring in the dress and to look at the fabrics we have upstairs. That way, we can determine if those work or if we have to order different materials." I want to make sure everything matches, and even if everything is black, using something that is just slightly off, a little too matte or shiny, would ruin the original gown.

"Wonderful. I knew we would work well together." She slips her arm through her Birkin bag and stands. I lead her over to where Cassy is perched on a stool behind the counter. After putting Em on the books for next week, we say our goodbyes, and I watch her *glide* out of the showroom. She approaches a shiny, gray Maserati waiting in front of the boutique and slips into the passenger side. The windows are too tinted for me to make out the driver. Curiosity tickles in my mind but is quickly replaced by irritation when Cassy informs me that Collin moved his meeting with Denis to the next day.

The coward didn't even call Denis himself. He called the mainline and had Cassy do his dirty work. He isn't feeling well. Riiight. My guess is that he partied a little too hard. Nothing I haven't heard before. While we were together, he either scaled back or hid it well. After all, he hid his ongoing affair(s) from me. I wouldn't be surprised if there were more than one.

. . .

WHEN I PULL into the garage, my insides feel like a thousand insects crawling through my veins. I texted Lilly about my first solo project, and she immediately replied, **We're going to celebrate!!!!!!!**

Not sure why this warrants seven exclamation marks, but oh well. She's happy for me. But celebrating with her also means Marcus since she doesn't go anywhere without her *Shadow*. If it were an outing not during his shift, he would swap with one of the guys. Marcus is a type *A* control freak. For Lilly's safety, I am all for it. Having to be in his vicinity, though, not so much. If it wouldn't raise a million questions, I'd ask if Ethan could take point instead—as the guys always called it. But I've never made a big deal about our mutual dislike. Starting now would be suspicious.

Why did he have to give me the best orgasm of my life?

I hang the keys to the G-Wagon on the board and stare at the garage door for a long time before I finally reach for the knob. He is off the clock. He is probably in the guesthouse. The chances of running into him are slim to none.

The deeper I walk into the house, the faster my breathing becomes. This is ridiculous. But I pulled one over on him this morning. Surprised him. That won't happen again. He'll make sure of it.

Sweat creeps across the insides of my palms, and I swipe them at the sides of my skirt—no Marcus in sight. My pulse slowly returns to a non-life-threatening pace, and I find my best friend on the patio. She's sitting with her laptop on one of the wrought iron sets, her signature Yeti with a tea bag hanging out next to her. Her head tilts up as I approach, and she beams at me.

"Hey, you! How was the rest of your day?"

"Hey." I let myself fall into the chair next to hers. Slipping my heels off, I tuck my legs under myself.

Lilly studies me with a crease between her brows. "You seem different."

"Oh?" My brows arch.

She taps her forefinger to her chin. "I can't pinpoint what it is. You've been so...withdrawn since you got here. But right now"—she gestures at me—"you're the Denielle I remember from high school."

Well, if that isn't interesting.

I shrug it off—or try to. "I'm in a good mood. I landed my first solo project. The woman is super nice, not like Denis's usual stuck-up clientele. Oli and Elena are visiting Friday..." I trail off.

A broad smile stretches across Lilly's face. "They are? I haven't seen them in ages."

"Just for the day. Elena's best friend from college is getting married."

"It'll be great to see them." Her good mood dims a little. "Do you have to work?"

I shake my head. "No, I've worked every day since last week, so I have Friday and Saturday off."

"Great, that means we can go celebrate your new job Thursday at *The Club*."

"Oh, Jesus, babe." *The Club* is one of the high-society places you go to be seen in LA. "Why can't we just go out to dinner?"

"Because I want to dance. We haven't done that in years."

"That's because you run a multigazillion-dollar empire and have a baby." The duh is implied.

She grins. "Doesn't mean we can't go party. The opposite, in fact."

"What do you mean?" I study my best friend. The devious expression on her face tells me she is up to something.

"I may or may not be in a bidding war over *The Club*."

"What do you need a nightclub for?" I'm confused.

"Margot tried to buy it as an investment." Her mouth is in a thin line, and she crosses her arms over her chest.

"No way." Margot Granger is a socialite that was involved with her brother at one point. When everything hit the press back then, she tried to push her way into the limelight by running a smear campaign against Lilly and her family. "I thought she fled the country."

"She's back." Lilly scoffs.

"And you made it your mission to make her life hell?" I chuckle.

This is unlike Lilly, but Margot is obsessed with her reputation. Being associated with Lilly's brother had stained her pristine image, and she attempted to rectify that by spewing awful lies. When Nate had no intention of setting things right, Lilly took matters into her own hands. She wouldn't let some spoiled rich bitch run her mouth—her words, not mine. Though, mine would've been even less *kind*. Lilly had unearthed every single unpleasant detail she could find about Margot and anonymously sent it to Lancaster, who happily published everything. The last thing I heard was that Margot had taken up residency in Europe.

She purses her lips. "It's just fair after what she pulled."

We stay outside until Rhys shows up with Audrey wrapped in a hooded bath towel and declares it is time for mommy to take over. His drowned-rat appearance explains his sour expression.

"Audrey still is not a fan of bath time?" I can't stop myself from mocking him.

He flips me off with the hand that isn't holding his baby girl. "How she can love the pool and hate bath time is beyond me."

"She's a woman. We don't make sense." I flash him my teeth.

"If that ain't the truth." He shifts so he can extend his daughter to her mother. As soon as Audrey changes hands, he whirls around and stomps into the house. "I'm going to work out."

"We love you, too," I call after him, to which he gives me the double finger this time.

After Tuesday turned out pretty damn great, Wednesday is a shit show.

I'm sitting in my office, assessing the fabric inventory and mentally going over what I will show Em on Thursday when he, who shall not be named, walks in without knocking.

Collin drops into the same chair he occupied at the beginning of the week. "You recovered from your little episode?" His tone is condescending at best. My spine stiffens, and I clench my teeth, forcing my shoulders to relax. I refuse to give him what he wants.

"How is the hangover?" I don't avert my eyes from my laptop, scrolling through my spreadsheet.

Silence engulfs the room, and after several more leisurely swipes on my trackpad, I finally grace him with my full attention. The vein in his neck is pulsing, and the bright satisfaction of pissing him off flashes through me. I lean back in my chair, crossing my arms. "What do you want, Collin?"

He rests his elbows on his knees and interlaces his fingers. "I want you to come off your high horse and come home. We had a future planned."

My brows shoot up. "Excuse me? You mean the future you shit all over when you stuck your dick in some purchased pussy?"

His lips press into a thin line, and I wait for his next move. "Do you think you can find a better match who would tolerate your little mental issue?"

Just...wow!

"My condition is not a *mental issue*," I bark, realizing that I'm defending myself too late. My brother's words repeat in my head: *You don't have to justify yourself to anyone.* I don't, but at the same time, I've been keeping it a secret.

Collin clicks his tongue like I said something stupid.

"Since when have you known?" Why I want to know, I'm not sure yet. Maybe because my father stabbed a knife in my back by bringing my ex into this.

"Your father needed someone to keep an eye on you," he replies casually, as if he was simply informing me of what he had for breakfast.

"That makes no sense." A flush of confusion begins to ooze

through me like lava slowly traveling down the outside of a volcano. I tense my fingers not to curl them inward.

"The first time we visited your parents, Victor invited me to his study, remember?" His posture is relaxed, which in return causes my stomach to clench. I don't like this.

I nod stiffly, the effort to keep my expression neutral being excruciating.

"He asked me what my intentions were. You had been hurt before, and he wanted to make sure this would not happen again."

I want to snort at the audacity. Even if his words (or my father's objective) are true, this would not explain Dad revealing the one secret he made us all swear to bury six feet under. I don't speak, wanting to know where this is going.

"I informed him that I believed you'd be the perfect addition to the Liberman family one day."

My skin crawls, imagining this future. "You mean I would've been your perfect beard?" Make him appear grown up and settled down while he whored his way through New York.

"Every marriage requires sacrifices." He steeples his fingers in front of his chest. "We would've been each other's *beards*, as you call it."

I'm starting to feel twitchy, wanting to dive across the desk and smack the superior smirk off his face. "That still doesn't explain why my father would let you in on my condition. I hadn't had an...attack in years." I bite the inside of my cheek until a coppery taste fills my mouth.

"Your father is a smart man. He was aware of my past. Marrying you would've put you at the top of the food chain—he very much liked that idea. He might be wealthy, but your father's meager surgeon salary has nothing on the Liberman fortune. He could've dropped the constant surveillance he had on you to make sure you wouldn't snap."

What. The. Fuck?

"I promised him I would keep your secret safe, and in return, I didn't have to give up my fun."

"Your fun?" I have no words.

"Your father cares about his reputation—a reputation that took an unrecoverable hit when you jumped in the pool that day. His career and monetary safety were nothing like what he could've had. Plus, all the money he spent on keeping an eye on you."

Wha—? My jaw drops.

Collin continues as if he hasn't just verbally slapped me. "He would've saved a fortune if I had taken over the watch."

I swallow against the lump in my throat. With a Herculean effort, I manage not to blink and give away the tears building in my eyes.

"Get out." My voice is calm, the opposite of the havoc raging inside of me. My father traded me for money. That was all it came down to. I knew he was a cold man, but this is unforgivable.

When Collin doesn't move, I push myself up with my palms flat on the desk. "You have five seconds to leave this room, Collin, or I will harm you. I don't give a fuck if I lose this job or go to jail, but you will be out of my life one way or another."

Collin challenges me by cocking an eyebrow, and my control snaps. I reach for the scissors peeking out of the pencil holder. For the past week, I've seen them as a decoration, with their pretty gold handle matching the rest of the accessories in the room, but they could do damage if necessary.

Wrapping my fingers around my newfound weapon, he jerks out of his seat. "What the hell, Denielle?" his voice pitches, and for some reason, Marcus's face appears in front of my mind's eye.

He drew a gun on Collin two days ago. Now, I'm threatening his life with a pair of scissors. And he does nothing. What did I ever see in this man? Oh right, a security blanket I thought I needed. Not anymore. Less than a month around Marcus, the only man who has the right to make me feel guilty for anything, has pushed me in ways I didn't expect. He brought the Denielle to the surface I thought I'd left behind along the way while watching my friends fight for their futures. I don't remember when I stopped fighting or even why, but that's over.

I sidestep the desk, and Collin bolts. "You will regret this," he hisses before he disappears into the hallway. I expect him to run to Denis, making him fire me on the spot, but when his footsteps echo down the stairs, I return to my original position and let my ass fall into my desk chair.

I slowly place the scissors on the tabletop and hold my trembling fingers out in front of me. Adrenaline is crashing through my body in waves.

I'm not sure how long I sit there, my hands now resting in my lap, staring at nothing, when a soft tap on the doorframe redirects my attention.

Denis studies me carefully before he approaches. "I heard all of it," he says quietly.

"I'm sorry. I'll pack up my things and—"

He holds out a hand, palm toward me. "You will do no such thing, Denielle." A soft smile tugs on the corner of his mouth. "I don't know what *condition* you have, and I told you I wouldn't intrude if it doesn't impact your ability to perform your job."

"But I—" He shakes his head, halting me once more. I want to advise that threatening the person he has a lucrative contract with would fall under *not doing my job*.

"Collin Liberman is a walking, talking sexual harassment lawsuit in the waiting. Not to mention his little recreational habit."

When he sees my stunned expression, he chuckles. "The fashion industry is worse than any high school clique or sorority house. Everyone talks about everyone."

"It seems I was the only one in the dark, then," I say, new humiliation clogging my throat.

"I've known you for as long as you've worked for Liberman, Denielle. You are very talented, which is why I hired you. Not for who you worked for before La Déesse or who you dated. My guess is, you never wanted to know because you didn't care enough for that little cretin to bother your pretty head."

Warmth spreads through my chest at his words, and I don't stop the moisture from spilling over this time.

He angles his head, folding one arm over his chest as his other palm touches the side of his neck. "Sweetheart, if your ex tries to kill my contract with his mother over this, I will inform Phyllis about why he missed yesterday's meeting. I know what's going on in this town. I may be an eccentric fashion designer, but I have my eyes and ears—especially when Little Man Liberman walks into one of my friend's clubs, asking for blow." Denis rolls his eyes, and I have no words.

I can't believe my luck with my boss. "I, um... Are you sure?"

He ignores my question and replies, "Show me what you have in mind for your client tomorrow."

AFTER MY APPOINTMENT with Em on Thursday, Denis *orders* me to take the rest of the afternoon off. I met Em at nine, and we narrowed down the fabrics. She left the dress, and we scheduled a fitting for the first round of alterations.

As Denis dismissed me, he declared he'd handle Collin for the remainder of his stay. He was scheduled to leave at the end of the day Friday, which meant he'd be back at the other end of the country when I would return to work. Not that I couldn't have taken care of Collin, but the possibility of me getting reckless with another sharp object was highly likely to very probable.

I walk into Lilly's house around noon and find Ethan rummaging through the pantry. He turns at my approach and glances between the clock on the microwave and me. "You're early."

I lift a shoulder and wink. "My boss gave me the rest of the day off."

A grin spreads across his face. "Nice. You're more of a worka-holic than Lilly."

A snorty laugh bursts out of me. "Yeah, right. Have you met the woman?" While Lilly and Rhys make sure to have a work-life balance and spend time together, as well as with Audrey and their families, both have their phones attached to them. Lilly is on call twenty-four seven.

"I heard you guys are hitting *The Club* tonight? I'm a little jealous." He wiggles his brows.

"Why's that?"

"B made me swap shifts, which means I'm pulling a double right now." As if on cue, he yawns and reaches for his energy drink on the counter.

I narrow my eyes. "I didn't think that was allowed. Don't you guys have to always be on high alert?"

He wiggles the can in response, and I purse my lips.

"Where is Ben or J?" Ben and J are the other two guys on rotation with Marcus and Ethan. While Marcus is their boss and the only one living on the property, two of the other three are always present.

"Ben got some stomach thing, called in sick last night. And J has a few days off. He headed home to visit a friend."

Lilly hasn't had any threats recently, but the guys are never careless with the security. Working a sixteen-hour shift is a lot.

Reading my mind, he elaborates, "Marcus called J back, but he won't be here until tomorrow. G ordered three guys from the Altman to the vineyard, and everyone else had their regular shifts at the hotels."

George brought more security up north? Does Lilly know about that?

"Well, I guess you stock up on those." I nod toward his liquid energy.

"Will do." He salutes me with the can as he passes me. "I'm gonna hit the cot downstairs once I'm off in an hour. See ya around, Den."

CHAPTER FIFTEEN

MARCUS

"Calla and D will be down in a sec." Rhys walks into the garage where I'm leaning against the Escalade.

Lilly and Rhys have their personal (favorite) cars they take when they are on their own, but the Escalade is the one used when they go places together or as a family. All the vehicles are outfitted with every possible security measure one could come up with, but the SUV is blacked out as well.

George and Tristen went slightly overboard in protecting these three—especially after Audrey was born. Do we really need bulletproof glass? Probably not. But there was no negotiation when Lilly announced her pregnancy. The cars were taken one by one to *The Garage*, disassembled, and put together with meticulous detail and enforcement. Audrey can safely be transported in any of the cars now.

I tap my phone to check the time. We were supposed to leave twenty minutes ago, but who's— My train of thought gets snuffed out like a candle dunked in a bucket of water when Keller follows Lilly through the door.

I vaguely hear Rhys complimenting his wife on her outfit. It can't be anything close to what Denielle just showed up in. Not that I could check, my eyes are glued to the silver romper-dress *thing* that barely covers her tits or ass. What is this? Leftover scraps from Halloween?

I trail her body from the thread-thin spaghetti straps down to the *V* that almost reaches her naval. The top half is covered with sequins, versus the bottom in feathers. A skirt of feathers? Shorts? I can't identify it. Whatever. I see her ass hanging out.

The irrational urge to tell her to change threatens to burst out of me. I clamp my jaw so hard I'm positive I've broken off the enamel of my molars.

She wears her signature twenty-five-inch heels. At closer inspection, I note that they're from the same red-soled label, but this pair has a peep toe. Her already long legs appear endless.

The tingling sensation in my lower half causes a surge of glaring anger to crash through me. The thudding in my chest becomes uncomfortable for multiple reasons, and I shove my phone in my pocket with such force I hear a ripping sound.

Fuck.

A low whistle brings everyone's attention to the garage entrance once more as Ethan appears.

"Damn, girl. You cleaned up nice since earlier," he drawls, and my now free fingers twitch to wipe his drooling smirk off his face. *Earlier?* When did he see her? What was she wearing earlier?

What. The. Fuck am I thinking?

"What are you doing here?" My clipped question turns all eyes on me.

Ethan crosses his arms, scanning me up and down like I have lost my mind. "J isn't back. We always have a detail of two when—"

"You already pulled a double today, you—"

"Just took a five-hour nap, B. I'm fine." He doesn't let me finish. In my peripheral vision, Denielle follows the exchange with interest. Her mouth is slashed, but not in an angry way—she is suppressing a smirk.

Every cord in my neck feels like it's about to snap.

"Let's go," my barked command echoes through the vast garage, and Lilly and Rhys jump into action like obedient children, not my employers.

Denielle has one hand tucked under her armpit. The crossed arm pushes her tits farther out of the nonexistent dress while she scratches her chin between her thumb and forefinger with the other. She is fully aware of what just happened.

Because you had your dick in her two days ago and are now acting like a jealous caveman, my inner asshole chimes in.

"You, too, Keller."

She arches a brow in a challenge—that little brat. How she was helpless against her ex but shows no fear toward me is a riddle I burn to solve.

I don't *ask* again. Either she gets in the damn car, or she stays. This night cannot get any worse. A voice inside my head cackles without further comment. I have the slight suspicion that tonight could make me lose my job.

WE GET to The Club without another *glitch*. I pull up to the back of the building as usual, and Ethan sweeps the perimeter for paps before anyone else exits. The Club has a small parking lot in the back that is exclusively reserved for VIPs, and I pull into one of the spots while Ethan leads Lilly, Rhys, and Denielle through the nondescript door blending into the black-painted concrete.

I find the others chatting in the dim hallway with the manager who came to greet Lilly. The guy nearly falls to his feet, and I suppress a gagging sound, witnessing his emasculating behavior.

Rhys turns slightly and meets Denielle's amused gaze. He rolls his eyes, and she snickers.

I haven't forgotten her standoffish behavior. Bridging the distance from the rear, I stand a little off to the side, yet close enough to feel her body heat on my exposed skin. My knuckles graze her naked leg, and Denielle sucks in a breath. Glee spreads through me as her spine goes rigid.

Lilly starts moving, but Denielle hesitates. Two can play this game. I lean down to her ear while flipping my hand. My palm wraps around the inside of her thigh. I glide my fingers against her naked flesh until I reach the seam of her panties. I tighten my grip, fingers pressing into her skin, and whisper, "Give me your worst, Keller."

Goose bumps erupt on her neck and back. Her eyes flutter closed, and a low moan escapes her lips. She takes one step forward, dislodging my hold on her, but halts. Blinking, she peers at her friends' retreating forms. Lilly and Rhys follow Ethan and the manager through the dim-lit corridor toward the staircase leading up to the second floor where the VIP lounges are located. In slow motion, Denielle pivots on her feet. She studies my face with her head slanted. Mimicking her expression, I refuse to break the connection first.

Her hand reaches up, and my shoulders automatically tense. The instinct of stepping back is overwritten by me shifting my weight evenly between both feet. I follow the movement she executes with such confidence I can feel my hold over her slipping. Breathless anticipation makes it hard to inhale. When her palm touches the side of my neck, her thumb slowly strokes up and down. The soft pad of her finger caresses my flitting pulse. I hold myself immobile, waiting for her next move.

She rises on her tiptoes until her lips align with my ear. "I fully intend to," she answers my earlier challenge. She drops back down, swivels on her heels, and strolls down the hallway. Her hips sway, making the feathers fan out. Her perfect ass is on full display, and my jeans become too tight within seconds.

I jam my hands into my front pockets, forcing the already

too-small cock space to become even smaller. We are not going to go there. Again.

Oh, we so are. FUCK!

I hold my breath at the painful constriction until she's out of sight. Exhaling in excruciating slowness, I pull my hands out of their confinement at the same time and rake them through my hair.

I challenged her, and she retaliated. Is this how it is now? And why do I like it? I shouldn't. But Denielle holding her own after all these years, even pushing back, stirs something alive in me. Something that had been dormant for a very long time.

When I regain some control, I stalk after them.

We always have the same private suite on the upper level of the club. The VIP areas are all separated from each other, with a small balcony opening to the dance floor below. Every so often, Lilly wants to be with the masses, but in general, she's content up here.

Bass thuds through the walls.

Aw, fuck. It's techno night.

The Club alternates between the different styles of music to please all its clientele. Lilly doesn't usually favor artificially produced tunes, but there is also no way she wasn't aware.

I find them, as expected, in our suite. Ethan has positioned himself next to the door. He side-eyes me when I enter before glancing toward our employers. Lilly and Denielle are in front of the balustrade, taking selfies with the crowd in the background. Rhys stands off to the side, engrossed in something on his phone.

"What's your deal tonight?" Ethan whisper-shouts at me, not averting his gaze from our charges. Following the rise of Keller's bird garment whenever she leans over to fit into the picture, I didn't notice he had stepped closer.

"I have no idea what you mean." Like hell I will admit to him that my cock wants a second round at the brunette in front of us while my brain still shouts insults at me.

"Sure you don't," he muses, retaking his post.

My fingers curl inward.

Fucking great.

FOR THE NEXT HOUR, Lilly and Denielle dance together, separate and with Rhys in the middle. The three are letting loose, and while I enjoy seeing Lilly and Rhys carefree, the opposite applies to the third person in front of me. With every shake of Keller's hips, the curve of her cheeks is on full display. My body vibrates from the craving to dig my fingers into the flesh of her ass, leaving marks and branding her with my touch, while I repeat every reason—the one reason—why this can never happen again. Is she attractive? Sure. Did her pussy feel like she was made for my cock? That would be an unwelcome hell to the yes. But did she also cause me to lose the only family I cared for?

Lilly sips on a flute of champagne, Rhys has a beer in hand that can buy me three cases in the store, and Keller has moved on to a bottle of mid-80s Bollinger. I check the time on my phone and skim over the messages I missed when something brushes my elbow.

I jerk my head around and latch on to Denielle's upper arm as she stumbles past me. "Where the hell do you think you're going?"

She tries to rip out of my grasp, but my hold is stronger. There is no fear, no terror like when her ex manhandled her.

"I have to pee. Let the fuck go, Baxter." She tugs harder, and I appease her, dropping my hand.

"Use the bathroom across the hall," I order, and she purses her lips. I wait for a retort, but instead, she just turns and high-tails it out, supporting herself against the frame before she disappears. Someone should probably go with her, or she'll break an ankle in her deathtrap footwear.

Ethan looks up from playing on his phone. Up here, we don't have to be on full alert. We have access to The Club's security cameras and get alerts about suspicious activity—a perk not every VIP has, but Lilly had a hand in it.

"Why do you hate Keller? It's been like that for years, and she's never done anything to you."

My stomach drops at Ethan's question. For years, I've been careful to keep my distance from Denielle for precisely that reason. Lately, my emotions control my actions. It used to be sole loathing, but my brain and dick are no longer on the same page, not even on the same bookshelf.

"That's none of your business." My voice is steady, and as my subordinate, he knows that means he's in trouble. None of this is his fault, but the rising pressure in my veins makes it hard to temper myself. I rarely get loud with my guys. Having trained under *The Ghost*, I learned the calmer you are, the more fear you instill in your opponent. They expect to evoke an emotion from you. Anger. Fear. Whatever their objective. But if there is nothing, when they don't achieve their goal, you have the upper hand. And I always have the upper hand.

Except when it comes to Denielle Keller.

Ethan clamps his mouth shut, nods, and sidles over to Rhys. They exchange a few words before he returns to his spot. "Lilly and Rhys are ready to head out."

I tilt my wrist and press the side button of my Garmin. "Copy. We'll leave as soon as Keller is back."

My scalp prickles. Where the fuck is she? It doesn't take this long to piss, especially when you have nothing to take off to do it.

Rhys has his arm around his wife's waist as he leads her over. "Calla's had enough." He chuckles as she leans into him.

Her eyes droop. "Oh, shut up. You were not up with Aud at four thirty this morning."

"No, I wasn't." He places a kiss on her temple. "And that's why you're the better parent."

She snorts but snuggles closer into his embrace. "Where is D?" Lilly scans the room.

"She went to use the bathroom," Ethan elaborates, which appeases her.

"Why don't we head to the car, and Ethan can—" Rhys begins, but I cut him off.

"I'll get Keller."

Lilly's attention snaps to my face, but she remains mute. She surveys me curiously. There is the roller-coaster sensation in my core again. Knowing her, she will interrogate me first thing tomorrow.

Her husband, on the other hand, is oblivious or doesn't give two fucks. "Sounds good. We'll see you outside."

Lilly digs her heels in and places her hand on my forearm. I can't decipher the message she's sending me. My thumbnail slices into the pad of my middle finger until the sting is enough of a distraction for my brain to spin on what my employer… friend is trying to tell me. Rhys urges her forward once more, and she complies. Our eyes remain locked until she is out of sight.

I CHECK the time on my watch again. Denielle has been gone longer than she should've been. Something crawls up the inside of my stomach walls, and I recognize it as the emotion that caused me to intervene three days ago: concern.

Reminding myself that she's a grown woman, whom I *don't* care about, I stride across the hall to the ladies' room. Knocking once, I push the door open. The two stalls are empty. The unease begins to expand, and coldness slithers through my veins.

Where the hell is she?

I slowly advance in the direction of the stairs leading to the main room below. She wouldn't have gone into any of the other lounges. Putting one foot in front of the other on autopilot, I take my phone back out of my pocket and log onto the app we use to access the cameras. Checking the one outside the bathroom, I go back ten minutes. I find the moment Denielle enters the bathroom. She disappears inside but reappears not a minute later.

What the hell?

I continue to watch. She aims at our suite but stops abruptly. Opening her clutch, she pulls her phone out. Thanks to the quality of the feed, the crease on her forehead is clear as day. She squints at the screen, then down the hallway. She's swaying on her feet. The bottle she pretty much single-handedly killed has hit its mark. Denielle chews on her bottom lip, and the mere action on the tiny screen shoots signals to my groin I refuse to acknowledge. She swivels on her heels and weaves down the corridor.

Confusion mingles with irritation and concern, shutting up the primal need to feel her teeth on me—my neck, my chest, anywhere. A combination I don't like but am starting to get used to when it comes to this woman.

"Sandstorm" by Darude shakes the building. Sounds like we've entered the nostalgia part of the night. The strobe lights bounce off the metallic black walls, and the closer I get to the archway blocked off by a red velvet rope, the more grateful I am that Lilly rarely comes here on techno night. I don't like people, much less a bunch of club hoppers in their midtwenties, jumping up and down to a song that's as old as them.

Callum, the bouncer manning the entrance to the VIP floor, nods at me. "Bax, good to see you, my man. Didn't know you were in the house. Not your usual scene." He smirks.

I pull the corner of my mouth up. The dude is greasier than the shit Ethan puts in his hair. "Don't tell me. The bosses had a night out, but we lost a friend of theirs." I scan the crowd closest to us. "See a dark-haired girl come through here? Silver dress."

"Hard to miss that one." His leery grin stretches, his teeth becoming the perfect target for my fist. "Headed that way."

I flex my fingers while following his outstretched, stubby digit.

Why do I care what he thinks or says about Keller?

He points toward one of the slightly elevated areas above the center dance floor. I don't spot her until a couple splits apart, and the sequins of her dress reflect the strobe lights like a beacon in the sea of bodies. Fire spreads through me like an inferno. Denielle's arms are above her head, her eyes are closed, and she's moving with the sound. I didn't know it was possible to dance to this music in a way that doesn't make you appear like you're having muscle spasms. Denielle's movements are fluid yet perfectly aligned with the bass and change in tempo.

I grind my teeth, refusing to let the smile that wants to show on my face appear. It's attraction—nothing more, nothing less. She's hot, that's all.

Liar, liar, pants on fire. Literally.

She twirls, falling into someone. She is fucking plastered. I take a step when her arms wrap around that someone. My foot hovers in the air, and my spine stiffens.

What the—?

"She your girl?" Callum's question registers in my brain.

No. "Yes."

Excuse me, what? *She is mine to torture*, I justify internally.

Yeah, right, sarcasm pipes up.

My feet start moving again. She's going home, and I don't care if I have to drag her by the— I'm closer and have a direct line of sight to the dude grinding on her. I bark a laugh, inaudible over the deafening sound coming through the floor-to-ceiling speakers. No fucking way. Is that? It is. Charlie York, her cheating high school ex. The woman has worse taste in men than Lincoln had picking theaters.

His hands are low on her hips, and as the song transitions to "Proximus" by Lauro Picotto, her fingers interlace at the nape of his neck. The beat slows, and so does she.

The heat of rage mingles with the heat surging to my groin, watching her sway. My focus morphs into tunnel vision with one goal. With my phone still in hand, I lift it to my line of sight. I pull up Ethan's last message and type. **Found Keller. She doesn't want to leave. Go ahead. I'll bring her home.**

After I bring her somewhere else.

Ethan can handle the trip back to the house by himself. I pocket the device, not waiting for his answer, and push through the crowd. As the distance between us shrinks, the buzzing in my veins increases.

As soon as I'm within five feet of Denielle, her head snaps up. She senses my presence the same way I know when she's near. Her eyes widen, and unwanted satisfaction spreads through me. Busted. I step between her and her dance partner, forcing him to drop his hands. Denielle has stopped moving, and I tilt my head, staring down at her. I keep my expression neutral. Neither of us says anything. Charlie attempts to move around me, but I block him, shooting my elbow into his ribs.

Something like a howl mingles with the rising sound of "The Nights" by Avicii. At least we've entered the last decade of music again. This DJ is all over the place.

Keller's eyes flicker to the side before settling on me.

"What do you think you're doing?" I don't have to shout for her to hear me.

She props her hands on her hips in the same manner I've witnessed so many times when she wants to stand up to me. "What does it look like?"

Do I dignify this with a response?

"Denielle, who is—" Charlie exclaims in all his unintimidating shortness. Fine, he's not short, but shorter than me, and that's all my possessive mind acknowledges at the moment. I refuse to analyze why I want to put a bullet between his eyes for touching Keller.

She is mine to torture.

I pivot so Denielle and I face the kid. "I'm her babysitter."

Her head whips up, a snarl on her lips. I wink at her before making eye contact with the other male in our triangle. I elaborate, bored, "It's her curfew." Not waiting for a response, I clasp her hand in mine. The electric jolt the connection gives me sends shock waves to my core.

Heading toward the second-floor stairs, I pull her behind me.

"What the fuck, Baxter?" she shrieks, trying to pull out of my grip, but my fingers wrapped around hers allow me to maintain my hold. Once again, she is nothing like during her interaction with Liberman. She doesn't show defeat. When she realizes she can't escape my grip, she claws her talons into the soft part of my hand. She acts like we're equals. We're not.

"Charlie, I'm so sorry. I'll call you—" I tune out the rest of her stammered apology as I drag her past Callum.

The way he ogles her makes it hard not to stop and knock a few of his teeth out, but I have other priorities.

Denielle stumbles, but I don't slow my pace. My jaw feels like it may break at any second. Where did Charlie fucking York come from? This club is not an establishment a guy like him, a.k.a. not filthy rich, frequents. The cover charge alone is more than most people make in a week. I'll have to check with whoever was controlling the doors about how he made it past them.

The beat of the music vibrating under our feet mingles with adrenaline thrashing through me. It's the fucking dress. It's the only logical explanation that makes sense. Can make sense. I allow to make sense. The swelling in my jeans is clouding my judgment.

We near Lilly's VIP suite, and instead of moving past it to the back exit, I reach for the handle, pushing the door open. Denielle resists my pull, but with one hard tug, she's over the threshold. She's lucky I didn't throw her over my shoulder like the child she acts like.

I slam the door shut and flip the lock. Whirling around, I prowl toward her. She backs up until her legs hit the leather couch situated against the wall to the right. Not letting up, I keep moving, and when she can't escape, she drops into the seat. Hovering above her, she blinks at me through her lashes. I have a direct line of sight down the *V* of her dress. The fabric hangs loose on her, covering her tits just enough not to show her nipples.

The tips of my fingers tingle with the need to feel her soft skin again. She props the heel of her hands against the cushion and leans slightly forward. Her eyes are unfocused, yet she's fully aware of her actions.

The silver sequins fall away from her chest, exposing more of her creamy flesh. Her hardened buds become visible, and my breathing picks up, my chest suddenly too tight.

No longer able to resist, I reach out and pinch the strap of her dress between my thumb and forefinger. She shudders, her lips parting. The rise and fall of her breasts mimic my own want. She parts her legs, and I step between them. Her face is perfectly aligned with my groin, and the sheer proximity of her mouth with my cock, imagining her plump lips wrapped around me, gets interrupted when her small hands touch the sides of my legs, slowly gliding up.

What is she doing?

CHAPTER SIXTEEN

DENIELLE

I'M DRUNK.

The champagne is making me do this. There is no other explanation as to why I would go there. Again. This is not one of our little mind games. Not anymore.

The first time, I wasn't myself. Allowing Marcus to fuck me in the most primal way I ever experienced was the mere solution to shutting off the overwhelming sensation of panic—the emotional state that used to drive me to do what my father hid from the outside world. Submerging used to be the only way for me to make it stop, numb myself and calm my speeding pulse until I could breathe again.

I had no control over my body, the panic draining me of all strength. I couldn't stand up to Collin. The helplessness against my physical reaction crippled me. Marcus... His touch didn't cause the same irrational feeling of being assaulted by thousands of needles. Even in my distress, the revelation registered. So, I used him—used his touch to come back.

What was *his* ulterior motive? Using my vulnerability to regain the upper hand that he was slowly losing in our battle of wills? Attempting to punish me differently? No, even with all his hatred, he is moral to a fault. Marcus wouldn't use a woman *that way*. What then? Does he find me attractive? His behavior when I walked into the garage would suggest that. But it can't be.

My hands move of their own volition. Touching them to his legs, the rough texture of his jeans sends a quiver from the nerve endings in my hands to my brain.

Stop touching him.

It takes effort to focus on his eyes. Have they always had those different shades? I used to think of them as brown—if I thought of them—but there are specs of green as well.

Maybe it's just the light. Yes, probably.

My mouth is too dry to swallow. Is that from the champagne or— The way he drinks me in sends signals to parts of my body that shouldn't react.

Fuck it.

I run my palms up his thighs, watching his jaw working back and forth. I'm waiting for him to stop me. He doesn't. When I graze his belt with my fingers, his nostrils flare. Marcus is unnaturally still. I freeze, not averting my gaze from his. His hold on the strap of my dress tightens.

"You're drunk," he states, void of emotion, his tone contradicting his physical cues.

"I am." No point in denying the fact. He saw me drown myself in a bottle that cost more than I currently have in my bank account—the new one, in my name, that I opened last week.

The groove between his brows indicates his internal struggle. After an elongated pause, his expression smooths out. He's made his decision.

Marcus releases my dress, and a voice in my head immediately objects. *No!* My heart shrivels in my chest as tears prick in my eyes. There is no reason why I would want to seek out Marcus Baxter. We're connected by guilt and hatred. Yet, him letting go feels like losing the ability to breathe. It makes no sense, but at the same time...it does. He makes me feel things I forgot I was capable of. But why would he want me? Other than to hurt me?

Blame it on the alcohol. I don't want this to be over. I don't want to go back to the house. Hooking my fingers through the belt loops of his jeans, I root him in place. His eyes flash, and he scans my face with an amused smirk.

The music reverberating through the open balcony into the room drowns out my accelerated breathing.

"What are you doing?" I read his lips, the low question inaudible over the earsplitting sound.

"What I want," I reply without hesitation.

The corner of his eye crinkles. Looks like he's proficient in lipreading as well. My already flushed skin burns from the inside out. The surge of power I get whenever I stand up to the man who has the ability (*and right*) to break me is exhilarating.

He doesn't push me away, walk out, or hurl cruel insults at my boldness. A month ago, he would've. Heck, even last week, he probably would've laughed in my face.

Instead, he slants his head, the corner of his mouth curving up. "Oh yeah?" he dares me.

To bring my point across further, I trail the leather with my nail, leaving a faint line from the loop to the front of his hips. Without breaking our visual connection, I unbuckle his belt. My palms are clammy, my skin ablaze with a need I can't describe or explain. It's as strong as the only other urge I've ever had in my life—the one I've always succumbed to when it became too much.

My veins are throbbing with my pulse rushing through them. I flip the button of his jeans, and Marcus sucks in a breath. I don't stop, though. In the back of my mind, a tiny voice berates me, telling me to end this before it's too late.

He will leave you high and *dripping*, like last time. High and dry would be an oxymoron for the state I am in.

There is no way to stop this, though. Marcus Baxter has

become my new addiction, his loathing a necessity for the old Denielle to break through.

Saliva pools in my mouth, and my objective turns single minded: I want to taste him. Having had him buried in my pussy, there is no way I can take him all the way in my mouth—I'd choke or suffocate. Yet, instead of it being a deterrent, it urges me on. My legs tremble despite sitting down. My thumbs hook inside his jeans, pushing at the hem until the denim is past his muscular thighs and hangs low on his legs. Marcus bends and wraps his hands around my wrists. He remains mute, but I'm starting to be able to read him. Heat battles with his distaste—his knowledge of what I've represented for the past two decades—against his desire. He doesn't want to go there again but can't deny that he wants me either. We're toxic for each other in every way imaginable, yet neither of us is willing to concede.

What does that mean?

My tongue darts out and swipes across my bottom lip. Marcus follows the motion greedily, and his hold morphs into ironclad shackles before he releases me. In the background, I register that the volume of the music has lowered, which is why I can hear his next words.

"Give me your worst." The dare is out in the open. He thinks he can dominate me. Maybe he can. Or perhaps I want him to? But first...

Need pools in my core, soaking my panties to an embarrassing level. I've never been a girl who has particularly enjoyed giving blow jobs. I've done it, sure, but most of the time, it was to reciprocate. Marcus, though...

My fingers curl into the material of his briefs, slowly tugging on the barrier and exposing Marcus's very. Hard. Length.

Fuck, this is never going to fit.

His hands land on my shoulders, but I can't avert my eyes from his cock.

It's the champagne.

The tips of his fingers glide across my collarbone and over

my neck. I have no doubt he can feel the thudding of my pulse against his touch. He continues his pursuit until his palms settle on either side of my face, tilting my head up slightly. My attention shifts to his face, and he studies me.

Marcus has been challenging me every step of the way since that night in the great room—the night I fell back into a habit I didn't know I still needed until my past came rushing back in.

We don't speak. Neither of us makes any indication to stop where this is headed. Does he want me to take charge? He said to give him my worst. What is my worst?

"Stop overthinking, Den." His words are spoken so softly. If we hadn't been between two songs, I would've missed him using the name my friends have for me. My eyes widen. There is an itch in the back of my head. He also called me Den when he got me away from Collin.

His thumb and forefinger travel to my chin in a featherlight caress. The calluses on them send waves of goose bumps down my neck and spine. He strokes up and down until he trails a burning path to my mouth. My eyelids flutter closed, and my lips part. Marcus pushes his finger inside, and my tongue swirls around it.

Letting go of his briefs, I circle my fingers around his dick. Hiding behind the security of my closed lids, I slowly pump him once, twice, while my other hand massages his balls. A hissing sound registers in my ears, and I pause.

"Don't stop," Marcus rasps.

Hearing the desire in his tone spurs me on. I let my legs fall open wider, and the scent of my arousal fills my nose.

He removes his finger from my mouth, smearing my saliva from my lips to my chin. He pinches the skin ever so slightly, a signal for me to look at him.

My body obeys of its own accord, every cell compliant to Marcus's whim.

I lift my gaze to his, the haze from the alcohol evaporating. A new form of intoxication takes over, and I rock my hips, my sensitive spot meeting the rough texture of his jeans where they hang low on his legs.

A moan escapes me, and a devilish grin forms on his gorgeous face. Marcus Baxter is sex in a male body. I've never denied how attractive he is. Our history simply never has allowed for the attraction to be anything more.

"Open."

He doesn't mean my legs. My fluttering heartbeat becomes painful with anticipation. I drop my hand from his balls and brace it against his thigh, the muscles coiling under my touch. *God, I want this. Him.* With the other still around his length, I lean in, never breaking our visual connection, and trail my tongue along the underside of his cock. When I reach the tip, I swirl it around once, licking the small drop off the head. Before he can give me another order, I do open.

I wrap my lips around him and take him until he hits the back of my throat.

"Oh, fuuuuck." His garbled expression of lust lightens the tightness in my chest.

I pump the part of his dick that's not in my mouth, pressing my tongue against the smooth skin, tasting him, sucking him. I want more. Need more.

His hips thrust forward, and my eyes water as he enters as far as physically possible.

"Touch yourself," he groans, finding his way into my hair with one of his hands and curling around the strands. The sting on my scalp is a brief distraction from the fullness in my mouth.

His gaze bores into mine. "I said, *touch yourself*."

What the fuck am I doing? enters my mind. I've never taken orders from a guy in bed—or on a couch. It is the one place in my life I've remained true to myself, even if I've lost myself in others. I'm not a vanilla kinda girl, but I also haven't experienced too much out of the box. I've never done it in public—until now. There was the occasional new position, but with there not being a deeper connection to my partners, there was never the trust for experimentation. Do I trust Marcus? I shouldn't. But I do. Why? Taking his orders (the last time and now) is not a sexual preference I saw myself enjoying. Craving. Submitting to someone. Maybe because I had to submit to my condition, to my family, keeping it hush-hush to not embarrass them. Following Marcus's *instructions*, I don't give up control, though. The knowledge that he would never force himself on me—should I choose to put a stop to it—is enough to allow myself to fall. And that's how it feels. Falling. Trusting. Being free. Taking the man, whom I shouldn't go near because of what I caused him and his family, would keep me in therapy for months—if I were still going.

Marcus withdraws from my mouth, fisting his cock in his free hand, forcing me to release him. He bends my head back so far my spine cracks. There is fire between his eyes. Not anger. Lust.

My nails dig into my naked thighs. My dress has ridden up, and Marcus has a straight line of sight to my black see-through thong. I lose the battle of holding his gaze, my eyes falling to where he strokes himself.

My core aches, and I bite the inside of my cheek.

"If you want more, do what you're told, Denielle." There is no disdain in the way he says my full name. Not like it used to be. He tugs on my curls, and my eyes fly back to his. "Do you want more?" Genuine curiosity is etched across his forehead, and I find myself nodding against his hold.

Retreating a few steps, my heart skips a beat. What is he doing? Did he want me to admit that I want him, just for him to — Before the doubt can fully manifest in my head, he bends at the waist, never letting go of my hair, and crashes his mouth to mine. I'm so shocked my body freezes. Oh my Go—

My heart trembles. His lips begin to move, possessive yet gentle. His tongue grazes the seam of my mouth, and I *fall* the rest of the way. I open up for him, and his soft tongue tangles with mine as I taste the cinnamon of his gum. My fingers curl into his shirt, trying to pull him closer.

Marcus chuckles, not breaking the kiss. "Are you ready to follow my orders now?" There is no condescension in his question.

I fist the cotton, taking charge of the kiss while one hand snakes behind his neck. I keep him in place as I explore his tongue with mine. He groans, and I have what I want. We're equals, neither of us in charge of the other. We give and take what we want. I nip at the corner of his mouth. "Give me your worst, *Bax*."

I release him, and he straightens. His eyes drop to my exposed, barely existent underwear, soaked through with need. I can no longer chalk it up to the champagne. I lean back into the couch, widening my thighs as far as possible, baring myself to him. Something snaps, a surge of endorphins rushes my body, and I can't suppress the shudder. I've never wanted anyone like I want Marcus Baxter at this moment. His breathing is labored, his nostrils flaring with each inhale. The fingers of my right hand glide over the feverish skin on my legs, from the outside, along the front of my thigh, until I reach the inside and feel the seam of my thong. I arch my back, cupping my breast with the left. I moan, watching him follow my every move. His own hand pumps his cock while the other hangs loosely at his side, his fingers flexing and unflexing. His glistening head invites me to lick it off. I pull the last bit of barrier aside and expose my needy pussy to him. His eyes roll back, and his fist tightens around his length.

I'm hyperaware of both of our bodies in the room, the strobe lights reflecting off the shiny surfaces in the lounge. As soon as his gaze finds me again, his features harden. "Now, Denielle." He's not angry but on the brink of losing it.

Not hesitating another second, I dip two fingers into my heat, pinching my nipple with the other through the dress. My whimper mingles with the bass shaking the club.

I withdraw from my folds, feeling my wetness coating my fingers. Pushing right back in, I circle my thumb over my clit.

Nerve endings in my body fire, and while pleasuring myself, I sit up on the couch. Releasing my breath, I beckon Marcus to step closer. A grin stretches across his face. He advances but remains out of reach.

"You didn't say please, *Keller.*" The usual sneer when he uses my last name is missing. His ability to tell me how he feels (about me) with the same word is not lost on me.

I pump in and out of my pussy. "Oh, god," my whimper turns to a moan as I apply more pressure to my sensitive spot. I shudder, not wanting to dip over the edge just yet. Not alone. I can barely focus on the man in front of me—him watching, stroking himself while I pleasure myself. I inhale slowly, forcing my body's urge to explode down. Nibbling on my lower lip, I flutter my lashes at him. "Please, Marcus. Let me taste you." I exaggerate my tone, and he barks out a genuine laugh. How we went from hating each other's existence to me begging to suck him off is not making any logical sense. But we're here, and my mind is fixated on one goal.

He takes pity, bridging the gap, and I reach greedily for him. Not withdrawing from my pussy, I wrap my free hand around his shaft and take him in my mouth in the same move.

"Jesus," he hisses as I bob my head back and forth. I swirl my tongue around his tip whenever I reach the top. Marcus's hands are back in my hair, and he guides me as he fucks my mouth.

"Fuck, D." His low groan sends a new tingling sensation to my core. "Yesss, keep going—just like this. Ah, fuck..."

His incoherent muttering is enough for me to pick up my own pace. I moan around the fullness of my mouth, pinching my clit between my thumb and forefinger as I feel him hardening against my tongue. I'm buzzing with the urge to let go. With every stroke of my tongue and swirling around his tip, he tightens his hold on my locks, guiding me how he wants it. He sets the speed, and I chase after him with my touches. I'm on the brink of diving over the edge, my clit so sensitive that there is no way of turning back, when warmth fills my mouth, and I taste his salty cum. He continues to pump inside me once, twice more before he halts. I'm on sensory overload. My own orgasm racks through my body, unable to follow its wanting to succumb to the tremor because Marcus is holding me in place as he empties inside of me. I let his release glide over my tongue, swallowing every drop while the flutter in my core signals my subsiding orgasm. He slowly withdraws from my lips, and I lick his cock until it is completely gone.

I remove my fingers from my dripping heat, tugging my thong back in place. My eyes sting, and I can't look at him. My post-orgasm flushed cheeks burn from a new sensation. A knot forms in my stomach, and I blink.

I sit on the couch, the leather sticky with my cum, preparing myself for some type of verbal stab. He can't leave me here. He needs to take me back to the mansion. But that doesn't mean he has to be kind all of a sudden. The pit expands, and I clench my teeth. Doing the walk of shame was not part of tonight's plans.

Two fingers guide my face until I have no choice but to look at the man in front of me. I let lust overtake my rational thinking. He's going to use this as a new way to—

"Stop." He squats in front of the couch, his elbows propped on his thighs. His jeans are back on, but the belt is still unfastened.

"Let's have it." I sigh, meeting his sudden scowl. Let's get this over with so we can both move on.

His lips press into a thin line. Is he really pissed at me for being realistic?

"Nothing has changed." His cold tone is like a stab right in the heart, worse than any insult he could've thrown at me.

My spent body tenses with its last bit of strength. I'm not going to give him the satisfaction. Pushing with the heels of my hands against the cushion, I stand, letting my dress fall back into place.

Marcus lands on his ass, not able to right himself fast enough. I want to laugh, but instead, I sidestep him, flip the lock, and walk out of the VIP suite and straight into the bathroom across the hall. I don't need to pee, and *freshening up* won't cut it. I brace my hands against the vanity, scanning my face in the mirror. My hair is a mess, my lipstick nonexistent, and my once smoky eyes have transformed into raccoon eyes after a night of clubbing.

Fuck.

All I have to do is make it home, then I can avoid him for the foreseeable future. Oli will be here tomorrow, and—

The door behind me swings inward and reveals Lilly's six-foot-four *Shadow*. "What's your problem?" His tone is hard, and for that alone, I want to knee him in the junk.

The junk you just happily fondled and had in your mouth.

My teeth clench, not wanting to lose it in front of him. My fury merges with the humiliation of my weakness and blends with the leftover endorphins from the second-best sexual experience of my life—the first also having been with this man.

He steps inside, letting the door shut, leaning against it with his arms crossed.

"Nothing has changed," I repeat his words to him, mimicking his posture.

I don't know what I expected. That he'd argue? Accuse me of acting like a scorned woman after I begged for his cock? Tell me that *everything* has changed? He does neither. He dips his chin, turns, and leaves. "I'll call us an Uber. Meet you at the back entrance."

I watch the door close in slow motion. With every passing second, white-hot rage simmers in my core. The clicking sound of the latch sounds like an explosion in my ears, and my control snaps. I hurl the little basket of soap sitting next to the sink across the room, hitting the wall next to the exit.

"MOTHER. FUCKER! AAARRRGH!"

CHAPTER SEVENTEEN

DENIELLE

"I thought you'd be happier to see me, Nelle."

I jerk my gaze to my brother sitting across from me, my fork hovering over the massacred salmon. I peer between my lunch and Oli. All that's left is flakes of pink between the steamed veggies, and I can imagine what's going on in his head. His statement was his way of inquiring about my mental state. Maybe I shouldn't have admitted everything to him on the phone the other day?

"I am happy to see you!" *I'm fine.* My defense is delivered with such false enthusiasm that Elena chokes on the water she is sipping on. I do not talk like a cheerleader on a sugar high. Her violent coughing fit briefly distracts everyone from the fact that I am as sociable as our father, a.k.a. not at all.

After I reassembled the soap dish in the club's restroom last night, I found Marcus standing with his phone in hand at the back entrance. He was typing something, swiping, typing again.

"Driver will be here in five." He didn't look up or acknowledge me further.

We completed the ride home in silence, him on one end of the back seat, me on the other. I would've gladly ridden in the trunk if it had been an option. The burn in my throat intensified with every mutinous mile. The only time Marcus glanced in my direction was when I pulled out my phone and typed out a message to Charlie.

Me: So sorry. Lilly's bodyguard is an asshole of epic proportions. Make it up to u?

I didn't know why I sent the last words. I had no intention of rekindling anything with Charlie. That train left the station eons ago and was on a different continent by now. Did he seem to want to? It appeared that way. And I let the alcohol take over my actions. He saw the picture I posted of Lilly and me at The Club and decided to show up. Weird? Maybe. But I chalked it up to us having a past and him feeling guilty about how our relationship ended.

I didn't expect Charlie to respond. It was late—or early, depending on how one wanted to see it. The three dots appeared almost instantly.

Charlie: No prob. Just let me know when and where.

I purposefully smiled at the screen. Call me petty, but somehow, I knew Marcus would care. I felt his glare in my direction before I started composing my response. The hair on the nape of my neck tickled, the same way I always knew when he was near —a reaction I used to blame on the guilt he evoked. Now...I wasn't sure.

Ignoring Marcus, I typed: **Great. How about Monday after work?**

Charlie: I'll be there.

We could have discussed the details over the weekend, but for the moment, I felt the satisfaction of trumping Marcus's, *"Nothing has changed."* At least, that was my goal.

As soon as the car pulled up in front of the house, I was out.

Racing up to the main entrance, I heard the other car door slam shut, followed by heavy footsteps stomping after me. I didn't bother closing the front door and sped up the stairs. Marcus wouldn't dare make noise at this time of night. I didn't know what I was hoping for, but when I reached my room, I paused. No sound came from downstairs, and I pictured Marcus standing in the foyer, staring toward the second floor. Did I want him to chase me down?

Don't be ridiculous, Denielle.

I have no idea how long I lingered in the hallway on the second floor, listening for a clue as to where Marcus went. But there was nothing. And I didn't see him again.

"HONEY, ARE YOU OKAY?" Oli pats his girlfriend's back.

Taking in my brother and Elena, my fingers that are not wrapped around the fork guilty of shredding my lunch begin to drum against the tabletop. Not once in my life have I been jealous of anyone's relationship. Never wished I could trade places with the happy couple. Today, though, it grates on my nerves. I don't like Marcus Baxter, let alone want to *be with him.* Yet, I can't stop my thoughts from spinning, spiraling toward him. How he felt inside of me earlier in the week. How he tasted yesterday. And even worse, how he made me feel. There was no self-doubt, not a shred of panic when he touched me, no need to run. What's so special about him and his damn cock that has me bent all out of shape?

"I'm fine." Elena pounds her chest. "The water just went down the wrong pipe." She eyes me suspiciously.

Elena Stevens (unfortunately) has been around me for the past six years. She has vacationed with us, spent the holidays at our house, and I visited her and Oli as much as my work schedule would allow. She's not just my brother's girlfriend. She is a friend.

I hold her gaze, begging her to let it go. She will catch me later, even if she calls me without Oli around. She dips her chin imperceptibly and turns to Oli.

"We don't have to be in San Diego until tomorrow afternoon. What do you say? Why don't we spend the night and then drive down tomorrow?"

Well, shit.

Both peer in my direction simultaneously, and I don't hide my eye roll. Pulling out my phone, I sigh and follow up with a smirk. "I'll call Lilly."

It isn't their fault that I'm in a shit mood over someone I shouldn't think about at all—other than how to avoid him. Lilly would love to have my family spend the night. Rhys and Oli get along great, and Lilly adores Elena. This is all on me.

WE'RE ON THE PATIO. Rhys and Oli are manning the massive built-in barbecue while Lilly, Elena, and I are lounging in our oversized, cushioned chairs around the massive outdoor table. I'm about to lift my glass of wine to my lips when a shiver runs down my spine, and Lilly beams at something behind me. *Someone.*

"Marcus! Come join us."

Footsteps come closer, and Elena's eyes widen. Her lips part as she ogles the man behind my chair. I don't have to look to be aware of where he is in my vicinity. Crunching in my ears alerts me to the fact that I'm grinding my molars as she continues to gape.

"Yeah, Bax. We're having steak and burgers. Veggie for Elena," Rhys exclaims, pointing tongs at the third girl at the table, and I groan inwardly.

What the fuck are they doing? Lilly knows why Marcus and I avoid each other. Why would she invite him? Plus, as if it wasn't awkward enough with me being here, now another Keller is reminding him of what our family has cost him.

There is an awkward pause, and Lilly studies me with her head slanted.

"Marcus, nice to see you again," Oli's voice breaks the silence, and I close my eyes.

Why, why, why?

A buzzing current slowly spreads from a spot behind my ribs, through my core, and into every limb. I jump out of my chair, the scraping sound diverting everyone's attention. "Oli, can you come help me with...something?" I struggle to keep my tone even as the sensation morphs into my muscles coiling and my breath quickening.

All eyes are on me while I do not acknowledge *he who fucked my brains out*.

"Uh..." My brother stares between me, Elena, and a spot slightly behind me.

"Now, Oli." I swivel on my heels and stalk into the house, still not making eye contact with the wall of muscle I almost run into in my retreat.

I march into one of the sitting rooms and wait with my back to the door. My chest is too tight, and inhaling is a chore. Fuck. I cannot afford another episode. Not with everyone in the house. I crouch down and put my head between my knees. Inhale, two, three, four. Hold, two, three, four. Exhale. Repeat. Needles prick my skin. My clothes are too tight.

"Nelle." My brother's voice is like a bullhorn, and I wince against my legs. "Nelle!" He comes closer, his feet appearing in my peripheral vision, but doesn't touch me. He's been through this with me too many times to count. He knows better, but he hasn't seen me like this in my adult life.

"You didn't tell me how bad it is." His disappointment, laced with concern, makes me wince.

"I'm fine. Just give me a moment," I mumble.

"Nelle, you are not fine. You're keeping it together, but you are not fine."

My vibrating pulse speeds up further. I unfold myself in a

jerked motion, whirling at my brother. "What do you expect, Oli? I live under the same roof as the man whose sister I killed!"

Oliver pales visibly before his cheeks turn crimson. "ARE YOU FUCKING KIDDING ME?" he shouts, and my shoulders scrunch up at his outburst. My brother rarely gets angry, let alone raises his tone at me. He doesn't let me speak before he continues, "You had nothing to do with McKenna Baxter's death. It was a fucking aneurysm. Dad probably couldn't have done anything for her either!" He throws his arms up in exasperation.

My throat burns. "What if he could've? If I hadn't jumped in the pool that n-night—" A sob bubbles up, and I cover my face with my hands. I don't want to lose it.

Arms envelop me, and instantly, I can't breathe. I struggle against Oli's hold. "P-please l-let go!" He could easily contain me. As with Collin, I've lost my ability to defend myself. My body is frozen, my skin burning where he touches me.

Oli immediately drops the embrace. "God, Nelle. I'm sorry." Anguish mars his features, and my tears fall freely. I don't want him to see me like this. To worry. I slash my lips, stopping them from trembling.

He softens. "None of that was your fault. That night was a string of random accidents. You witnessed Mom drown when you were five years old. What child wouldn't be traumatized? And you had the predisposition for... Celine didn't know." Through my own blurry vision, I can see his eyes become glassy, and he breaks off.

"Babe?" Lilly's muffled call of my name startles me, and I pivot on my heels, finding my best friend in the archway of her living room. Her hands cover her mouth, and a tear is running down her cheek. "What does he mean you saw your mother drown?" she whispers, her brows pinched.

Lilly doesn't know that Celine Keller is not my biological mother. No one would suspect because we look so much alike, plus Lilly never had a reason to check on the year my parents got married. I can't speak, can't explain to her our fucked-up family dynamic.

I open my mouth. "I..." I shake my head. "I'm sorry." Rushing past her, I race up the stairs and to my room.

It's four thirty in the morning. Sleep hasn't come.

By a miracle, I didn't have to utilize my bathtub. Probably because I didn't go into a full-blown panic attack. I'm just glad, because there would've been no way to convince Oli to leave me after that. He is my big brother, and while he never agreed with my parents' approach of medication, he wouldn't leave me alone in LA.

I'm lying in my bed, staring at the ceiling, when footsteps outside of my room alert me to another person being up. I hesitate a moment before throwing the covers back. I grab my duster cardigan that's draped over the foot of the bed and slip my arms in it. Slowly opening the door, I walk into the dim hallway. Built-in night-lights in every other outlet ensure that the house is never in the dark. Peering left and right, I pad toward the staircase. Light illuminates the foyer, and I make my way downstairs.

Entering the kitchen, I find Rhys leaning with a water bottle against the island.

"Hey." I tug the front of my cardigan closed, wringing my hands into the fabric.

His attention snaps to me, and his brows shoot up. "Hey, D."

We stare at each other, and I curl my toes under, rocking back on my heels. "I, uh... I'm sorry."

The arch of his brows dip. "For what?"

I chuckle. "Don't play dumb. You could never lie."

He purses his lips and waits.

"Your secret about Lilly doesn't count," I declare with a grin.

"The hell it doesn't. None of you had a fucking clue." He puffs his chest out.

Our banter eases the tension in my limbs. I step closer, taking the bottle out of his hands and take a big gulp. "Fiiine."

Handing him the bottle back, he shakes his head. "I don't want your cooties, D. I love you, but the only bodily fluids I let in my mouth are my wife's."

"Ew, gross!" I shriek and punch him against the shoulder.

Rhys doubles over, and I can't help but join. When we've both regained our composure, he sobers. "I know why I'm up this early, but why are you?"

My throat thickens. "What did Lilly tell you?"

He hesitates. Rhys and I have never been on a deep secret kinda level. That was always Lilly, and later Wes, but for some reason I feel the urge to talk to him.

"She said Celine isn't your mother."

"She is not." I walk around the island and perch on one of the barstools. "She is my aunt."

Rhys's eyes bulge. "What the fuck?" He places both palms on the counter, his full attention on me.

"She's finally back asleep. Let's go back to—" Lilly rounds the corner and halts. "Oh, uh... Hey, babe. Did we wake you up?" She tilts her head.

The corner of my mouth quirks without me having to force or fake it. "I couldn't sleep. I heard someone walk by and came down to check what was going on."

Her shoulders visibly sag. "Oh, phew. Good. I'm glad. Audrey is teething and has been up every two hours. She, uh..." She stammers, and the awkwardness between us puts my stomach in knots. I hold my hand out toward her. Lilly doesn't hesitate and takes the stool next to mine. I wrap my arm around her shoulder.

"I just revealed to your hubby here that Celine is not my mother, but my aunt," I blurt out, and my best friend jerks out of my embrace.

"Excuse me?" Her jaw drops.

I lift a shoulder. That part of my past has never bothered me.

Celine is a genuinely good person—apart from her one mistake and how she became my mother, but she has always cared well for Oli and me. "My father had an affair with my mother's sister. I never knew the full extent of it, like how long, etc. But after my mother died, Dad and Celine got married within a few weeks. We moved to Westbridge soon after." I neglect to mention the fact that my father moved us to Westbridge after everything went down with McKenna, and I started having more and more episodes.

"What was your birth mother's name?" Even in the quiet house, Lilly's question is barely audible.

"Bianca." I lift my hands to my sternum and rub. "I don't talk about her."

Both of my friends nod in understanding. It's clear what Lilly is not asking but is dying to know—not that she couldn't find out on her own if she really wanted to.

"My mother drowned the summer before I turned five." The ache in my chest expands. I'm not having an episode; it's a different kind of pain. Sorrow? Regret? "I was the one who found her." I wring my hands together on the marble counter, unable to look at either of them. "My father was at work, and Oli was at a friend's house. Mom and I were alone." I inhale slowly. "I screamed for help." *Exhale.* "But no one heard me. We lived on a large property that used to belong to my mother's family. Our neighbors were miles away." *Inhale.* "Dad and Oli found me by the pool. My voice was so hoarse from crying for hours that I couldn't tell anyone what happened."

"Oh, my god," Lilly whispers. She reaches out, her fingers hovering above mine. She saw me with Oli earlier and witnessed how he was unable to touch me. Is that why she is waiting?

I flip over my palm, signaling to her that it's okay.

"What happened?" Rhys voices the question I was waiting for.

I squeeze my best friend's hand, drawing strength from her. "My mother wasn't doing well. She was on medication. Dad and

Celine never talk about her, and Oli was just as young as me. He has more memories of her, but he can't remember her...bad days, as Celine called them. I overheard her and my father sometimes when they thought we were asleep, but they never said anything in front of us."

"Do you know what kind of medication?" Lilly returns my tight hold.

"I have a suspicion." *One I am not ready to explain.*

"Is that the reason you disappeared the night McKenna..." She trails off. I'm about to respond when a shudder runs down my spine. I whip my head to the side and take in Lilly's expression. She's focused on a reflection in the kitchen's patio door. Slowly turning my head, I lock eyes with Marcus.

No one speaks, and a hollow void settles in my core. How much did he hear?

"I came early to relieve Ben. He's still not a hundred percent," Marcus explains his presence. His face is a blank mask, eyes never straying from mine, and my heart flips.

"Sounds good, man." Rhys breaks the awkwardness, and everyone's attention shifts to him. "Well, I'm gonna go work out, then. Calla, you should try to get another hour of sleep. I have a suspicion that tonight will be another repeat of the last few."

It's then that I notice the dark circles under his eyes. "Is there anything I can help with?" I offer.

He waves me off. "Nah, it's all good. That's what caffeine is for, right?" He trudges over to Lilly, wrapping his arm around her shoulders. "Let's go get you to bed, babe. I'll have to change, and maybe we—"

Lilly slugs him in the arm. "If you ask me to have sex with you right now, you can take care of your daughter alone tonight." Her outrage is fake, but Rhys gets the message.

I can't help but snicker, and when Marcus walks past me toward the fridge, I notice a smirk on his face. Seeing him smile causes my stomach to flip.

Lilly and Rhys disappear, and it's only Marcus and me.

Unsure what to do, I slide off my seat and walk over to turn on the espresso maker. I flip the switch and am about to grab a mug out of the cabinet when Marcus steps in my way. He opens the door, taking a mug out and handing it to me. My heart halts in its tracks. What is he—

When I don't reach for it, he says, "It's just a mug, Denielle."

He is correct on that fact, however, besides two orgasms, the man has never given me anything voluntarily. The way he enunciates my name contradicts the meaning of his statement, and my insides warm. I don't dare think that the time we spent together has put us on at least friendly terms.

I take the offering from him and turn toward the machine. "Would you like a cup?" If he can extend an olive branch, I can as well.

"Uh, yeah, sure." A thermos appears next to me, and I press my lips together to not show him the smile he doesn't deserve. Not yet.

I SPEND my morning highly caffeinated (and jittery) with Oli and Elena. By the time they got up, I was four shots deep in the espresso. I've assured Oli numerous times that I am fine and he doesn't have to come back to LA after their friend's wedding.

"Hearing what happened with Kelly just brought back a lot of memories I had suppressed," I tell him to justify my relapse.

"You don't have to tell Dad, but do you think you should call Dr.—"

"NO!" Poor Elena jumps at my outburst, and I mouth a *sorry* in her direction. I am convinced my therapist reports back to my parents. "How about I call you if it happens again, and you can come babysit me?" I plaster a false smile on my face. While he could technically work from anywhere and has the ability to watch me, I wouldn't call him unless it got bad *bad*. What's gone on the last few weeks has been a cakewalk compared to my childhood.

Needing to hit the road, Oli grudgingly agrees to our new arrangement. We hug goodbye outside, and as their rental car rounds the corner and I turn back toward the house, I catch a glimpse of Marcus standing in the window of Lilly's office.

My heart jumps at the sight, and as soon as our gazes collide, my body turns feverish.

This is ridiculous.

I avert my eyes and speed inside and to my room. I'm not supposed to work, but I could always swing by La Déesse to get a head start on next week.

CHAPTER EIGHTEEN

MARCUS

"What are you looking at?" Lilly questions, amused.

I turn as if I didn't follow Denielle's every move as she walked her brother and his girlfriend to their car and saw them off.

"Oliver left." I keep my tone neutral.

"I'm sorry I didn't give you a heads-up yesterday. I totally spaced out." She hollows her cheeks.

Her concern for my well-being always gives me a sense of belonging. Lilly and Rhys are not my family, but they are. Which is also why I hate that she has been put in this conflicting position between her best friend and me.

"It's fine. I guess having Keller here on the regular has desensitized me," I play it down.

Lilly crosses her arms over her chest, pursing her lips at me disapprovingly. She sits behind her desk, surrounded by her gazillion monitors. "Marcus, Denielle has no fault in McKenna's accident or the blood vessel bursting in her brain."

My heart squeezes, and I pause midstep. While I know Lilly is aware of my past and my sister's accident, we've never openly addressed it. I don't address the topic, period. Adrenaline shoots through every cell, and I root myself in place, fighting against the flight instinct spreading through me. I have the sudden urge to call King. With everything going on this past week, I've missed two calls, and her texts have gotten gradually pissier. She is my best friend, but if I can't admit the change between Keller and me to myself, how can I bring her into it? I do what I do best: avoid and ignore. She's going to stab me with her favorite toy next time we see each other for that.

Instead of aiming for the door, I continue toward the two chairs opposite Lilly's desk, dropping into one and crossing my ankle over my knee. I focus on my breathing, calming the thrashing in my veins. I came in here to talk about the shift changes George and I discussed, not have a fucking therapy session.

"I am aware that she did not cause McKenna's accident or the aneurysm." I'm not arguing the belief that has me kept going for two decades. If Victor Keller hadn't left—

"Did you know that Den watched her mother drown?" Lilly catches me off guard.

Drown?

Images of Denielle gliding into the pool at the vineyard flash in front of me. The amount of time she stayed underwater before she resurfaced. Her face when she did. It was...blank. A shell.

"No, I was not aware of that." My tone is the opposite of what is happening inside of me. I had managed to calm my pulse until Lilly dropped that bomb. As if my unwelcome liking for her wasn't already enough.

"It's not my place to tell—"

"Then why did you start?" I cut her off.

Lilly jumps at my sudden outburst. I don't want to direct my anger toward her, but she's the only one here. She brought it up.

"I...I don't know." She sighs. "Denielle is my best friend. I worry about her."

I narrow my eyes. "Worry how?" Don't they share everything with each other?

"Something is off." She chews on her lower lip. "Has been for a long time, but with her in New York, I didn't realize how much."

I remain mute. This conversation is more for Lilly than it is to set me straight.

"The whole secret engagement with Collin. It's not like her. After Charlie... She didn't let anyone in. She didn't talk about it, but he hurt her to the point that we—Wes, Rhys, and I—were worried she would never date again. She told me she was dating, but why would she get engaged to him? He's..."

"A douche?" I supply helpfully, a sheen of green settling in front of my eyes. I blink, and it disappears as fast as it came. I'm not capable of the emotion the color represents.

Lilly smirks. "That's an accurate description, I guess." She stares out the window, tapping her finger to her chin. "She is hiding something. Something she doesn't want me to know. And it scares me." Her eyes swivel back to me. "Oli knew how to, uh...handle her, which means it's been going on for a long time."

"What do you mean?"

"He tried to hug her, and she was freaking out. She..."

"Acted like a cornered animal?" The scene with Liberman in front of the house replaces the memory of the vineyard.

"Yes!" She sits up straight. "How do you...?"

"I've been around enough people with PTSD. She probably never processed what happened with her mother." I almost tell Lilly about the incident with Liberman, but at the last moment decide to change gears. If Denielle hasn't told Lilly herself, there is a reason for it. A switch inside of me flips.

Why do I care if I reveal her secret?

Because you would kill anyone who dug into your past without your knowledge.

That's not all. I want to shoot myself in the knee for even considering the possibility that I *care* for Denielle Keller.

"You're probably right," Lilly drops the topic.

That was too easy.

LILLY and I finished our conversation, and I decided to get my workout in as soon as my shift was over, exhausting myself to the point of being unable to think about my earlier revelation.

Caring didn't mean liking, let alone forgiving her. I spent too long blaming her family for what happened to mine. Not my father's hand in it. That was never part of my hatred for Victor Keller or his daughter. I took care of my father. Even Oliver wasn't on the same level. I focused all my energy on Denielle once she entered my life six years ago. She was an easy target. An available target.

But living on the same property with her for the past month...things have shifted. And not just because I had my dick in her or she gave me a blow job that will never compare to anyone else. The woman has the mouth of a goddess.

I've received quite a few oral favors over the years, especially when Ethan and I hit *The Club*. Being part of Lilly's team, we never paid the cover charge. We used her suite whenever we wanted. Chicks assumed we were swimming in dough, and who were we to correct them? The thought of hitting *The Club* now is as appealing as shaving my balls with a dull razor.

Fuck

I MANAGED to avoid Denielle for the rest of the weekend. Whenever she was already in a room, came from upstairs, or the one time I was heading to the main house and noticed her dark hair in the window situated over the sink in the kitchen, I made a U-ey like a freaking pussy. It was getting ridiculous.

Sunday afternoon, after another grueling workout to distract my mind, I peered into the garage. Why? I told myself it was to check on the McGuires' cars. But let's face it, I never do that—

that's what we have the home security feed for when needed. Plus, I was off the clock. The G-Wagon was not in its usual spot. Being a diligent employee, of course, I activated the tracker.

Denielle was at work. On a Sunday. Was she avoiding me as well?

I didn't have much time to think about it after that. Or her. George kept me on video calls for the remainder of the day. Something had crawled up his ass, and he was getting on my nerves. He normally let me run my team however I saw fit. Suddenly, he wanted to make all kinds of changes that made no fucking sense, which didn't sit right with me.

LILLY IS WORKING from home on Monday. Rhys is at the office, so we don't have to worry about him. The security there would put any federal prison to shame. When he's ready to leave, one of us will follow the tracker in his car.

I'm downstairs in the kitchen when my phone buzzes across the countertop. I keep pouring my coffee as I peer over at it, and my fingers clench around the handle of the mug. Lilly's name lights up the display. What the—?

She's upstairs, sitting with Audrey. Baby McGuire won't go to sleep alone these days, and Lilly has to lie in front of her crib, holding her hand while working on her phone with the other.

I let go of my mug and tap the text, ready to race upstairs to eliminate any possible threat that could have found its way into the house. *Which is impossible*, logic attempts to reason.

D called 4x. Can't answer, Aud just fell asleep.

As I scan her words, three dots appear again.

Something is wrong. I can feel it.

The blood inside my veins turns to ice. Why would Denielle call her four times in the middle of the day? I'm trained for situations like this. I don't panic, don't let emotions take over my actions, yet as I exit out of the message and switch to my phone book, I have to tap twice because my finger misses the icon.

I have all of Lilly's friends' numbers. We all do. It's part of covering our bases. After Thursday, I even had Charlie York's digits—though, that had less to do with my employer.

I tap on her name and wait. Adrenaline rushes my body. With every ring, it becomes harder to breathe.

Something is wrong, I hear Lilly's voice in my head.

The ringing cuts off, and I want to scream.

"He-ohhh," Denielle slurs into the phone.

"It's me." I don't bother announcing myself properly. "Where are you? Lilly said you called her four times."

"—arcus?" She sounds far away, as if speaking takes effort.

"Yes," I gentle my tone, even though the urge to yell at her to fucking tell me what's going on overwhelms my senses. "Den, what's going on? Are you okay?"

She groans instead of answering, and my control snaps. I race toward the garage, grabbing the keys to the Escalade from the board, and hit the garage door on the way. "Please tell me where you are."

"—ork." Then something clatters, and there is silence.

No, no, no.

"DENIELLE!" I'm losing it. I don't lose it, not even when I found my sister on the road. Not like this. I throw the SUV into reverse and plow out of the garage at a more than unsafe speed. "Den, answer me! Are you there?"

No response. Fuck, fuck, fuck. Disconnecting the call feels like someone is stabbing me in the heart. Peering between the road and my screen, I pull up Ethan's number. He's not on shift until tonight, and I have no clue if he's sleeping or what. It takes two calls before his drowsy voice answers. "B?"

"Get someone to La Déesse. Something is wrong with Denielle," I bark the command and hang up, dialing Denielle's number again. No answer.

I repeat the call attempts until I pull into the alley behind the boutique. I don't bother parking properly. I stop the car in the middle of the small lot, abandoning it with the motor still running.

Thankfully, the back door is not locked during store hours. I'm in the building two seconds after exiting the car.

"DENIELLE!" I race down the hall. "Jesus, woman! Where the fuck are you?"

A girl comes around the corner from the main showroom. "Who are you?"

"Where is Denielle?" I'm in front of her in three strides, and she cranes her neck up at me. She must see that I'm not in the mood for shit talking.

"Upstairs in her office," she supplies in a mousy tone. I follow the direction she points to the stairwell behind me.

Whirling around, I take two steps at a time. "DEN!"

"Third door on the right," the girl calls after me, and I increase my speed. The drumming in my ears mimics the pounding of my shoes against the hardwood. I find her door open and am through it before I can take another breath. She's not there. I scan the room. Her laptop sits open on the desk. Her chair is too far away, though. I cross the distance, and what I discover catapults me back two decades. Denielle's unconscious form lies facedown on the ground. Her phone is next to her, her open palm upward. I fall to my knees, ignoring the pain shooting through my legs.

Oh, god.

Placing two trembling fingers on her neck, I close my eyes. Bile rises in my throat. Where is her pulse? I withdraw my hand, shaking it out. Concentrate, fucker. She is not dead. She can't be. I place my fingers once more against her skin and hold my breath. There! Her pulse is slow but strong. Oh, thank you, Jesus. Relief like I have never experienced before floods me.

"Oh, my god! Denielle." My head whips up. The girl from downstairs stands in the doorframe.

"Call an ambulance." I carefully turn Denielle around and fall on my ass. Pulling her into my lap, I cradle her head. When I don't hear footsteps, I peer up. The bimbo is still standing with her mouth open in the hallway.

"CALL A FUCKING AMBULANCE!" I roar, and she finally jumps into action.

"—arcus?" Denielle's whisper is barely audible.

I touch my hand to her cheek, stroking her hair with the other. "I'm here. Everything will be okay."

She leans into my touch, and my heart skips a beat.

"Th- ank -ou."

Waves of hot and cold rack through me. One second, sweat seeps across my skin, and the next, I'm shivering. "What for?" I lean closer. She's weak, and if the damn ambulance is not here soon, I will take her myself.

"Com— for me." Her eyes blink open, and when our gazes collide, my chest squeezes. She moves her hand ever so slightly, and I interpret it as her attempt to reach for me. I remove my hand from her face and take her fingers. Interlacing mine with hers, she smiles softly.

"Of course I came."

Commotion in the hallway is followed by a breathless Ethan in the doorframe. He takes in the scene, and his eyes bug out. I'm sitting on the floor with a mostly unconscious Denielle Keller—the girl I swore to hate—in my lap, holding on to her hand like it's a lifeline. For her or me is the question.

"What the fuck happened?"

Before I can answer him, sirens alert us to the arrival of the ambulance.

"Fucking finally."

Ethan squats down next to me, scanning Denielle's face. "She's pale," he whispers.

I nod, unable to take my eyes off her usually tan face.

We sit in silence until the paramedics appear in the room. When one (*I name him EMT-One*) asks me to let go, I don't budge. I can't. My muscles are in full lockdown. I didn't get to hold Ken. Logic tells me Denielle doesn't need surgery, she's not going to die, but I can't let go.

"B, let the guys help her." Ethan's careful command registers. Hands wrap around my upper arms. "Come on, man." He shakes me ever so slightly. "She's right there. You can see her."

"Sir, please," EMT-Two addresses me as well.

I must've done something, or said something, because he jumps back. My control is slipping.

"Okay, B." The grip on my biceps shifts to my armpits, and I'm being hurled up. One of the EMTs holds Denielle's head as my legs are being pulled out from under her.

I struggle, my vision becoming hazy. The scene in front of me flips between present and past. I'm in Denielle's office. The next second, I can smell the hot asphalt covered in my sister's blood. My lungs cramp, the stench from the past burning into my nose.

"Whoa, B!" The grip on me tightens. "Take a breath."

We watch the two men work on Denielle, and it feels like an eternity until one of them blinks up at us. "It appears that Miss Keller has been drugged. Based on her symptoms, I would suspect some type of sedative. We will know more once we get her to the hospital and can run more tests."

"Drugged?" My blood is thrashing in my ears. And Ethan must've heard something in my one-word question, because I'm suddenly unable to move.

"Are you saying she got roofied?" Ethan peers around the room, incredulous.

"Miss Keller exhibits symptoms of it, yes."

One of the paramedics stands and disappears in the hallway, just to reappear with a stretcher. Watching them lift Denielle up and strap her to the thing is pure torture.

My fingers curl and uncurl. Ethan finally loosens his grip, and I shrug him off. "I'm coming with you."

EMT-One's head jerks up. "Are you family?"

"I am coming with you," I repeat myself slowly. Panic is

replaced by an even more dangerous calm. The dude's eyes widen, and he jerks his head up and down.

Attaboy.

Trailing after them rolling the stretcher out into the hallway, I address Ethan. "Call Rhys. Lilly's going to freak out, and she can't leave the house because of Audrey. Rhys needs to be the one to tell her."

"On it, boss." Ethan already has his phone in hand when a male voice echoes through the narrow staircase.

"Dear Lord, what happened?" Denis, the owner of this over-priced fabric shop, stands at the bottom.

My gaze shifts to the person hovering behind him, and every muscle in my body coils. Behind Denis, Collin Liberman observes the scene with expressionless eyes—no concern, no shock, no...nothing.

"Easy, B." A hand lands on my shoulder. "Did you just growl?" Ethan's chuckle fills my ears.

I throw a death glare behind me, and Ethan drops his hand.

"I get it, man. I'm worried, too."

No, you don't.

I don't tell him that he has no fucking clue. I'm supposed to hate Denielle Keller, yet I fucked her, let her blow me, and am about to go out of my mind from seeing her unconscious. I want to sucker punch her ex. Something is off about the guy. Why is he still here?

I avoid Denis, who flattens himself against the wall of the corridor with his hand on his chest. The man is near tears. Liberman is less considerate. He makes enough room for the paramedics to wheel the stretcher past him, but they have to avoid him, not the other way around. My adrenaline level has reached an unhealthy and irrational high. When it's my turn to move past Liberman, he steps in my path and stares at me.

Oh, no you don't.

"Move." My tone is low and calm despite the constriction in my chest and the thrashing in my ears.

When he doesn't comply, I reach for—

"Okayyyy." A hand lands on my chest, and Ethan maneuvers himself between Liberman and me. Our eyes lock, but no words are spoken. We don't need to. I nod, and when he's sure I won't shoot the New York high-society coke whore, he turns and tilts his head at the guy.

"I suggest you step away, or my man here will remove you, which will result in a call for another ambulance. And I can promise you, it won't make it in time." I snort because E perfectly imitates the voice of the Joker. He sounds like he is the insane one, not me—the one who was ready to draw a gun in Denielle's place of work.

We all have our damage. Ethan's is as disturbing as mine is tragic.

Collin Liberman's face drains of color. I don't have to see Ethan to know his *smile* is anything but friendly.

He pats Liberman's cheek. "Good boy. Now run along." With that, he pushes him out of the way with one finger against his forehead.

We follow the paramedics, who just finished loading the stretcher into the ambulance. One is about to shut the doors when I climb into the back and settle next to EMT-Two.

Before we're locked in, I call out, "Follow us to the hospital and let me know what Rhys says."

Ethan salutes me before our visual connection is severed.

CHAPTER NINETEEN

DENIELLE

Beep. Beep. Beep.

What the hell is that? I turn toward the obnoxious sound, but as soon as I move my head, dizziness rolls through me in waves, making vomit burn in my throat. Oh, god. Cold sweat slithers across my neck and back. I swallow, but my throat is too dry, and I choke. Lifting my hand to my mouth, I'm stopped by a sharp pain in my hand.

"Oww." I keep tugging, ignoring the sting in my arm getting worse. My heart rate picks up, my breath coming in sharp bursts. Why can't I move? What is going on?

"Hey, hey," Lilly's voice penetrates my cloud of panic. "Slow down, babe." Fingers wrap around my arm. "Hold on, D. Your IV is caught somewhere."

IV?

The sting transforms into a burn spreading through the top of my hand.

"What hap—?" The scratching in my throat is agony. "Wat-r..."

"Sure, okay. Hold on. Let me raise the bed."

My lids feel like they're glued shut. It takes several tries to peel them back. Blinking slowly, a dim room comes into view. I don't recognize my surroundings. Where the fuck am I?

"You're in the hospital," Rhys explains.

Did I say that out loud? I tilt my head to the other side and spot him leaning against the windowsill. The drawn shades put his face in shadows. His arms are crossed, and his foot is propped against the wall underneath the window. He reminds me of his younger version, lounging in the hallway of Westbridge High, Wes by his side, and observing his surroundings—a.k.a. watching Lilly without anyone's knowledge. All those damn secrets. A giggle bubbles up at the memory, resulting in another coughing fit, and he raises a brow.

Why am I so out of it?

Shifting my focus back to my other side, Lilly is fussing with wires and tubes that disappear under...

"Where are my clothes?" I'm draped in one of those flimsy hospital gowns. Panic rises in my core, and my eyes fly around the room.

Lilly presses her lips together, throwing a glance at her husband. When she meets my eyes again, she puffs out her cheeks. "You were drugged."

My brows shoot up. "I was what?" Disbelief mingles with sheer terror. My arms and legs begin to tremble, and my already strenuous inhales become impossible. Finally able to move freely, I rub my fist against my sternum in small circles.

"What do you remember?" Rhys steps closer, perching on the edge of the bed near my feet.

Lilly places a hand on my leg. "Shhh. The doctors checked you out. Nothing happened."

This one sentence releases the pressure in my lungs, and the oxygen finally flows again. The erratic thudding in my chest slows. *Nothing happened.* "I..." my voice cracks. I have the urge to check my entire body myself to make sure. I don't feel injured or... "How did I get here?"

"Marcus found you," Lilly explains.

"Marcus?" Why on earth would Marcus—? I'm suddenly too hot. My stomach dips. This is all too much. I squeeze my eyes shut.

"You called Calla. She was with Audrey and couldn't answer," Rhys begins.

Lilly's hand strokes up and down my thigh. "I texted Marcus to have him check what was going on. You called several times, and I was worried."

I search for my last memory. "I had lunch with Charlie."

"Charlie?" Lilly and Rhys exclaim simultaneously.

"We went to the bakery around the corner. We were supposed to meet after work, but he asked if I could meet for lunch instead."

"Why are you hanging out with him again?" Rhys's harsh tone startles me, and my eyes pop open. His hard expression is not what I expected. He and Charlie used to be friends back in school.

I lift a shoulder. "I...I don't know." I can't tell them that getting back at Lilly's *Shadow* was part of the reason. "I'm not mad at him anymore. I just felt like I owed it to him after Kelly..."

"That makes no fucking sense, D." Rhys's jaw works back and forth.

Everything halts. Even the little dust particles hovering in the air seem suspended, unmoving as it clicks. "Are you saying Charlie drugged me?"

"We just want to figure out what happened. We're still waiting on the lab results, but the doctors told Marcus that you show all signs of a sedative."

"A.k.a. roofied." Rhys throws his hands up.

This time, his words don't have the same impact. I'm hung up on why Marcus knows all of it.

Lilly must've seen the confusion on my face and turns toward her husband. "Babe, can you call Laurin and check on

Aud? Then, make sure Ethan got someone to help with the cars."

Rhys slants his head at her, and silent communication passes between them. *I'm not that far gone. She's trying to get rid of him.*

"Fine. I'll go get a coffee while I'm at it." Rhys reaches out and pats my hand before leaving the room.

When we hear the door hit the frame, I blurt, "I slept with Marcus." I clamp my eyes shut.

Fuck, fuck, fuck.

"That explains some...things." Lilly's calm, unsurprised tone is enough for me to look at her through slitted lids.

"What do you mean?" I mumble, scared of what her answer might be.

She purses her lips. "D, do you think I'm blind?"

"Um, maybe?" I pull one shoulder up.

"Ha!" She shakes her head. "Well, I'm not. Something changed between you guys. That much was obvious. I just couldn't put my finger on it. Marcus was the one who went to find you at The Club. Ethan told Rhys he discovered Marcus with you in his lap in your office. Marcus nearly lost it when he had to let go of you for the EMTs. He rode with you in the ambulance, and..." She pauses, a blush staining her cheeks. "When I arrived earlier, he was holding your hand and had his head resting on your bed."

A different kind of warmth spreads through me. Marcus held me. He stayed with me. The person who swore to hate me came to my rescue. The flutter in my belly expands to my chest. "Where is he?"

Lilly's face falls. "He went home."

Home? He left. Left me. The flutter stops. The butterflies disintegrate like someone aiming a flamethrower at them and are replaced by a hollow emptiness, the ashes of their burned bodies floating to the ground. "I see."

Her hand moves from my thigh to the one with the IV, and

she interlaces our hands carefully. "Can you remember anything that happened during lunch?" She drops the topic, though I'm sure it's not the last conversation we'll have about it.

Rhys bursts into the room before I can respond. "The fucking lab results are still not in. What kind of shit show is this?"

He stalks with two to-go cups in hand toward the bed, and I study his scowl. He's worked hard to rein in his temper over the years, but I can see parts of the old Rhys breaking through. He hands the one with the tea bag tag hanging out to Lilly and takes a big gulp from the other. When our eyes meet, his brows dip. "You're not allowed to have any, D. Sorry."

"Just wonderful," I mutter.

Lilly holds my gaze, answering Rhys. "I'll have Jax make a few calls."

"Why are you getting Jax involved?" An icy shiver runs down my spine. This hot/cold thing my body is doing is irritating, to say the least. Tanner Jaxon Weiler, a.k.a. Jax, is part of Lilly's legal team. I first met him when he came to Montana after King was accused of murder. He is anything but your typical attorney. Physically, he gives any male model a run for his money. His sarcastic, smart mouth has gotten him in trouble on numerous occasions in court. But where Lilly's brother is a genius with computers, Jax is one when it comes to legal matters. If he argues a case, you have no chance. I've seen him on and off when I've visited, but probably not in over six months. He's also not just one of Lilly's employees but a friend *and* George's nephew.

"He went to college with someone in administration. He can have them put some pressure on the lab. Your nurse checked three times already, but they're dragging their feet," Lilly explains.

"Let's go over what happened." Rhys pulls a chair to the side of my bed.

I inhale slowly and let the memories run through my mind. "I got to work around nine. I met with Denis to discuss some issues we had with a fabric delivery and how to handle a large bridal party scheduled later in the week. My client dropped off her dress for her appointment on Wednesday. I went over some invoices and then met Charlie for lunch." During my recollection, I kept my eyes trained on the ceiling.

"What did you guys talk about?" Lilly prods.

"I apologized for Thursday, leaving him standing at The Club and—"

"Wait, what?" Rhys sits up straight. "When was he at The Club?"

"He texted me that he saw our post"—I peer at Lilly—"and came by."

My friends exchange a look.

"What?" I flip-flop between them.

"Don't you think that's a little odd? He keeps popping up wherever you are. It's like he's stalking you on social media," Rhys accuses.

I shake my head, and a wave of dizziness washes over me. "This is Charlie. He can't hurt a fly."

"No, but he can cheat on you for months, which no one ever suspected. And don't forget what you did to retaliate. I'm sure he didn't like finding all his shit in the dumpster." Rhys crosses his arms.

"That was years ago. We were kids," I defend myself (and him).

"And we all know how long people can hold a grudge." Rhys glowers at his wife, who has remained mute throughout the exchange. He's not angry with her. He's simply reminding us of what she went through because of something that happened before she was born.

"He wouldn't hurt me," I emphasize once more, my fingers curling into the thin blanket covering my body.

"Would you be upset with me if I looked into what he's been up to the last few years?" Lilly carefully asks.

If I say no, she won't do it. She isn't that kind of friend, but at the same time... Simmering paranoia and suspicion steadily turned to a boil the more Rhys argued his point. I nod slowly. "Go for it."

"What did you do after lunch?" I focus back on Rhys. All that's missing is him pulling out a small notepad, taking my statement.

I fill my lungs with air and chew on my lip. Things are starting to get hazy, and I have to concentrate. "Charlie walked back with me. We said our goodbyes, and I went inside. I talked to Cassy for a minute, then went upstairs."

"Did you eat or drink anything you didn't get yourself?" Rhys has taken on full interrogation mode.

"What are you now, the police?" I roll my eyes, using sarcasm to mask my overpowering feeling of being violated—even if it didn't go *that* far.

"No, they will have their own questions, but someone fucking drugged you. You can bet your sexy ass on us finding who is behind that." I'm stunned by his speech.

A knock on the door redirects everyone's focus. The door opens, and a woman in scrubs walks in, followed by Ethan.

"Hello, Denielle. My name is Dr. Palmer." She carries a folder in her hand, and her warm smile eases some of the knots in my stomach.

"Hi." I force the corners of my mouth up.

Ethan positions himself next to Rhys and squeezes my foot through the covers. "Hey, girl. You scared us half to death. Don't do that again, 'kay?" He grins crookedly, and I laugh. His easy-going attitude manages to lift the weighted blanket covering me since waking up.

"I'll do my best."

"Denielle, your brother is on his way. He permitted us to disclose your medical condition with your friends."

"My brother?" my voice turns shrill. My father's face flashes in front of my eyes.

"Yes. He was listed as your emergency contact." She appears confused at my outburst.

I rack my brain, trying to remember who else is on the list. Living on the other side of the country, I never put Lilly on it—something I should do ASAP. "You *just* called Oli?" I need her to confirm to me that my father is not coming to LA.

"Yes, is there a problem?" Dr. Palmer peers between the other people in the room and me.

"No. I'm sorry." Embarrassment keeps me from facing my friends. I'm acting less than sane. I give her what I'm hoping is a reassuring smile.

"Well, uh, okay then. Would you like your friends to be with you when we go over the lab results?"

"Yes, please." For once, I am not trying to be strong. My eyes gloss over as the realization hits that the one person I need to be here is not. I want Lilly to call Marcus. He's been the one giving me strength. If it is because he pushes me or for a reason I'm not willing to admit to myself...

A finger swipes at the tear trailing down my cheek. "Um, would you guys wait outside?" Lilly addresses Rhys and Ethan, who both cock a brow. "Please?" she pushes more sternly.

Hesitantly, both guys start drudging toward the door. When both are gone, Lilly takes my hand. "Do you want me to call him?"

My heart skips a beat. "How do you—?"

She smiles softly at me. "Babe, how long have we been friends?"

"No, it's fine."

My poor doctor must be beyond confused by our cryptic conversation.

"Are you sure? I can order him here." Lilly shrugs with a smirk.

I shake my head and face Dr. Palmer. "What do the results say?"

She peers at the folder in her hand. "The urine and blood

sample both showed a low dose of Flunitrazepam in your system. It wasn't as much as we normally find in sexual assault victims, which explains why you were able to call for help and were in and out of consciousness."

Marcus's face flashes in front of my inner eye, him stroking my cheek and holding my hand. *Of course I came.* He stated it with such confidence that it makes me want to believe he's moved past his hatred.

"Isn't it odd that someone would drug her and then leave her alone? I mean, if someone tried to, uh...you know..." Lilly doesn't finish her sentence, but Dr. Palmer and I both understand what she indicates.

"I'm going to be blunt with you. This is a unique situation. I usually don't get these types of test results unless there has been at least an attempt of physical assault. Could this have been someone playing a terrible prank on you?"

A prank? A tremble spreads through my limbs.

"I wouldn't know who." I glance at Lilly, following the twitch in her arm to her fingers flicking against her thumb. *What is she not saying?*

"Well, okay. You will have to give your statement to the police later. They have been notified, and someone will come by before you are released tomorrow."

"Tomorrow? Why can't I go home today?" I don't want to stay here.

"You need fluids, and we need to keep you under observation." Dr. Palmer's calm voice does the opposite of soothing me. I hate hospitals. They remind me of— My chest feels too tight, and my gaze darts around the room.

"D, calm down. You'll be okay. You won't be alone." Lilly takes both my hands in hers, and I focus on her face. The crease between her brows will cause a permanent wrinkle. I inhale slowly through my nose and hold my breath before expelling it, repeating the motion.

"Would you like me to get the nurse to give you something to relax?" My eyes fly to my doctor.

"NO!"

She jumps back, and I wince. *Now she's going to give you something to calm your ass down.*

"She'll be okay. It's just a lot. I think rest will be all D needs," Lilly interjects herself, and suddenly, she's in mom-slash-business mode. Sometimes I'm still surprised by the different faces she has mastered and taken on over the years. It all seems to come naturally to her. But things are never how they appear from the outside. I'm the best example of that.

The woman in scrubs studies us for a moment too long before nodding. "Don't hesitate to call for a nurse. I will leave a prescription with them, just in case. I will check on you before my shift ends, and the night nurse will take your vitals in a bit." She squeezes my forearm before leaving the room.

Lilly and Rhys stay for another hour before I kick them out. Even if their sitter has everything handled at home, they need to be with Audrey. Ethan remains back per Lilly's orders, and I'm glad not to be alone. My mind has been all over the place. I was drugged. *Roofied.* Why? By whom? Was it a mistake? Was someone else the target?

"You look like you're about to lose it." Ethan steps closer, holding something out to me. I drop my gaze from his face and trademark grin to his hand. My phone. "I figured you might want a distraction. I also grabbed your purse when I had the cars picked up." He drops himself into the chair Rhys had pulled over earlier and props his feet on the mattress.

I tilt my head, taking in his profile. His eyes are trained on the TV on the opposite side of the room. "Ethan?"

"Mhmm." He glances at me from the corner of his eyes.

"Thank you." The lump in my throat makes it hard to speak.

He gives me a tight smile and holds his fist out toward me. "Anytime."

I bump his knuckles, laughing. "You're a dork."

"Nicest compliment I've ever gotten," he mumbles, and I scan his features. Ethan always has a joke on his lips, but something tells me a lot is going on behind his pretty face that not many people know about.

It's clear that our conversation is over, so I swipe my phone open. One text from Oli, informing me he is on the next flight out and will be in LA by morning. A pang of guilt spreads through me. I hate for him to have to fly across the country again—a day after he just left San Diego.

I scroll to my call log and see the four outgoing calls to Lilly earlier in the day. Above her name is a number I didn't have—until now. My phone shows one accepted call and then several unanswered ones. I save his number to my contacts and then stare at the name. Why did he stay with me but then leave? The question reverberates through my head until I could scream. It's not like we are in a relationship or even dating. Fuck.

I place my phone on top of the covers next to me and focus on whatever Ethan has playing on the TV. My nail picks at the case of my phone, itching to send him the question. Not once in my life has a guy made me feel this...nuts. And I have enough mental baggage that should do it for me. No, Marcus Baxter makes me feel powerful and insecure at the same time. The urge to hurl the device across the room in a temper tantrum makes me twitchy.

Letting go of the phone, I cross my arms over my chest and close my eyes. My frustration toward Marcus distracts me enough from today's events to relax and eventually drift off.

CHAPTER TWENTY

MARCUS

LILLY AND RHYS ENTER FROM THE GARAGE AS I PUSH through the door coming from the gym. I've spent the last several hours exerting my body (and mind) in every possible way to not think about...*her*. My stomach was demanding nourishment after what I had just put myself through, but seeing them home, my nonexistent appetite turns into a wave of nausea.

Who is with Denielle?

Why do you care? You couldn't leave her side fast enough.

"Hey!" Lilly smiles when she spots me rooted in the hallway.

Rhys scans my face, claps my shoulder as he passes me, and heads straight for the stairs. "Hey." His greeting is less enthusiastic.

Lilly stares at me with her head slightly tilted. "You okay?"

Ignore and avoid.

I turn toward the kitchen. "Yeah, why wouldn't I be?"

"Marcus, stop," she raises her voice just slightly, but enough to make me halt.

I don't face her. A hollow sensation spreads through me. I

know where she's going, and I don't want to head in that direction. I'm not ready. Will I ever be?

"Can we talk?" She's giving me an out.

I should take it.

"Sure." I start moving again and aim for the fridge. I get busy with my original plan and suppress the gag the inside of the fridge causes.

Lilly pulls herself up on the counter, sitting next to me as I crack eggs into a bowl. I breathe through my mouth to not smell the yellow-orangey substance, or I may throw up. I've never experienced such uncontrollable turmoil. I don't like it.

"She asked for you."

I roll my lips under. How am I supposed to respond? "How is she?"

"She's...confused."

I snort, shaking my head noncomically. "Confused? Someone roofied her."

"There is that as well, yes." She kicks her legs, staring at the ground. "We left Ethan with her until Oli gets here."

My head jerks in her direction. "Why is Oliver coming back?" The thrashing in my ears makes it hard to hear Lilly's response.

"The hospital called him. He was listed as her emergency contact."

My fingers twitch, and one of the eggs explodes in my palm. Fuck. Lilly narrows one eye at me, and I have to focus on uncurling my fist, relaxing the muscles in my back. Without missing a beat or even acting surprised, Lilly reaches beside her and hands me the roll of paper towels. I abandon the meal prep, focusing on cleaning the mess I created.

"What about her father?" If Victor Keller shows up, I can't guarantee anything. While things between Denielle and me are... different, the man still causes my vision to cloud. Plus, something isn't right between him and his daughter—something beyond him marrying his dead wife's sister.

She shakes her head, and the rest of the tension melts away.

"Do you want to head back to the hospital? We're fine here." The hopefulness in Lilly's tone gives her away.

"What did Denielle tell you?" I hold the air in my lungs, waiting for the bomb to drop.

Lilly chews on her cheek, not meeting my eyes.

Jesus, this is not good.

"Lilly?" I growl.

"She said she slept with you," my boss blurts, her eyes flicking to me before aiming back at her feet.

"That's it?"

"We got interrupted."

I expel my breath with a whoosh, and Lilly bursts out laughing, circling a finger at my face. "I don't think you could've appeared more relieved."

The lightness between us in this situation solidifies, once more, why I consider the woman next to me a friend more than an employer. She never judges. I attempt not to smile (and fail) and pull my shoulder up casually.

Her laugh dies down. "It's okay if you like her, you know?"

The corners of my mouth drop, and I shift toward my abandoned bowl again. Picking up the whisk, I start scrambling the eggs, stirring so forcefully that I spill it all over the counter.

"Shit." I should just give up. I'm not hungry anyway. I reach for the paper towels again when Lilly's hand lands on my forearm.

"Marcus."

I halt midaction. "I can't, Lilly."

Her fingers tighten. "She had nothing to do with your sister's death."

Her words hit me like a bullet. McKenna's face flashes in front of my eyes. Her eyes laughing with joy. Her smile that could light up a room just by it being aimed at you. We had a childhood no kid should experience. We never experienced the love of a parent, just the fists of our father, yet it never diminished her light.

"Be happy, big brother!" her voice echoes in my mind, and my throat constricts.

How can I be happy when you're gone?

Lilly and I remain like this for the longest time. Footsteps in the foyer fill the silence, and Audrey's squeal enters the kitchen. Lilly drops her hand and jumps off the counter. "Hey, my love."

The smile in her voice causes my chest to compress.

She takes her daughter from Rhys, who kisses her in return before heading toward the gym. I've never thought about having a family. Never wanted one. With the change between Denielle and me, more things have shifted. There is something like... possibility?

Lilly comes back over, standing next to me with her daughter in her arms. I peer to the side, meeting Audrey's big hazel eyes. "Hey, Baby McG." I boop her nose, and she giggles.

"May I give you my honest opinion?" Lilly begins, then shifts Audrey to her other side before eyeing me again.

"I'd prefer you to give me your *dis*honest opinion," I state blankly, and she gives me a dirty look. I grin at my boss, the expression genuine. It feels good.

"Asshole." The laughter in her wannabe insult makes warmth spread through me. "I think you like D but have spent so many years hating her and her family that you won't let yourself see all the good you both could have."

"Could we?" I challenge. "What kind of *relationship* would we have?"

"One that could heal both of you."

I let her words sink in. Would it? I can't form a response. The ever-present cockroaches when I picture Denielle Keller crawl up my stomach walls, beginning to feel more like the dreaded flutter of...*hope?*

"Just...think about it." She has to lean away from Audrey's hand patting her face. "You've brought the Denielle back to the surface that disappeared years ago. And you...you seem...I don't know. Lighter? Less driven by hatred." She peers at the ceiling. "Sorry, that sounds terrible." She starts rambling. "You're a good friend. I just want you to—"

"I get it, Lilly." I drop the whisk into the bowl of over-scrambled eggs and turn toward the two females. Wrapping my arms around both, Audrey wriggles against her mom and me. "You're a good friend, too."

I SPENT the rest of the night overthinking things. I almost went back to the hospital but then changed my mind. I replayed the last few weeks in my head over and over. The night I first saw her at the pool. The denial over accepting that everything changed in that moment. Denielle's pushbacks had become an addiction—an itch I needed to scratch. Witnessing the strong-willed woman I met six years ago reemerge whenever she was in my vicinity. The urge to wrap her in my arms when she crumbled in front of my eyes. The need to figure out what made her so self-conscious when she should be the opposite.

What was the one secret she kept close?

WHEN OLIVER BRINGS Denielle back to the house in the early afternoon, I am sitting in the living room of the guesthouse, following her on my phone. Ethan had left the G-Wagon at the hospital when J picked him up on his way this morning. Watching Oliver navigate the Mercedes up the driveway and toward the garages, my leg bounces so hard I can't keep the small screen steady. I switch to the next camera, which is positioned over the door leading from the garage into the house. Lilly and Rhys have made sure to have all entrances covered and the windows secured with sensors, but inside their home, there are no cameras—unlike the vineyard where one can't take a shit without it being recorded.

Denielle gets out of the passenger side door. She's dressed in leggings and a loose-fitting tank top, the duster cardigan I've seen her wear around the house draped over her arm. She looks pale, and a knot forms in my stomach.

Who did this to her and why?

Ethan and I discussed our two prime suspects: cheating frat orgy ex Charlie York, and cheating coke whore of an ex, Collin Liberman. But what's their motive? Scaring her into getting back with them? Charlie appearing everywhere Den went was certainly a red flag. Liberman was supposed to have left last week, but there he was yesterday. Why did he stay? I've considered asking Denielle if either of them has made advances or comments that would point in one direction or another. My jaw tenses. The thought of her back with either of them... My hand tightens, and the case of my phone crackles.

Denielle disappears into the house, Oli slowly following with a plastic bag and Denielle's purse in one hand. I have the urge to switch to the foyer camera to see if I can catch her there, but I shut down the feed instead. My behavior is ridiculous. I'm acting like a stalker, all because I can't figure out what I want—to resent and blame her or fuck her until she screams my name. I'm too old for this. That's why I have avoided emotional relationships my entire life. If you don't get attached, you have no problem walking away.

You've always been attached to Denielle.

The truth. I've been fixated on Denielle Keller.

I get up to get a bottle of water from the fridge. With every step, thoughts slam into me. Dad using Ken and me as his personal punching bags for his fucked-up life. The times his fists would descend on me while I'd scream for Ken to run. I told her to climb out the window that night. Me. Not Denielle. The driver going too fast when Ken ran into the road in the pitch dark. Not Denielle. A blood vessel bursting in Ken's brain when everyone thought the surgery was pretty much over. Denielle had no hand in that. She is *my* punching bag. I channeled my anger and rage at all the things I could not control in my first eighteen years of life on her—a five-year-old girl at the time. None of this was Denielle's fault. My fingers clench around the water bottle, the plastic about to burst. I whirl around and fire the bottle like a missile against the wall.

"FUUUUUCK!"

WHEN I WALK into the kitchen the next day, Rhys and Lilly are in the middle of preparing lunch—something they started doing a few times a week while Audrey would nap to spend some alone time together. I'm on second shift, and Ethan texted that he is downstairs in our little command center room off the gym.

Rhys is standing behind his wife, nuzzling her neck as she stirs something on the stove. My chest constricts at the sight. I picture a certain brunette in front of me, nothing but my shirt on while my hands roam her body.

"You guys need a moment?" I quip, mentally wiping away the vision, and they both turn.

Rhys grins. "Feel free to watch and learn."

I flip him the bird while Lilly elbows him in the side.

"Jesus, Calla. I'm joking. I'm sure Marcus has it all covered."

That makes me halt. "What are you talking about?" Suspicion slowly rises in my core.

"Nothing, man." He turns back around, and I meet Lilly's gaze. She averts her eyes, and I have my answer. She discussed Denielle and me with her hubs.

Guess there is no point in beating around the bush, then. "Where is Denielle?"

Rhys steps to the side, leaning against the counter next to the stove. He snatches a piece of sautéed veggie from the pan in front of Lilly, chewing it with a grin that makes me want to clock him.

"She's at work," Lilly supplies as she throws a glance in my direction.

I was about to drop onto the bench seat when her words hit, and I halt, hovering like I'm about to take a dump. "What did you say?" I can't keep the seething out of my tone.

Lilly fully turns, with one hand still stirring their lunch. "She said she needed to get back to work. We tried to tell her to take it easy. Denis told her he's got it covered, but she just got dressed and left."

I straighten back up. "Where is her brother?" How can Oliver just let her do that?

"He left early this morning."

"He...left? His little sister got fucking roofied. We have no clue why or how, and he left?" Rage surges up inside of me. "Is anyone with Denielle?"

"No." Lilly's low tone makes it even worse.

"You of all people should know that shit like this can escalate quickly." My voice rises with every word, and Rhys takes a step in my direction.

"Whoa, hold it right there." His hands are raised in a disarming gesture, though his face conveys a different message. "You cannot compare what happened to Calla with yesterday." He points to his wife and back at me. "Maybe if you wouldn't be so set in your fucking Denielle-Keller-is-to-blame-for-everyone-who-pissed-in-your-coffee-over-the-last-twenty-years attitude, maybe she wouldn't have to flee the house. Why don't we also fault her if it rains tomorrow?" His face turns crimson. He's on a roll—an irrational one, at that.

I press my lips together not to lash out. My stab against Lilly was uncalled for, but what does he know about my life?

"Rhys," Lilly calls his name.

"I'm starting to get really tired of your little vendetta. We've accepted it for what it was for years. We all have someone we can't stand—"

"Babe!" she tries again.

"But Denielle is one of our oldest and best friends and—"

"BACK. THE. FUCK. OFF." I didn't realize how close I had

moved as Rhys spewed his words. My blood is boiling for more reasons than him laying into me for something he can't comprehend. Fingers curling, it takes every ounce of self-control not to punch his lights out.

Lilly pushes her way between us. "Guys, enough." She puts a hand on Rhys's chest while looking at me—probably checking to see if I'm about to lose my job.

I inhale slowly through my nose, never breaking eye contact with Rhys. He does the same, and the sizzling tension in the room slowly simmers down.

He's the first to break the stare down, and my shoulders sag in response. I retreat and finally settle in the breakfast nook. With my head in my hands, I sort through my thoughts.

"Rhys, that was uncalled for," Lilly chastises him.

"No, it wasn't," I correct her, never averting my gaze from the surface in front of me. "He's right. I've blamed Denielle for everything." A choking sensation makes it hard to verbalize what I should've realized long ago. "Things she had no part in." Admitting this to someone else, not just myself, is like finally allowing myself to grieve Ken.

"Marcus..." Lilly whispers.

I shake my head, unable to look at them. "Let me say this... You're both right. I've held on to my rage for so long that I couldn't distinguish where my guilt and Victor Keller not being able to save Ken began or ended. But in either case, Denielle had no part in it." I lift my head, meeting first Rhys's then Lilly's concerned gaze. "I apologize for bringing up..." I don't need to finish the sentence. We all know what happened to Lilly McGuire.

The room is eerily silent. My jaw works, emotions I haven't allowed in slowly clogging my throat. I never learned to show vulnerability. Admitting weakness would've meant giving up, not fighting.

Lilly pushes the pan off the burner and pads over. She drops in the seat across from me and scoots in to make room for Rhys. No one speaks.

"I..." Rhys begins. He places his palms flat on the table, splaying his fingers. The tips press into the wood, turning his knuckles white. "I'm sorry for belittling your past. I can't comprehend what it would mean to lose my little sister. Natty... she... It would kill me."

Lilly puts her hand on Rhys's and wraps her fingers around his.

"I shouldn't have brought up what happened with—" I stumble over my next words, my heart thudding against my ribs. "I'm worried about Denielle." I peer at my friends—not my employers, my family. Lilly's eyes soften, and she glances at Rhys, who returns the look.

"So are we," she admits. "I always drew the line at looking into my friends' lives, but I'm..."

Lilly could find out what Denielle is hiding—if she wanted to.

I surprise myself by saying, "Give her more time. She will tell *you*."

Rhys's brows shoot up. "What makes you say that?"

"Last week, when Liberman brought her home. She...she was not herself." I probably shouldn't mention that I fucked her senseless between his washer and dryer that day.

"Do you think Collin has anything to do with it?" Unease rings in Lilly's question.

"I'm not sure. But he is on the top of my list."

"Maybe I should look more into him," Lilly considers.

"I'd say that is a perfectly reasonable idea." I nod with a corner of my mouth quirking.

In the meantime, I need to figure out what I want to do about my newfound *caring* for Denielle Keller.

CHAPTER TWENTY-ONE

DENIELLE

Arriving home from the hospital, I took a long and very hot shower, scrubbing my skin until every inch looked (and felt) like I had used steel wool to apply the body wash. While I was physically clean, my soul was stained—tainted with violation and fear. I was falling, spiraling into losing control over my mind. And the one person who could make it stop...he had left me.

Why did he have to be the one to find me? Why couldn't Lilly have called Ethan? Or J? I would've taken the gardener over Marcus *"The Spineless Shadow"* Baxter. Irrational rage began to slither like venom through my veins, numbing every cell poisoned by whoever did this. I was going to use the red haze to cover the gray of anxiety for as long as I could. This was better than the helplessness blanketing me since I woke up yesterday.

I didn't venture out of my room again, and the only time Oli left my side was to grab us food. We lounged in my bed, watching one of our favorite childhood TV shows until my lids started drooping. While it didn't numb the havoc racking my body, it distracted me enough to not think of *him*.

Halfway through the season, I announced I would go back to work in the morning. To say my brother disagreed with my decision was an understatement. Oli argued until he was blue in the face. He probably would've caused less of a scene if I had gone into a full-blown episode in front of our father in the middle of one of his lectures. Unfortunately for Oli, he had to be back home for a work engagement. Missing it could risk his job, and I would not be the cause of that.

I assured him that I'd be fine. "I basically live in a fortified stronghold."

"Which you would be leaving to go to work." Oli cocked a brow and crossed his arms.

"I'll check in with you every day. I'll make sure someone knows where I am, and Lilly can keep the tracker on in the car." Why was I entertaining him? He couldn't do anything about it. He was getting on a flight in the morning.

Because you would want your brother, or Elena, if it had been her, to be safe if the roles were reversed.

I remained calm through the entire *discussion*—one of my best performances in weeks. Oli was unaware of the panic-inducing thoughts flashing one after another through my mind, but I needed to do this. I couldn't let another circumstance handicap me. Fear was an emotion. Nothing more, nothing less. If you didn't let it in, it couldn't immobilize you, prevent you from living.

This only lasted, though, until we called it a night. As soon as the room was shrouded in darkness, my carefully constructed facade crumbled. I had zero clue who was behind the...attack? Was it an attack? The person who drugged me. The mere thought of someone touching me without my knowledge or consent made bile rise in my throat. Dr. Palmer assured me I showed no signs of assault. It was less than ten minutes between answering Marcus's call and when he arrived at La Déesse. Enough time for someone to...get to me, but I also thoroughly inspected my body in the privacy of the hospital room's adjacent bathroom the minute I was allowed to get up. Nothing. No bruise or blemish. I felt fine—physically. Mentally, the craving of a distraction, of numbing myself, coated my flesh. But I couldn't give in. Oli lay on the sofa across the room. We used to share a bed a lot as kids, but not in a decade and a half. I probably wouldn't have objected if he had wanted to sleep next to me. I needed his proximity as much as he needed the reassurance that I was okay. The more the urge spread, the more my mind kept wandering to the guesthouse, to the man whose arms I wanted wrapped around me to make me forget. My earlier anger gave way to another emotion...longing? He was so close, yet it felt like he was on a different continent. Why did he have to be the one who gave me the strength to face my demons? Why did he stay with me and then leave? And no word since. I should expect it by now. Yet, it still hurt.

Sleep didn't come until the early morning hours. Caffeine would be a necessity to make it through the day.

"DENIELLE." Denis's eyes widen as he notices me climbing the stairs. He just stepped out of the kitchen with his favorite purple ceramic mug that his niece made for him in pottery class. "What are you doing here?"

I plaster a smile on my face and chirp, "Working. What did I miss?"

He sees right through my act. I wonder what happened to him for tolerating the drama I brought upon his business without demanding an explanation and continuing to give me a job.

"You shouldn't be here. You should be resting." He stops, our toes almost touching.

My shoulders slump as he scrutinizes me. "I need the distraction," I admit, talking to his tea instead of him.

When there is no response, my gaze slowly travels up until I meet his concerned eyes. He doesn't speak at first, and I expect him to send me home. His expression suddenly shifts. "I won't keep you, then. Please, let me know if you need anything."

I dip my chin, relief crashing through me. "Will do." I slip past him and dash to my office before he can change his mind.

Entering the room I don't recall exiting two days ago, a cold shiver runs through me. Charlie texted twice yesterday. I ignored both messages. I didn't delete them, but I also didn't read them. I couldn't see him being behind it, but who else would it be? And how? I've been going over the day repeatedly. Everything is clear until I got back to La Déesse.

Charlie never touched my food or drink during lunch. He bought us each a bottle of water on the way out, but that was brand new, the seal not broken. I drank most of it on the walk. Back at the office, I remember dropping my purse on the desk. There was a little bit of water left in the bottle, and I dumped it into the orchid.

My eyes drift to the flower with no origin. My heart begins to thud against my ribs. Was the flower from the same person? Why didn't I think of it before? I pivot on my heels, racing down the hallway to Denis's office.

I burst into the room, startling my boss. He jerks and splashes his tea over one of his sketches.

Shit!

"Oh my gosh, I'm so sorry." My reason for chasing him down is briefly forgotten. I reach for the box of tissues at the end of his desk and pull a wad out. Patting the drawing frantically, I keep mumbling apologies.

Denis stops my cleaning attempts with his hand. "It's fine. This is one of the rejects." He laughs, and my eyes prick. Maybe I shouldn't have come after all?

He withdraws his fingers, and I straighten up, balling the wet tissues in my hand and holding them against my chest.

"Is everything okay?" He scrutinizes me, concerned.

I curl my lips under, digging my teeth in until I can no longer stall. "Did you put the orchid in my office last week?"

A crease appears between his brows, and I have my answer. *No, no, no.*

"What orchid?" His tone is wary.

I wet my lips. "Someone delivered an orchid to my office. It had a note but no signature."

He slants his head. "A note?"

"Yes, uh…it said, *'You deserve everything you get.'*" I start shredding the soaked tissues.

Denis leans back in his chair, steepling his fingers. He glances at my busy hands and then between my eyes. "May I give you my advice?"

"Of course." I dip my chin.

"Throw it in the dumpster." His dry delivery makes me pause.

"Excuse me?"

"No one with genuine intentions would not sign their name. Get rid of it." His tone has gone icy, and my nerves buzz with dread. Without another word, I whirl around and speed walk to my office.

I aim for the flower, pick it up by the stem, and beeline for the trash in the kitchen. I don't want it anywhere near me. Even this is too close, but if I race past my employer's office, choking a plant, he'll officially think I've lost my mind.

Back behind my desk, I place my palms flat on the top and close my eyes. My chest heaves as if I just ran a mile on Lilly's treadmill. Inhaling slowly through my nose, I repeat the same three words over and over in my head. "You are okay. You are okay."

Once my breathing has calmed to its normal rhythm, I simply sit. Snippets of Monday fade in and out of my conscious mind. Trying to remember feels like digging through mud with a toothpick.

. . .

I ANSWERED EMAILS.

I checked on Em's dress that she had dropped off earlier, wanting to make sure it was stored properly until she came back.

I reviewed some orders and appointments for Denis, and then...

NOTHING.

I squeeze my eyes shut. I know I called Lilly, but not because I remember. They told me. I saw the unanswered calls in my phone log. Hazy pictures of Marcus hovering over me, his face blurring in and out, his eyes dull with worry flash through the black of my lids.

The ringing of my phone jerks me out of my self-torture. The showroom's number rolls across the screen, and I answer the call.

"Hello?"

"It's Cassy. You have a call on line two."

A call?

My heart stutters. Who would call the boutique instead of my cell? Everyone has my number.

Not everyone.

"Yes." Cassy's high-pitched voice, which normally puts a smile on my face (the girl is always in a good mood), irritates me to no end today. "It's your client."

Oh. The thundering in my chest slows, and I draw in a deep breath.

You are okay.

"Thanks, Cassy." I disconnect with her and switch to the other line. "This is Denielle."

"Denielle, hello. It's Em. I'm so sorry to do this, but I have to reschedule my fitting to next week. I had to unexpectedly go out of town for business. I hope that doesn't cause too much trouble?" The background noise of traffic is muted by a shutting car door.

"Not at all. What day would you like to come in?" I pull up

my calendar on my laptop.

"Do you have any openings on Monday?" Her calm tone settles my nerves more.

I smile to myself. There is nothing not perfect on the woman. "Yes, Monday works great."

We reschedule her appointment, and as I hang up, my eyes flick to my cell phone. My thoughts drift to my other best friend, who—due to the distance—is completely in the dark about what is going on here. I doubt Lilly or Rhys would fill Wes or King in without my knowledge. If they had, I would've already heard from Wes. I would have to face him sooner or later. But for now, I will focus on the friends I can't avoid. Though, I haven't spoken to Lilly today.

Rhys was downstairs when I left this morning. Lilly had gone to the office for a meeting, which meant I had missed Marcus as well. *Missed* being the accurate descriptor here. A hollow emptiness slowly spreads through me as I stand. How could I miss this man? Marcus came for me, and he stayed with me at the hospital until Lilly arrived. He didn't have to stay, yet he did.

But then he left.

He saved me from Collin. I pick a cuticle with my nail. Not having any nail polish on, I need to pick at something. The night at the vineyard flashes back to me. The dark hallway leading toward the great room. I was soaked, my dress dripping across the dark floor, goose bumps rippling in waves over every exposed inch. I was numb inside. Shocked at what I had just done. The first time in years. Then, Marcus moved out of the dark, his shadow breaking through my barrier of disbelief. The second he stepped close, something shifted. In me. In him. I felt...like me. I didn't talk back to him that night—too stunned at what had just snapped into place. It took days—until we left Northern California—until the shock had morphed to a newfound strength. The guilt his presence always instilled in me was still there, but it was accompanied by something new. And I craved the feeling. The sensation of power.

Marcus didn't loathe me for pushing back. No. He liked it as much as I did.

CHAPTER TWENTY-TWO

MARCUS

Denielle wouldn't meet my eye yesterday when she came home from work. J and I were in the garage, testing the cars' trackers—something we did once a month. Denielle pulled the G-Wagon into its spot, got out, and sped past us as if her overpriced shoes were on fire. A mumbled, "J. Marcus," was the only indication that she noticed us—not that that would've been hard with us basically blocking her path.

J glanced at me out of the corner of his eye before returning the *greeting*.

Watching her disappear into the house, something became painfully clear. She was pissed. At me. The hair on the nape of my neck tingled, and I lifted a hand to rub the sensation away. Her avoidance was anything but the duck and run she used to do. After our forced proximity this last month and a half, she didn't cower to me, which left one conclusion—and I didn't like it. I brought it on myself. I left her unconscious in the hospital. Part of me wasn't proud of it, but at the same time, I couldn't seek her out. Not yet.

. . .

THIS MORNING WAS another repeat of the previous day. Denielle acknowledged me with a semi-polite greeting, but that was it. Everyone else she treated just fine. Lilly and Rhys exchanged a look but remained mute otherwise.

Now, I'm lying on the couch, my head resting on the back and my feet stretched out on the coffee table. My gaze is trained on the TV without actually watching what's flittering across the screen. I've been in a constant state of annoyance since a certain brunette drove off the property this morning.

My phone buzzes next to me on the cushion and redirects my nonexistent attention.

What now?

I peer to the side without abandoning my position. Reading the caller ID, my heart slips in my chest. What the—? Denielle's name rolls across the screen, and I jerk upright, grabbing the phone. I stare at her name, my chest constricting with every vibration ringing through my palm. My thumb hovers over the display, not accepting or declining the call.

Ah, fuck it.

"Hello?"

"Hi, uh...Marcus?" Her reluctance conjures a picture of a blush creeping across her features, my face suddenly equally feverish. Jesus, this is why I've never done the whole relationship thing.

Not that we are in a relationship.

"Yes, you called *me*." I chuckle, the warmth expanding to my core.

She answers with a huffed laugh but cuts herself off as soon as it starts. "Um, would you, uh...could you pick me up at work? Please?"

The excitement of her reaching out is snuffed out, unease cracking open a pit in my stomach. Something isn't right. "What's wrong with the G-Wagon?"

There is silence on the other end, and my grip tightens around the phone.

"Denielle?" I prod. I don't want her to hang up for pushing, but at the same time, I need her to tell me what's going on.

"Could you just come, please?" Her plea, combined with the dip in her voice, is all I need to fly off the couch.

I wrap my hands around the strap of my holster draped across the back of the armchair and am out the door before she can say another word. "Are you safe?" My question is rushed as breathing is suddenly impossible. I race to the side entrance of the house and the garage.

It takes her as long as I need to reach the car to answer. "I think so."

She thinks so?

"Where are you?" I'm getting louder.

"In my office."

I don't ask more questions. "I'm on my way. Stay on the phone with me." I have no clue what's going on, but I need to know she is with me.

"Okay," she whispers.

I'm speeding down the driveway, and the guard has the gate open before I reach it. Neither of us speaks as I drive to Denielle's place of work.

"I'm almost there," I inform her, making my last turn into the alley behind the row of high-end stores.

I hear a crackle and then footsteps. My heart stutters before its thudding becomes painful. "What are you doing?"

"I'm coming down." She doesn't say anything else.

I pull into the spot next to Lilly's Mercedes. The cars are to the left of the back door of La Déesse, with mine being in the closest spot. The door opens as I exit the vehicle, revealing a pale Denielle. She halts, meeting my eyes, and I freeze with my hand on top of the driver's door, one foot still inside. We stare at each other. Having her brown eyes finally trained on me again snaps everything amiss in place, and a sigh escapes me. Suddenly, she takes off in my direction, and I only manage to righten myself, having both feet planted on the asphalt, when she rounds the hood and plows into me. Her arms wrap around my midsection, and her nose nuzzles against my chest. I pull her closer. She shudders against the embrace, tightening her hold. I place my cheek against the crown of her head. Our bodies fit like she was always meant to be there.

We stand like this for minutes. I wanted her to tell me what was going on. Why she called me of all people. But I can't let go. This moment, her nearness...

Eventually, she loosens her hold, but I don't let go. She leans back and peers up at me, a soft smile tugging on her mouth. I untangle one arm from her and place my palm on her cheek. She leans into my touch, my thumb stroking across her soft skin. The contact sends a tingling current up my arm, but when her eyes flutter closed, she presses her lips into a thin line. The smile vanishes, and so does the sensation in my limb.

"The car," she murmurs without looking at me.

My eyes narrow, and I study her face, letting the words sink in—the car. What ca— My eyes swivel to the G-Wagon in slow motion. I trail the body of it but see nothing out of place until— the tire. I shift to the next one, and my fingers on her back grip her side. Denielle winces but doesn't make a sound.

The two tires visible to me are shredded. Not just slashed. *Massacred.* They look like someone took a hatchet or axe to them, the rubber sliced into strips and pieces covering the asphalt. What on earth could've done that? *Who* could've done that? Every muscle in my body goes on high alert. We're in an alley, but all the stores use it for customer parking. There is always a chance of someone coming or going.

I force my arms to drop Denielle and slowly make my way to the other side of the G-Wagon. I'm met with the same scene.

What the fuck?

Looking at Denielle across the car, she's chewing on her bottom lip. She's hugging herself, following my every move.

"Where is Denis?" I can't keep the hostility out of my tone. Why is no one else here with her? It's not even six.

"He had an appointment and left early."

"What about the blonde chick?" No clue what her name is.

Denielle's eyes widen. "She left at five when we closed."

"Then, why did you stay here by yourself?" I bark. None of this is her fault. My own fear is overtaking my senses. I fill my lungs with air and hold it until my chest begins to burn. I want to shout at her about how irresponsible that was. We still have no idea who drugged her just days ago.

Tears pool in her eyes, and I take a step toward her. I hate seeing my strong woman like this. *Mine?* My foot hovers midstride. Mine. I am waiting for the objection, some type of voice telling me that I've lost my mind. There is nothing.

I bridge the gap, and she is back in my arms. "You can't be here alone." I cup the back of her head. "Not until we find who tried to hurt you," I gentle my tone, and she shakes against me. With my other arm around her waist, I lead her to the passenger side of the Escalade. I deposit her in the seat and close the door. With one hand still on the outer frame, I face away. My heart is pounding, and it hurts to breathe. If I had a suspicion about Monday's incident being targeted and not a random accident, I have my confirmation. I peer over my shoulder at the woman in my car. She sits with her head bowed, her hands wringing together in her lap. Her eyes are closed, and her jaw works as if she's trying not to cry.

I need to make a call, but I'm not sure I want her to hear what I have to say. At the same time, I don't want her to be in there by herself.

I round the SUV and settle in my seat. Denielle won't look at me, and I can't hold back any longer. Reaching over, I clasp both of her hands between my larger one. She flips one hand over and interlaces her fingers with mine. Her other palm is on top of our joined hands. Reaching across, I take my phone out of the middle console, where I dropped it when I pulled into the parking spot.

I inhale deeply, deciding that now is not the time to spare

anyone's privacy. Unlocking the screen, I tap on my phone log and then Ethan's name. He's on duty at the house, but with Lilly and Rhys both there, he's probably downstairs in our office.

It rings twice before he picks up. "Where did you speed off to?" His tone is curious, but his usual playfulness is missing.

"I need you to contact Jenn." In my peripheral vision, I see Denielle's head swivel in my direction.

The line remains silent.

"E." I don't have the patience for this.

"Why?" His reluctance is to be expected.

Ethan left his former life behind for a reason, and with that, he left his family—not family by blood, but by being raised by the infamous Marshall Davis. He was the fourth brother in the group—Jenn being the only girl. Ethan and Jenn had a thing during their teen years, but that ended as quickly as it began. They were too much alike and realized they'd kill each other (most likely literally) in the first few weeks. He was closest to her, even though he and Corbin, the oldest, were just a month apart.

"Someone slashed Denielle's tires." He'll see the extent of it when we pick up the car. Maybe Ethan has an idea what the fuck was used. He knows his weapons like no other. "George pulled too many resources for me to delegate one of the guys to take over Den's security." Denielle's nails dig into the flesh of my hand, but I ignore the bite. Whether it is for me going over her head and assigning her a detail, or if it's for using her nickname, I don't know. Calling her *Den* rolled naturally off my tongue. I didn't have to think about it. "Can you get in touch with Jenn?"

Jenn would blend in, being a girl and around the same age. Plus, she's the only one of the siblings that could disappear without raising questions. Marshall had the boys on a short leash. She went on little vacations all the time between jobs, which is how I met her one day when she showed up at Ethan's doorstep.

"I can try." Ethan pauses. "She's been off-grid for a few

months." His wariness doesn't sit well with me. While my vest is not clean, Ethan's is bloodstained and smells of corpses.

"Try. I want an update when we get to the house." Without waiting for his answer, I hang up and drop the phone back into the console.

I start the SUV and pull out of the parking spot.

"What are we doing about Lilly's car?" Denielle asks meekly as if it was her fault for the tires being unusable ever again.

I let go of her fingers and let my hand settle on her thigh, stroking it with my thumb.

"I'll have someone tow it. I want to know what did that."

"What do you mean, *what*?" Her voice quivers, and she hugs herself again.

"What tool. The tires were shredded. You can't accomplish that with a simple knife or even a hatchet. Those tires are too thick." It takes effort not to slip into business mode, the part of me that is trained to shut off the emotional distractions to do my job, but this is more. I don't think Denielle would handle that well at this point. She teeters on the verge of breaking, and after what I witnessed the last few weeks, it is a miracle she is holding it together the way she currently is. But then, she's had years of perfecting her facade, from what I've gathered.

"I see." She leans her head against the window.

Despite my wanting to reassure her, we don't talk until we reach the house. I pull into the garage and throw the Escalade in park. Ethan appears in the door before I pull the key out of the ignition.

Denielle eyes him suspiciously, thumb picking on the middle finger of her hand.

I reach over, letting my knuckles caress her cheek. "Hey."

Denielle slowly turns. She gnaws on her lip, and following the action, my thoughts stray from the task. A picture of her dark hair splayed across my pillow, her body writhing underneath me, appears in front of my mind's eye, and I have to push it away forcefully. *Not now.*

Her attention on me, I shift my grip to the back of her neck. I don't hold her in place, but I signal to her the severity of the situation. "I will keep you safe."

Her gaze moves between my eyes and lips, then flicks over to Ethan. I have the suspicion her thoughts went where mine went just a second ago. The corner of my mouth turns up for the first time since she asked me to come get her. "We'll get to that later..." I leave the sentence hanging, but the heat in her eyes tells me she understands the meaning. And she doesn't object, either. I pull her closer and let my forehead touch hers. "Let's go."

"Okay," she murmurs so close to my lips that, if Ethan wasn't right there, I would show her how serious I am about keeping her safe.

We pull back and simultaneously open our respective doors. I wait for her to round the SUV and reach for her hand on autopilot as we walk toward the door to the house.

Ethan's gaze is trained on our joined hands, but he remains mute. His expression is grave, but if it is because he reached Jenn or if he couldn't get in touch with her remains to be seen. My order for him to contact his little sister was a lot to ask.

He leads the way to the kitchen, where Rhys and Lilly are eating dinner with Audrey. Three pairs of eyes swivel toward us when we enter.

The two adult pairs dip toward our hands, and Rhys's brows shoot up while Lilly presses her lips in a thin line but can't hide her smirk.

I guide Denielle over to the breakfast nook, and she scoots in. I follow her onto the bench, facing Lilly and Rhys. Audrey sits in her high chair attached to the tabletop, and Ethan leans against the island. Lilly slowly scans everyone's faces before she settles on mine. "What is going on?" All amusement has left.

Rhys narrows his eyes at his wife before he turns to me.

"Someone vandalized the G-Wagon behind La Déesse." I'm playing it down. "I'm going to have it towed to the garage to have the guys look at it." I don't have to elaborate on which garage—I'm not referring to the one on the property.

Lilly's eyes grow wide, and she turns to her friend. "Are you okay?"

Denielle nods slowly. "I'm sorry about—"

Rhys snorts. "D, if you think one of us will even dignify that with an answer, you disappoint me." He redirects his attention to me. "What are you going to do?"

I peer over to Ethan, and he nods.

I squeeze Denielle's hand under the table, and she presses her leg against mine in return. "I'm bringing someone in who will stay with Denielle until we figure out who is behind this." Rhys opens his mouth, but I continue, "With the changes George made in staffing, I can't pull anyone from their current position to follow Denielle." I glance at Denielle with a smirk. "And I doubt she'll agree to quit and stay put until we find the guilty party."

She rolls her eyes, and Lilly chuckles.

"Who is this outside party you're talking about? Can we trust him?" Rhys looks between Ethan and me while holding the spoon to his daughter.

"Her," Ethan interjects.

"Her?" Lilly parrots with a question mark etched on her face as she lifts her glass to her lips.

"I called my sister," Ethan elaborates.

Lilly spits the water across the table while Rhys lets the spoon drop to the high chair tray with a clatter.

His daughter immediately begins to fuss, and he picks it up. "I'm sorry, princess." When Audrey has a mouthful and is happily chewing again, he hisses at me. "What the fu— 'dge?"

I'm not surprised Lilly and Rhys are aware of Ethan's past and his relationship with Marshall Davis and his kids. We're here to protect this family, and they should have full transparency into our damage. Though, E's is the one that left the most scars —not just metaphorically.

"What if Davis comes looking for her?" Lilly glances between Ethan and me. She won't look at Denielle. She wants to protect her best friend, but bringing in *The Cleaner* is a bold move, even for us.

"He won't." Ethan steps away from the island and positions himself in front of our employers—wide stance, hands clasped behind his back. "I vouch for Jenn. She will not bring harm to you or your family." He nods at Audrey.

"I don't know, Calla." Rhys scans Lilly's face. Her eyes are fixed on Audrey, who's now playing patty-cake with her mashed potatoes and peas, using the adults' distraction to change her dinner's consistency to mush.

"Who is Jenn?" Denielle's frustration breaks the silence.

"She's my adopted sister and a friend," Ethan answers, resulting in Rhys and me snorting. Understatement of the century.

"Jennifer Ann Davis is *The Cleaner* for one of the most lethal CTH syndicates in North America," Lilly explains calmly.

"CT..." Denielle's brows draw together.

"Contract to hire." I rub Denielle's thigh, and her eyes fly to mine.

Her mouth opens and closes several times before she spits, "You called an assassin to be my babysitter?" Her eyes jump between mine.

"Technically, Jenn is their cleaner," I state. This world might be old news to me, having worked in it half my life, but not everyone shares our acceptance of the lifestyles and occupations of others.

I fully expect Denielle to throw a fit. Instead, she shoves at me until I slide out of the bench seat. As soon as she's upright, she looks at Lilly. "I'm going to be upstairs if you need me." Turning to Ethan, she says, "Let me know when my new *friend* arrives." She won't acknowledge me when she exits the kitchen with her back straight.

This is not how I expected this evening to go.

CHAPTER TWENTY-THREE

DENIELLE

The door clicks shut, and I lean against it with my back. The tremble in my chest makes it hard to draw in a full breath. This is not how I meant for this day to end. How is this happening? To me of all people? *Who* did this? And why? Question after question bombards me, yet no answer will form.

I haven't felt this...helpless in a long time. Not that I am helpless. I have Lilly and Rhys. Ethan. And now a female bodyguard whose day job is to clean up after her assassin brothers. That's as far as I let my mind wander. And I thought my family was fucked up. Did any of us have a normal family these days? Wes and his parents flash in front of my eyes. He literally is the only one. Even Heather and Tristen, while being loving parents to their children, kept so many secrets from Lilly, Rhys, and Natty that it took them a long time to rebuild the broken trust.

A knock on my door makes me jump. My hand flies to my chest, my thundering heartbeat vibrating under my touch. My eyes flutter closed, and I inhale slowly. I'm safe.

"Babe? Can I come in?" Lilly's voice drifts through the barrier.

Drawing in one more shuddering breath, I turn and reach for the knob. Letting the door swing inward, Lilly appears. She stands in front of me, one arm hugging her midsection while the other is bent, chewing on her thumbnail. Scanning her from top to bottom, her toes are curled, and she rocks back on her heels. She looks years younger.

I wave her in. She walks past me, not breaking eye contact. Once we're alone, away from prying ears that could listen from somewhere down the hallway, she drops onto the sofa, and I follow suit. I pull my legs under and wrap my arms around myself, leaning my head against the back. Lilly mimics my position, and I can't suppress my smile.

"This was one hell of a weird day," I admit.

She sucks in her cheeks. "That's about as accurate as saying the way G introduced himself to you was a *little odd*."

"Touché." I point a finger at her, and she grins.

Lilly reaches out, placing her palm on my knee. "How are you? Really."

I roll my lips between my teeth. How am I? "Confused? Scared?" A sting alerts me that I picked at my cuticle too hard. Red pools around my nail. *Shit*. I wrap the hem of my top around it, not caring if I permanently stain it. "Who do you think is behind all this?"

"I don't know, babe." She pulls her hand back and tucks it under her armpit. "What about Charlie? Or Collin? Could it be one of them?"

I shake my head quickly but then pause. Could they? But why? "Charlie is a good guy. He wouldn't..." He did appear out of nowhere every single time. But he never gave any indication that he was upset with me or wanted something I wasn't willing to give. As opposed to... "Collin wanted me to come home." I stare at the crimson seeping through my shirt.

"He what?" Lilly sits up straight.

"When he drove me that day, he said I needed to come home, that we had a future planned." I neglect to say, once again, why he brought me back to the mansion or the fact that my father had filled him in on our family's skeleton, a.k.a. me.

"A future he shit all over," Lilly's tone rises. "Please tell me you are not consider—"

"Oh, fuck no!" I don't have to think twice about it. Even if I had deep-rooted feelings for Collin Liberman (which I don't), the fact that he and my father went behind my back is an absolute deal breaker.

My mind wanders to the man downstairs, and heat creeps up my neck. Not lifting my head, I peer at Lilly through my lashes.

She studies me for a moment before the corner of her mouth turns up. Neither of us spells it out, though. She wants me to take the lead, but I'm not ready. So much has changed in such a short time. Do I care for Marcus? Yes. I can no longer refuse acceptance. The mutual denial of "Nothing has changed" has officially been overwritten. Was he the first person I called when I discovered what had happened to the G-Wagon? Also, yes. There was no one else I wanted. Needed. He gives me power, strength, while letting me be vulnerable. When I am with him, I can handle the darkness that has been following me since I was five years old.

"Sooo... I never expected to need my own *Shadow* one day, let alone someone who operates on the other side of the law." I quirk a brow at my best friend. While Lilly has bent the rules of legality at times and, technically, protected a felon, her being okay with this Jenn person is surprising to me.

Lilly rubs her palms over her face and peers at me between her fingers. She lets her hands drop into her lap, and her shoulders slump. "Trust me, I have no idea how I feel about this."

"Do you think we are safe with her?" After a pause, I amend, "Saf-er?"

She shrugs a shoulder. "Honest answer?" There is a dramatic pause. "I hope so. I'm aware of how the Davis family operates. The services they...provide for the right price. I never met—" Lilly halts, and something flitters across her face. It disappears as fast as it came, and she continues, "*Jenn* personally. Marcus has, though. And if he and Ethan trust her, then I trust them."

"When has Marcus met her?" A bitter taste coats my tongue. Is this...jealousy? Did he and this woman...

Lilly can read me clear as day, and her brows shoot up. "Denielle Keller, are you...?"

"No!" I burst out before she can finish her idiotic question. My stomach drops. Is it idiotic, though?

"That was a little too fast, D," she chuckles. "We will talk about your love life eventually—especially your confession at the hospital."

My cheeks turn feverish, and a wave of goose bumps runs down my spine, remembering. Does she have a suspicion where —? No. She can't.

"Jesus, D. I don't think I want to know what happened between you two. You're all hot and bothered just thinking about it." She waves me up and down.

"I'm not hot and—" Sweat breaks out on my forehead.

"You look like you're about to have an orgasm," she cackles.

It's my turn to cover my face. "Can we not talk about it?" Pulling my hands away, I fan myself dramatically, and we both burst out laughing. At this moment, we are two twentysomething girls gossiping about our love life. How did the tension shift to a lighthearted conversation about a boy? Man! Marcus is anything but a boy.

I shake my head. "Okay, back to the original topic." I pathetically attempt to redirect our conversation, but Lilly indulges me.

"Here is what I can tell you." She draws in a breath and holds it before expelling the air with a whoosh. "Ethan had a pretty rough childhood. He lost his parents when he was little and ended up in foster care. He got placed with a wealthy family when he was four or five. I forget the exact age. But, as it turned out, the head of the family took in orphans to train them."

"Train?" My mouth runs dry.

"Marshall Davis has a successful *business model*. You want something done without anyone asking questions or finding out? Marshall is the person you contact. His services range from forgery to making someone disappear."

"How do you know all that?" I'm stunned.

"About ten years ago, Ethan wanted out. He doesn't talk about the reason. In that sense, he's like Marcus. They refuse to burden anyone with their past. They'd rather suffer in solitude."

An ache forms in my throat, and I press my lips together, listening.

"George recruited him from Marshall. I don't know the details. Neither G nor Ethan would ever divulge how this arrangement came to be. Ethan cut all ties with his old life, with his brothers. The only person he occasionally speaks to is Jennifer. She's a little older than us, and the two have met up over the years. G has assured me that none of the Davis kids or Marshall are a threat to my family. It's sort of a live-and-let-live agreement."

"But you know what they're doing?" I ask incredulously. "How can you—?"

"I have no knowledge about any specific business deals. This is...a gray area, D. I have my own skeletons. Altman is not just a posh hotel chain. We provide privacy and security. While Rhys and I set rules around it, not all our guests have reputable careers." She pauses for a second. "I faced my demons. I'm not willing to bring a new monster into my family's life."

Her tone has gone cold, businesslike, and I realize there are things I've missed while being across the country. "I understand." We sit quietly until there is another knock on the door.

"Come in," we both answer simultaneously, and Lilly laughs. "I'm sorry, babe. Force of habit."

I wave her off. "It's your house."

Lilly purses her lips disapprovingly but then shifts her gaze to the door. "Hey." Her face lights up as Rhys carries Audrey into the room.

"We just wanted to say good night." He struggles to hold on to his daughter as she wiggles for her mom.

"Go put your baby to bed," I nudge her, and Lilly reaches for Audrey.

She turns back to me. "You sure?"

"Of course." This time, I don't have to force a false smile on my face. Seeing my best friend with her family makes me genuinely happy. If someone deserves happiness, it's her and Rhys.

The three disappear, and I slowly walk over to where I dropped my phone on the comforter earlier. Tapping the screen, Marcus's name appears. My heart leaps in my chest, and a flutter spreads through my body.

I open the text and scan his words.

Marcus: I'm heading with Ethan to the garage. J and Mark are in the house. Do not leave the premises.

Marcus: Please.

A laugh bubbles up. Adding "please" must've been excruciating for him. Marcus Baxter is not used to being disobeyed. A challenge I've begun to crave—not counting the times when I *did obey* him. Heat flushes to my core, recalling those moments, and I bite my lip. This day has been a nightmare, yet my mind goes back to the few stolen moments with him. His presence overshadows the darkness even when he's absent.

Hovering with my thumbs over the keyboard, I debate how to respond.

I was pissed earlier. Assigning me a babysitter (not considering who this babysitter was) felt too much like what my father did to me all my life—taking away my choice of how to handle a situation. My father had me watched, and now Marcus will have this Jenn person follow me.

She is here to protect you, not to spy on you.

I close my eyes, reminding myself that this is not the same. My irrational feelings are just that. Irrational. Remnants from today's events—this week. Someone has it out for me. For what reason, I have no idea. Marcus and Ethan are protecting me, which apparently includes having a new friend. I refuse to let this break me. I've been crippled by my mind my entire life. A person's attempts to cause harm are no competition to one's mind rendering them helpless.

Me: Are you coming back tonight?

I hit send before I can overthink it.

When there is no immediate response, I glance over at the clock. It is after eight. I let the phone fall back on the comforter and head to the bathroom for a hot shower.

Walking inside, I pass the tub. Stepping in front of the mirror, I begin to remove my makeup. Wiping with the cotton pad over my lid, I zero in on the reflection of the tub with my open eye. I halt midmotion, waiting for the need to feel the burn. Today's events should've sent me spiraling. I should be craving the numbness, the urge to float. It's not there. The only explanation I have is that Marcus has changed things. For some reason, he anchors me.

I finish my skincare routine, take a shower, and then check my phone once more. Nothing. I peel the covers back and climb into bed. It's early, but leaning into the pillow, exhaustion weighs me down and before I can shift to turn off the light, I feel my body drift into sleep.

I startle awake by my phone buzzing across the nightstand. My heart is thundering, and my body is anything but rested. Groggily, I blink at the lamp.

What time is it?

I reach for the device as the vibration of the repeat notification begins to resemble a motor next to my ear. My head is pounding, and I click on the message without looking at the sender. The text doesn't have a name, just a number.

I informed your father of your little issue resurfacing. He will be in touch. Time to come home, sweetheart.

I jolt upright. What the—? I narrow my eyes at the digits above the three sentences. I know the number. How he got mine is another question.

My pulse thrashes in my ears. The covers are suddenly too heavy, my pajamas too tight. No, no, no. I refuse to let Collin do this to me when someone slashing my tires didn't.

You had Marcus there when Lilly's car got mutilated. You're alone now.

I glance at the bedside table. The red numbers on the alarm clock show 5:32 a.m. I exit out of the message and see that Marcus had texted at one point. How did I miss his but heard Collin's? I must've been out cold for most of the night.

I click on the message.

Marcus: Heading back now. You're awake?

That was at 11:13 p.m. Clearly, I wasn't. *Shit.*

Eyeing the comforter, the unpleasant sensation of tightness begins to constrict my chest. I swing my legs off the mattress and don't bother with shoes. I'm in sleep shorts and a camisole. Goose bumps roll down my naked arms, but my mind is set on a singular goal.

I throw my door open and take two steps down at a time. Before I can aim for the French patio doors, hushed voices drift into the foyer from the kitchen. The lights are off, the rising sun already bathing the rooms in a warm glow.

I slowly pad toward the archway, and my breath hitches. Marcus leans against the kitchen counter, his chest bare, workout shorts low on his hips, and in front of him is a dark-haired girl I've never seen before. She's too close to him, their voices too low for me to hear their conversation. I'm frozen in place. Did I interpret the change in our...relationship all wrong? The thudding in my chest slows and becomes painful with every passing moment.

What the fuck is going on here? I want to yell out my confusion, but my jaw is so tense that I can't form words.

All I see is her long, dark hair cascading down her back. She's dressed in tight black leggings and a formfitting long-sleeve shirt —also black. Combat boots complete the outfit, making her look like a cat burglar or... *The Cleaner.*

Suddenly, Ethan rounds the corner from the hallway leading to the garage and gym. "I got your bag, J." His eyes lock on me, and he halts midstep, letting J's duffel hover between them. "Oh, hey, Den."

Marcus's head jerks around, and the brunette—no. J? Jenn? Whatever—turns as well. All eyes are on me, and I swallow audibly. I wish I would've at least grabbed my cardigan.

I don't know what I expect to happen, but it is not Marcus sidestepping our guest and stalking toward me with so much determination I stagger backward as soon as he reaches me, and he wraps me in his arms, my face resting against his naked chest. I'm acutely aware of our lack of clothing at this early hour, but at the same time, I can't bring myself to care. He smells of sweat, something that would repulse me on any other man. On him, though... I press closer, digging my nails into his back as I return the embrace. A rumble in his chest indicates his approval, and I lean back in his arms. Craning my neck, our gazes lock, and the heat in his brown eyes causes my skin to tingle.

"Baxter, either take your little make-out session to a room or introduce me," a female voice calls out, and my shoulders tense.

Marcus rolls his eyes and smirks without looking at her. "Denielle, this is Jenn. Jenn, meet Denielle."

Relishing his sole attention, my earlier insecurity vanishes into thin air. I've never been the jealous type, but this man wakes all kinds of new traits. Leaning to the side, I peer around Marcus's large frame and face my babysitter. Marcus shifts so his arm is draped around my waist and guides me toward Ethan and Jenn.

Jenn stretches her hand out, bouncing on her heels. Her eyes shine with warmth, and her smile is sincere—both in complete contradiction to her appearance *and occupation.* "Hi. Denielle? May I call you D?" She cocks her head. "Your name is quite the mouthful." Jenn shrugs. More bouncing. "Wild Bill here tells me you've got yourself a little stalker situation." She dips her head in Ethan's direction.

I take her hand, my brows arching as my gaze swivels to Ethan. "Wild Bill?" I enunciate the words slowly. Is she messing with me? On my side, Marcus shakes with silent laughter.

Ethan shoots daggers at Jenn's back and drops her bag with a thud. He cuffs his biceps. "It's a nickname. One I stopped using years ago." He purses his lips.

Jenn peers over her shoulder, my hand still in hers. "Oh, come on." Turning back to me, her perfectly shaped lips turn into a wide grin. "The WK Wild Bill was Ethan's tool of choice when he and I worked together. He trained me, you know? When he and Cor—"

"Jennifer!" Ethan hisses, and she stops midsentence.

Jenn lets go of my hand and turns to him, poking him with her forefinger against the chest. "What? Stop pretending your past didn't happen. Man up." She shakes out her hands and rolls back on her heels. "Jesus, you've been working out, big brother. And what kind of espresso do you guys have here? This is worse than the one time T and I got into Cor's secret stash."

She pivots back to me. "I'm so sorry. I haven't slept in forty-some hours, and your man here made me a triple shot of espresso. This shit is legit. Jeez." She puts her palm against her sternum. "Do you guys have a gym here? Please tell me you do. I need to get this buzzing out of my body, or I'm going to lose it."

I have no idea what to say. This is not how I pictured a girl—uh...woman—cleaning up dead bodies. I...like her.

"We do. Let's go." Ethan takes her by the elbow and leads her toward the hallway. Almost out of the kitchen, Jenn turns one more time. "I promise I'll be in better shape when you see me again. We'll get your little problem handled."

With that, they disappear, and it's only Marcus and me.

CHAPTER TWENTY-FOUR

DENIELLE

MARCUS'S FINGERS BITE INTO MY SIDE WHEN WE HEAR THE door to the gym click shut. He slowly spins, bridging the small gap between us so his hips connect with my belly. With *him* pressing against my stomach, a familiar flush of desire ignites between my legs. I keep my eyes trained on his still naked chest, which is not helping. This man has not one gram of body fat, and my mouth runs dry. I force my thoughts in a different direction.

We haven't discussed anything that happened since he found me in my office days ago.

Confusion about him staying with me—*"Of course I came"*—and then disappearing kept me from demanding answers. While I *felt* we had moved forward—his hatred toward me no longer in the foreground—a nagging voice in my head kept whispering that this was all just a game. A long con to finally get his revenge.

Could it be?

With both hands on me, he takes a step forward, forcing me to retreat. He continues the advance until my lower back hits the edge of the kitchen cabinets. I don't feel the impact. The connection of his calloused fingers to my skin overpowers my pain receptors, sending every nerve ending into a frenzy. Leaving a blazing path behind, Marcus's hands glide down until he cups my ass. His grip digs into my flesh, and I'm quite literally painfully aware of how thin my sleep shorts are. He lifts me to sit on the counter. My exposed cheeks against the cold marble send a shudder down my spine.

Marcus's index fingers trail twin paths along my legs until his palms are pressed on my thighs. "What are you thinking?" He slants his head, and I meet his gaze for the first time.

Before I can stop myself, I blurt, "Is this all part of your revenge plan?"

The crease between his brows deepens. "Revenge plan?"

"For my hand in your sister's..." The last word lodges in my throat, and I chew on my bottom lip.

I've never brought up McKenna, and I'm not sure it is a good idea to confront him. He pulls away, and the sudden distance between us opens a chasm in my stomach.

Marcus recoils until he leans against the island across from where I'm perched. I watch the muscles in his biceps flex as he cuffs his fingers around them. The space is no more than a few feet, but it might as well be miles.

Raking his hands through his hair, he rests them on the top of his head. He studies me, unspeaking. My palms are planted on the countertop, and I press the tips of my fingers into the cold surface. I tilt my head, peering out the patio doors at the blue water of the pool shimmering in the rising sun.

"Is that what you think I'm doing?" he breaks the silence.

"I don't know what to think," I admit.

With lightning speed, his hands wrap around my wrists, and he's in front of me. My head jerks around, and I meet his unreadable gaze. He roots me in place as he steps between my legs. With his height, his groin is perfectly lined up with my pussy, and I suck in a breath. The mere proximity to... I can feel my own wetness betraying my resolve.

"Come with me," he orders as he pulls me off the counter.

"Wha—"

He doesn't elaborate, just keeps one wrist shackled and drags me after him. Before I can protest, we're through the patio doors and across the lawn. My heart is hammering in feverish anticipation and confusing uncertainty. The grass between my toes tickles, the cool morning air making me shiver. Marcus doesn't stop or release me until we're in the guesthouse.

I've been in here a few times, stayed here when we all visited and Wes and King had the suite I currently occupy. But I haven't been back since. Not since Marcus moved in. Not much has changed besides a few dishes in the sink and an arsenal of weapons on every visible surface.

He disappears into one of the bedrooms, leaving me standing in the short hallway. I tremble, slowly placing one foot in front of the other until I'm in the middle of the open-concept living area. Marcus reappears and, as he passes, reaches for my hand. Clasping my fingers in his, he guides me to the couch, gesturing for me to sit.

I drop onto the cushion and place my palms on my knees.

What am I doing here?

He lowers himself beside me and holds out a tattered shoebox.

My gaze swivels between him and the object. "What is this?" Sweat slithers across my palms.

"Open it."

I take it carefully. This is something of value. Cradling it in my lap, he lifts the lid, and I peer inside. The first thing that comes into view is a faded photograph of a boy, maybe seventeen or eighteen, with a younger girl tucked under his arm. Both are too thin, and he has a bruise on his jaw. I take a closer look and jerk my gaze to Marcus. "This is you." My eyes water as his form blurs.

Marcus nods and points at the girl. "And that's Ken."

At him speaking her name, the lump in my throat becomes

unbearable. I've known about her for so long, but I never allowed myself to look her up on the remote chance I would put a face to the guilt.

I scan her every feature. She had Marcus's eyes. They shone with happiness despite their life having been anything but. The appearance of both made that clear. A sob chokes me. "I'm so sorry," I rasp the apology.

His thumb swipes away the lone tear that is running down my cheek. "That is not why I'm showing you this."

My hold on the photo tightens, the skin around my nails turning white from the pressure.

Marcus draws me to his side. "Ken was all I had. Mom died when Ken was two. An aneurysm."

My eyes widen, and I scan his face. Marcus closes himself off as he continues to speak. "Aneurysms are generally not hereditary. However, if there have been cases in your family, the risk of you having one is higher than the average." He draws in a shuddering breath. "I have no idea if what happened to Ken was caused by the accident or because our mother died of...*one*, or if it could've been prevented. But your father left the operating room, and it was easier to blame someone rather than accept that it was an unavoidable fluke or coincidence. Your father...and *you* became the enemy."

I can't control the stream of tears wetting my cheeks, and Marcus guides my face toward him with one finger. "I see now that it was not your fault."

His cloudy form becomes hazier, and I can no longer contain my quivering lips.

"I owe you an apology." His thumb strokes over my cheekbone, stopping the tears from falling.

I shake my head, blowing out a shaky breath. "What if she could've been saved?"

Suddenly, I'm catapulted into the past, and that night replays in my mind in vivid detail.

. . .

Celine is pacing the small, sterile-smelling room for the hundredth time. We arrived at the hospital's emergency department what feels like hours ago. Being out of immediate danger, I got transferred from the stretcher to this bed and hooked up to monitors that will not stop making sounds.

Celine has her cell phone plastered to her ear. She's still drenched, her clothes clinging to her thin frame. "No, you don't understand. You need to page Victor NOW! Denielle—"

I tune her out again. Oli sits on my bed, clutching my hand that doesn't have the IV between both of his. He's dressed in scrubs that one of the nurses brought him, and they are too big. Celine had refused the offering, continuing to call my father's department.

"Oli, I'm fine," I whisper hoarsely. My throat feels like the time I had strep throat and couldn't swallow for days without gagging.

My big brother looks so small. "I know, Nelle." His fingers tighten their hold.

I heard the paramedics talking to each other. Oli found me. He jumped into the pool, trying to drag me to the edge. He wasn't strong enough, though, and Celine went in as well. I was breathing on my own before the ambulance arrived, but they took me to the hospital anyway.

The entire time they checked me out next to the pool, Celine wouldn't stop repeating, "This is all my fault."

It wasn't. That much I know, even at my young age. What exactly happened, I don't understand. Not yet. I was upset over something... What had I been sad about? Mom's picture.

I had flipped through a book before dinner and had found one of Mom's photos tucked between the pages. She was smiling at the camera. Memories assaulted me like a tidal wave.

I WALKED out on the patio to ask Mommy for a snack. Daddy had taken Oli to play golf. She didn't respond to my calls. Where was she?

I rounded the house to the pool, and that was when I saw her. *Her hair.* The dark strands floated under the surface in waves, like the mermaids' hair in my favorite fairy-tale book. But this wasn't a mermaid. This was my mommy. I ran to the side of the pool, ready to help her.

My parents' voices filled my ears as I kneeled at the side, fingers curled around the edge and dipped in the water. "Don't ever get in the pool without one of us, Denielle. You can swim, but you never know when you'll get tired. We don't want anything happening to you."

My mom needed me. But I promised them not to get in alone. I did the only thing possible: I screamed. And screamed.

CELINE'S ARMS *closed around me, and I dropped the photograph. She kept patting my hair, repeating that I was safe. Had I screamed out loud?*

"I'm here, honey. Everything is fine."

But it wasn't. I didn't help my mommy. She was...gone. How could everything be fine?

I can't breathe. Why can't I breathe? *Her hold was too tight. Her touch felt like knives slicing me over and over. She was hurting me. No, no, no. I began to thrash, fighting against her hold until she released me, and then I took off. Black spots appeared in my vision as I fumbled my way through the house. I was drawn to the one place I last saw her. The sliding glass door was closed. It was too heavy. I pulled on it until it opened far enough for me to slip through. My bare feet hit the walkway to my destination, the rough surface of the cobblestones biting into my soles. But it didn't stop me. When I reached the edge of the pool, I halted only for the briefest of moments.* I don't want to hurt myself. *The smooth surface rippling in the moonlight beckoned me.* The water will stop the pain. *I jumped.*

I EXPERIENCED the numbing peace for the first time in my life. The burn in my lungs became a sensation I began to crave more than air over the years. The night it all started.

. . .

"HEY." Someone shakes me, not hard but enough for my head to flop back and forth. "Hey, hey, Den. Baby."

Hands frame my face, and my eyes zero in on... I blink. *Marcus.*

"There you are." He breathes a sigh of relief and rests his forehead against mine. My eyes flutter closed as I inhale his exhales. My pulse slowly calms. My lids pop open as he shifts and takes the box from my lap. He places it on the coffee table before gently prying the photo from my fingers and dropping it next to it. He picks me up by the hips and pulls until I'm straddling his lap.

His hands find my face again. "Where did you just go?"

I lift my trembling fingers. Only the tips connect with his skin as I slowly trace the contours of his face—across his forehead, down his temples, and along his sharp cheekbones. Marcus shivers under my touch. My thumb glides across his bottom lip and stops at the corner of his mouth, with the rest of my hand splayed across the side of his neck. The vibration of his speeding pulse against my fingers mimics my own. He watches me carefully while I drink in his features.

The man who hated me with every fiber of his being has become my savior.

My gaze lifts from his mouth to his eyes. "Are you playing with me?" I need to know. I can't describe the awareness of certainty as I push for the answer. I already know, but I have to hear the words. He won't lie to me.

Marcus stares a moment longer, void of emotion. "No."

I dip my chin once and peer at a spot on the wall behind us before turning my attention back to him. His blank mask is replaced with concern and...

He grips the back of my neck, leaving imprints on my skin. I don't resist as he guides me closer. The instant our lips meet, heat lights my core. My fingers rake through his hair, curling into the strands, and I press myself to him, surging my hips, and Marcus bucks.

I feel his hardened cock, locked in his pants, pressing against its confinement, and need dampens my underwear.

Parting my lips, I graze his with my tongue. I can't suppress the moan, and he opens up. Our tongues collide in a tangle of sensation. I grind my hips into his lap, and he groans. "Fuck, baby."

Clasping my sleep shirt, he tugs on the hem. I untangle myself, and my top is gone before I fully lift my arms. Cool air caresses my skin, my nipples pebbling. Marcus snakes one arm around my waist and tugs me closer. His other hand finds my breast, his palm forming to my curves. He pinches my nipple, and my eyes roll back inside my head. The sting turns the flutter in my core into an inferno of raw desire. I grind my heat against his groin, and his grip on my hard bud disappears. I'm about to protest when his fingers are replaced with his mouth. I whimper as he sucks and nips on my sensitive skin. "Oh, god."

He chuckles, never removing his mouth from me. "You will be screaming *my name* soon."

My nails dig into his muscles as I cling to his shoulders. "Make me."

With one swift move, I'm on my back with him hovering above. "Is that a challenge, *Keller*?"

"Bring it on, Bax—"

His phone begins to buzz in his pocket, and he closes his eyes. His forehead drops to mine in resignation.

The inferno extinguishes. "I assume you can't ignore that?"

He sighs. "No, I'm on first shift, and I was already on duty when I brought you here."

I press my lips in a thin line, not wanting him to see my disappointment. He shifts to sit back on the couch with my legs on his lap. He peers sideways, stroking my chin with his fingers. "We should probably talk anyway before..."

I understand his meaning. He brought me here to show me something—something my little trip down memory lane interrupted.

I push myself up with one arm, the other covering my breasts. I pull my legs from his lap and behind his butt, tucking them close to wrap my arms around them and cover my nakedness. "Yes, we should."

I didn't mean for it to come out as cold as it did, but before I can correct myself, the shutters drop behind his eyes. He nods, stands, and leaves me sitting on his couch.

Shit.

Marcus disappears into the bedroom, and I hear the water turn on a second later. I'm rooted to the cushion, unsure of what to do. I feel cold, inside and out, the warmth from moments ago like it never existed. We have so much to work through, even if he no longer blames me for...Ken. I have my own baggage—baggage that has resurfaced and steadily grown.

I slide my feet off the couch and plant my soles on the hardwood floor. He probably assumes I'll leave. I reach for my discarded top and pull it over my head. My eyes travel to the front door and then to the bedroom. Marcus Baxter is thirty-seven. I'll be twenty-five in a little over a week. We're too old to play games. I don't want to play anymore.

With my feet grounded, I lean back into the couch and cross my arms over my chest, ready for whatever will happen next. But if I have any say in it, Marcus and I will battle it together. Conviction replaces uncertainty. Peering at the clock on the wall, only an hour has passed since waking up to Collin's message, and yet, it feels like, once again, *everything* has changed.

The water shuts off.

Goose bumps erupt on my arms and legs, and I scan the room. A throw blanket is draped over one end of the couch. I reach over and pull it over my lap. Who knows how long—

"You're still here." I lift my gaze from adjusting the throw to Marcus standing in the doorway, a dark-blue towel wrapped around his trim waist.

"I am." I fold my hands in my lap.

"Why?" He appears genuinely confused, but not in an annoyed, angry way.

I pull the blanket aside and stand. Marcus follows the movement as I slowly walk over, giving him the chance to kick me out. His head slants, and he scans me from head to toe, lingering on my bare legs.

I stop right in front of him, our toes nearly touching, and place a hand on his still glistening chest. His earlier stench is replaced by an equally delicious scent. I have no idea what shower gel he uses, but the fresh smell of a *clean Marcus* has my mouth watering.

He looks down.

My thumb caresses his pec, and I glance up at him. "I don't want to play games."

His eyes narrow, waiting for me to elaborate.

"You are the first person I don't have to hide from. I don't understand why you're different. Maybe because you already hate me."

"I thought we established that I no longer...blame you." His gruffness causes lightness to settle in my chest.

"Hated me," I correct. "But you...you challenged me in a way no other ever has. It became an addiction." I can't stop the chuckle at my words. "To see your reactions when I pushed back. Then you...helped me."

"You mean I fucked you in your best friend's laundry room?" He smirks devilishly, and a flush flourishes up my face.

I smile. "That, too. And I appreciated that more than you might think—for various reasons."

Marcus barks out a laugh and lifts his palms to frame my face. His hardened features melt, and I see the man that he hides from everyone—except me.

"What I'm trying to say..." I bite the inside of my cheek, grasping for the right words. "I...shit." I blow out a breath. "I don't want this to end."

I don't think I've ever been this inarticulate.

His gaze jumps between my eyes as he slowly lowers his face. He gently touches his lips to my mouth, just the slightest of caresses before he withdraws again. My lids are hooded, and I can barely make out his form in front of me.

"Then let's not play games," he says softly.

It's my turn to frown. That could be interpreted either way.

"Stop overthinking, baby." He kisses me one more time. "If I can handle it, you definitely can accept that this is happening."

My body buzzes from the inside out. This is really happening. But that also means I eventually will have to come clean with the one secret I've been keeping to myself.

Can I do that?

I SIT in the passenger seat of...

"What car is this again?" I shout over the roar of the engine mixed with "Steal my Romance" by Ghosts on the Radio. My nails dig into the dark-gray leather as Jenn takes another turn toward La Déesse. Maybe I should've taken off work after all. I have my doubts that we will arrive there alive.

"It's a Bugatti Centodieci. Isn't she a beauty?" *She? This monstrosity is a girl?* Jenn beams, and I want to scream at her to pay attention to the road. "It was a birthday present from my brother." She trains her gaze back to the traffic.

Thank God!

I force my fingers to unclench before I cause damage to the interior that I most definitely cannot afford to replace.

After Marcus had led me back to the main house and I got ready, I found everyone downstairs eating breakfast like it was the most normal thing in the world to have a *cleaner* in the house.

Lilly was laughing as Jenn had Audrey propped on one hip, tickling her and making the little girl squeal in giggly hysterics. And here I thought I'd seen it all.

Jenn had showered, her hair had been damp, and her leggings were replaced by black skinny jeans.

With my own coffee in hand, I had joined them, and my babysitter declared that she'd be driving me to work—if I wanted to go in, that was. Denis was unaware of what had happened behind his store, and I didn't want to give him another reason to consider firing me. So, I had told her we'd be leaving by nine.

Marcus's grim expression had been a clear indication that he didn't like the idea, but he brought the girl in to protect me. He couldn't object to me going to work.

When we walked out to her car, the guys all fell over each other. Even Marcus seemed impressed, which told me this must be something special. Material possessions have never interested him—a trait I picked up on years ago.

We pull into the alley, and I expel a sigh of relief. We made it. Alive. Though my elevated pulse could easily result in a heart attack.

Inside, I introduce Jenn as my cousin and ask Denis if it would be okay for her to hang out at the boutique while she is in town, promising that it won't interfere with my job. As expected, my boss has no objections. How I got this lucky with my employer is a miracle. Jenn also is surprisingly good company, and her knowledge about fashion is as extensive as someone who has worked in the industry. I show her the designs for Em's alterations, and when she suggests adding a sheer layer with embedded black crystals to the lower back, I clap my hands like a lunatic. I can totally picture it, and Em will love the additional detail.

MARCUS ISN'T ANYWHERE to be found as Jenn and I arrive home that evening. Rhys announces that Marcus and Ethan went to the garage to check on the progress of the G-Wagon. They have their bi-weekly video call with George and would take it from the hotel's main security office.

Jenn has taken over one of the other guest rooms, and I promise to let her know if I leave the main house. I am under twenty-four-seven surveillance.

I've just crawled under the covers, the early wake-up catching up to me, when Marcus's name lights up my phone.

Marcus: How was your day?

Me: Are you making small talk?

As much as I enjoy having normal conversations with Marcus and talking about things that don't revolve around either of our pasts, a tiny voice in the back of my head keeps me from opening up all the way. And that includes truly believing that there is no ulterior motive. While my heart tells me Marcus does believe that what happened that night did not cause Ken's death, the whispers of, *What if he changes his mind?* continue to be present.

Marcus: Isn't that what people who don't dislike each other do? ;)

Heat creeps up my cheeks, reading his words. I lean back into my pillows and hold the phone in both hands.

Me: You're right. And I did. Jenn knows a lot about fashion. How come?

Marcus: Not sure. Ethan doesn't talk about his past. Or her.

Me: That doesn't sound good.

Marcus: Whatever happened probably wasn't good.

I stare at the screen, watching the minutes tick by at the top.

Me: Is there any news on the car?

Marcus: Not yet. They have a few ideas, but it'll take time to confirm them.

When I don't respond, the three dots indicate he is typing again.

Marcus: We'll figure out who did this.

Me: I know you will.

I exit out of his message, and the number Collin texted from sits in front of me. I need to tell Marcus, or Lilly, about this. But that would also mean I would have to let them in on my condition. My jaw clenches, and my rib cage constricts. Soon. What's Collin gonna do? Abduct me? I want to see how that's gonna go over with Jenn following me, even to the bathroom, when I'm not here at the house.

CHAPTER TWENTY-FIVE

MARCUS

It's been three days since I told Denielle this was happening. This. *Us.* While I didn't see her during the days, things fell into a rhythm.

She went to work, with Jenn following her every move. Saturday afternoon, Denielle sent me an all-caps text message to *inform her babysitter* that if she followed her one more time to the bathroom, she would hurt me in my sleep. I barked a laugh and got an odd look from Ben. He wasn't used to me being...happy.

I had moved to second shift, and once I got off work, I showered at the guesthouse where Denielle was already waiting. We spent the night together and repeated the pattern the next day. Even though nothing happened, it was the most content I'd felt in...ever.

Monday morning, I woke up before her alarm and watched her sleep. Her constant guard was absent, and she looked so much younger. Lying on my side with my elbow bent under my head, I scanned her features. My steady heartbeat suddenly slowed, and a hollowness took over my chest. How could I be happy when my little sister would never get the chance? The muscles in my neck and shoulders coiled, and I rolled on my back, staring at the ceiling.

A small hand suddenly landed on my arm. "Talk to me," Denielle's sleepy whisper relaxed the tension instantly.

I wanted to respond that everything was fine, but the words rolled off my tongue. "I was thinking about Ken. She'll never have a future, find someone she'll..." I trailed off.

Denielle's thumb began to caress my bicep, and with every pass, I relaxed under her touch.

"Ken would want you to be happy. The same way you would wish that for her," she declared softly.

She was right. "It's hard to let go," I admitted.

Denielle snuggled closer, resting her temple on my shoulder and draping her arm over my stomach. "No one is asking you to let go." She tapped the spot over my heart with her index finger, causing a flutter to drive out the darkness that had lived there for too long. "She's right here."

I wrapped my arms around her and placed a kiss on her forehead. Neither of us spoke until her alarm signaled us to start the day.

After Denielle left for work, I unlocked my phone and pulled up my best friend's number. This would be the first time I had spoken to King in weeks.

"Are you ready to explain yourself, Bax?" I winced at the sneer when she answered. Despite being a grown-ass fucking man, King had my balls in a vise from day one—not in a romantic sort of way.

She laid into me before I could form a reply, even threatened to withhold Haddie when she came into town on Friday—a threat I did not take lightly. I loved my goddaughter like my own, and she knew it. For her to resort to such drastic measures warned me how disappointed she was. My insides knotted. I owed her an explanation. We used to talk several times a week until the vineyard. After that, my attention was captured by a different woman.

"So?"

It was my turn. "Do I have a choice?"

"No." Footsteps in the background and a door clicking indicated that she ensured the privacy of this conversation. "Talk to me, Marcus. What's going on?"

Marcus, not Bax.

"Denielle."

"What did she do?" she asked low, hesitant.

"She didn't do anything." I wasn't going to reveal what I witnessed whenever Denielle disappeared in her head. That wasn't my place. "I... Things have changed."

"How?" Suspicion coated the question.

I grasped for the right words. "You never asked why I hated her."

King didn't speak for a moment. "If you wanted me to know, you would've let me help carry your burden."

Her choice of words hit hard. *My burden.* "Victor Keller was Ken's surgeon the night she..."

"Denielle's father?" she cried incredulously.

"One and the same. He left the OR because Denielle had jumped into the pool and almost drowned. She was in the emergency department. The aneurysm ruptured after he left, and they couldn't save her."

"Oh, Bax." The quiver in my name told me how she felt for me. For Ken. For Denielle.

"I see now that it wasn't her fault, King." Drawing in a deep breath, I repeated what I had already admitted to Denielle. "It was easier to blame them than accept my guilt in telling Ken to run or that it was all a coincidence."

The silence between us elongated. "This was no one's fault but your abusive, son of a bitch father's. He came after you. You protected your sister."

The lump in my throat made it hard to speak. "You're right."

There is another pause. "So, what changed your mind?"

Do I tell her what I witnessed? I swipe my palm over my

mouth, pinching my bottom lip between my thumb and forefinger.

"I got to see a different side of Denielle." Denielle needed to come clean to Wes first. Letting King in before her husband found out felt like betrayal.

"Can you be a little less cryptic?" There was no anger in her tone.

"It's Denielle's story, Monroe." Using the name she went by when we met was my way of telling her how much she meant to me. Addressing Denielle by her last name was a means to execute my dominance and distaste over her. With King, it had always been the opposite.

"Okay. Please be careful. I like Denielle. She's great, and Wes will kill me if he hears me say this, but something isn't right. I know when a person is hiding something, and I don't want you to get hurt." I pictured her chewing on her bottom lip—a habit she had when she was giving someone the truth despite the possibility of it hurting their feelings.

"I will. Plus, we have some additional security on the property these days."

"Explain!" The order was clear. This woman was—well, used to be—the only one allowed to demand anything from me. Now there were two, which is still a surreal concept.

I had no choice but to fill her in on that part of what had been going on. By the time I finished, I had spoken for minutes, and my mouth felt metallic and parched.

"Does Wes know about this?" Of course her first concern was for her husband. He and Denielle were as close as King and I were.

"I have no idea." I doubted Denielle had told him, but I couldn't know for sure.

"Bax," she breathed out. "I can't keep this from him. Is this Jenn person trustworthy? A cleaner? For real?"

"She is. And you do what you have to do. Den will rip me a new one, but—"

"Den?" Her shrill inquiry told me my blunder. "Since when do you call her Den?"

"Well, I actually have been calling her baby, too," I admitted sheepishly. And it felt good. Great, even.

"WHAT? Marcus Baxter, what the fuck? Now I'm starting to understand what *different side* you meant. Jesus, Bax. Wes is going to fucking blow a gasket." Padding sounds in the background told me she was pacing.

"Your husband can go sit on a cactus and rotate for all I care."

That made her laugh. "I know, Bax, sorry. This is a ton to take in. I saw you four weeks ago, and—"

"You know yourself how much can change in four weeks." That was a low blow, but I was not going to have her or Wes judge my sex life or relationship—definitely not after how theirs started.

"OK, shutting up now. I'm just...wow. You and I will have a very long conversation when I get there this week."

"I wouldn't expect anything else from you, Monroe," I chuckled. "I'll see you Friday, 'kay?"

"Yes, we'll get in midday. See you then."

WHEN I DIDN'T FIND Denielle in the guesthouse after my shift, I took a quick shower before heading back. I spent most of the day and evening downstairs in the security office, reviewing paperwork and discussing a new recruit with George. The McGuires were home, so we didn't have to keep the constant surveillance up. The property feed played on the screens, which Ben monitored, and we would know if anyone was coming or going.

· · ·

STRIDING INTO AN EMPTY KITCHEN, I follow the voices to one of the living rooms, where I find Lilly on her laptop, Rhys playing on his phone next to her, and Jenn—

"What the fuck are you doing?"

Jenn sits on a white tarp, one leg straight, the other bent in front of her, cleaning a rifle. Not just any rifle. A Bergara HMR Premier 6.5 PRC. In the middle of the fucking living room.

She peers between me and her task innocently. "What does it look like? I went to the range after dropping your girl off."

No one blinks at her choice of words. And I notice that I don't mind it either. *My girl.*

"Where did the tarp come from?" We don't have anything like that lying around.

"My car." She shrugs.

"Oh, sweet Jesus." I rub my palms across my face. I glance at Lilly and Rhys, who both smirk at their respective devices. "And you two are just cool with this?" I gesture to the absurd scene.

Lilly peers up for the first time. "What do you want us to say? She's keeping my carpets clean."

"Yeah, it's not like she used the gun to..." Rhys pipes up, then glances at Jenn. "It hasn't, right."

Jenn just rolls her eyes.

"Where is Denielle?" I ask the room. If they are all congregated down here, why isn't she with them?

"I haven't seen her since dinner," Lilly informs me. "She went upstairs to check on a package."

"A package?" The hair on the back of my neck stands. "What package?" My rising tone brings everyone's attention to me.

"She got a delivery at work. I put it in her room," Jenn informs me casually as she inspects the barrel for gun powder debris. She slowly places the part on the plastic in front of her. "It was one of those post office, flat-rate boxes. I scanned it, checked the outside for foreign substances. It was harmless."

I feel the color drain from my face with every new word.

"Marcus, what's wrong?" Lilly sets the laptop between her and Rhys.

"How long has she been up there?" My pulse thrashes through my veins, challenging me to remain in place.

"Maybe an hour?" Jenn peers at the watch on her wrist.

An hour. Fuck!

I whirl around and race up the stairs, taking three at a time. Behind me, footsteps follow. I twist the knob as soon as I reach Denielle's door, but it doesn't budge. I hammer against the solid oak. "Denielle, open up!"

No response.

"KEL-LER!" My spiking adrenaline prevents me from taking a normal breath, and her name comes out chopped. My eyes fly around for something to unlock her door. I'm about to kick it in when Jenn holds out her Leatherman. Relief surges through me. I take it without hesitation and flip open one of the blades. Lining it up with the coin turn, I twist and am through the door in seconds.

The bedroom is empty. My stomach drops at the sight. The package Jenn mentioned sits on Denielle's bed, but she is not here—not in this room. Something hangs out of the box, but I don't waste time checking it out. I know where I'll find her.

I still have the knife in my hand, ready to use it again. Thankfully, she didn't barricade herself in. Pushing into the bathroom, I find my worst fear come to life.

My heartbeat stutters and slows before taking off in a thundering rhythm. My mind catalogs the visual, at the same time I refuse to believe the pictures my eyes send to my brain.

The bathtub is filled to the rim with water, and puddles pool on the tiles around the claw feet. Denielle's feet hang over the far edge, the rest of her body submerged. All that's visible is her long, dark hair floating around her form. Her face is hidden. The sound of the Leatherman clattering to the tiled floor faintly registers. I lunge forward, plunging my hands in the water. Several things run through my mind at once. I need to get her out. I have to protect her from her friends witnessing her like this. My body covers Denielle from view as I try to find the right hold to pull her out. No, no, no. I'm shaking and slip as I attempt to hook my fingers under her arms. Water splashes everywhere as I lean over the side of the tub. My upper body skims the surface as I finally get ahold of her, and water drenches my front. Pulling her from the water, she doesn't struggle. The blood in my veins turns to ice.

Please don't let me be too late.

I land on my ass, Denielle's weight pushing me off balance. Her legs are the last to follow and drop with a loud thud to the floor. The irrational thought that this will cause her heels to bruise flitters through my mind. Cradling her lifeless form, water seeps from her clothes, creating more puddles around us.

"Oh, my god!" Lilly's shrill shout announces her arrival.

I glance up as Jenn shoulders into the bathroom and drops to her knees next to me. "Marcus, let me check her."

Logic tells me I need to look for a pulse, make sure she is alive, but my arms are locked around her. I can't move. Now that I have hold of her, I can't let go. My breath comes in short bursts, causing black spots to fade in and out in front of Denielle's ashen face.

Rhys also crouches at my side. He lightly touches my shoulder as Lilly's sobs fill the room. "Put her on the ground so Jenn can look at her." He is weirdly collected. Why is he so calm?

For the first time, I manage to remove my gaze from the woman I used to hate with every fiber of my being. I have spent so many years letting anger and revenge rule my life, not allowing myself to see the good. Denielle Keller chases the darkness away. She deserves the world.

Jenn has her eyes trained on Denielle's chest. Flicking them to me for a fraction of a second, she reaches out and slowly guides me to place Denielle flat on the ground.

"She's breathing. It's shallow, but she's breathing," Jenn

announces, and I inhale shakily. I hold one of her hands between both of mine as Jenn checks her pulse. She produces a small flashlight from God knows where, pulling Denielle's lids apart.

"Come on, baby. Wake up," I murmur more to myself, squeezing Denielle's fingers.

Rhys has retreated to Lilly's side. She clings to her husband, her face buried in his shoulder, with muffled cries racking her body.

Jenn pats Denielle's cheek. "Come on, girly. Not cool to let your man wait like this."

"I'm going to call an ambulance," Lilly hiccups. She's turning out of Rhys's grip when Denielle convulses in a coughing fit. She retches, and water splutters from her mouth. My entire body sags forward, the tension draining from every muscle that has been holding me upright.

Jenn smiles. "Good girl." She guides Denielle to the side and looks up at me. "Support her. She needs to get it all out."

Jenn scoots back, holding the hand Denielle pulled out of mine as she shifted. "There you go, let your body do the work. You'll be okay." Jenn's soothing words are like a calming blanket covering the room. I position myself behind my girl, allowing her to lean into me for support.

When she finally catches her breath, Denielle curls into a fetal position and begins to cry. My heart breaks at the sight, and I want to take away whatever is causing her such pain.

Jenn straightens and touches the back of her hand to Denielle's cheek. She meets my blurry gaze. "I'll be outside. She'll be fine, but she needs you."

I dip my chin, unable to form a reply. My throat has closed up, and I swallow over the razor blades in the back of my mouth. Three sets of feet slowly pad out of the room. I don't hear the telltale click of having complete privacy, but I can't bring myself to care.

With my ass on the wet tiles, my jeans cling to my legs. I reach my arms around Denielle and pull her into my lap, where she curls into a ball. She fists my shirt between her trembling fingers. Rocking us back and forth, I lean my cheek to the crown of her head. I don't wipe away the moisture on my face. The mere thought of not having come up here in time...

Eventually, her sobs slow, and she calms. "I'm sorry." Her apology is barely audible.

My heart squeezes, hearing her voice. "What for, baby?"

"That you saw me like this." She sniffs, pulling me closer. I adjust my hold and gently tip her chin up until her eyes meet mine. Even red rimmed and puffy from the ordeal she just went through, she is still the most beautiful woman I've ever seen.

"Why are you smiling?" Her brow puckers.

"You're beautiful," I tell her, making her laugh. The amusement quickly turns into another wheezing coughing fit, and I stroke her cheekbone until she settles back down.

"We need to get you out of these clothes." As if on command, she shudders.

I ignore my own clothes clinging to my body as I help her stand. I hardly notice the damp material. She has my full attention. Denielle pads, with my help, to the small bench seat in the corner. It was probably meant as decoration or to drop your discarded clothes on, but it comes in handy now. She is wearing another of those barely there sleep outfits, making it easy for me to get her out of the soaked material. I wrap a towel around her as I search the room for something to wear. Nothing.

"I'll be right back." I graze my knuckles against her cheek, and she covers my hand with hers before tucking the towel closer.

"Okay."

In the bedroom, I find Lilly and Rhys on the couch. Jenn and Ethan stand next to the door to the hallway, heads bowed and arguing in hushed tones.

I stop. Where do I look for clothes?

"I grabbed a pair of sweats for you." Rhys points his finger at something hanging over the armrest without abandoning his forward position with his elbows on his knees.

I nod. "Thanks, man." I glance at Lilly. "Could you help me find something for Den?"

Lilly's gaze jerks up. She sits similarly to her husband with her arms hugging her midsection. Tears glisten on her face, and she bobs her head.

Rhys rubs her back as she stands. Knowing where to go, she opens one drawer, then another. Then, she heads into the walk-in closet. An overpowering sense of helplessness roots me in place. I teeter between a soul-crushing need to help Denielle and self-doubt about what I have to offer her. I haven't been able to take care of myself, emotionally, since...well, never.

Lilly reappears and holds a pile of clothes out to me.

As I reach out, I force the nagging contradictions aside. I take the offering with a tight smile and head back to the bathroom.

Denielle's gaze lifts, new tears brim in her eyes, and my chest aches for her.

I place the change of clothes on the vanity and kneel. Placing my palms on either side of her thighs. "Do you want me to send them away?"

Denielle shakes her head. "It's time they know."

I carefully untangle the terrycloth from her, grabbing the dry clothes. "Do you need help?"

Denielle gives me a small smile. "No, thank you." After paus-ing, she adds, "Would you give me a moment?"

My chest constricts, and my gaze automatically finds the still-filled tub.

Denielle places her hand on my jaw, her skin cold as ice. Gently forcing me to focus on her, she emphasizes, "I'll be right out. I promise." A wave of goose bumps erupts on my arms.

I watch her carefully, trying to find a hint of deceit in her features. Her other palm also touches my cheek, and she leans in, never breaking eye contact. Right before her mouth meets mine, my eyes close of their own volition. Her lips are as equally chilled as her touch, but the soft caress ignites a fire in me I've only ever experienced with her. The kiss is over too soon.

Her thumbs swipe over my bottom lip, and I blink.

"I'll be right out."

CHAPTER TWENTY-SIX

MARCUS

WHILE DENIELLE GETS DRESSED, I CHANGE OUT OF MY WET jeans in the walk-in closet. Not having a dry alternative for my upper body, I enter the room shirtless. No one bats an eye. Everyone's thoughts are occupied elsewhere. Denielle exits the bathroom not long after I settle on the bench seat at the foot of her bed.

Jenn and Ethan have positioned themselves on either side of the door, arms behind their backs—a maneuver that seems almost rehearsed, as if they've stood like this many times. Lilly curls herself into Rhys's side on the couch, her phone in hand with the baby monitor on display.

Denielle hesitates in the doorway. All eyes are on her, yet she doesn't look at anyone but me. I can only imagine how uncomfortable she is. I stretch my hand in her direction, gesturing for her to come over. She bridges the distance in fast strides, and I turn her to settle between my legs. The seat is not deep, but I want her as close as possible. Seemingly needing the same, Denielle melts against my chest. Once again, the surreal thought of, *This is where she belongs*, reverberates through my mind.

My arms cross in front of her midsection, and Denielle rests her hands on top of mine, interlacing our fingers. For the first time since walking into the house tonight, I feel lighter.

Lilly's eyes drop to our joined hands, and a small smile toys with her lips.

"I owe you an apology," she begins, and her fingers tighten around mine. "And an explanation."

Rhys cocks his head, meeting my eyes, before dropping his gaze to her. "Explanation, yes. Apology, no. We're worried. We care for you, D."

Denielle's shoulders hunch slightly. "I know."

I can't see her face, but having learned her mannerisms, she either chews on the inside of her cheek or her bottom lip.

"OK, uh..." She inhales deeply before blowing out a breath. "I have haphephobia."

What the hell—?

I measure everyone's reaction. Everyone but Jenn displays equal expressions of confusion. Jenn doesn't give anything away. I know what it is, but I've never actually met anyone with the... condition.

It all begins to make sense.

Denielle must see as well that half of the occupants in the room don't know what it means. "Haphephobia is also called fear of touch."

Lilly's hand latches onto Rhys's forearm, her jaw locked.

Rhys's brows sit near his hairline. "I've touched you since the first day we met." Rhys peers at Lilly. "I mean...you know, not touched *touched*, but...you know." His awkwardness—something you rarely get to see on the guy—results in a collective chuckle.

"It doesn't work the way you think." The amusement in Denielle's voice thaws the last bit of ice in my veins. "At least not for me."

"Are you sure you want to talk about it?" Lilly probes carefully.

"Yes. It's time that someone outside of my family knows the truth. I don't want to hide *it* anymore."

A bitter taste slithers across my tongue. Is that what Victor Keller did? Made her do? He made her feel like she has to be ashamed.

"Why would you hide it?" Anger coats Jenn's question.

Denielle turns her head, and I get the profile of her pinched smile. "The night Marcus's sister died was the night I had my first episode. My father wasn't there to save her. He was called out of the OR because of me."

My body heats with white-hot rage. Her father had drilled into her that this was something she had to hide from the world. Did he also make her believe that Ken's death was her fault? Was this why she took my hate all those years? His pristine scrubs got a stain. He was the one embarrassed and put the burden on his daughter—after everything he had already put his family through with his affair. The pounding in my ears mutes Denielle's next words as she shifts in my arms.

She talks to the room but speaks only to me. "It's not recognized as a mental illness. It's only diagnosed as a phobia. There is no known cause for it. Some believe one is born with it, or that it's triggered by a change in brain function. Others believe it's a result of a traumatic experience." She regards me, waiting.

"Your mother," I complete the statement for her.

"Yes," her voice cracks. "Mom's death was ruled an accident, but...I don't know."

No one dares to breathe.

"I found her journal during the move and hid it. I didn't read it until years later. I have no clue how long they'd been going behind Mom's back, but she knew of the affair. She'd also been on antidepressants for years. In some entries, she wrote how she hated the way the meds made her feel."

Denielle's nails bite into my hand, but I welcome the pain. I'd take anything that helps her work through this.

"There has always been the nagging thought of *what if it*

wasn't an accident?" She pauses again. "Oli refuses to acknowledge the possibility, and I stopped pushing. He had enough to deal with, keeping my...secret."

"But why keep it a secret?" Lilly's agitation is palpable.

Denielle slips out of my embrace and positions herself next to me. Pulling her legs up, cross-legged, she takes my hand and clasps it between both of hers. "Pride?" She lifts a shoulder. "My father and Celine got married just a few weeks after my mother's death. It was a courthouse ceremony. They kept our new family dynamic hush-hush. I pieced the time line together over the years. At four or five years old, I didn't understand a lot of what was going on. We stayed in my mother's family home at first. Celine inherited it after Mom's death. It had been in their family forever. But then I had the..."—she licks her lips—"accident. I never tried to hurt myself. Self-harm has never been the reason," she quickly adds and makes eye contact with everyone.

"Then why?" Lilly whispers.

"The night of... I found a picture. Of my mom. Dad and Celine had removed all her photos—to make it easier for us."

Rhys snorts, and I couldn't agree with him more.

Denielle hollows her cheeks. "I remembered everything. The helplessness. Watching my mother float underwater, unable to do anything about it." A lone tear spills over. "I screamed. The same way I cried for help that day. Celine came running in and tried to comfort me. But her touch... Her arms were too tight. I couldn't breathe. It made me...sick. I can't explain it. I lose control. It's like my body turns against me. Everything from nausea, to utter panic, and sometimes even physical pain. It's..." She breaks off, her fingers wringing together in her lap. "I got away from Celine and ran through the house. I ended up at the pool. It was like the water was calling for me, so I jumped in, and..." She peers sideways at me. "When I'm underwater, the fear, the panic, and...the pain goes away. I'm in control. I control how long I stay under. The sensation of floating, the burn in my lungs. I'm in charge of it all."

"You stayed under a bit too long, though," Jenn inserts herself. She is oddly composed, but then, she grew up in an environment no kid should experience. Hell, most adults couldn't handle it.

Denielle dips her chin. "Yes. There have been a few occasions where I've lost track of time, needing the burn. But I've always come back up—with the exception of the first time. I don't know if I got too tired?" She side-eyes me briefly. "McKenna's death was ruled an accident. Aneurysms can't be predicted, but my father's career took a hit, nonetheless. I'm not sure if the hospital blamed him. Maybe some of his colleagues said something, or it was because I was brought in that night for possible drowning. Who knows what the rumors about me were, but my father moved us to Westbridge within a few weeks."

"So, in short, he blamed you." Jenn steps away from the wall and muses noncomically to Ethan, "And here I thought we had an asshole for a father."

Ethan, in return, just inclines his head but remains otherwise void of emotion.

Denielle scoots closer, and my hand drapes around her lower back, slipping under the long-sleeve shirt. My fingers draw circles on her naked skin, and she leans her head against my shoulder. She shivers as goose bumps erupt under my touch.

Lilly stands and *marches* over to us. She takes her friend's hands in hers, studying them with her mouth in a grim slash. "I'm only going to say this once. You are my best friend. Have been for the past twelve years. You were there for me when I doubted my feelings, thought there was something wrong with me. None of this is your fault. Don't. You. Dare let anyone ever make you feel ashamed. We love you. And fuck everyone else. Who gives a shit?"

Denielle bursts out laughing, in complete contradiction to the waterworks running down their faces. "The only thing missing is a bunch of naked girls and a stinky drain." She hiccups.

Lilly grins, and my brows draw together.

What the—?

Denielle smiles at me, wiping under her eyes. "She's repeating my words back to me. From the day she figured out she was in love with Rhys."

Oh.

Rhys stands, pulling his wife to her feet. He hugs her from behind and rests his chin on the top of her head. "And I will forever be grateful for you, even though you hid her for the next twenty-four hours."

"Sorry?" Denielle shrugs.

Lilly opens her arms, and Denielle steps into them. Rhys embraces both the girls. I hear the door open and watch Jenn and Ethan disappear.

"We're going to leave you two alone. But promise me that you won't fight this battle alone anymore. We're family. Call one of us," Lilly instructs and begs at the same time.

Before Denielle can answer, I reply, "She won't need to." All three glance toward me, and Rhys nods appreciatively.

"Let's go, Calla. Let's give them some privacy." He winks, and I want to clock my boss's jaw.

Freaking twenty-some-year-old kids.

Alone, Denielle pads over to her bedside, turning on the lamp, followed by flipping the switch by the door.

My ass has gone numb from the damn bench seat, so I move to the side, leaning against the mattress. Denielle keeps her back to me for an elongated moment, and I'm about to inquire what's wrong when she pivots and slowly saunters over. I quirk a brow as she steps between my legs and rests her forearms on my shoulders. Her fingers play with the strands of my hair, and a tingling sensation shoots from my scalp down my spine. My toes curl into the hardwood.

She tilts her head, studying me intently. "Why did you come for me?" After a short pause, she amends, "Tonight."

My breath hitches, the comfort of her touch vanishing to the background as the memory of the knowledge that something was wrong nearly made me stagger downstairs. The back of my throat aches, and my gaze swings to the wall opposite us. "A feeling."

When she remains mute, I ask the question no one dared. "What happened?"

What triggered her to...submerge... I can't finish the sentence, bile rising in my throat.

Denielle inhales through her nose, holding her breath at the top. Before she can reply, though, she begins to cough. It sounds like she's hacking up a lung, and every muscle in my body tenses. Lifting her arm, she coughs into the crook of her elbow, and I hold myself still. The urge to throw her over my shoulder and deliver her to the nearest emergency room surges to the fore-front. The wait for her to settle down is excruciating, even though it probably isn't more than a minute.

"Maybe we should take you to get checked out?" I phrase it like a question, even though I'm not asking—not really.

Shaking her head, she steps closer. "No doctors. I'm fine." She clears her throat once more.

I scan her from her hairline to her bare toes, unease mingling with concern.

Her palm settles on my cheek. "I'm okay, Marcus. Honest. I just inhaled too deeply. I'm good."

I want to believe her, but I vow to myself that if it happens again, I will carry her fireman style into the ER if necessary. "Okay. So...what—" I start again, but she cuts me off.

"Can that wait until the morning?"

Can it?

Not really.

"Sure." Before I can reconsider, her hands drop to the hem of my pants. "Uh, what are you doing, *Keller?*"

She leans in, her nose trailing my jaw to my neck. She nips the skin before lining up her lips with my ear. "Give me your worst, Baxter."

I'm unable to suppress the tremble she evokes.

Denielle pulls back, a devilish smirk on her lips. I zero in on her mouth, watching her pull the bottom between her teeth. Her eyes sparkle in the dim illumination of the room. Visions of her sprawled out on the bed, at my mercy, flitter through my mind. Heat shoots through my body.

As much as I want to punish her for giving me the second worst scare of my life, the thought of giving her my worst doesn't sit well. "I don't think we should—"

Her fingers curl around the band. "I want you to make me forget," she exclaims as she tugs on the material. "Be the only thought on my mind." She burns a path into my skin where her nails graze my thighs. Leaning closer again, her warm breath fanning across my lips. "Make me scream your na—"

Jesus, fuck!

I don't let her finish, every cell of my body crackling with electric need. I am aware that this is a distraction, a way to not deal with what happened. And while it is probably the wrong decision, I refuse to stop. I need her as much as she wants me.

I grab her hips, thrusting my hardening cock against her heat.

Fuck gentle.

"I'm going to fill more than just your mind if you keep that up." My tone is low and threatening.

She leans in, her lips hovering over mine. "Bring it on, *Bax*."

Releasing one side, I glide the tips of my thumb, fore, and middle fingers up her spine. Denielle hums her approval, never breaking our visual connection. Reaching its destination, my hand wraps around the back of her neck, applying pressure and confirming she understands who's in charge. I force her mouth to mine, biting her bottom lip, not enough to draw blood but to bring my point across further. Denielle whimpers, and I watch her eyes flutter closed. She licks across the spot I just nipped before sinking teeth into the same spot.

God, this woman is going to kill me.

I let myself fall back on the mattress, pulling her with me. Her eyes spring open as she braces her palms against the comforter. The air between us ignites with pent-up...need? Anger? Frustration? The emotional overload from the last hour short-circuits all rationale. Her gaze finds mine, desire swirling in the brown of her irises. My hand releases her neck as she climbs the bed, her legs straddling me.

Denielle grinds into my groin, and I thank the heavens that I'm no longer wearing my jeans, but the borrowed sweats. Her heat burns through the minimal barrier, and my fingers dig into the flesh of her ass.

Clasping the bottom of her shirt, she pulls it off in one swift move. My cock twitches. My mouth waters at the sight of her perky tits. I cover one of her breasts with my palm, kneading her soft flesh.

She begins to lower her face, and I'm forced to readjust my grip to a different body part. When her naked chest connects with mine, I apply pressure to her taut ass, and she rocks into me. A feverish heat spreads through my veins, wanting to taste every inch of my woman.

My woman. Nothing has ever felt so right.

Her hands cup my face before her thumbs stroke across my forehead. She scans my face before leaning in. Her tongue swipes across the seam of my mouth, seeking entrance. She explores me with feverish desire, spurning on my hunger for her.

Denielle's moan when my fingers slip into her pants reverberates through the room. Finding that she never put on the underwear I had left in the bathroom for her snaps my last bit of self-control.

CHAPTER TWENTY-SEVEN

DENIELLE

Marcus's hands disappear from my ass. Before I can protest, I'm on my back with him hovering above me.

He slants his head, sizing me up like an animal about to devour his prey. I wait for his next move. His gaze dips to my rapidly rising and falling chest. Drawing in air has become increasingly harder.

Suddenly, Marcus retreats. Cold air hits my flushed skin, and I shiver. Propping myself up on my elbow, my brows knit. What is he doing? Did he change his mind about—

He slides off the bed, hooks his thumbs into the waistband, and pushes his sweats down. His movements are almost too smooth. No one should be able to undress this gracefully, yet fast. But I only have eyes for one body part. His hard cock stands erect, glistening at the top. Saliva pools in my mouth, remembering the club and how he tasted on my tongue.

I push up farther, pressing my palms into the mattress, but Marcus shakes his head.

"Uh-uh." The way the corner of his mouth quirks, a quiver

somersaults in my stomach. He lifts his hand and twirls his fore-finger in the air. "Turn."

At the menace in the one word, my bent legs drop inward, pressing together from my knees to my needy pussy. I don't recognize myself, but then I've never experimented or let go before.

I hold his gaze, and Marcus blinks once. "Who is in charge here, *Keller*?" He's running out of patience.

Jesus Christ, why does this make me so wet?

"You are," I breathe out, unable to speak at a normal volume.

"Then, why are you not on your knees yet?" He fists his dick, stroking up and down.

In slow motion, I shift, not leaving him out of sight until I find myself facing the headboard. My hands and knees press into the soft comforter as I wait. When nothing happens, I begin to turn my head, but suddenly, something wraps around my eyes from behind. Shifting my weight to the right, my left hand reaches up to identify the object—one of my silk headbands.

"Do you have anything to say, baby?" His breath fans over my ear, and I jump. I didn't realize how close he'd come.

"No."

"If at any point you want to change...pace, just say the word." His sudden gentle tone contrasts his commanding persona from a moment ago. Marcus Baxter would never force me to do some-thing I didn't want. He's merely giving me what I asked for.

A new voice pushes its way into my conscious thoughts. *What does this say about you? Wanting to submit to him.*

I sit back on my heels, covering my breasts with my arms. If I weren't already *blind*, my eyes would've squeezed together, not wanting to face Marcus. The mattress shifts, and Marcus's arms sneak around my chest, covering mine with his.

"What's wrong, baby?" His chin rests on my shoulder as he draws me against him.

Embarrassment makes my tongue thicken. "Why do I like when you tell me what to do? Give me orders?"

"Why do I like *being in* charge?" he counters.

I don't speak.

"There is nothing wrong with surrendering to another person on your terms. It's an act of trust. And confidence." I interrupt him with a halfhearted laugh, but he just squeezes me tighter. "You telling me what you want shows your trust. In *us*. You're willing to let go because we can stop whenever we want. Surrendering is not putting me in charge. It's taking control of what you desire and need. This doesn't make you weak or reflect a lack of self-esteem or whatever a guy like your ex would tell you. It also doesn't mean that this is the only way we will have sex for the rest of our lives."

He shifts and places a kiss underneath my ear. My pulse surges through my veins. *The rest of our lives?*

"What are you saying?" I whisper.

"You used to be the person reminding me of every reason why I never wanted a relationship. Caring for someone...loving another human meant you could lose them. Loss equaled pain— something I refused to experience again. You changed that when you went into the pool that night at the vineyard."

My heart skips a beat. *He saw that? How did he—*

"I saw you on the cameras. Something happened that night. For both of us. I didn't want to admit it for the longest time, but I'm done avoiding it. Avoiding you." He loosens his hold, his fingers drawing circles over my collarbone. "You are one of the strongest women I've ever met. Your...condition doesn't define you."

"You make it sound so simple." I drop my hands and reach back, placing my palms on his thighs. Marcus cups my breasts, and my head falls back against his shoulder.

"It is that simple, baby. You and I share a connection that was born out of tragic circumstances, grew by hate and guilt, and finally transformed into something I refuse to give up now that I have it."

He rolls my nipples between his fingers, and a low moan

escapes my lips. My nails claw into the sides of his legs. "When did you become so poetic, *Baxter*?" I tip my head to the side, and his lips hover over mine.

"There are many sides of me you haven't seen yet, *Keller*."

"I can't wait."

"Good." Marcus releases my breasts, and his body heat disappears, instantly depriving me of his nearness.

"Now, get on your knees," he orders, and a smile tugs on my lips as I comply.

My little moment of insecurity could've easily ruined the mood, yet it did the opposite. I've never felt more powerful, and it's all because of the man who hated me for years. Moving across the country to start over resulted in not just one new beginning.

My heart hammers in my throat, waiting for his next move.

"Are you ready *to be* in charge?" Fingers curl into my leggings as he begins to peel them over my butt in excruciating slowness.

"Give me your worst," I pant with anticipation.

Marcus pulls them down my thighs but then lets them bunch at my knees, restricting my movement.

My fingertips press into the mattress, fisting the comforter underneath. Desire like I've never experienced before pools in my core.

A whoosh of air is the brief warning before a sharp ache explodes on my right butt cheek. My spine stiffens, but I swallow my sound of surprise. Marcus's knees cage my legs, his cock nestling in my crack. He leans down until his naked chest is flush with my back. "That was for challenging me this past month."

He breaks the connection, rubbing the heat from the impact of his palm. My chest expands with air at the soothing motion but catches in my lungs as another strike comes down on the left. He leans in again. "And that was for the kiss you *took* that morning in the kitchen."

This time, I can't suppress the whimper as his thumb

caresses my biting flesh. The tips of his fingers slowly move from the ache to between my butt cheeks, stopping where I am not prepared for. I finally understand what a friend from New York once divulged to me after one-too-many drinks: *If you think your clit is sensitive, you need to try anal play.* Back then, I just laughed her comment off. Right now, I'm not laughing. I hold my breath as nerve endings coming from this one part of my body fire up at the same time, and holy—my eyes roll back inside my head. But as Marcus applies the slightest bit of pressure, my eyes squeeze shut beneath the blindfold, every muscle going on high alert. Do I want this? No. Yes. *No.*

He pushes the tip of his finger the tiniest bit inside my ass, and my elbows nearly buckle from the sensory overload, bliss and discomfort sending my body into a frenzy. "I would never do something you didn't like." He withdraws, settling his palms on either cheek. "You will like this, though," he purrs. I expel the breath I involuntarily held. "But not yet. Tonight, I have other plans for you." He shifts to the side so my leg is trapped between both of his as he plunges three fingers into my heat, making me cry out at the intrusion.

"Shhh, baby. We don't want to wake the whole house, do we?" He strokes his fingers in and out as my head falls forward.

"Fuck." I inhale through my nose in a failed attempt to stay quiet.

"Not yet, baby." His grin is audible, and he stops, buried in my folds.

"I'm go-ing to fuck-ing k-kill you." I can't articulate between panting and trying not to come from his damn fingers.

"Bring it on, *Keller.*" The heat of his legs radiates against mine.

The tip of his cock rests against my ass while Marcus continues his assault on my pussy.

My eyes roll back inside my head, and a ripping sound reaches my ears. I owe Lilly a new duvet. "Are you going to finger fuck me to my orgasm, or will you use your dick like a big boy?" I'm quite proud of how well I managed to get the words out, not coming in the process.

The overstimulation stops, and his fingers are gone with lightning speed. There is no sound in the room besides my own breathing. I freeze, unable to even blink with the scarf wrapped around my head.

What is he doing?

The mattress behind me dips and—

"Ahhhhh," I cry out as Marcus enters me in one thrust. His hard length hits my insides, and my arms cave. My face impacts with a pillow, and his palm lands on the back of my head, keeping me down.

He pumps in and out with such force I turn farther into the pillow to muffle my moaning.

"Is." *Thrust.* "This." *Thrust.* "Big Boy." Thrust, thrust. "Enough for you?" His fingers curl into my hair, and he tugs, bending my head back.

I bite my bottom lip to silence myself, but it's no use. "Oh, god, yesss."

Marcus releases my strands, and both of his hands find my hips. "I didn't hear your answer, baby." He mocks me in a way that is anything but insulting. He enjoys this as much as I do.

"Har-der, *Bax*." My breath comes in spurts, and it's a miracle I get the words out at all.

He chuckles and slows his torturous movements. He bends down until one of his hands covers mine, and our fingers interlace. The heat of his chest burns into my back as he nuzzles my neck. His other fingers find my clit, rubbing my sensitive spot in circles. "Where have you been all my life?"

"You're going to make me come if you keep that up."

His hand disappears, and he withdraws.

"What are you doing?"

The blindfold slips off my head, and I blink.

"Turn around."

I peer behind me and find Marcus kneeling on the mattress,

stroking his cock covered in my juices. My gaze dips, following his movement.

He lets go and drops to all fours, covering my backside again. "Turn, or we'll try out how much you'll like anal tonight."

He's not serious—*I think*—but I flip on my back, nonetheless.

Marcus's eyes shine with amusement. I kick off my leggings and widen my legs. His gaze dips to my center before he lowers himself and lines up with my entrance.

"I want to see your eyes when you come this time." He places a gentle kiss on my lips. "Before, though, I'm going to do something I've wanted since the laundry room."

I quirk a brow. "And what's that?" The gleam in his eyes makes my stomach flip.

Marcus slides down my body, trailing kisses along his way. When he reaches the spot between my legs, my body vibrates—literally. I have to lean my head up to be able to see him and meet his gaze. Without breaking eye contact, he leans in, and his tongue swipes across my seam.

Oh, god.

My lids flutter closed, and my hands reach up, fisting the pillows beneath my head. Stars explode as he swirls my clit.

My legs bend, pressing my heels into the mattress. "Fuck, ahhh." I have no idea where top or bottom is as my mind spins in a sexual vertigo of desire and release. My body is burning from the inside out.

Marcus hooks his arms around my thighs, applying the slightest pressure on my lower abdomen as he continues his exploration. Every time I manage to peel my eyes open, I find him watching me. He blows cool air against my overheated flesh.

Goose bumps erupt on my arms and legs. I unclench my fingers from the pillows and reach down to rake them through his messy hair. Curling into his blond strands, I guide him back, and he chuckles. The hum of his laughter against my clit nearly pushing me over the edge.

"Yesss, keep doing that." I tug on his hair.

"Who's in charge, huh?"

Does he really want to have this conversation now?

"We are." The two words leave me in a breathy moan.

"Mhmmm, I like the sound of that." I can hear his smile. "Tell me what you want."

Implicit trust puts us both in charge. "You. All of you. Now."

"You sure? I could—"

"If you don't fuck me right this second, we're done."

Marcus sits up, wipes his mouth with the back of his hand, and slants his head. "Is that so?" He's declaring a challenge.

"No, but I'd really like your dick inside my *cunt*." I flutter my eyes, and he shakes his head. I've never talked like this before. But with Marcus, everything is different.

"Jesus, woman." Instead of making me beg, which I expected, he mounts my body, holding himself on his elbows.

My knees fall to the sides, allowing him to align himself with my opening. The atmosphere in the room shifts, and the feverish desire morphs into a slow-moving stream of incinerating lava.

I cup his face, my thumbs stroking across his cheekbones.

Our mouths connect, and Marcus sweeps his tongue across my bottom lip. My arms intertwine behind his neck. I part my lips, and he enters me—tongue and cock. My hips roll as he fills me to the hilt, and a groan rumbles in his throat. He hooks one arm under my back while the other glides down my rib cage until he has a firm grip on my thigh. I'm hyperaware of the path where his calloused skin trails mine, the sensation burned into my flesh. This is nothing like the previous times. The laundry room was about dominance and numbing. *The Club* to fulfill a desire we didn't allow ourselves to acknowledge. Tonight is about us. About passion and...feeling. Marcus has the ability to let me drown without the need for submerging. I begged him to make me forget, be the only one on my mind. He's done just that. As our bodies tangle together and he moves on top of me, all I can think about is that I'm falling. For him.

CHAPTER TWENTY-EIGHT

MARCUS

FOR THE SECOND TIME IN A LITTLE OVER A MONTH, I WAKE UP in a bed that's not mine—my room in the main house. Today, I don't care, though. My face is buried in one of the many pillows Denielle keeps in her bed. What is it with her and the excessive need to have more pillows than my boss has the same model rifles? My hand travels across the sheet to find the other side cold.

Where the hell is this woman now?

I lift my head. She's nowhere in sight. Peering toward the room I will forever dread after yesterday, the door is wide open and empty as well. I push myself up and groan. Fuck, I'm tired. I consider myself in good shape, but after last night, I need a break. I'm emotionally and physically drained.

I left my shirt and jeans balled up in the closet, so I don't even bother checking if they're dry. Slipping out of bed and peering around, I spot my borrowed sweats.

I make my way downstairs. I hear everyone talking over each other before my feet hit the foyer.

Jenn is the loudest of all. "You called me to keep her safe, so let me do my fucking job, Ethan!"

"I called *you*. You're not bringing Paycen into this." I round the corner just as Ethan points a finger at Jenn's face.

I wouldn't be surprised if she snaps his digit off. Jenn has a temper of her own. Ethan's scowl complements the grim line of his mouth. He only ever lets his carefully controlled mask slip if he's about to blow.

"T and Cor are on a job. He is close and—" Jenn starts again, her fists propped on her hips.

"Unstable," Ethan barks. "Our little brother is as trustworthy as Dahmer, Shipman, and Bundy combined. If you call Paycen, you're out. P is a ticking time bomb. He's not setting foot on this property."

Jenn folds her arms. If I hadn't already been in the room, I wouldn't have heard her reply. "You know it's not his fault."

Ethan bridges the gap and hugs her to him. "I know, J." He props his head on hers and meets my eyes. "But he cannot be here."

"Okay," she concedes.

Lilly and Rhys sit on the barstools, with Denielle on the other side of the kitchen island. She has a mug between her hands, holding it right under her chin and staring at nothing.

With everyone following the argument, I went unnoticed. I clear my throat.

Her head turns, and a soft smile graces her lips. Walking around, I stop beside her and pull her to me. She snuggles close, as if it's the most natural thing ever. In a way, it is.

"Hey." I peer down, and she rests her temple against my chest.

"Good morning."

Glancing over to Lilly and Rhys, who have equally grim expressions, I address Ethan and Jenn. "What's going on?"

Denielle places her coffee on the countertop and wraps both

arms around my midsection. Her open affection surprises me, but no one else even blinks.

"We were discussing what to do about the package," Jenn explains.

The package. I forgot about the reason Denielle...

I dip my chin to see her face. She doesn't look at me, so I address the room. "Where is it?"

Ethan reaches behind him and reveals the object. It's a standard flat-rate box one can pick up at any post office. The flaps are cut open, and E pushes it over. Peering inside, some type of check-patterned material comes into view.

Jenn pulls it out, and I identify it as a scarf, or a small blanket, or something along those lines. Denielle buries her face into my chest, her spine stiffening. The hair on the back of my neck stands, and I tighten my hold.

While Jenn places the scarf-blanket on the counter, Ethan reaches in again. He pulls out a piece of paper.

My brows draw up. "What's that?"

Denielle's nails dig into my backside.

What the hell?

"This is the Burberry scarf Kelly, Charlie's mother, gave Denielle for Christmas during our junior year," Lilly elaborates, void of emotion.

Understanding sets in. "And this?" I tip my chin toward the rectangle Ethan now has face down on the countertop.

His gaze bores into Denielle's back.

"Show him." Her muffled permission doesn't sit right with me. What the hell is this?

Ethan and Jenn exchange a look before he flips the paper and holds it up for me to see. A photograph.

In my peripheral vision, Lilly turns into Rhys and hides her face in the crook of his neck.

I scan the picture, and my mouth runs dry. A pit opens in my stomach, and I no longer wonder what set Denielle off. It's an evidence photo. I don't have to ask who the person in the picture is. The resemblance is uncanny. Denielle's mother's life-less form lies on some type of tiled ground. Her hair and clothes are wet. The exposed skin of her face and bare arms is pale, blending between blue and gray. But worst of all is her lifeless eyes. They're open, staring at nothing.

If I had seen Ken like this... "This is what was delivered?" My voice matches the ice in my veins.

Jenn glances around the room before looking straight at me. "Yes. I'm sorry, Marcus. I checked it for weapons and chemicals, but not..."

I shake my head. "You did nothing wrong."

"I took it last night," she amends. "I figured you two needed some time, and leaving it upstairs— I wanted to examine it more."

There's a sour taste against my tongue. "What did you find?"

She regards Ethan for a moment. "Not much. It was addressed to Denielle at La Déesse, no return address. The tracking showed it got dropped off at a post office here in LA. No traces of anything that I can find—with what I have available to check it out. The only prints on the photo were Denielle's."

I'm about to start a full-blown interrogation when Denielle shifts. She untangles herself and leans back, her brown eyes boring into mine. "I dropped it in Collin's car that day..." She trails off, and I scowl.

That day.

"The day he drove you home?"

The day I should've put a bullet between his eyes.

"Yes."

Ethan shoves the photo back in the box and covers it with the scarf, placing it on the other countertop behind him.

I survey the room. Lilly sits up straight again, nodding at her friend. An unspoken message passes. Denielle shifts in my embrace. Her arms snake around me, and she intertwines her fingers.

"The day Collin drove me home..." She pauses and draws in a

deep breath. "Charlie met me outside of La Déesse. We had just gotten back from lunch with Denis. Charlie gave me the scarf. He said he thought I might want it back since it was from Kelly." Denielle recalls how seeing the present triggered her *condition*, how Collin intervened and drove her home. Every so often, she squeezes my midsection. When she reveals that Collin knew about her haphephobia, that her father had used Collin to spy on her, and that the little shit tried to blackmail Denielle to come back to him, my body goes rigid. My skin is too tight, my fingers itching to wrap them around the throat of a certain upper-crust shit stain.

My hold on Denielle turns to a vise, and she winces.

"I'm sorry, baby." I hug her gently.

"So, you're saying Collin threatened you?" Jenn's neutral tone causes my jaw to clench. This woman is scarier than my boss when she is in her natural element: violence.

"I...guess. I haven't seen him in almost two weeks, though. Not since I pulled a pair of scissors on him."

Jenn chuckles, and she holds out her fist. "Attagirl."

Denielle bumps her knuckles against Jenn's, and I shake my head.

"*We* saw him." Ethan redirects everyone's attention. "When Denielle was, uh... He was there when we left for the hospital."

Denielle recoils from my embrace, staring up in shock. "Why didn't you tell me?" She scans everyone's faces. "That was on Monday. He was supposed to have left the Friday before."

Was he now?

"I had other things on my mind," I point out, not admitting that I forgot about the little twat. My mind was spinning from what Denielle did to me by simply breathing the same air—not something that should happen in my line of work.

"I want to speak to Denis," Jenn declares. "If he wasn't supposed to be in town, yet he was when all this happened, we would have our main suspect."

"What about Charlie?" Rhys inserts himself. "He's been showing up everywhere D has been. It's fucking weird."

Agreed.

"I left the scarf in Collin's car," Denielle defends her ex. "How would Charlie have gotten hold of it? Let alone a picture of..." She cuts herself off, a visible shudder running through her body.

"Maybe they work together. Two scorned exes." Ethan shrugs.

"This is not like Charlie." Lilly looks at her best friend, who gives her a pinched smile.

"Have you talked to Charlie lately?" I inquire.

Denielle shakes her head. "No, not since the day we had lunch, and I..."

"Let's figure out what Liberman's deal is first. Then, we look into ex number two." Jenn takes charge. She glances at her wrist, pressing the button on the side of her watch.

Huh, The Cleaner *and I share the same watch.*

"Let's get you to work." She looks pointedly at Denielle. "But first, you need to change. I don't think this outfit is suitable for your high-end clientcle." Jenn winks, and for the first time, I acknowledge Denielle's appearance.

She wears wide sweats that oddly look like the borrowed ones I'm wearing. No, they are mine. What the—?

Denielle nods. "I'll be ready in thirty."

She steps out of my arms. Twining our fingers together, she strides toward the foyer. I follow, too baffled about where she found my sweats.

In her room, she closes the door and leans against it. My gaze drops from her eyes, to her lips, and down the rest of her body. Whereas my pants are about to fall off her frame, not to mention the numerous times they're rolled up at the feet, her tank top is painted on. The contours of her tits reveal that she's not wearing a bra, and sudden heat floods my body—from the fact that Ethan saw her like this or the knowledge that I could tear the top off her and latch on to her erect nipples in one move, I'm not sure.

I need to redirect my thoughts.

"Wanna explain how my sweats ended up covering your ass?" I cock an eyebrow, placing both my hands on either side of her head against the door.

Denielle's fingers trace my abs, her touch scorching my skin.

"You left them in the dryer," she remarks cockily.

My dick twitches at her attitude. Instead, though, I hollow my cheeks. "So...you thought it was reasonable to steal them?"

She lifts a shoulder. "I thought it was fair, given how you left me standing in the laundry room that day."

My brows shoot up. "You've had my pants since we...?"

How did I not notice that?

"Maybe." Her sheepish grin makes me laugh.

"You are one of a kind, *Keller*." I lean in, my mouth hovering over hers.

"I prefer when you call me baby." She flutters her eyes.

"You do, huh?" I slowly move my lips along her jaw, relishing the tremble that racks through her until I reach her ear. My nose strokes the shell, and I whisper, "What is my baby going to do if I don't cooperate?"

Her fingers curl, leaving scratch marks down my belly to the hem of my pants. "I might withhold some of your favorite activities from you."

"My favorite?" I nip on the skin of her neck.

"That's what you called it last night—after round number three. Or was it four?" With her thumb on the outside, her fingers dip under the waistband. Reaching all the way in, she wraps her hand around my hard cock, pumping up and down. "Am I wrong?"

My lips part, and I groan into the crook of her neck. What is this woman doing to me? "*Baby*," I warn. "Don't start something you can't see through."

"Why not?" She innocently swipes her thumb over my head,

already covered in precum. Heat shoots from head to toe, and my gentle nip on her soft skin morphs to me sinking my teeth into her flesh.

"Mhmm," she hums.

Ripping my body away, I retreat until she has to pull her hand out of my pants. "You need to get ready for work."

Why the fuck do I care if Denis fires her? One less variable where she could be attacked. But at the same time, I know how much this job means to her—to her independence. I'll be the last person to take that from her.

Denielle's pout almost changes my mind, but I shake my head. "Go shower. I'll be here, and tonight, we'll finish this conversation."

Denielle slowly walks past me, never dropping her eyes from mine, challenging me, so I amend. "At the guesthouse, where no one will hear your screams."

Her step falters. My momentary satisfaction is punched in the junk when she reaches for the hem of her top. Pulling it over her head, she follows the motion by releasing the drawstring of her stolen sweats. The material drops to the floor, and she steps out of them, spinning to stand in front of me, butt naked. She forwent the underwear again. Blood rushes to my cock like rapids.

I hold myself motionless to not lose control and take her against the wall, possibly damaging the drywall in the process.

"Well, until then, don't forget how you feel right now," she quips, pivots, and disappears into the bathroom.

I swipe my hands over my face, shaking my head.

What have I gotten myself into?

ONLY AN HOUR after Denielle and Jenn arrive at La Déesse, Jenn's name lights up my phone.

My shift doesn't start until one, but after showering and changing into my own clothes, the walls closed in. So, when our cleaner calls, I'm with Ethan in the main house, going over the shifts for the next month.

Lilly is on a conference call in her office, Rhys downstairs in the gym, and Audrey with her nanny.

I answer on speakerphone. "What did you find out?"

"Hello to you, too," she huffs.

"Come on, J," Ethan sighs, probably used to her sass.

"Fiiine," Jenn whines. "I had to explain to Denis why I was interrogating him on STD boy, but I left it vague."

"Oh, so you didn't tell him you make dead bodies disappear for a living?" Ethan chimes in.

"This is me flipping you off, *Bill*," Jenn bickers.

I have to look up this thing Ethan got his nickname from.

"As I was saying before I got so rudely interrupted," Jenn drawls, and I peer at Ethan, who rolls his eyes, "I informed Denis that I was Denielle's detail and hired to protect her. Did you know she got an orchid with a creepy note?"

Where her words choked me, Jenn oozed excitement. "What are you talking about?"

"When I alluded to the package and that Denielle did not just faint the day the EMTs took her to the hospital, he asked if she had told me about the flower. Clearly, she hadn't. And neither did you guys."

"That's because this is the first time I'm hearing of this," I snap at her.

"Oh, well," Jenn glosses over my anger. "Denielle threw it in the dumpster, so no dice on getting any prints from that. The note was super cryptic. Could've been a compliment or a threat. Either way, it's gone."

My chest cramps, and I rub my fist up and down its center. I don't bother asking what it had said. There is nothing we can do about it now. "What about Liberman?"

"Denis hasn't heard from him since Tuesday after they had lunch. Denis said Collin stayed longer because one of the fabric shipments was delayed, and Mama Liberman wanted to ensure the stuff was to her satisfaction. Denielle confirmed that the materials were supposed to be delivered the week before but didn't arrive until Tuesday morning. Collin checked them out and then left a week ago."

My head hurts. "So, is he back in New York?" I'm losing my patience.

"I don't know." Jenn's confident attitude takes a dive.

"Explain." Technically, she's not one of my subordinates, and she could easily tell me to go fuck off, but I have a hunch that she likes Denielle and wants to figure out who's after her.

"Denielle texted some of her New York friends who still work at Liberman. No one has seen him since he left for LA. However, he did check out of his hotel the day he was supposed to leave."

"Then where the fuck is he?" My palm uncurls and hits the desk. My phone jumps at the impact, and Ethan raises a brow.

"Should we ask Lilly to *explore some angles*?" he suggests.

The pounding in my ears makes it hard to concentrate. "No, she has enough going on. Unless Denielle wants to bring her in, let her role be Denielle's friend." I inhale and close my eyes. "I'll call the boss."

There is a sharp intake of breath on the other end of the line.

"Do you have anything to say, Jennifer?" I sneer, having had it with everyone's attitudes.

"Nope. Your decision."

"Do not let Denielle out of your sight, and report back if there is any unusual activity."

"You got it." She disconnects, and I sit with Ethan in the quiet of our office.

Denielle's birthday is this weekend. Lilly has it all planned out. King and Wes will be arriving with Haddie on Friday. Elle and her sister will fly in Saturday evening right before the surprise party. I refuse to let anything or anyone ruin this weekend for her.

"What does Jenn know about *the boss*?" I turn to Ethan.

"What do you mean?" His face pales.

"Don't play dumb." I cross my arms, leaning back in my chair.

"Jenn might have mentioned something," Ethan replies, subdued.

"Define *something*." Is this why George changed schedules and reassigned additional personnel to the vineyard?

"Jenn's heard rumors of his handle popping up in *Thanatos3*. You know Corbin is in charge of—" Ethan cuts himself off.

Thanatos3 is a dark web chatroom Marshall Davis uses for his ventures. The man is obsessed with Greek mythology, hence he named his preferred communication platform after the personification of death.

"All the more reason to keep Lilly out of it." If there is something else going on that George has kept me in the dark from, I will make sure Lilly and Rhys are safe from it—especially if it involves Lilly's brother and the Davis clan. Together.

"Whatever you say, B."

CHAPTER TWENTY-NINE

DENIELLE

AFTER MARCUS GOT OFF WORK WEDNESDAY EVENING, WE extensively *discussed* my theft of his favorite sweats. Somehow, I doubted they were really his favorites.

We're lying next to each other in the tangled sheets when he orders me to wait for him here. He throws on a pair of running shorts that have materialized from somewhere on the floor and disappears into the living room. The sound of the front door causes me to sit up in his bed.

What the—?

According to the alarm clock, ten minutes pass before I hear footsteps again.

I picked on a frayed thread on the corner of the comforter and slipped my feet out several times but then decided against it. Whatever he was doing seemed important to him.

Marcus appears in the doorway, leaning with his shoulder against the frame. "Get up."

"Excuse me?" I arch my brows. "It's one in the morning."

"So? What's your point? *Baby*." He's been using the endear-ment at every possible chance, with the occasional *Keller* thrown in between. But even using my last name has morphed into something more. The way he enunciates it, it is like a challenge, and a swarm of butterflies explodes in my belly—challenges I happily accept every single time.

Before I can protest, he turns and walks back out. I clench my jaw, a jab on my tongue, but move to follow. As my feet hit the carpet, another demand stops me in my tracks.

"Oh, and don't bother putting clothes on." His call comes from somewhere in the house.

Has he lost his mind?

My pulse speeds up, and I pull the sheet from the bed with me. I don't mind being naked in front of him, but having no idea what his plans are...

I find Marcus in the living room, his shorts replaced with one of the pool towels from the hall closet. He holds a matching one in my direction. "Let's go."

I bristle as my gaze jumps between the offering and his face. "Where?"

"You'll see." His smirk tethers between mischievous and... like something momentous is about to happen. There is a gleam in the depths of his eyes I can't decipher.

Putting my trust in him, I cross the room, drop the sheet, and cover myself with the towel.

Marcus opens the door and gestures to go ahead. *We're leaving?* My heart thunders in my ears. My ass peeks out of the bottom of the towel, and I peer toward the camera under the pool house's roofline. It's one of God knows how many monitoring the property's exterior.

The moonlight reflects on the surface of the pool. A small camping lamp sits on a low table between two lounge chairs, providing the only illumination. None of the other lights on the patio are on.

Marcus turns me to face him, wrapping his arms around my waist. I clutch the towel over my chest, and my stomach churns watching him chew on the inside of his cheek. His eyes flip between mine, and with every passing second, the nervous swarm of butterflies morphs into an angry murder of crows flapping ferociously.

My confident man never acts unsure of his actions.

"I..." he starts, glances between the smooth surface of the water and back to me. "I want you to show me what you do when..."

I inhale sharply. "But I don't need to...right now."

What is he asking of me?

"I know. I figured if you show me, explain it to me when you don't have to...maybe over time, we can work on finding something less...hazardous." This time, there is a tiny tug on his lips.

Less hazardous.

My breath stalls, and I slash my mouth, not wanting him to see the tremble. He wants to help me, not just accept my condition. No one has ever done that. I've always just suppressed and hidden it. An odd giddiness rolls through me, and I step closer until we're toe to toe. Interlacing my fingers behind his head, I pull him to my level and bridge the gap. It's the softest of touches as his mouth begins to move against mine, and I automatically open up to him. This man is like a drug I didn't know I needed. Marcus's tongue enters my mouth, and I let him take the lead as we tangle in synchronous movement. My body burns from the inside out until a cool breeze reminds me where we are.

I pull back, peering up at him. "Thank you."

He leans his forehead to mine. "Drop the towel, baby. If we're doing this, we're doing it the right way."

I burst out laughing. "The right way involves skinny dipping?"

"Absolutely, it does." He reaches to the spot where the towel is tucked together over my breasts. "I figure if it ends up becoming too much, I can distract you a different way."

Desire flickers at the thought. "What about the cameras?"

"Turned off. J knows not to leave the office or turn the pool feed on until he gets my okay. He can watch the rest of the property from the inside." Marcus grins against my lips.

With one move, he whips the towel away from my body and stifles my shriek of surprise with his mouth.

WE SPENT HALF the night outside. Thankfully, the pool was heated.

When I slipped into the water, he was right beside me. The thundering rhythm against my rib cage made it hard to concentrate. My adrenaline was through the roof, and I waited for *the need* to set in. It never came.

Marcus challenged me with endless questions. He forced me to face my demon—my mind. The knowledge that I could stop at any point, that he would never push me over the edge, allowed me to talk him through every thought, sensation, and urge that went through my mind when I craved my unconventional coping strategy. This was the first time I voluntarily put it in words, without being prodded by a therapist or my father. The liberation was exhilarating. With every sentence, I felt lighter, breathing became easier, and I became...free.

While I subconsciously was aware of the why, the risk of judgment—or worse, pity—had kept me from verbalizing it. It was etched into my soul that *we* didn't talk about it. We didn't admit to not being perfect.

"How... What do you feel when you look up at the world above?"

I pulled my bottom lip between my teeth. "I'm in charge."

This wasn't enough of an explanation, so he simply waited.

"I, um... I'm in charge of how long I remain submerged. How sharp I let the burn get before...surrendering and resurfacing."

Marcus nodded in understanding, and his acceptance reignited a flame I never expected to feel again.

He held me as I drifted to the bottom of the pool, staying with me until we ran out of air. The familiar ache morphed into a completely new emotion. I didn't chase the numbing pain. I shared it with him. He became part of my way to...heal.

I had gone from helpless to the situation to Marcus being the only one whose touch I could bear. Sharing that night, my pain, made him become part of it. Where my condition overtook my mind and body, he held my soul.

When we were both spent from the continuous deprivation of air, he wrapped me in a towel and carried me back to the guesthouse. The sway of his slow walk lulled me to sleep. I rested my cheek against his shoulder, and he hummed contently. The surrealness of this, us, was still hard to comprehend.

It was too good to be true. To be permanent.

SITTING behind my desk Friday afternoon, I get ready to pack up. With it being my birthday weekend, Lilly made me promise not to work.

A knock on the door draws my attention away from the task at hand, and a squeal erupts in my throat. I can't get out of my chair fast enough. Rounding the desk, I almost catch my foot on my purse but manage to sidestep it at the last minute.

I plow into the male body, and a sudden wave of emotion makes my eyes water. I hold on as tight as possible, fear of him vanishing overpowering my senses.

His arms wind around me, holding me just as tight. After a moment, he tries to draw back, but I tense my muscles, locking him in place. "Not yet."

"I missed you, too, D." Wes's voice is like a soothing blanket.

Finally regaining control, I pull back, holding on to his arms. "What are you doing here?" A tear escapes my eye.

My best friend pulls his mouth into his usual crooked grin. "What kind of best friend would I be if I missed your birthday?"

I press my lips together, but it's of no use. A sob bubbles up, turning into a half laugh, half cry.

"Hey." Wes wraps his arms back around me. "Why are you crying?"

"Who are you, and why is Denielle in tears?" a stern voice comes from behind, and I glance around Wes at Jenn. She doesn't have a weapon on him, probably assuming that he is safe due to the hugging, but she has become oddly attuned with my emotional state and knows when I so much as hiccup.

Wes steps to my side and slants his head. "The question is, who are you?"

Jenn's eyes narrow, and I insert myself into the standoff. "Jenn, this is Wes, my best friend. He lives in Montana with his wife and daughter. Wes, this is Jenn. She's, uh...my babysitter."

Jenn snorts at her job description. "The infamous Weston Sheats." She appreciatively scans him up and down, and I narrow my eyes. Noticing my territorial behavior, Jenn shakes her head. "Are you ready to head out soon?"

"Yes, would you mind if I drove with Wes?" I turn to him. "If you have a car here?"

His features take on boyish excitement. "I borrowed the R8."

"Oh jeez." Noticing Jenn already rubbing her palms together, I point a finger at her. "Not happening. Forget it."

She purses her lips in a pout. "You're no fun, Keller."

"You will not race back to the house."

"Huh?" Wes glances between both of us, and I pat his forearm.

"You'll see."

Not truly satisfied, Wes nods and waits for me to finish packing up.

Closing my laptop, I notice him typing on his phone. "Is King here, too?"

"Yes, she's at the house with Haddie. She wanted to come, but Haddie has been...challenging lately. She wasn't having it."

"Threenager?" I repeat the phrase King had used at one point, and Wes huffs.

"Understatement, D. If this is a preview of her teenage years,

I'm moving in with Kiwi and Zeke. Maybe Marcus can take over some parental duties, being the godfather and all." He strokes his chin, and a pang hits my chest. I've never considered Marcus as a father, but I've seen him with Haddie. He adores the little girl.

"What's with the face?" Wes's question snaps me out of it.

A blush stains my cheeks. "Nothing," I answer too fast, and Wes's brows shoot up. "A lot has changed in the past few weeks," I explain pathetically.

"Define *a lot*?" He leans against the wall next to the door, hands in his front pockets and feet crossed at the ankles.

"I'll tell you when we're back at the house."

And I figure out where to start.

THANKFULLY, Wes was too preoccupied with driving Rhys's little toy to continue the interrogation.

Jenn pulls up in front while Wes heads straight to the garage. I laugh as we enter the house. He didn't want to exit the car and kept stroking the steering wheel.

"Why don't you get one? You can afford it."

"Because it's completely impractical for where we—"

"HADDIE MONROE SHEATS, I SWEAR TO— Bax, please take your goddaughter while Mommy takes a time-out," King's raised voice interrupts Wes, and we both stop in our tracks.

Uh-oh.

"Fuck!" Wes whisper-shouts to himself. "If she takes a time-out, that means it's bad, and she separates herself from the situation."

I curl my lips under, rubbing Wes between the shoulder blades.

We make our way into the kitchen, where Marcus stands with Haddie sitting on the counter. "Nugget, that was uncalled for." His head turns toward us, and his stern expression changes. "Hey, baby. How was work?"

Wes goes rigid beside me, his gaze slowly swiveling from Marcus and his daughter to me. His stare bores into me, and I fight the urge to cringe.

"Baby?" His jaw works back and forth, and I swear I hear his teeth grinding.

I peer over at Marcus, whose amused expression does nothing to help the situation. "I told you a lot has changed," I murmur, staring at my Louboutins.

Ignoring me, he turns toward Haddie. "What happened?"

The little girl crosses her arms over her chest. "Mommy was mean." The serious expression on her face makes it hard not to laugh.

The two men also seem to struggle, because it takes a moment before Wes asks his daughter, "And why is that?" He walks over, picking her up.

"She said I can't have a granola bar." The pout on her lips is Oscar-worthy.

"Well, did she say why?"

I'm truly impressed with how my friend handles the situation.

"I already had two." Her meek admission is too much, and I cover my mouth with my palm, meeting Marcus's eyes over Wes's head.

"I'd say that's a good reason. It's almost dinnertime, remem—"

"NO!" Haddie narrows her eyes.

"Ooookay, Nugget. Why don't you and I look for Ethan? I'm sure he is here somewhere. You haven't met his friend who's staying with us yet." Marcus takes Haddie from Wes.

"Marcus," I hiss, widening my eyes at him. Taking a three-year-old to meet a cleaner as a distraction? Really?

"She'll be fine. You know she loves Ethan."

"Jenn?" I clarify with brows arched.

Her voice interrupts any further objection to his plan. "Someone call my name? Sorry, I was on the phone with— Oh, we have another guest. And who are you?" She beams at Haddie.

Haddie cocks her head at the newcomer. "Nugget, this is Ethan's friend, Jenn. Let's have her help us find Ethan. Your dad and Denielle have a few things to discuss." He throws me a glance over his shoulder, and I want to punch him.

The three disappear from the room, and Wes slowly swivels toward me. His face is expressionless, and I inhale until my lungs are filled to max capacity. Letting the air out, I point toward the breakfast nook we've had so many serious conversations in over the years. "Talk?"

Wes jerks his chin up and down, walks over, and drops into the seat.

BEFORE I CAN START my confession, King reappears and slides in next to Wes. Once he explains where their offspring is, she leans into him. "She is pushing my buttons today."

He places a kiss on her temple. "Let Uncle Bax handle it for a while. It seems there is a lot we've missed since leaving California."

The strain in my chest intensifies. His snide tone is not lost on me, and as much as I want to flip him off, I deserve the attitude.

I open my mouth, but King interrupts, "Marcus filled me in on a few...things earlier this week." When she sees my bulging eyes, she amends quickly, "Not everything. And only because I threatened him to withhold Haddie."

Wes peers down at his wife. "And you didn't think to give me a heads-up why?"

"The same reason Marcus didn't elaborate on anything concerning Denielle. It wasn't my place. Den is your best friend. Marcus is mine." She looks back at me. "Not that you're not my friend—"

I wave her off. "I know what you mean." I stretch my hand across the table, and she takes it.

With my fingers interlaced with King's, I start my confession with the secret I hid from my friends for over a decade. To say Wes and King are shocked is an understatement, but the disappointment reflected in Wes's eyes is the worst. My heart shrivels, and I word vomit the rest.

We sit in silence when Marcus and Rhys appear with the kids and announce that it's time for dinner. I'm grateful for the distraction but am fully aware that this is not the end of the conversation.

Unfortunately (or fortunately for me), Wes and King are busy with Haddie after we clean up the kitchen, and I take the cowardly way out, sneaking off to the guesthouse. I need a break from the topic.

My birthday starts with waking up to Marcus nestled against my back. His hands slide into my sleep shorts, applying the slightest pressure to my clit. He is insatiable. But so am I.

"Good morning to you, too," I breathe, suppressing the moan that wants to break free.

"Happy birthday, *Keller*." He bites down on the skin under my ear. Not nipping, he sinks his teeth in, then soothes the pain with his tongue.

Waves of pleasure travel down my back, and I press my ass against his hard cock. "Is this my birthday present?" I turn my head to see his face.

His nose trails along my cheek. "One of them."

"One?" I laugh, raising my brows. "Are they all orgasms?"

His lips find mine. "Who says I'll let you come?"

I turn in his embrace, forcing him to adjust his hold. My fingers slip under the waistband of his briefs, curling them into his butt, and reciprocate his teeth with my nails. "I do."

And I do get my first present, straddling Marcus's hips, not soon after.

LILLY AND KING have prepared a feast for breakfast. When Marcus and I enter the kitchen, his arm around my shoulders, both exchange looks.

"What?" I stop short, forcing Marcus to halt half behind me.

"Nothing." Both quip in unison, and I narrow my eyes at my best friend and my other best friend's wife.

"Stop scowling, or you'll need Botox before you're thirty," Lilly retorts, and I stick my tongue out at her. Carrying over a plateful of pancakes, she says, "You look happy. That's all."

Warmth spreads through me, and I lean into Marcus. "I am." I tilt my head to meet his eyes. He bends down, placing a kiss on my lips.

"Can I have my birthday hug now, or do I have to give Marcus an extra assignment for him to let go of you?" Lilly mock pouts.

I step away from Marcus and walk into my friend's arms.

"Happy birthday, D." She places a kiss on my cheek.

"Thanks, babe."

"My turn." King hip checks Lilly out of the way and places a kiss on my other cheek. "Happy birthday." Leaning in, she whispers, "And thank you for making Bax happy." A little louder, she adds, "He hasn't scowled once since I've been here," and winks over my shoulder.

During breakfast, Lilly reveals the plan for today. She went all out.

"We have a girls' night at The Club. I'm picking Elle and Hazel up after dinner, and we'll meet you and King in the usual lounge."

I glance over to Rhys and Wes. King wraps her arm around her husband. "The guys are on babysitting duty tonight."

"Not all of us," Rhys grumbles, side-eyeing Marcus.

"Marcus is working. Stop pouting," Lilly chastises. "Plus, Marcus will be outside of the suite. No men allowed."

Marcus's head whips up, ready to protest.

"Jenn will be with us. You and Ethan will be outside the door. Nothing will happen." Her smug expression falters when Marcus glowers at her.

AFTER LOUNGING by the pool all day with everyone, I'm getting ready in my bathroom. I didn't bring the makeup needed for a night at *The Club* to the guesthouse, which is why Marcus is now hovering behind me with a perma-scowl grooved between his brows.

"I would feel better if Ethan was in your car." Marcus has me caged between his arms as he watches me apply my mascara.

"You guys are Lilly's security," I say, switching the wand from one eye to the other. "Jenn is armed to the teeth. No one will get past her." I blink a few times before reaching for my lash brush. "Plus, there have been no new deliveries or vandalism. You'll be right behind us."

Marcus steps closer, wrapping his arms around my waist. "How can you be so at ease about this?" He studies me in the mirror.

My excitement to toast and dance the night away with my friends vanishes. "I'm not at ease. I'm worried. We don't know who is behind this. It feels too much like what happened with Lilly, but..." I place my hands on top of his. "Things have changed. *I* have changed. Because of you."

"I don't like it."

I turn in his embrace and lift my hand to smooth out the crease between his brows. "Everything will be fine."

CHAPTER THIRTY

MARCUS

"They're not here." Lilly halts in her tracks. She hovers in the door to her suite and peers over at Elle. "I texted them forty minutes ago. D said they already left."

I have my phone pressed against my ear before she finishes the sentence. With every ring, my chest constricts more.

Why isn't she answering?

"Maybe they got held up in traffic?" Hazel supplies *un*helpfully.

I should've never let her drive alone.

"Have J activate the tracker in the BMW," I bark, not taking my eyes off her name still lit up on my screen. My thumb hovers, trembling above the red button. I can't cut the connection, despite knowing, deep down, that no one will answer.

It takes a whole inhale and exaggerated exhale before I press my finger down. I watch the skin around my nail turn white, not easing up the pressure. I can't allow my mind to go where my thoughts are headed.

Lilly stands in the middle of the room, chewing on her

bottom lip. Worry shines in her eyes, and my stomach drops. I'm not overly paranoid. She feels it, too.

Pulling up the app that supplies us with the property's security feed, I select the garage camera. The spot for Rhys's sedan is empty.

Before I can check the time they left, Ethan provides the answer I don't want to hear. "They left the house forty-six minutes ago."

I raise my head, meeting his eyes. "Tracker is loading."

We stand in the VIP lounge, bass vibrating the floor beneath us. I watch Ethan for his reaction as he listens to J on the other end. The second the skin across his knuckles stretches, I have my confirmation. My worst nightmare has come to life. *Again.*

His eyes are on the far wall, and he stops breathing. In slow motion, his eyes shift to mine, and instinctively, I want to crouch and put my head between my palms. Instead, I pull my shoulders back, locking my body in place.

Lilly's tiny hand slips into mine, and I jump. Fixated on E, I didn't notice her approach.

She squeezes my fingers, addressing Ethan. "Where is the car?"

"Second and Alberts. Has been there for the last twenty minutes." His dark expression mirrors the black void slowly taking over my mind.

My pulse beats violently as I pivot and pull Lilly with me. I don't give a fuck if the rest follow, but Lilly is my responsibility, and I won't leave her, even for the woman I—

I already have the Escalade in drive, Lilly in the seat behind me, when Ethan climbs into the passenger side. Elle and Hazel slide in the back, neither bothering with the third row.

I peel out of the lot.

"It's me," Lilly's voice fills the interior of the car. "Where is Wes?"

Rhys's question reverberates through the cabin. "We just put the girls down. What's up?" She put him on speaker.

"Wes?" Lilly hesitantly addresses their friend.

There is rustling in the background. "I'm here. What's up, Lil?"

"Um, have you heard from King since they left?" We know the answer, yet a sliver of hope in me wants to believe that this is all a bad dream.

The silence on the other end is like a knife plunging into my gut, twisting to inflict the most damage.

"No. Why?" His tone is low.

"They're not at The Club." Lilly inhales. "J said the BMW has been at the same intersection for twenty minutes," she supplies carefully.

"What intersection?" Wes's agitation spikes my own adrenaline.

"We're already on the way," I insert. Taking charge distracts me from the flickering images assaulting my mind's eye: Ken lying in the road, Denielle submerged in her bathtub.

No one speaks as I navigate the SUV through the streets.

"What?" Rhys suddenly exclaims.

My gaze jerks to Lilly in the rearview mirror, finding her focus trained on the screen.

"Dude, spit it out. You're scaring me," Rhys shouts, and the girls in the back seat wince at the outburst. Everyone is on the verge of hysterics, with Lilly's husband about to cross the line.

"King is pregnant," Wes announces in an oddly robotic tone.

Ethan whips around in his seat, and I watch Lilly's free hand fly to her mouth. My jaw locks. This just got way more serious.

"We're almost the—" I turn onto Second Avenue, and the word gets lodged in my throat.

"Oh no," Elle breathes out.

"Fuck," Ethan curses.

"What's going on? Calla, talk to me," Rhys demands. "It's okay, man. Everything is fine," he calms his friend. "Calla, tell me that everyone is okay."

I hit the brakes right behind one of the cruisers, its flashing lights still on. I dive out of my seat before Ethan can reach for the handle.

My ankle rolls as I trip over a curb, looking for someone with answers, yet I don't feel anything. My pulse pumps terror through my veins. The BMW is a mangled hunk of metal. The entire passenger side is pushed in, as if it has been T-boned by a semi. The airbags are out and deflated. Some of them show tears.

They cut the nylon to get to the passengers.

"HEY!" I yell at one of the cops, who turns and is most likely going to tell me to get lost until his eyes land on Lilly. She's on my heels, and we face off with the man. She is a known individual for many reasons, and clearly, the guy recognizes her.

My lips part, but she beats me to it.

"What happened here?" Everything slows down as we wait for his reply. She puts her hand on my forearm—her signal to let her do the talking.

My airways are too tight, my temper wearing thin. Lilly has slipped into her other persona, the one she uses when dealing with public matters or her board members. I pride myself on my control, the ability to do my job under any circumstance. Falling for Denielle was not something I ever expected, let alone handling her being taken from me like Ken. No, not like Ken. Denielle is not dead. She can't be.

"Mrs. McGuire. We, uh...we just ran the license plate." He's visibly confused about how we got here so fast.

"This is my husband's car," she states calmly, her fingers warming my skin where she holds on to me. "He was not driving it, though. A friend borrowed it tonight."

"Calla, what the fuck is going on?" Rhys's faraway voice draws everyone's attention to the phone in Lilly's hand.

She ignores her husband and hands the device to Ethan, who materializes out of nowhere. He disconnects the speaker and stalks away.

The cop peers over at one of the firefighters. "There were no direct witnesses. However, we got a call from someone walking their dog a block away. The caller reported that he witnessed three individuals being taken from the car and loaded into the vehicle that had run into them."

Subconsciously, I wonder if he should be telling us this.

Who cares? The more we know, the faster we get them back.

Lilly's nails dig into my skin, yet, scanning her features, she appears unaffected and composed. She nods. "I will have the car towed to our garage."

"Ma'am. You cannot—"

"She holds up a finger. My attorney will be in touch to file whatever is necessary for us to take my husband's car." She turns to me. "May I use your phone to call Jax?"

My actions are on autopilot. Reaching into my back pocket, I surrender not just my phone to my employer but also myself.

She starts delegating like the leader she has become over the last few years.

Standing next to her, I follow everyone's moves like a movie. My thumping pulse drowns out my surroundings, and I struggle to focus on what's in front of me. Peering toward the curb, Ken materializes, lying in a pool of blood. I watch myself kneeling beside her, unable to touch my little sister's contorted form. Cold sweat breaks out over my forehead, and I swallow over the needles in my throat. Static in my ears accompanies the simmering bile.

Just when I'm about to bend at the waist to vomit all over the accident scene, Ethan joins us. "Rhys and Wes want an update. I kept it as vague as possible, but Wes is a mess."

The thundering in my ears quiets, allowing me to make out their exchange.

For the first time, emotion flitters across Lilly's face. "They cannot come here. Whatever you say, do not let them leave the property. They can't see the scene."

Ethan cocks his head, and Lilly explains, "This is almost identical to when I *left*."

She never uses the word *kidnapped*.

Ethan nods. "Do you want me to take Elle and Hazel back to the house?"

I throw a glance over my shoulder. The two girls are watching from a distance.

"We're leaving as soon as Jax arrives. He can handle the rest and ensure the BMW gets delivered to the garage," Lilly declares. "There is nothing we can do here."

As soon as Jax takes over, Ethan steers me to the Escalade. If I'd had to stare at the totaled car much longer, I would've lost it.

Lilly pulls me into the back seat beside her, never letting go of our interlaced hands.

She strokes her thumb back and forth, quieting the voice in my head that accuses me of being at fault for this. Logically, I know that my absence didn't cause the accident. It would've happened no matter what. Whoever is after Denielle has made their move. Not being in the BMW enables me to hunt them down and kill them one by one.

Rhys and Wes wait for us in the garage. Wes has his arms wrapped around his midsection, not looking away from the floor. He only untangles himself to catch Lilly, who races straight into his embrace. Rhys clamps his hand on his friend's shoulder, looking at me with hollowed cheeks.

"We'll get her back," she reassures her friend, then turns to me. "All of them."

I dip my chin, unable to speak. Meeting Wes's eyes, I see my anguish reflected in his.

"What am I going to tell Hadd—?" his tone cracks.

"We'll cross that bridge when we get to it." Elle walks up to them and takes Wes's hand. She leads the way into the house. Lilly remains in the garage, addressing her husband. "I need to call Nate."

"I already tried. He's not answering. Neither is G," Rhys whispers.

Lilly slants her lips. "Okay. That's fine. It's fine. We don't need them. It would've been easier, but...we can manage without him." Lilly rubs her temples. "I'll be upstairs." She walks past Rhys into the house.

Rhys holds my gaze for a moment longer. "You go with her. I'll stay with Wes."

LILLY SITS BEHIND HER DESK, two keyboards in front of her, and every monitor is lit up. At that moment, she resembles her brother to a T.

I mutely position myself against the wall behind her. The adrenaline rush has left me drained, making the thumping beat of my heart feel like a strenuous exercise. I refuse to let myself rest. I may not be able to do much until we have a location and bodies to eliminate, but until that happens, I will be in this room.

The continuous rhythm of slow inhales and exhales is the only calm I allow my body to have. Watching her type gives me a sense of peace—the knowledge that she's looking for Denielle, King, and Jenn. Occasional curses are followed by more typing.

She *accesses* the CCTV feed in the area, but that particular intersection is not monitored. The ambush was not far from *The Club*. Everything points toward it being meticulously planned. The surrounding area contains a lot of converted warehouses and not many residential properties. It's pretty much dead at night. It was a miracle that someone had seen the accident at all. Searching through the screens is like digging for a needle in a haystack.

A few hours in, Rhys shows up with a cup of Earl Grey. Lilly receives it gratefully. She's been yawning nonstop for the past thirty minutes.

"How is Wes?" My voice is hoarse despite not having used it.

Rhys leans against the desk next to his wife and folds his

arms. "He's with Haddie. He said to call him when we find anything."

When. Not if.

It makes sense that he would try to find comfort or distraction with his daughter. My breath comes in coarse spurts. I would do the same if I could. But I don't have anyone to lean on. The only person I'd want with me is the one that was taken. I swallow rapidly as I return to my original position. Rhys pulls up a chair and joins Lilly while I peer over their shoulders.

WE'VE BEEN SCANNING traffic cameras for six hours when Wes bursts into the room. His face is flushed yet pale. His forehead glistens with a sheen of sweat. "It's King." He's extending a shaking hand, and my eyes drop to the rectangular object.

I push away from the wall, but Lilly snatches the phone before I can rip it out of his hand.

"Are you okay?" the question explodes out of her mouth. She stands stock-still as she listens, and I strain my ears. Why isn't she putting King on speaker? Suddenly, Lilly's free hand flies to her mouth. "Are you sure?" Her eyes gloss over, and she whispers, "What about Jenn?" No one in the room dares to breathe as we wait. "Okay. Ethan is on his way."

She heads out of the office without a backward glance.

What the—?

We race after her, and with every step, my pulse thunders in my ears. I want to demand to know what the fuck is going on, but Lilly rounds another corner before I can formulate the words.

The three of us trail her to the first floor. Elle is asleep on the couch in one of the living rooms, with Ethan next to her in the armchair. He is on his phone, but his head snaps up at the sound of our footsteps. Lilly gestures for him to follow, and he stands in a fluid motion.

She doesn't stop until she's in front of the door to the garage.

Pivoting toward Ethan, she explains, "They released King. I just sent the address to your phone. She's waiting for you inside a twenty-four-hour gas station."

The hallway begins to tilt, and I press my palm against the nearest wall to steady myself.

"What about Jenn?" Ethan studies Lilly's face.

In all of this, I didn't consider his relationship with Jenn. She is missing, too. She is his sister, for all intents and purposes.

"King never saw her." Her monotone voice sends chills down my spine. *How can she be this...disconnected?*

"I'm going with him." Wes blows past me, but Lilly plants a hand on his chest.

"No."

"What do you mean, no? She's my fucking wife." Wes tries to sidestep Lilly, but Ethan blocks his way. Adrenaline chases my thumping heartbeat, and my attention shifts between everyone in the hallway. None of this makes sense.

"If Lilly says no, the answer is no." Ethan lets a mask slip into place that I've only heard of. I recognize the person he used to be—before he started working for George.

Wes wants to argue, and Rhys side-eyes me. Even though he knows as much as the rest of us, he's ready to hold his best friend back if necessary. He trusts Lilly implicitly.

Wes's shoulders slump. He gives up. "How far is this place?"

"About an hour from here. King will call you as soon as she's with Ethan. She is safe, but we're not risking anyone else. He's the one best equipped for this. And you need to be here in case Haddie wakes up."

Lilly's cryptic answers are getting on my nerves. Before I can order him to take me, Ethan pushes through the door, and a moment later, we hear the motor of the Escalade come to life.

"You're really expecting us to sit here for the next two hours? What are you not telling me?" Wes flicks his eyes at me. "Us," he amends. He has come to the same conclusion.

"King will explain. I don't have all the facts. I..." She seeks out her husband. "I'm going to sit with Audrey while we wait."

My legs threaten to give out. She's not going to continue to look for Denielle. Lilly is rattled to the core. I watch her head toward the stairs with one arm across her chest and the other covering her mouth.

I REMAIN rooted in the hallway as Wes goes back to Haddie. Rhys trails after Lilly, and I am...alone. Elle and Hazel are asleep —not that I would've sought either of them out.

On autopilot, I climb the stairs to the second floor and find myself in front of Denielle's door. My thrashing heartbeat has slowed to an almost alarming pace. Is this normal? I should be pissed at Lilly, worried for Denielle, relieved that King is on her way home. I'm waiting to feel something. Anything. But all I do is stare at the barrier separating me from the room Denielle has called home since moving to LA. Entering feels wrong and right at the same time. I twist the knob, letting the door swing inward. Her bed is made because she spent the last few nights in the guesthouse with me. Stepping inside, I quietly close the door. Part of me wants to lie down on her bed and press my nose into one of her pillows. Another part of me has an entirely different urge. I put one foot in front of the other until my shins meet the claw-foot tub. I stare at the white porcelain surface. Reaching down, I turn the little wheel. The water rushes from the faucet and immediately begins to rise. I press the plug down. Pulling my fingers from the water, I study the tiny droplets running down my fingers and falling onto the floor.

I don't think, just follow what my body directs me to do. Stripping out of my clothes, I stand only in my briefs in Denielle's bathroom. The harsh light from the vanity is too bright. I lean over and flip the switch, the illumination from the bedroom enough. I'm doused in darkness—in more ways than one. The space behind my ribs shrinks.

Where are you, baby?

Stepping into the tub, the water nearly sloshes over the rim. I turn the faucet off and sit down. My wet underwear instantly clings to my frame. The tub isn't large enough to hold Denielle, let alone me. The memory of how I found Denielle four days ago forms. I lift my feet and prop them on the far edge. Wrapping my fingers around the edges on either side, I slide as far forward as necessary for me to lean my entire upper body back. I hold my breath as the water slowly closes over me. Blinking my eyes open, I stare at the blurry darkness above. Relaxing, the water weighs me down. Denielle had described every sensation to me in detail. I wanted to learn it all. What went on in her head when she let the water pull her down into its depths. How it felt when every cell of her body was deprived of oxygen. How it numbed her mind from the thoughts overpowering her control. She never hesitated once. She told me everything.

That night...I fell in love with Denielle Keller.

CHAPTER THIRTY-ONE

DENIELLE

I HURT—EVERYWHERE.

I'm trying to lift my head, but pain assaults my skull. *Owwww.* I squeeze my lids together, waiting for the cutting agony to subside. My neck is stiff, and when I finally manage to move, a crack between my vertebrae sends a fresh wave of torment through my nervous system. The sensation of someone continuously stabbing an icepick in both ears simultaneously causes me to groan.

I attempt to lift my hand to rub my temple, but—*what the?* I tug. My pulse speeds up, the pain momentarily forgotten. *No, no, no.* I can't move. My wrists are restrained. Every muscle in my body tenses. Taking stock, my breath accelerates to the point of my lungs burning. It's a sensation I've chased too many times in my life, but today, at this moment, it's not caused by my own doing. Several thin straps bite into my wrists and forearms, forcing me to remain motionless on a cool, smooth surface. My arms are bare and— Didn't I wear my blazer when I left the house with—King. Oh, my—King. And Jenn. Jenn was driving. Where are they? I struggle to open my eyes, but...it's of no use.

I'm trapped in the dark. Where the hell am I? A whimper escapes my lips, and I slash my mouth.

The ache from my lungs spreads through every cell of my body, and I strain against whatever holds me in place. The new trauma doesn't register until warmth trickles down my exposed flesh. I broke skin. Blood slowly seeps across my arm and drips onto my legs. Panic overtakes my mind. My legs are bare as well. Someone took my clothes. I'm tied up and...naked? No, not completely. My chest and...privates are covered. I can taste the bile as tears prick at my eyes.

I can no longer contain the sobs. Marcus's face flashes against the black curtain like a mirage.

Everything will be fine.

Nothing is fucking fine. What the fuck happened?

I rack my brain, but sorting through my memories feels like wading through neck-deep mud. Everything is dark and murky, every step causing me not just physical but emotional agony.

WE MET IN THE GARAGE.

I SQUEEZE my eyes shut in the hopes of it easing the ice picks— it doesn't. The stabbing just shifts from the sides to the front, like the point is being shoved up my nose into my brain.

MARCUS KISSED ME GOODBYE. *He got behind the wheel of the Escalade.*

THE ICE PICK TWISTS.

. . .

ETHAN BRUSHED PAST ME. *"Looking good, Den. See you in a few."* He *went to the passenger side, redirecting Marcus's attention as he said something I couldn't hear.*

POUNDING in my ears numbs out the puncturing of my brain matter.

LILLY HUGGED *me and headed to the door behind Marcus. "I'll text you when we leave the hangar. From there it should only take us about thirty minutes to get to The Club. Just head out whenever. They know you're coming." Lilly stood with one foot inside the back seat, her arm propped on the door.*

I met Marcus's eyes through the windshield, my chest squeezing.

MY HEAD DROPS FORWARD, my spine no longer able to support it. The weight pulls me down, my body sinking in the mud I just sifted through. Marcus's face begins to dissolve. I want to reach out, make him stay.

Don't leave me.

He's gone.

I JERK AWAKE, unsure what catapulted me out of the pain-free void.

"Oh god," I groan as bile pushes its way up my throat. A bitter taste settles on my tongue, and I swallow against my better judgment. My throat feels like I've ingested a chain of barbed wire that's now lodged in my esophagus. I gag, but the cutting sensation only gets worse, resulting in a retching cough.

"Oh, goody!" Footsteps come closer. "You're awake."

My head is forced back by the hair, and the excruciating sting in my scalp drives me to cry out. "Ahhhh!"

My pulse thrashes through my veins. I try to clamp my mouth shut and not scream again, but the angle of my head doesn't allow it.

"Let's not be overdramatic, Denielle." The tension on my strands eases the slightest bit.

The voice is too loud. Too close to my ear. Too chipper.

Why does the voice sound so familiar?

I attempt to twist my head, but I get wrenched back and whimper.

I try once more to peel my lids back, but it's like they're glued shut. My lashes stick to each other. "C-an't s-ee," I choke on the words.

"Oh, I know." Something scratchy swipes at my cheek, no doubt leaving marks on my skin. I try to draw away, but *The Voice* still has my hair in her hold. "The blood from your head wound ran all over your face. It's quite gross. I had to have them cut off your clothes to make sure there were no other wounds."

Them?

The relief of apparently not being injured anywhere else is doused by The Voice's next words. "I can't have you die of injuries I didn't cause." A giggle follows the declaration, and I freeze. My heart rate resembles the speed of a hummingbird's wings.

What?

All the pain is pushed into the background, and I tear on the restraints anew. I need to get out of here.

"Stop that! I just cleaned the floor from your last tantrum."

I can't, though. My body has taken over of its own accord. I want out. Scream. For King, Jenn, anyone. Where are my friends? My rapid inhales are chased by even faster exhales, yet no air reaches its target. Can you see black spots in front of a curtain of blindness? The answer is yes. The dark fuzzies simply turn white as my starved lungs demand relief.

The Voice yanks my hair back, and my head follows the motion. A crack echoes in the room, and I sob.

"I. Said. Stop." My head gets thrown in the opposite direction, and it slumps forward. Tears run down my face, cleaning the blood obscuring my vision.

My glued lashes peel apart, and light hits my retinas for the first time since I lost sight of Marcus in my memory. It's too bright, and I squeeze my eyes shut. It takes me several tries before I can tolerate the glare. We're in a warehouse-style room. The overhead lights reflect against the white walls and polished concrete. There is nothing in here besides me and... I turn in the direction of the voice.

My eyes are still sensitive to the commercial lights, and I focus on the ground. Shoes are the first thing that comes into view—black wedge pumps strapped to the ankle of slender, tan legs. I follow the legs to the hem of a black, skintight dress. Raising my eyes further, feminine curves are emphasized by a wide Gucci belt. Despite my brain fog, the designer labels register. Following the lines of the cream seam in the center of the material, I finally reach the face of the speaker.

My eyes widen, and my heart comes to a halt before it takes off, racing a mile a minute. "Em?" my voice cracks, and another wave of coughing racks spasms of pain through me.

How is this—? Why would she—?

Em waves me off with a Tinkerbell laugh. "I know, this must be a surprise. We'll do full introductions soon. We have to wait for King to wake up first."

King? I can't breathe. My chest feels like someone put a hundred-pound weight on it.

"Whe—?" *Where is my friend?*

"Over there, silly." She dips her head to my left, her glossy curls bouncing with the motion. "You should assess your surroundings in a hostile situation."

Hostile situation? What the hell is this? She uses terms like a soldier yet talks like this is a cocktail party. My skin suddenly feels too hot. It doesn't make sense. I'm freezing. They took my clothes. Nothing is as it should be. I should be with Marcus, celebrating my birthday with my friends. My gaze flicks to her shoes. Why am I looking at her shoes? I force my attention back to Em's face. Her cheery tone doesn't match...anything. Her lips are pursed as if she is waiting for something. *Oh.* I carefully turn my head in the direction *my client* indicated, the throbbing in my head preventing me from moving as fast as I want.

Next to me, a little set back, King is strapped to a similar chair. Her head is slumped forward, her eyes closed. The only difference is that she is still fully dressed. The only thing missing is her jacket.

Having read my mind, Em explains, "King sat on the other side of the car during the impact. She didn't have any visible injuries."

Impact. Injuries. I taste the words on my tongue, let them settle. Suddenly, the missing pieces appear like camera flashes in front of my mind's eye.

THE CLUB WAS JUST a few blocks away. We drove Rhys's BMW.

King sat behind Jenn. I was in the passenger seat.

We halted at a stop sign, Jenn and King bickering over the music. Jenn took her foot off the brake, and we rolled into the intersection where...headlights shot at us from the right.

"LET'S WAKE HER UP." Em snaps her fingers, and a guy appears from behind us. Fear settles in my stomach and metastasizes like a slow, infectious disease through my body. I bite the inside of my cheek to prevent myself from making a sound. He's huge, tattoos snaking out of the top of his black tee, up his neck, and over his shaved skull. He glances in my direction dismissively, and I notice the ink extending to half his face. He catches me staring, and his lips peel back, revealing a row of silver teeth. His impassive stare turns to a leer, promising me things I never want to think about. It takes every ounce of control not to avert my gaze. What is he going to do to King?

He handles her with equal roughness as Em treated me, bending her head back and holding something under her nose.

"Watch it, Cal!" Em snarls, and he...*gentles?*...his hands on my friend.

Confusion mingles with the terror rushing through my veins.

"Sorry, boss." His deep voice contradicts his dismissive apology.

King's eyes snap open, and she bucks against her restraint. Her eyes fly around wildly. She takes in her position, then sweeps her surroundings. Her eyes land on me, and we stare at each other. I want to apologize to her, but the biting in the back of my throat chokes the words. King continues her scan of our surroundings until she finds Em. She visibly pales, and her mouth opens and closes several times. "Rae?"

She breathes the name I've only heard King and Wes use on a few rare occasions. Rae. Rachel. King's sister.

My gaze jumps from my friend to our captor. "Rae? But—" I block out the effort it takes me to speak. She introduced herself as *Em* at La Déesse. The edges of my vision become blurry, and I have to close my eyes to regain my focus.

Rae/Em snaps her fingers again, and Tattoo Guy rolls a cream-colored leather desk chair over. She lowers herself with the same elegance I saw when she came for her fitting. "Technically, you're both wrong." She crosses one knee over the other and leans back, resting her manicured fingers on the armrests.

"What the fuck is going on here? Rae, what the—?" King tugs on her restraint, making her chair jump forward. "Cut me loose."

If she's afraid, she doesn't show it.

I try to remember the few facts I know about King's sister. Rachel is ten years older. She abandoned King when she was eleven, leaving her and their mother to fend for themselves—more than they already were. Stephanie Monroe had worked multiple jobs for years until she was diagnosed with cancer, and King was forced to sell her dignity at *The Pole* to help pay her mother's hospital bills. King's father had been out of the picture long before Rae took off.

"I can't do that Roe-Roe." The reply is calm, almost affectionate. "You were not supposed to be with *her*," Em...Rae sneers, pointing a manicured finger in my direction.

Wha—? I was her intended target? The scene in front of me slows. Why? What did I ever—

"And Jennifer Davis?" King's sister glowers at me. "How will I explain to Marshall what happened to his beloved daughter?" The previous warmth directed at King is snuffed out when her eyes are trained on me. *Happened to his...* Did she kill—"You didn't make this easy, did you?" Rae's eyes narrow.

This? What is this? I want to yell at her. The room begins to lean, and I feel like I'm experiencing the worst case of vertigo.

"You said your name was Em," I whisper—my only way to get the words out.

Her expression morphs again, this time to the person I met at La Déesse. "It is, but not *Em*. It is M, as in the letter *M*." She rolls her eyes, exaggerating the mmm sound.

"What the hell are you talking about?" King's voice has become less furious, and a crease forms between her brows. She still doesn't seem afraid. I'm not sure if this is a good or bad development.

"I guess you never heard my full name from your mommy, did you?" She swivels the chair toward King. "My name is *Mara* Rachel Turner," she elaborates, waiting for us to catch on.

Mara?

"Mara?" King repeats slowly.

"Think, Roe-Roe," Em, Rae...*fuck*, Mara continues to address King with her childhood nickname—the only one still using it these days is Kiwi.

I'm getting nauseated.

"Please tell me you didn't believe your whole life that I was your biological sister? Stephanie was only six years older than me. You're smarter than that." Mara's warmth mingles with condescension.

King has gone pale at the mention of her mother, but eventually, she whispers, "I knew."

"And what exactly is that?" Mara cocks her head at her sister. Half sister? I swallow the sickening feeling down. I guess it makes sense, seeing them together, but I never thought about their age difference in combination with King's mother. But I also never knew her exact age, just that she was much younger than King's father.

"I knew they adopte—" King begins, but Mara cackles a manic laugh.

"Adopted? They didn't adopt me," she spits the word at King, spins, and jerks out of her chair. She suddenly holds something between both hands. Where did—? It's a knife. And not just any knife. The same one King used to carry everywhere: a CRKT Du Hoc.

Mara has the hilt in one hand and the point poking into her forefinger of the other. She whirls around, stabbing the chair with the curved blade before she peers at King across her shoulder. "My father was R.J. Turner, Kingsley."

King's eyes widen, mimicking my own shock. More bits of information I'd heard over the years catapult to the forefront.

Of course I'd heard of R.J. Turner. He was King's dead criminal uncle. He started as a small-town drug dealer before expanding his operation to more lucrative ways to make money. He used Gray, his little brother and King's father, as one of his distributors while getting him hooked as an insurance policy— until Gray killed him.

Does that make them....?

Before I can put things in order, Mara drops the blade and starts pacing in front of us, her heels clicking against the concrete. "Daddy always had a temper, you know? Everyone feared him." She pauses, examining her manicure with a diabolical smirk. Dropping her hand, she props her fists on her hips. "So, one day, the mood struck him to have some fun"—she puts air quotes around the word—"with his little brother's girl crush."

She looks pointedly at King before continuing her track in front of us. "Which resulted in..." She stops abruptly, pirouettes, and waves at herself. "Moi."

She taps her finger to her chin. "Unfortunately, said girl had some issues." Mara holds up a finger. "She was only a teenager herself." Finger number two goes up. "She grew up with a violently drunk father that beat her on the regular." Finger number three joins the first two. "And getting raped by her friend's brother doesn't result in a healthy mental state. Ergo, she wasn't able to care for her baby."

Dropping her hand, she starts moving again. "The baby ended up in a foster home—multiple, actually—but that's not important." She waves us off as if we are catching up with a long-lost friend.

All I can do is stare. The pain I woke up to is momentarily forgotten.

How is this real?

"A few years later, the girl found herself a nice, boring husband. Clueless schmuck." Mara clucks her tongue. "She hid her damaged past from him, suppressed the urges that fought to break free." Mara swirls her finger next to her head.

The spots in my vision are back.

"So..." Mara looks at King as she continues our *conversation*. "One day, she tracked down her daughter and convinced your father—her childhood friend who didn't protect her from his brother—to take her daughter in. The baby was his niece, after all. Gray always did her bidding, no matter how much he loved Stephanie." She shakes her head. "Anyway, Gray convinced Stephanie to raise his niece alongside their one-year-old daughter. Stephanie really was a pushover." Mara purses her lips, propping her hands on her sides.

I peer at King for the first time. Her face is flushed, and her mouth is pressed so tightly I can barely make out the red. She's fighting against her better judgment of letting Mara finish her story.

"What's with the talking in third person?" King lost the fight.

"I tell my life's story the way I want to tell it, sis," Mara snaps.

"According to your little trip down memory lane, it's *cuz*," King challenges.

"Touché." She smiles genuinely.

This woman is as unstable as...

"Wait." The missing link finally forms. "If R.J. Turner is your father," I state, and Mara turns to me, brows raised. "The *girl* you're talking about...the one he raped..." All the air gets sucked out of my lungs. "Your mother is Emily Sumner," I breathe the name.

"Ohhh, look at your deductive skills. You are not so dense after all." Mara regards me proudly.

Emily Sumner. Birth name: Emily Kaczmarek. "That makes you..." I can't bring myself to say it.

"I'm your bestie's big sister, yes!" She steeples her hands under her chin.

Mara Rachel Turner is Lilly's half sister and King's cousin. Dread knots my stomach.

How is this possible? Why has no one ever found the connection?

"Emily couldn't take care of me herself without revealing the remnants of her damage to her husband. Plus, she was dealing with *the burden* of another baby." She trains her attention on King. "So, I became your big sister instead."

"Did Uncle Ronnie—?"

"He knew about me, but he didn't care much. I was a nuisance. A hindrance in expanding his business. Which is why his untimely demise didn't faze me. Actually, it worked in my favor."

"What do you mean?"

I follow their *chat* with fascination, ignoring the tingling warning in my chest.

"His second took over and kept the chair warm for me until I was ready to take over what was mine. The Turner territory belonged to me. I was the rightful heir." Mara pokes her chest. "After leaving you, I stayed with Emily for a few months until we decided I was more useful in the States."

"But his original team took over after Uncle Ronnie...died."

My throat aches, watching King trying to piece together what part of her life has been another lie.

"Until your father killed him. Say it, King." When King doesn't respond, Mara sighs dramatically. "You were too preoccupied with your daddy resurfacing. Plus, he couldn't really tell you that I was running the show, could he?" She rolls her eyes. "Your father was in my debt. He had nowhere to go after the shitstorm he caused earlier that year. He was lucky I didn't kill him on the spot. He took my last living parent. Having him at my beck and call made it easy to keep an eye on him—and you."

"You were the jobs he mentioned?" King's eyes gloss over, betrayal shining in them.

"I kept him busy, yes. But then you got cozy with Weston Sheats. Why, Roe-Roe? He's not that—"

"LEAVE MY HUSBAND OUT OF THIS!" King roars, pulling forward. "Fuck." She winces, and my insides coil at the sight. The restraints are stronger than her fury, slicing into her forearms. Blood trickles from under the plastic and drips onto the floor.

"Kingsley," Mara chastises. Turning to her goon standing against the wall, she orders, "Bring me something to clean that up. And some bandages."

Her tattooed gopher jerks his chin robotically and tracks out of sight.

Tears stream down King's cheeks. I am the intended victim of this, and she is the one in pain—physical and emotional.

"Why did you stay with Mom and me? You and Mom never got along." King hiccups. She wants closure for things that happened years ago.

"Because of you, Roe-Roe." Mara kneels in front of King, placing her hands on King's thighs and rubbing them. "I love you. You are my family. I always saw you as my little sister, even when we were not blood sisters. But you had Kiwi. You were going to be okay. It was my time to be with my other family."

Mara swipes the tears away from under King's eyes. My friend leans away from the touch but, at the same time, lets the woman she had believed to be her (adopted) sister comfort her.

Tattoo Guy returns with a full medical kit and begins to treat King's wounds. Cutting one cable tie at a time, he sets to work. When the cut is cleaned and bandaged, he puts a new restraint in place.

"Cal is also our medic. You are lucky he is here and not one of the other guys. They don't know a Band-Aid from sandpaper." Mara smiles fondly at her *sister*.

Adrenaline courses through every cell of my body. "What are you going to do with us?" I lift my chin and speak for the first time. My throat feels better, though I would kill for a glass of water.

Mara trains her eyes on me. "My sister is going home as soon as we're done with Jennifer. You, on the other hand..."

"What did you do with Jenn?" King demands.

"Nothing. Yet. One of my guys has some business to settle with one of her brothers, so I let him have at it." Mara puckers her lips.

"When did you get so cold?" King inquires, resigned.

"I was born this way." She steps closer, stroking King's cheek. "The difference is, I love you, little *sister*. You are the exception. You and, by extension, your family, even if your husband is friends with the person who prevented me from having the life I deserved."

"What do you mean?" Confusion mars King's features.

"If Emily hadn't gotten pregnant with Lilly, I would've been able to be with my mother."

She blamed Lilly for not growing up with her mother. Not that Emily would constitute a mother to Lilly either. She hadn't been around since Lilly was six years old, only ever caring about Lilly's biological father's money.

"Lilly didn't take Emily from you. You got to be with her."

"As an adult, Kingsley," she snaps. "And even after that, Emily's focus was always on my brat of a sister. She had your father check on her, who in return checked on you. I was left with my dead father's *legacy*." She gestures wildly around herself.

"You could've left this life behind any day," King argues.

The familiarity between the two allows King to talk back, but Mara's temper is wearing thin. Her facade slowly cracks. "What do you know?"

"What do I know? I was a fucking stripper before I finished high school. Do you have any idea how many times we got our electricity shut off? Or ran out of food? Do you think my childhood was all sunshine and roses?"

"Lilly will pay for everything."

She's deranged.

"What do you mean?" King peers over at me.

"I can't get to my little sister, thanks to her *Shadow* and constant surveillance. So, I'm taking the next best thing." Mara looks over at me, her dead eyes sending chills down my spine. "But don't worry"—she turns to King and smiles—"you won't witness any of it."

King's brows draw together, but I read between the lines. King will be leaving here alive. I will not.

Mara focuses on me. "You followed the plan like a puppet. It was too easy."

My newfound realization shifts reality. I should be afraid, scream, fight. Anything. There is nothing. My next words sound monotone. "Too easy?"

"Who do you think sent the escort your dimwitted fiancé

hooked up with? Repeatedly." She snorts. "The man is hornier than a teenager discovering the function of his dick for the first time. He might want to have that diagnosed."

"You..." I can't form the words. Where is the hurt, the betrayal one should feel in a situation like this?

"All me," she beams and bows to me with a wave of her hand. "I put the plan together the day you became engaged to Collin Liberman. He didn't question anything as long as we supplied him with enough coke and pussy. And Gianna had him wrapped around her naked body from day one. We had to time it right, though, so we didn't expose him too soon."

Expose?

"The STD." This time, there is a physical reaction. Vomit coats my tongue. More pieces fall into place. "You drugged me." I have too much saliva in my mouth. "You sent the flowers."

Mara was behind all of it.

"And the scarf," she says proudly. "That part I didn't see coming. While I knew about your little issue—your ex-fiancé talks a lot when he's high—Charlie York's role couldn't have been planned more perfectly. Gianna followed Collin to LA, and we gave him a little treat the day after you had your public melt-down. He handed the scarf over without question. When you left on your little lunch date, I went back, pretending to need to use the bathroom. You had left your water bottle on your desk. I knew you would drink it eventually. Collin whined about your meticulously calculated water intake each day. You did a number on this dude."

A memory of taking a few sips from my reusable bottle flashes in front of me. I had forgotten about it until now.

"The photo?" I want answers.

"That was a little harder to procure. I had to pay a good chunk of money for that. Nice touch, wasn't it?"

"Why? Why did you torture me like this if you're just going to kill me for revenge?"

"For fun, Denielle. What else?" She reveals her perfect white teeth.

"Rae, you don't have to do—"

"Cal, please bring my sister to the room I prepared for her. Once H.T. is done, have him take her somewhere where she can find her way home. He knows what to do." She talks over her head and dismisses her sister.

Cal tilts King's chair back and drags her out of the room by the back. I hear King's shouts and curses alongside metal scraping against concrete until a heavy clang separates us.

I'm alone in the room with the woman who wants to use me as payback against her biological half sister.

CHAPTER THIRTY-TWO

DENIELLE

I HAVE NO IDEA HOW LONG MARA HAS BEEN GONE.

After Tattoo Guy—Cal—dragged King out, Mara just stared. A slow smile turned the corners of her mouth, but it wasn't so much a smile as a promise—a dark and painful promise. The shaky quiver in my chest turned to thundering terror. For the second time since waking up, I felt truly afraid. The affection she showed King was gone. In its place was...nothing. The lack of emotion was worse than if she'd openly hated me for my friendship with her sister.

Her sister. I couldn't wrap my head around it. Lilly had a half sister.

Suddenly, Mara looked toward the door. "I'm hungry." The casual lightness was a testament to the soulless evil inside of her. Peering back at me, she amended, "We'll continue our *chat* later." With that, she stalked out of the room. The clicking of her heels against the polished concrete faded with every step until there was no sound at all.

A shiver rolled along my arms and legs, and I watched the tiny bumps rise and then disappear. I was alone. Letting my eyes close, I pictured Marcus, the way he studied me when I woke up and he had already been watching me for God knew how long. It should have been creepy, observing someone while they were the most vulnerable. Instead, I felt safe.

You need to know your environment, baby. Find a weak spot.

I squeeze my lids together. All I want is for the void to pull me under so I can be with Marcus a little longer. But his hallucination is right. I need to know where I am. So, I force myself to scan my surroundings. Cataloging every detail is the distraction I need to slow my heartbeat to a bearable rhythm.

This place must have been a warehouse at one point, but it's been remodeled, painted, and cleaned up. The white walls and polished white floor make it appear almost sterile. What does Mara do here?

The large windows farther down the long room begin to brighten. The sun is coming up. We left the house at eight last night, which means I've been gone for ten-ish hours. Automatically, my eyes begin to droop, and I struggle to stay alert. With my slowing pulse, the adrenaline rush has also smoothed to a tranquil stream. Exhaustion quickly seeps through every cell. Falling asleep is a bad idea. Not just for my safety. The throbbing in my head is also concerning.

I wiggle my arms against the cable ties, not applying too much pressure after seeing how deep King's cuts were. There is no way I can get out of this on my own. Every time I feel myself slipping into unconsciousness, I apply more pressure to my broken skin, forcing my pain receptors to fire up. Cold sweat pools in my pores while every cell of my body is a blazing inferno. I clamp my teeth and turn my wrist ever so slightly, slicing into the open wound. The pain forces me to grind my teeth to not cry out. But it's the only way to stay awake.

A pool of blood has collected on my legs and the floor when the telltale sound of Mara's heels alerts me of her return. My spine tenses, and I hold myself still.

"Where have you been?" *Click, click, click.* "You made sure she is safe?" *Click, click.* "She'll be fine. My sister is resilient." *Click, click, click, click.* "Kingsley is more my sister than the little bitch ever will be," she snarls, and I suspect whoever spoke said something Mara didn't like.

Mara comes into view, her phone no longer to her ear and the Birkin bag she had carried at La Déesse hooked in the crook of her elbow.

"Good morning, Denielle." Her eyes drop to the crimson stains below my chair. "Oh, you already started without me. How rude."

Wha—?

"I've been looking forward to this for weeks." She huffs, then waves me off. "Oh well, I'll just make it more painful."

Swallowing, a thousand needles puncture my throat. I attempt to get rid of the excessive amount of saliva in my mouth, but the slicing sensation causes me to retch.

What is she talking about?

Mara puts her purse on the chair she sat in last night, ignoring the damage she did to it with the knife. She unclasps the locks and pulls the top apart. Reaching in, she pulls out a folded leather case.

I gag again. *What the hell is that?*

She strokes the worn *skin* affectionately, and panic runs down my spine. I find myself watching her. Her movements morph to slow motion. My mind is playing tricks on me. The case is held together by a long leather strap. As she unravels it, she begins to hum to herself. The sound snaps time back to a normal speed again. She places the unfolded object on the chair next to her purse, which costs more than a small car. Something reflects the overhead light, and I squint.

Identifying the tools in front of me, my body begins to tremble. Please, no. *No, no, no.* Inside are different-sized scalpels and other instruments I can't name but recognize that they have no business outside an operating room.

Mara steps back and tips her fore and middle finger to her

chin. Flicking her eyes at me, she scans my body, then reaches for one of the smaller objects in the case.

I press my tongue to the roof of my mouth as I watch her pull out a thin scalpel. Mara regards it in the light before putting it back in and pulling out something else.

Oh, god.

She pivots in my direction, holding the scissor-looking instrument up. They're not scissors, though, more like...spreaders. "You shouldn't have done that," she chastises. "Now I have to work with what you started."

My eyes burn, and a fuzzy frame takes shape around Mara's form. *No, no, no.*

"Let's see." She steps closer, scanning my bloody arms. "Are you a lefty or a righty?"

"What?" I croak. I can't take my eyes off her torture instrument. I'm going to be sick.

"Actually, it doesn't matter. You won't be using either hand much longer."

She turns away, and I want to sigh in relief at the delay, but then she spins, and I notice she also grabbed the scalpel she put back earlier.

My heart thrashes in my chest, the increase in speed not gradual, but as if someone simply flipped a switch. I start pulling on the restraints, throwing my body back and forth, causing the chair to almost topple over. Mara steps closer, and my stomach rolls.

"Stop moving. You're just making it harder on yourself." She clucks her tongue. Her hand shoots out, and her fingers curl around my hair near my forehead. She leans in until we're nose to nose. Her warm breath fans over my mouth, and I can taste the coffee she drank. "You either stop moving, or I will start carving the skin of your pretty face first."

First?

I whimper as she releases me with a flick of her wrist, and

the force makes my head snap back. My breath comes in bursts, and my lungs begin to cramp.

As if watching from the outside, I follow as Mara lines up the scalpel with the middle restraint. I brace myself for the cut, but then the pressure on the tie falls away. I blink and see that she has cut the plastic. The brief relief is replaced with the worst possible horror when she sticks her fingers through the holes of the *not-scissors*, opening and closing the clasps in the front. She steps parallel to the chair, and all I can do is watch. I've lost all control over my body. My brain commands me to fight, to scream, to do anything but sit there. My muscles won't obey. They have locked up and won't budge. My thrashing pulse is the only conscious sensation left. I can see it rippling through my veins under my skin.

Mara's manicured fingers wrap around my wrist as she lines the spreader up with the cut. My heart thunders against my ribs, and a new sheet of sweat forms over the dried layer coating my forehead. She slowly lowers the instrument to my self-inflicted wound. As soon as the cool metal connects with the torn flesh, my brain short-circuits. Pain receptors explode all over my body, not just where Mara is starting her torture. She digs the edges deeper into the cut, and I can no longer hold back the agonizing scream.

"Ahhhhh!" My voice doesn't sound like my own, not having used it in hours because of the soreness in my throat.

Tears stream down my face as she twists the instrument first, then proceeds to use them for the intended procedure. She spreads the skin apart, locking the clamp in place. Scream after scream bursts from my lungs as she does the same on my other arm. Halfway through it, I bend over and begin to retch. I haven't eaten since dinner last night, so my stomach holds nothing I could throw up. A sour taste fills my mouth between crying and gagging.

Mara says something, but the rushing in my ears makes it impossible to understand. A palm impacts my cheek, my head flinging to the side. I have nothing left. I can't lift my gaze to hers.

Muted shouts register in my mind. "I asked you how you were, you little cunt."

Another slap. This time, my head lolls in the other direction. "You are no fun."

My last conscious thought is wondering if she just stomped her foot.

THE NUMBING void begins to lift, and I want to sob for being thrust back into my torture chamber.

Unmoving, I strain my ears. My spine feels about to snap from being in this contorted state for however long I was out. When there's no sound, I slowly blink. The floor comes into view first, dried blood staining the white and making it look pink where the glossy surface shines through.

What a pretty color.

Pretty? I've lost my mind. This is my blood. I lift my head enough to see that no one is near me—at least, not in the front.

My stomach rolls, and my mouth is too dry. At the same time, I can't bring myself to worry about dehydration. I let the weight of my neck fall forward again. My spine cracks, but its pain is less than the strain of keeping my head upright. With my eyes still open, I notice that the spreaders are gone, and the two wounds are halfheartedly taped up.

Probably to stop me from bleeding out slowly.

Too soon, the sound of footsteps registers, and I hold my breath, making the familiar burn spread through me. Never in my life did I want to die. Not once. Even when I pushed myself to the limits underwater, refusing to resurface. I don't know how much I can endure, though.

Her heels come into view, and she taps her foot. "I know you're awake. I saw you move on the camera."

A wretched snort escapes me. *Surveillance really runs in Lilly's family*. With the little rational thinking I have left, I'm aware of how ridiculous this epiphany is.

"I thought I'd let you choose what we play with next," Mara chirps. Fingers touch under my chin and lift it. I want to rip out of her grasp, but her nails dig into my jaw, and I have no strength left. When my eyes land on hers, the comprehension that I will die at her hands slams into me. My parched lips begin to tremble, and a crease forms between her brows.

"Can't you fight a little more? I see your resignation. How pathetic are you?" she huffs and drops my chin.

Her feet disappear from my vision, and I hear the umph sound of the chair when she drops herself into it. "I guess we'll wait until you regain some energy. I've been looking forward to this for years."

I peer up and see her pulling out her cell phone. She scrolls and types, scrolls some more. Occasionally, she comments with, "Oh, that's nice."

Is she...shopping?

Time has no meaning anymore. I could've been listening to her for five minutes or hours when a new voice fills the room. "Mara Turner."

Surprise makes my head snap up, and I see Mara stare at something behind me with shock. Someone. She looks...afraid?

Who is there?

I can't turn my head. I used my last bit of strength to lift it forward. Slow steps come closer, calculated and confident.

"You know who I am?" the male voice asks.

"Yes." The woman who threatened to carve my face off has gone pale, and my adrenaline level rises slow but steady.

Do I need to be afraid?

"Good." The voice stops beside me. In my peripheral vision, I see him pivot. He crouches down with his forearms propped on his knees. Tilting his head, he scrutinizes me. "Did you do this to her?" He doesn't look at Mara but continues to study me with a disturbing type of interest.

The newcomer is young. Probably a few years younger than me. He has the face of an angel and the eyes of a demon. Where Mara is cold, he is...dead. There is nothing, no empathy for what he found in this room, yet I know he is not here to harm me. Mara on the other hand...

He holds out a hand, palm up. When Mara doesn't move, he cocks his head. "I'm not asking again."

He didn't ask anything.

Mara reaches behind her and picks up the scalpel.

Oh, god, no.

I whimper as the angel of death takes the sharp instrument from her. I squeeze my eyes shut, but instead of more pain, my restraints fall away. The clang of metal against the concrete tells me he dropped the scalpel. He leans close to my ear. "My sister will take care of you shortly."

I suck in a breath.

Sister?

With those words, he stands back up and addresses Mara. "You have a one-minute head start."

That's all. But apparently, it is all Mara needs, because she takes off to where he came from. He doesn't speak as his eyes are trained on his wristwatch—a similar one to Marcus's. Marcus. Will I see him again?

"Paycen, did you let her run?" Jenn's exasperated voice fills my ears. Jenn! I want to turn, to see her, but the jerked movement results in me toppling off the chair. Right before I would've impacted with the ground, arms wrap around me and brace my fall. I look up at the man, Paycen's emotionless eyes.

"Fuck," Jenn exclaims. "Good catch, little brother."

Paycen lowers me to the floor, the cold surface like ice against my naked skin. Jenn sinks to her knees beside me. "I'm here now. You're safe." She pulls me into her lap, and I curl into her embrace. An emotional tidal wave crashes down on me, and I can't hold back any longer. Sobs rack through my body, shaking both of us as Jenn hugs me tightly.

I hear her exchange a few words with her brother, and then it's only the two of us. Jenn holds me with one arm while she types on a cell phone she procured from somewhere. She lifts the device to her ear, and I listen to her speak. With every word, the reality that I will get out of here etches itself into my mind. I'm going to live.

"It's me." Someone on the other end shouts. "T, shut up," Jenn barks. A little softer, she says, "I'm fine. Thank you for sending him." She listens. "Nothing I couldn't handle." Her expression tells me she's lying to whoever is on the other end. "I need you to send me a package. Medium size is sufficient." Pause. "Thanks. Then call Ethan. Tell him I have Denielle and that she..." Jenn peers down. "She's alive and will be okay. I also need a medic." The voice on the other end says something. "Paycen gave Mara a head start." There is quiet on both sides before *T* speaks again. Jenn chuckles. "Let him play. It'll keep him busy, and we know she'll get what she deserves." Pause. "Love you, too. I'll call you tonight."

Jenn drops the phone and strokes my cheek with her knuckles. "I'm so sorry, Denielle. I didn't do my job." I laugh at the ridiculousness of her statement. Her face is blue, her lip is split, and her right eye is so swollen you can't see her lashes.

"Who did this to you?" I rasp.

"Someone who will soon be no more. Don't worry your pretty head about that. We need to clean you up before Marcus sees you." She glances at my arms. "May I take a look?"

No. I nod, and Jenn gently peels one of the bandages back. Her wince tells me it's not pretty, but as soon as her eyes find mine, she composes herself. "It'll heal," she states with confidence.

"How did your...Paycen find us?" I whisper as she continues to stroke my caked hair.

She smiles softly. "My family is very paranoid. I talk to my brothers every day. Usually T, since he's my twin, but when he's on a job, we check in with the others. I missed my morning call."

"But how did he know where—" I start coughing and can't finish my question.

She smirks. "Let's say Mara's little friend didn't do his job well enough. She lifts my hand gently and places two fingers on a spot behind her left ear. There is a tiny little bump under her skin, and when her eyes meet mine, she explains, "It's a tracker. We all have one."

"All?"

"My brothers and me. Marshall usually doesn't bother checking where we're at unless we miss an assignment. He put them into place after Ethan left. It's a precaution as well as a safety measure."

I process what she just revealed to me. And I thought my father was controlling.

The phone dings next to us, and Jenn picks it up. "Ethan and Marcus are on their way."

At the sound of Marcus's name, fresh tears gather in my eyes. I cling to Jenn as I drift off from exhaustion. The soothing motion of her fingers against my hair is my last memory.

I JOLT awake as I transfer from one set of arms to another. It only takes me a second to relax my coiled muscles. I would recognize these arms anywhere. The flutter in my chest welcomes *his* embrace.

"Hey," I breathe, not yet ready to leave the dark comfort of my closed lids.

"Hi, baby," Marcus's voice cracks as his knuckles caress my jaw.

I lift my chin to give him better access. It takes Herculean effort, but as his warmth sinks into my bones, the ice that ate itself through my body melts. A tired smile forms on my lips. *Home.*

"Bax?" Jenn keeps her voice low, probably assuming I'm asleep again. He must've given her his attention because she continues. "My medic will be here in twenty. He'll take care of her wounds."

Marcus stiffens, his hold tensing for a fraction of a second. I'm fisting his sweater, loosening my grip lightly and letting my thumb glide back and forth across his stomach.

I'm okay. Now that you're here.

"Thanks," his reply rumbles against my ear.

"We probably shouldn't take her to a hospital unless you want to answer a lot of questions. Make law enforcement look for Mara's..." Jenn trails off.

Mara. At the name, I curl deeper into Marcus's chest.

Marcus mimics the signal I just gave him. *You're safe.* "You will take care of her?"

Her as in Mara, not her as in *me*.

"Paycen's already got her. No one escapes him. He just likes to play with his toys before he disassembles them." I hear a cold smile in her tone. Disassemble. Something tells me Mara met a fate worse than what she had in store for me.

I can't bring myself to care.

CHAPTER THIRTY-THREE

MARCUS

A knock on the door woke me, and I jerked to a sitting position. Disoriented, I dug the heels of my hands into my eyes.

Wha—?

Denielle. The accident. Denielle was missing.

Images of last night tore across the backs of my covered lids, appearing and disappearing like a slide show. Dropping my hands, I blinked. I was in Denielle's bedroom. Sluggish thoughts of, *I didn't turn the light off*, and, *I'm thirsty*, mingled with the slowly lifting fog.

Sleep had eventually pulled me under. My little experiment in the bathtub did what I'd hoped. And more. I had felt a connection to Denielle, as ridiculous as it seemed. It had exerted me. After drying off, I had put my pants and shirt back on, foregoing my drenched briefs, and lay down on top of her comforter.

That was where I was when Rhys opened the door. He scanned the room, settling on me. He looked like death warmed over—probably hadn't gotten much rest either. "I figured I'd find you here," he stated solemnly. "Ethan just pulled through the gate."

My parched throat and mouth became even drier. King was home. Safe. I was happy. I loved her, but the nagging thought of, *Why had King been released and not Denielle?* made my stomach churn. I nodded and swung my legs off the mattress.

"Any *other* news?" The meaning in my rasped question was clear.

"Not yet."

I couldn't make eye contact. "I'll be right down."

Rhys disappeared from the gap and left the door ajar. I rubbed my palms across my face one more time. King was safe. She was home. This was good. I would not let the relief and elation be overshadowed by resentment and despair. King was my best friend.

But Denielle is the woman you love.

Before I could go down the rabbit hole, I set my feet on the floor and stood. Not bothering with shoes, I padded downstairs and reached the kitchen the moment Wes led King through the door from the garage.

Lilly and Rhys stood to the side, watching their friend guide his wife down the hallway. Ethan trailed them slowly, his face a closed-off mask. My heart sat in the pit of my stomach as I was rooted in place. I was unable to take my eyes off King's face. Half was shadowed with a massive bruise, but other than that, she seemed fine.

Was Denielle uninjured? Where had she been in the car when the impact happened?

King slowly lifted her gaze. As soon as she found me, her lips began to tremble. She stepped away from Wes, and I met her halfway.

"I'm so sorry, Bax." She clung to me, sobs shaking her small frame.

Everything slowed. *Sorry?* What was she saying?

"I didn't want to leave her. She didn't give me a choice," King mumbled between cries, and dizziness made me sway.

She?

"Who is *she*, princess?" Wes had placed a hand between her shoulder blades.

King turned in my embrace and looked at Wes, then at Lilly. "Rae...I mean, Mara."

Who the fuck is Mara?

"Your sister?" Wes exclaimed in shock. His tone was too loud, and my shoulders pulled up.

Her gaze flicked to him before returning to Lilly. "Not my sister. Lilly's."

Lilly's face drained of color, and Rhys's eyes jumped between his wife, King, Wes, and me.

It was clear that we had a lot to talk about.

WE HAD RECONVENED to the living room, fatigue fast taking over everyone.

Thank fuck Laurin had already arrived at the house to keep the kids entertained and oblivious. Audrey was less of a worry than Haddie. My goddaughter was smart and would pick up in no time that something was off.

For the moment, both girls were still asleep, which allowed us to talk uninterrupted. Elle and Hazel had joined us, and we were spread across the various couches when King recalled what happened over the last few hours.

Wes had pulled King into his side. With her legs draped across his, he held on like a lifeline—a need I could understand too well. I dropped into one of the armchairs, unable to bear anyone's closeness. I needed space—to distance myself to function. I concentrated on my breathing as I listened to King, always making sure my inhales matched my exhales.

Lilly sat next to Rhys, her thumb flicking against her fingers while their friend spoke. Her gaze was trained on something on the ground. She was paying attention, but at the same time, she was far away. Given her shoulders' rapid rise and fall, I had a suspicion where. Rhys's arm was around her waist, and his other hand gripped her thigh. His white knuckles were an obvious indicator that he had trouble handling this.

Ethan positioned himself next to the door—wide stance and arms behind his back. He didn't lean against the wall. He stood straight, his chin tipped up and his eyes unfocused. This was not the Ethan I worked with. It was like he was thrust back into a life he so desperately wanted to leave behind.

WHEN KING FINISHED, Lilly blinked, and her eyes found her friend's. "Emily mentioned Mara once. But I never..." She let the sentence hang, pressing her lips into a thin line before whispering, "I have a sister."

Everyone's life in this room was somehow connected, webbed in ways no one could've foreseen. The coincidence of King ending up with Wes, of all people, formed a link that allowed us to find a pattern that would've remained hidden otherwise.

"You didn't see Jenn," Ethan inquires. It was more a statement than a question. While he was present physically, his mind had put up a barrier between himself and us.

"No, I'm sorry."

My pulse stuttered at her apology, and I leaned forward, resting my elbows on my knees. Before I could say what was on my tongue, Elle reasoned, "None of this has anything to do with you. Mara targeted Denielle because she is a psychotic sociopath and had no other way to get to Lilly."

King bobbed her head, but guilt was eating her up that she was home and Denielle and Jenn weren't.

We sat in silence until Lilly excused herself. She wanted to research her sister's name and speak to her brother. If someone could help track Mara Turner down, it was Nate. I was just hoping whatever had been keeping him unavailable lately would not prevent him from being there for her today.

King went to shower, not wanting Haddie to see her in

yesterday's clothes, and Wes trailed after her. It would take him a long time to move past this.

I SPENT the next few hours in Lilly's office. Again.

Staying busy was the only way to keep my shred of sanity. Lilly's brother was as shocked as everyone else and immediately set to digging into Mara's past. This was his specialty, while Lilly, Rhys, and I pulled out file after file she compiled years ago, hoping for a hint toward Mara's whereabouts. Who she could be.

There was nothing.

Nate confirmed that Mara Turner didn't exist past her twenty-first birthday. She vanished the day she left King. And even before, there was nothing but superficial facts. A yearbook photo posted on her school's website. A handful of old social media posts she had been tagged in. Mara's profile had long been deactivated, but the internet didn't forget. And who would've looked into a name no one knew or remembered existed? She had no reason to wipe those few traces. The alias she used at La Déesse also was a dead end. M. Jones returned a million results, none of them remotely resembling Mara.

R.J. Turner's drug empire continued to operate after he was killed, but with the key players gone, we had nowhere to start.

At one point, Ethan settled into a chair in front of Lilly's desk. He mutinously observed as Lilly grew more and more frustrated. The lack of...concern made the hair at the nape of my neck stand. He was no longer my friend or subordinate. He had shut himself off.

With every blank wall, blind alley, name it what you want, my throat constricted until it felt like a noose cutting off my airways.

Rhys eventually left to give Laurin a break and spend time with Audrey.

"I'm going to find her," Lilly mumbled as her husband gave her a kiss. She refused to stop or leave her office.

I admired her determination, but even I had to admit that our chances were dwindling.

My stomach growled, and turning my wrist, I wasn't surprised to find that it was almost noon.

Maybe I should go get something to—

"What the—?" My head jerked up at Ethan's voice. He sat up, gaping at his phone. His gaze shifted to mine. "It's T."

Theo Davis?

"Answer," I barked. *What is he waiting for?*

Ethan lifted the device to his ear. "T?"

I stared at his face, waiting for some type of reaction. Why was Jenn's brother calling him, if not to...

Ethan's eyes grew wide. "Why the fuck didn't you—?" His free hand curled inward as T snapped something on the other end. Ethan bared his teeth at a man who wasn't in the room. "We could've already been there."

My spine stiffened. What did he say?

"That's bullshit, T. Just becau—" He pulled the phone away. "Fuck!"

I waited for him to explain what was going on, but Ethan shot to his feet. "We gotta go."

My heart skipped a beat before thundering in my chest.

"What?" Lilly stood with her palms flat on her desk.

"Go where?" Confusion mixed with irritation.

"I know where they arc."

WALKING INTO THE WAREHOUSE, I had one singular goal. I ignored my surroundings and aimed for the location Ethan had received from Jenn's twin.

On the way, Ethan had explained how they found Jenn and that he had no idea about Marshall Davis's new measures to secure his assets—that was all his children apparently were. Ethan assured me he would've contacted *his brothers* if he'd known. I didn't reply, battling between the numbness and terror of what I would find.

I hadn't *felt* in so long. My body didn't know how to process the time period since finding the VIP lounge empty. Denielle was alone with Mara for eight hours after King was dropped off. From what King divulged to us, Mara was as unstable as her birth mother. Deep down, I was sure she didn't tell us everything —not to keep secrets, but to protect us. *Me.*

There were multiple rooms on the first level but only one on the second. Bursting through the door at the top of the stairs, I immediately spotted the two huddled forms.

My stomach twisted, dread and relief fighting with equal strength for dominance.

Denielle's pale skin blended in with the white floor. She was in the boy shorts she had put on last night and the black tank top I *ordered* her to wear. The taste of bile slithered across my tongue.

Where the hell are her clothes?

Her eyes were closed, Jenn cradling her in her lap.

The Cleaner's head snapped up as the soles of my feet pounded against the concrete. When my shoes reached the dried blood, I couldn't move. There was so much blood. Too much.

"Marcus," Jenn whispered, and my eyes snapped to hers. "She'll be fine." She nodded her chin to Denielle and indicated for me to take over. "She needs you."

I kneeled next to the woman I needed more than air. Jenn shifted her carefully to my arms, and Denielle stirred instantly. A smile tugged on her lips. "Hey."

JENN BRINGS us a blanket and informs me that Ethan is checking the rest of the building. It appeared empty when we arrived— her little brother most likely the reason. No one voluntarily remained in reach of *The Coldblood*. He had earned the name with his reputation.

With the blanket and my arms around her, Denielle's breathing has evened out, and I watch her rest. Jenn takes position in the corner near the door, giving us space and typing on the phone Paycen had left her.

"My medic is about to pull up. You should move her downstairs. There are several bedrooms," Jenn announces just loud enough for me to hear.

Bedrooms? What is this place?

Just as we hit the stairs, Ethan comes into view. "You will not believe what I found." He looks at me, but Jenn answers.

"Spit it out. We don't have much time. My package will be here with the medic."

"Liberman."

"Excuse me?" My steps falter, and I pivot with Denielle in my arms. I peer down at her, finding her focus on me.

Ethan shakes his head, the crooked smirk we know from him back. "He's all coked out with some chick in one of the bedrooms. Smells like he hasn't left that room since he went missing last week."

My brows shoot up.

"Mara kept him locked away until her plan was completed. She probably would've blamed it on him in the end," Jenn deadpans.

I automatically scan Denielle's features and have to clench my jaw to not growl at her to watch her mouth. How she can be so caring and kind one moment and stone cold without remorse or emotion the next is disturbing.

"We'll have the medic drop Liberman at the nearest hospital and call his mommy." Jenn smirks. "Let's have her deal with him."

"What if he talks?" Ethan questions Jenn's decision.

"If Mara kept him as drugged up as I'm assuming, he either

won't remember, or no one will believe him. We'll drop his whore off with him. It'll solidify his *un*believability."

While they formulate their plan of action, I carry Denielle the rest of the way downstairs.

The place is outfitted with multiple bedrooms containing a twin bed, chair, and dresser.

Not more than a minute after I lower Denielle on the mattress, a man in an EMT outfit strides in. Jenn's medic is an actual paramedic with his own ambulance. How far do the Davis connections reach?

"My name is Josh," he says as if we're doing introductions at a dinner party.

"Marcus Baxter," I reply stiffly.

Josh gives me a curt smile and sets his bag next to the bed on the floor. Hesitantly, I take a step back and let him get to work. When he pulls out a syringe, my hand clamps down on his shoulder. He glances at me, unaffected. "This will take some of the pain away and keep her calm. I need to clean and stitch her cuts up."

"Marcus," Denielle whispers hoarsely, and I scan her tired face. "It's fine. Jenn trusts him."

I want to agree with her, but worry clogs my throat. For the remainder of Josh doing his job, I lean against the far wall, arms crossed over my chest and my fingers wrapped around my biceps. When Denielle winces and squeezes her eyes shut, I'm ready to rip Josh's head off, but my brave girlfriend just shakes her head. "I'm okay."

Girlfriend. There is no doubt in my mind that she is just that and will be more one day.

Jenn flits in and out of the room to check on us. At one point, she pulls me into the hallway, informing me that she'll stay back to clean up. The warehouse belongs to someone who Airbnb's it to criminals needing a place in LA. That's all she would reveal.

Her ensuring to erase all traces of what happened here tells me this is a player she doesn't want to piss off or mess with. I don't care as long as Denielle and I leave as soon as we can.

TWO HOURS LATER, we're in the back seat of the Escalade with Ethan in the front. Denielle is nestled under my arm. Her hair is still a tangled mess, but her face and wounds are cleaned up. Once the blood was washed off and the small head wound cleaned, all that was left was the bruise from where Mara hit her. I made Jenn swear Paycen would seek the appropriate punishment for that.

"I let Lilly know we're on the way," Ethan declares as he pulls out of the warehouse gates.

"Is Lilly okay?" Denielle peers up at me. Of course her concern is for her friend, not for what she endured because of her friendship with Lilly.

"She's confused and upset, but mostly she's worried about you," I tell her, interlacing my fingers with hers in my lap.

"I still can't believe that Mara is...*was?*"—she scans my face —"her sister."

I ignore the unspoken question. Whatever happens to Mara or has already happened is nothing I will lose sleep over. She doesn't deserve anyone's empathy, least of all Denielle's or Lilly's.

"You and Lilly will help each other heal. You are her sister. Blood doesn't define family."

Denielle curls farther into me, her eyes drooping. "You're right. Let's go home."

I place a kiss on her head. "Home."

EPILOGUE

DENIELLE

Two weeks later

I wake up to the incessant buzzing of my phone on the nightstand.

"Baby, if you don't turn that off, your phone will learn to fly—or better, swim." Marcus's groggy threat is muffled by a pillow. Marcus was on third shift and didn't get to bed until an hour and a half ago.

I chuckle. A flutter in my stomach replaces the emptiness trying to pull me under every time I leave the blissful void of sleep. Each morning since leaving the warehouse, it takes me several breaths to remember that the nightmare is over. I am safe.

Everything is healing nicely. Between Lilly's physician and Jenn's *medic,* who keeps checking on me daily, I am cared for better than in a hospital.

It also helps that Marcus waits on me hand and foot. Two

days after returning home, he announced that I would no longer live in my room in the main house. Marcus was permanently moved into the guesthouse, and a few hours later, he, Ethan, and Rhys had carried my belongings across the lawn as well—not that I was objecting. Waking up next to Marcus every day has become my new addiction.

Despite what happened, I hadn't had one episode—not when the doctor asked me questions to better assess my injuries, and not when Jenn came to the property last week.

I WAS in the kitchen with Lilly and Audrey when Ethan walked in. "Jenn just pulled up outside. She wanted to say goodbye."

Pictures of the white room and Mara flashed in front of me. My heart immediately began thumping against my ribs, my fingers tingling from the adrenaline, but as soon as Marcus's arm snaked around my belly and I felt his strong body against my back, calm blanketed my nerves, and my muscles relaxed.

Together, we walked to the front door. Jenn had one arm on top of her Bugatti, leaning down to the passenger side window. Glancing past her, I saw Paycen in the seat. His eyes were trained forward and, as the last time, void of anything.

At our approach, Jenn pushed off her car and strode toward us. Ethan lingered near the entrance.

Stopping just inches away, she scanned me up and down. Jenn's mouth pulled up on one side. "You look good. *Medic* said you're healing well."

I cocked a brow. "Medic? His name is Josh."

"I don't get to know them. The names change with every location. Their duties don't." She shrugged, showing the side she hid well when she and I had been thrown together.

"JENN!" Paycen's barked shout turned everyone's attention on him.

His face was still forward, and Jenn rolled her eyes. "He's

pissed because he's not allowed to smoke in my car." She chuckled.

"Where is his car? I thought he came from Vegas that day he —" Lilly cut herself off, peering at me.

"He did, but not in his own car." The way Jenn answered a question without answering it, a.k.a. incriminating herself or her family, was impressive.

She hugged me, then moved to Lilly. "You have my number if you ever need *assistance* again."

Lilly nodded with a small smile. "Thank you."

Jenn reached for my friend's hand. "I'm sorry you had to find out the way you did. You are better off without her, though. You have a family and friends that are more than she could've ever been. Plus, you have your big brother." She glanced over her shoulder. "*Those* are the best," she declared, raising her voice.

Paycen's hand appeared in the open window, flipping her off. Jenn barked a laugh but winked at me. "He loves me."

"I don't love anyone, Jenn-Ann. Let's go. Tobias Underwood requires your services, and you know how much Marshall hates when you're late for a job."

Jenn rolled her eyes. "Work never stops." She then zeroed in on Ethan behind me. "Can I talk to you for a minute?"

Her expression had shifted, and Ethan must've noticed it as well because he followed without a word. They headed to the driver's side, where she spoke in hushed tones, and Ethan's hands flew to his head. He appeared upset, but his focus on Jenn didn't waver.

Studying the man who had become *Angel of Death* to me, our gazes met. Once again, his dead eyes sent chills down my spine. Nonetheless, I mouthed, "Thank you."

He dipped his chin curtly before facing forward and closing the window.

Jenn hugged Ethan and climbed into her car. Waving, she took off with screeching tires.

. . .

I GRAB my phone off the nightstand and swipe without looking at who it is. My father's face fills the screen, and a chasm tears open in my stomach.

Fuck.

"Did you think I wouldn't hear about it?" His livid accusation causes my heartbeat to falter.

I take a deep breath. He has no power over me anymore. The knowledge settles my buzzing nerves almost instantly. "Hear what?" I push myself up and sit against the pillows, rubbing my eyes with one hand.

My father's face turns redder than it already is. "That you relapsed. And not just relapsed, you embarrassed yourself in public."

My hand falls to my lap, and Marcus's head lifts out of the mound of pillows. My excessive need for head comfort also moved into his bedroom with all my belongings.

"Relapsed? *Embarrassed*," I say the word slowly, tasting it on my tongue. Anger begins to simmer in my core. "The only one embarrassed by my condition is you. You brainwashed me to believe that it's something to be ashamed of, that I have to suppress and hide it instead of deal with the triggers. Well, guess what, *Daddy*, I am handling it now. My way."

My father's jaw drops. I don't think I've ever seen Victor Keller speechless. In the background, Celine covers her mouth, but I continue, "You no longer have to pay for anyone to look out for me or use a person's own issues to pressure them into being with me."

No matter how much I despise my ex-fiancé, my father had used Collin's issues to his advantage, planting the idea of how marriage would benefit everyone. As expected, Phyllis had taken care of her son. She had him shipped off as soon as word got to her where he was found and in what state. Rumor has it that Collin is in a private facility that will help him deal with his dependencies. Not just the drug addictions but also his physical compulsions. While his behavior was unforgivable, I hope, for his sake, he gets the help he needs.

I peer over at Marcus, who pushes his hand onto my thigh under the covers and squeezes. He is making sure I am okay. I relax farther into the bed, my chest having never felt this light.

After Collin, I closed the last chapter that was preventing me from moving on the previous week as well. I called Charlie. I didn't tell him what happened, but I let him know (as gently as possible) that I couldn't see him anymore. I wished him the best, but he was part of my past. I was leaving the darkness that had followed me for almost twenty years behind, ready to embrace the future.

I train my attention back to the screen.

Instead of showing remorse for his betrayal, my father's eyes narrow. "And how do you think you will handle your *condition*?" he spits the word at the camera.

He hasn't always been this...hateful—or at least he hasn't shown it as he does now.

The phone disappears out of my hand, and I whirl just in time to see Marcus lift it to his line of sight. "Good morning, Victor." Marcus wipes his hand over his mouth, appearing nonchalant on the screen, but his coiled muscles tell a different story.

"W-Wha—?" my father sputters.

"Denielle has me to help her deal with her condition." He crosses his free hand over his bare chest. "Not that there is anything wrong with her. Everyone deals with trauma differently, and your daughter chose the one way that made her feel close to her mother. If you had thought, for just two seconds, about it, you would've seen that instead of blaming her for something she has no control over. And maybe you would have even been able to help her. As a medical professional, you should know that no two humans are alike."

Marcus's tone is calm and collected, his words raising my body temperature.

"What do you know about her condition?" my father sneers. He's lost control, and now he's in attack mode.

"You're just—"

"I'm just what?" Marcus's brows rise in a challenge. "Let's get one thing straight here, *Keller*. Your daughter had nothing to do with your tanked career or my sister's death. Blaming her for McKenna is something I will spend the rest of my life regretting and making up to her. Here is my advice for you: pull your head out of your ass and love your daughter the way she is. I intend to do just that, so get used to seeing my face around."

He disconnects the call and throws the phone toward the end of the bed. I sit on the mattress, speechless, opening my mouth, but no sound comes out.

"Don't catch a fly, baby." Marcus chuckles.

I snap my lips together with a smacking sound. Marcus shifts to all fours and crawls over to me. I fall back into the mattress as he hovers above me. "Do you think your father is mad that I hung up on him?" He smirks.

I burst out laughing. "Probably."

Marcus shrugs. "Oh, well. Good thing that I don't give two shits about his blessing."

Blessing. My eyes widen. "What are you saying?"

Marcus lowers himself until his chest is flush against mine, his elbows caging me in without dropping his weight on me. "I'm saying that you're stuck with me. For as long as you'll have me. And I don't care if your father has a problem with it."

My eyes water. I wriggle my arms until I can free my hands and cup his face. "I love you."

Marcus bridges the distance between our mouths, his lips grazing mine. "I love you, too. And I will make you mine."

"I'm already yours. Was from the moment you pulled me into the laundry room." I smirk.

"Good, because I was thinking about testing out every room in the pool house as well." He pulls back, his eyes darkening.

"Now?" I press farther into the pillow.

Marcus cocks his head and grinds his groin against my core.
"Any objections, *Keller*?"
"Give me your worst, Baxter."

Dear reader,

Thank you so much for reading FBTD.

I would be honored if you considered leaving a brief review (or star rating) for Denielle and Marcus. Each review helps indie authors to be considered for audiobook deals and other amazing opportunities.

Make sure to check out the **Acknowledgments section** for any unanswered questions that will be revealed **soon**.

BUT FIRST,
keep reading for **TWO** exclusive previews.

REZONED
(Prologue)

ETHAN

PRESENT

SAYING goodbye to my foster sister is never easy. It makes my chest constrict as much as my (in her presence, permanently coiled) muscles relax. I care for Jenn, love her—on a non-romantic, platonic level. Out of the four Davis siblings, she's the only one I remained in touch with.

However, over the years, we drifted apart. Our lives don't blend well. I work security for the Altman Hotel empire, and she is *The Cleaner* for one of the biggest organized crime families in the western hemisphere. A family I used to be part of—not that I ever asked for it. Did I want to be out of the foster system? Of course. What five-year-old wouldn't want to belong somewhere?

But at what cost? A price I didn't understand until it was too late.

"Can I talk to you for a minute?"

My eyes flick to Jenn, and a sour taste forms on my tongue. As good as she is in her profession, she doesn't possess the mask our brothers wear, which is why she is *The Cleaner*, and the guys execute the jobs. She is about to deliver the news I never wanted to get.

My pulse thrashes in my veins as I follow her to the driver's side of her Bugatti. She studies me, and with every passing second, I fight the urge to latch onto her arms and shake her. I don't want to hear what she has to say, but I don't have a choice.

"He found her." Her tone is level. While she visually can't hide shit, she is a professional in her area of expertise. The groove between her brows contradicts her voice. The sorrow and fear for me are etched across every inch, but no one would know just by hearing her speak.

"How?" I choke on the one-word question.

"By sheer coincidence." She peers over to where my employer and her friends stand but continues her recap. "Cor called just before we got here. He overheard Marshall on the phone with Tony. He was on assignment in Maine and stopped at a diner on the drive back."

My fingers flex and curl as I listen. "Don't tell me she works at a diner." Why would she do that? A vision of her red hair behind the counter flashes in front of my mind's eye.

"Not work. She owns it," Jenn states. "It's all she's ever known. Can you blame her?" Her gaze jumps between my eyes.

"And you're telling me Tony stopped at her diner, of all places?" This is the most fucked-up coincidence in the history of random occurrences.

Jenn nods, and my hands fly up, fisting the strands of my cropped dark hair. I get ahold of enough to pull, causing a sting that distracts me momentarily from the pit that has been ripped open in my stomach.

"Why didn't Tony eliminate her on the spot?" Not that I'm not glad he didn't, but she should've been dead a decade ago. To Marshall Davis's knowledge, she was.

"Marshall ordered him back to the compound. He probably wants to figure out what happened before taking action." She chews on her bottom lip.

"Are you going to be okay?" What I'm asking is, *will you be safe?*

"He won't kill me." The corner of her mouth quirks, and my snarky little sister is back.

I slant my head, not dignifying her attempt to make light of the situation.

Jenn rolls her eyes and places both hands on my shoulders. "You know Father doesn't tolerate disobedience. That's what started this mess in the first place. But Mother will not allow him to harm me. To him, I wasn't even there."

"Maybe not you, but Corbin was. *I* was. He sent me there to watch Ju—" Saying her name constricts my airways, and I have to pause. "How can he not think we had anything to do with her surviving?"

Her expression softens. "I will call you once I have more details. Cor is working on getting the exact location."

Jenn hugs me, and despite returning the embrace, I feel nothing. A hollow cold has taken over my body.

They found Jules.

Rezoned is a dark, (love-to) hate-to-love, second-chance standalone novel and prequel to **The Davis Order**.

KEEP READING

**I Am the Dark
(Prologue)**

Note:
This chapter is subject to change in the final version of
I Am the Dark.

HIM

Present

Arms snake around my stomach, jolting me out of the memory.

"Something's burning." Her muffled statement is accompanied by nuzzling her nose into my back. Her breath warms the spot under my white long-sleeve shirt, and the hair on the nape of my neck stands in pleasure.

Then, her words sink in. My vision comes back into focus.

Fucking shit.

Letting my gaze drift from the wooden spoon in my hand to the stovetop, another red droplet falls slowly onto the burner. It instantly turns into a crusted black circle, dark smoke rising into the air, and she tightens her hold. Her thumb caresses the muscles of my abdomen, and I grasp the edge of the industrial stove, closing my eyes. My abs tense automatically where she makes contact, despite the thick cotton providing an ample barrier.

"Where did you just go?"

The corner of my mouth tilts up in a sneer. "*Back.*" I don't have to elaborate. Back equals TLPH. Twin Lake Psychiatric Hospital. The place I called home for the past six years. Home. As I roll the word over my tongue, a noncomical snort erupts in my throat. I deserved to be there. Wanted to be there. I needed to get better. For myself and my family. TLPH wasn't one of those dingy, horror-movie-style asylums with walls covered in blood and bodily fluids. There were no wheelchairs from the fifties in which the patients were rolled around, drugged out of their minds—no, the opposite, in fact. Of course my attorneys managed to get me sent to one of the most upscale mental hospitals in the country. Its patients were all wealthy one-percenters with a little anxiety or a recreational habit that would bring them bad press down the line if not fixed. I had walked into the place with bad press. I was *The Babysitter*, a title the staff never let me live down. I was the only criminal within those pristine white walls with its marble floors—until her.

I turn off the burner and push back, forcing her to loosen her hold. She retreats but doesn't fully let go. She only allows me to pivot to face her.

Leaning against the stove, I fold my arms over my chest. Her forefingers hook into the belt loops of my jeans, and our gazes meet. The gray in her irises is so light it borders on white, an attribute that makes her striking features even more breathtaking—no matter how much she attempts to hide who she is under makeup and hair dye.

I lift my hand, tugging on one of the black strands peeking out from under the blonde. When I first saw her, her face was caked in smudged makeup—smeared from fighting the nurses. The lower half of her hair was died black, while the top half was its natural light blonde—untouched. "You dyed it again," I state the obvious. The black had grown out over the last fifteen months, but somehow, she managed to obtain fresh color as soon as I *broke her out*.

"I made G add it to the last grocery order." She shrugs nonchalantly, and I chuckle.

"Of course you did."

She peers down, and I follow her line of sight. My phone vibrates across the countertop, lit with a missed text.

She picks the device up and holds it in front of my face, unlocking the screen. For someone who lives and breathes tech, adjusting to an everyday thing like my phone has been harder than expected. The message opens, and I scan the words.

George: On our way. 10 min out.

Ten minutes.

"They'll be here in ten," I inform her, and she drops the phone back on the counter.

Wrapping my arms around her shoulders, I draw her close and place a kiss on her forehead. "You have everything you need?"

She tips her chin up, signaling to me what she wants. A flutter erupts in my chest, and I indulge her—not that it would be a chore. As soon as our lips connect, she swipes her tongue across the seam of my mouth and purrs, "Now, I do."

I can't help but roll my eyes. "You're impossible."

She steps out of my embrace, and I let my arms fall. Intertwining her fingers under her chin, she cocks her head and flutters her eyes. "Isn't that why you brought me here?" She grins like a lunatic.

Shaking my head, I bark out a laugh.

I try to reach for her again, but she blows me a kiss and swivels on her bare feet. The abrupt motion flares her short plaid skirt, and the lace boy shorts underneath become visible.

As her foot hits the first step, she peers over her shoulder. "I'll be upstairs when you come to bed tonight. I'll text you or G if I need anything."

I bite the inside of my cheek, sudden heat burning in the pit of my stomach. *Bed.* Not letting my mind go there, I call out, "Harley?"

Her brows rise, and I continue, "I have to tell her. I don't keep secrets from my sister."

The corner of her mouth tilts up. "I wouldn't expect anything less from you."

ACKNOWLEDGMENTS

This is the first time since I started writing that I am struggling with the acknowledgments. Not because I don't know who to thank (*or acknowledge*), but because I didn't expect Denielle and Marcus's story to be like...*this*.

I've said it before: ***I don't write my books. My characters do.*** But this time, I wasn't prepared for it. When I first sat down to write *Followed by the Dark*, the only thing I knew was that Mara would be revealed. I've been waiting for this moment since *Out of the Dark*. Denielle and Marcus, their combined and individual backstories... I didn't see them coming.

You got to experience sides of Denielle I never anticipated when she first "came to life" in *The Dark Series* trilogy.

I was genuinely hoping that I could make this book a standalone so readers who do not necessarily enjoy any of the tropes from the previous four books would be able to pick up *Followed by the Dark*.

However, after working with my alphas and betas and having lengthy conversations with my team, I decided not to market FBTD as an interconnected standalone. While Denielle and Marcus's romance is standalone, the suspense plot is a <u>continuation</u> of the previous books in *The Dark Series*.

I have a few bonus scenes I still want to write.

- **How did Lilly and King deal with the revelation of Mara?** A few of my early readers asked me that question, and at first, I debated adding a chapter but then decided against it. Lilly and King need to tell you that themselves and not through Denielle's or Marcus's eyes, so I decided this will be one of the future bonus scenes.
- Another scene that has been playing out in my head is **a sparring scene between (grown-up) Lilly and Rhys**. You may remember the sleeve-choke scene if you've read *In the Dark*. This time, it will be...less innocent. *(I think ;-))*

If there are any bonus scenes you would like to see (for any of the books, not just FBTD), please feel free to email author danahloganpa@gmail.com, and my PA will add them to my list.

Once again, I know there are some **unanswered questions**, but I can <u>promise</u> they will be answered. Bear with me and the series. Everything will come to a close in *I am the Dark*, but you will also get more glimpses into my next world, which will begin with *Deadzone*.

If there are other loose ends and you would like to know when they will be tied up, **message me** at danah@authordanahlogan.com. I'd love to hear from you.

Okay, now to the thank-yous. WOW, the list keeps growing. I have such an amazing team backing me up, and I couldn't do this without any of you!!

My husband & daughters: Chasing this dream would be nothing without you. You are my world! I love you!

My family and friends: I can't begin to tell you how much your continued support of my dream means to me. Thank you for cheering me on every step of the way.

Mary: My PA and friend. Please stop throwing new plot ideas at me. You'll keep me busy for the next thirty years. Just kidding! I love our plotting sessions and finding new ways to expand the web in my head. The setting for *Deadzone* was your idea, and I cannot wait to start on that book with you. I couldn't do this job without you.

Sammi: I never expected to find such an amazing friend when I picked up *Chasing Ivy* on a whim three years ago. I adore you more than words can describe and cannot wait for when we finally cowrite our book together. But for now, thank you for letting me borrow Tobias. :-*

Jim: You've been my best friend for over a decade, helped me through some of the hardest times in my life, walked me down the aisle, and now you're proofreading my steamy scenes for the male POVs. Thank you, thank you, thank you! What are we going to do next?

Kezia: I wouldn't have been able to write this book without your expertise and feedback. Thank you for lending me your brain, alpha reading Denielle and Marcus, and making sure I keep my sanity.

My alphas: Mary D. and Lil. Thank you so so much for reading this story chapter by chapter, tolerating my deadline changes, and providing me with your valuable feedback.

My betas: Lyndsey, Maggie, Ellie, and Tiffany. Thank you for taking time out of your busy lives to beta read Den and Marcus's story and helping me polish it. You are an integral part of my process, and I can't begin to tell you how grateful I am for you.

Bethany from Weaver Literacy Agency: Thank you for being the wonderful agent you are. I appreciate your hard work and letting me run all things TDS by you day and night.

Jenn from Jenn Lockwood Editing: Thank you for once

again adjusting to my crazy schedule and making my words clean and pretty.

Rosa from My Brother's Editor: Thank you so much for proofing Denielle and Marcus's story and ensuring FBTD is ready for the world.

My ARC Readers & Street Team: THANK YOU!! Thank you for reading and reviewing my books before they're out in the wild and spreading the word. I'm blown away by your support and wouldn't be here without you!

And finally, you, my Readers: Thank you for reading my words and escaping with me into the world(s) my crazy head cooks up. Seeing you fall in love, like (or dislike) my characters makes me so happy because it means I created something you can identify with in one way or another. I can't wait to give you many more books and to hear what you think about them.

I know everyone is waiting for *HIS* book, but first comes Ethan.

Let's find out what his story is, and then let's finish this series.

xoxo
Danah Logan

Born and raised in Germany, Danah moved to the US, where she met her husband, eventually trading downtown Chicago's city life for the northern Rockies.

She can be seen hanging with her twin girls and exploring the outdoors when she's not arguing plot points with the characters in her head.

But it's that exact passion that has produced *The Dark Series* and continues to keep her glued to her laptop, following her dreams.

Scan the below QR code to sign up for my newsletter and be the first to know about upcoming releases, sales, and new arrivals.

Add me on Facebook
www.facebook.com/authordanahlogan/

Follow me on Instagram
www.instagram.com/authordanahlogan/

Visit my Website for more content
and other places to stalk me
www.authordanahlogan.com

Or scan this second QR code for all the links:

ALSO BY DANAH LOGAN

The Ghost
The Beginning.
A Dark Series and Davis Order Novella
(George & Lou)

The Dark Series

In the Dark, Book 1
Out of the Dark, Book 2
Of Light and Dark, Book 3
(Lilly and Rhys)
A Dark, New-Adult, Romantic-Suspense Trilogy

Because of the Dark, Book 4
(Wes and King)
A Dark, Hidden-Identity, Romantic-Suspense Novel

Followed by the Dark, Book 5
(Denielle and Marcus)
A Dark, Enemies-to-Lovers, Age-Gap,
Romantic-Suspense Novel

I Am the Dark, Book 6
(HIM)
A Dark, Age-Gap, Romantic-Suspense Novel

<u>**The Davis Order**</u>

Rezoned, Prequel
(Ethan)
A Dark, Hate-to-Love, Second-Chance,
Romantic-Suspense Novel

www.ingramcontent.com/pod-product-compliance
Lightning Source LLC
Chambersburg PA
CBHW031203010826
48971CB00013B/1298